JFP 198M

C000184763

OLIVER LEESE

by the same Author

Edith Cavell
Ravenstein

OLIVER LEESE

by
Rowland Ryder

HAMISH HAMILTON · LONDON

This book is dedicated
to the Coldstream Guards.

First published in Great Britain 1987
by Hamish Hamilton Ltd
27 Wrights Lane, London W8 5TZ

Copyright © 1987 by Rowland Ryder

British Library Cataloguing in Publication Data
Ryder, Rowland
Oliver Leese.
1. Leese, Oliver   2. Great Britain. *Army*
– Biography   3. Generals – Great Britain
– Biography
I. Title
335.3'31'0924   DA69.3.L4
ISBN 0-241-12024-1

Typeset by Rowland Phototypesetting Ltd,
Bury St Edmunds, Suffolk
Printed and bound in Great Britain by
Butler & Tanner Ltd, Frome and London

CONTENTS

List of illustrations   vii
List of maps   viii
Acknowledgments   ix
Foreword   xi
 1 FATHER TO THE MAN   1
 2 DISTINGUISHED SERVICE   15
 3 TEACHING AND LEARNING   27
 4 A MARRIAGE HAS BEEN ARRANGED   34
 5 LETTERS FROM QUETTA   45
 6 A TOWN LIKE ARRAS   61
 7 GUARDS ARMOURED   86
 8 CORPS COMMANDER   93
 9 ALAMEIN   107
10 ALAMEIN TO SFAX   116
11 SICILY   133
12 ARMY COMMANDER   146
13 CASSINO   163
14 KING'S GENERAL   180
15 THE FINEST FIGHTING SOLDIER   194
16 MANDALAY AND RANGOON   217
17 A RAW DEAL   235
18 POST WAR   259
19 LAST POST   286
    Appendices   293
    Select bibliography   299
    Index   301

LIST OF ILLUSTRATIONS

1 The Eton Eleven in 1914.
2 The German Officer who shot Leese.
3 Jack Lambert.

4 Leese with his Divisional Commanders (*reproduced by permission of the Imperial War Museum*)
5 Leese with Ion Calvocoressi.

6 Alfresco luncheon in Tripoli.
7 Leese, Alexander and Mark Clark.

8 Leese knighted on the battlefield by George VI.
9 Leese and Churchill.

10 Leese and his Staff on his last day with the Eighth Army.
11 Leese with Wood, Christison and Kent.

12 Mountbatten, Slim and Leese.
13 'Thank You, Sir Oliver' – cartoon by Jon.

14 Oliver Leese and Margie at Worfield.
15 At Lord's with the Queen (*reproduced by permission of Sport and General Press Agency Ltd*)

16 Leese standing by the de Laszlo portrait of Margie.
17 Frances Denby.

LIST OF MAPS

Alamein. Situation and Plan, 23 October 1942.   110

The Eastern Mediterranean in 1942.   117

Plan Olive suggested by Leese, 4 August 1944.   184

The Battle for Burma. Diagram to show Leese's journeys.   204

The Race for Rangoon.   233

ACKNOWLEDGMENTS

Mrs Frances Denby, Edmund King and Ion Calvocoressi, friends and trustees of Sir Oliver Leese, invited me to write this book. Edmund King, alas, died before the book was completed.

Mrs Frances Denby has given me unrestricted access to Oliver Leese's papers and complete freedom as to how I went about my task. I owe her my warmest thanks for her unfailing help.

Ion Calvocoressi, ADC to Sir Oliver Leese during the Second World War, and friend until the latter's death, has shown unlimited kindness in translating his general as he saw him. I am indebted to him for the loan of relevant documents.

Former members of Sir Oliver Leese's staff have been most liberal of their time, recalling the past and, in many cases, reading and commenting on chapters of this book. I owe my sincere thanks to General Sir Victor Fitz-George-Balfour, General Sir John Gibbon, Major General Sir Edric Bastyan, Brigadier Sidney Kent, Colonel Peter Dunphie, Colonel Victor Cowley, Lord Killearn, Lord Tweedsmuir, the Hon. Luke Asquith, the Hon. Bernard Bruce, Nigel Barne, David Butter, Petre Crowder, Ian Weston Smith, John Stimpson, James Beer, Wilfred Kershaw, John Lamb, Leslie Mavers, Ralph Warren.

My thanks are due to the General's family for their help, especially to Lt-Colonel A. J. M. Drake, his nephew, who has read the work in typescript, for his occasional suggestions and for his encouragement; and to Lt-Colonel Hilary Leese, WRAC, his cousin, for her notes and information.

It has been an unforgettable privilege to have the benefit of Field Marshal Lord Harding's wisdom and experience in his comments concerning the chapters on the Italian campaign; and, equally, to have the help of General Sir Philip Christison, the only surviving General involved in the series of incidents following the fall of Rangoon.

I would like to express my gratitude to Major General O'Carroll Scott and Brigadier Neville Chesshyre, who provided invaluable material for the Quetta chapter; Lord Bridgeman and General Sir Frank Simpson for their help over the Dunkirk period; General Allan Adair and General Sir Randle Feilden (Guards Armoured); Major General Douglas Wimberley and Major General Sir Julian Gascoigne for reading the Middle East chapters, and for their counsel, exposition and advice. Harold Macmillan (Lord Stockton) gave me of his time with a spirited assessment of General Leese in Italy, and General Sir

Sidney Kirkman gave me the benefit of his memory and his diary in connexion with Operation *Olive*. I would like to thank Harry Verney for his kindness in lending me his father's papers connected with General Leese's campaigns.

While apologising for accidental omissions I would like to thank for varied help: Mrs Moran Ainscough, Miss Elizabeth Bache, Robert Bent, Ernest Bishop, Mrs Rosemary Blackham, Major Gregory Blaxland, Mrs Catherine Brodie, David Brown, Brigadier Lorne Campbell, VC, Colonel James Carne, VC, Field Marshal Lord Carver, Eric Caswell, General Mark Clark, Colin Cowdrey, Sir Geoffrey Cox, Mrs Hilda Davey, Mrs Diana Farmer, General Sir David Fraser, Lord Freyberg, Anthony Gell, Mrs Diana Goddard, Cyril Golding, Lt-General Sir George Gordon-Lennox, Miss Lilias Graham, Miss Joyce Grenfell, Lord Hailsham, Nigel Hamilton, John Henderson, Denis Hills, Major General Burt Hoffmeister, Brigadier David Houchin, Richard Howe, Field Marshal Sir Richard Hull, Brian Johnston, Gordon Lambert, Miss Judy Lampson, Miss Penny Lloyd, Prince Eugen Lubomirski, Brigadier Maurice Lush, Colonel J. M. McNeill, Viscount Montgomery of Alamein, Prebendary Stanley Moore, Dame Anna Neagle, General Sir Richard O'Connor, Sir Antony Part, Anthony Powell, Mrs Grace Randall, Major General G. P. B. Roberts, General Rudnicki, Gordon Shepherd, M. J. K. Smith, Mr and Mrs John Sutton, Prebendary Thomson, Major General Vokes, George Wareham, Judge White (NZ), J. W. Williams, Colonel S. Zakrzewski.

My warm thanks are due to Miss Rose Coombe, Roderick Suddaby and Terence Charman of the Imperial War Museum; Miss Patricia Methven of the Liddell Hart Centre; the Master, Fellows and Students of Churchill College, Cambridge, Mrs Mollie Travis of the Broadlands Archives; Colonel Peter Tower, Lt-Colonel Frank Betts and Major James Innes, RHQ, Coldstream Guards; Patrick Strong, Eton College Archivist; the staff of the Public Record Office and the staff of the Birmingham Reference Library.

I am grateful to Sir Robert Armstrong, Secretary of the Cabinet, and to the Trustees of the Broadlands Archives, for permission to quote from Lord Mountbatten's letters to Oliver Leese and from the exchange of telegrams; and to the Trustees of the Liddell Hart Centre for permission to quote from the Alanbrooke Diaries.

I am grateful to John Claughton of Eton College for permission to use the picture of the Eton Eleven; to Gordon Lambert for the pictures of the German Officer and Jack Lambert; to Ion Calvocoressi for the picture of himself with Leese; to John Stimpson for the picture of Leese with his staff; Brigadier S. H. Kent for the picture of Lesse with Wood, Christison and Kent; and to Frances Denby for the cartoon by Jon.

I would like to thank Leslie Deakins, who first suggested that I should write the biography, and Alan Smith, who provided me with an office to work in at the County Ground, Edgbaston. My thanks are due to Mrs Hedda Heathcote, who typed the manuscript in its various stages; I am very grateful to Miss Hatty Sumption, of Hamish Hamilton, for her work on the book as Editor, and to Patrick Leeson who did the maps. Finally, I would like to thank my wife for her limitless help during the six years that the work has been in progress.

Rowland Ryder
Edgbaston   1986

Foreword by Field Marshal Lord Carver

In writing this biography of Oliver Leese, Rowland Ryder has filled a gap in the history of the Second World War, making it possible for historians and others to obtain a better balanced picture both of the campaign in Italy and of the final stages of that in Burma, by seeing them from Leese's point of view. Sir Oliver's misfortune was to find himself competing, in one way or another, with more glamorous figures who were not averse to seeking the limelight. Neither his family and military background – an Etonian Coldstream guardsman, scion of one of those families whose industrial success had provided an entrée into landowning aristocracy – nor his personal inclination urged him to compete with Montgomery, Mountbatten, Slim or Horrocks in the popularity stakes.

He was the master of the set-piece battle: the operation in which the action of all arms and weapons was coordinated in an intense clash with a well-prepared and organized enemy: the Second World War equivalent of the battles of the First. He had an eye for detail and was a first class executive manager of military operations. His strong character, immense reserves of energy, determination and courage, supported by a natural optimism, acted as a dynamic force in executing the plan which his managerial skill had evolved. Montgomery recognized this when he asked for him to come out to Egypt and take command of 30th Corps, which was given the major rôle in the Battle of El Alamein. From that time on, until Montgomery left Eighth Army to return to England and assume command of 21st Army Group, he made it clear that Leese was his most favoured corps commander, and it was on his recommendation that Leese succeeded him in command of Eighth Army in Italy.

Allied to these characteristics was an open friendliness, applied to all ranks, nationalities and types, which endeared him to all those with whom he came into contact, whether in military operations, on the cricket field or in the specialized form of horticulture, known as succulents, in which, in his retirement, he became expert.

It was a tragedy for him that these characteristics made no impact on either of the strong-minded men, one his superior, Mountbatten, the other his subordinate, Slim, when, in October 1944, he was transferred from command of Eighth Army in Italy to succeed Giffard as Commander-in-Chief Allied Land Forces South East Asia, the equivalent of an army group. Oliver Leese never established happy relations with either of them. The chances of doing so were never high. Mountbatten's headquarters, in its ivory tower of a hill station in Ceylon, not only exercised an almost one-over-one command of Leese's, but was almost as far removed as it could be, physically and psychologically, from Leese's practical one in the steamy, unromantic atmosphere of Barrackpore near Calcutta. His predecessor, Giffard, had been to Slim very much what Alexander had been to Montgomery in the Middle East. Although technically his superior, he had acted almost as a subordinate, restricting himself to coordinating matters with Auchinleck at GHQ India and the American-Chinese operations along the Ledo road, the contribution of which to the campaign in Burma is almost universally overlooked by British historians. Leese's more forceful and dynamic activity, notably in successfully pressing for and achieving the direct capture of Rangoon by an airborne and amphibious operation, upset Slim and his Fourteenth Army headquarters, who were accustomed to getting their own way and receiving overall priority. Leese's arrival with a personal circus of staff officers soaked in Eighth Army lore was bound to cause resentment in the sensitive self-styled 'Forgotten Army', fundamentally of Indian Army origins. Bluff and outgoing himself, Leese failed to detect and make allowance for their sensibilities.

All military headquarters tend to treat the one superior to them with disdain, as being remote from the realities of the battlefield and insensitive to their needs. Slim so treated Leese, as Leese did Mountbatten. By 1945 all were set in their ways, reinforced by being surrounded by admiring staffs, whom they had gathered round them as Wolseley had his Ashanti Ring, inflating their masters' egos. The result was the affair, which has been wrongly described as an attempt by Leese to sack Slim. On the facts of the case, Leese had all reason on his side. The state of Slim's health and his request for home leave have not previously been revealed. But a more subtle touch, advised perhaps by a senior staff officer of Indian Army origin, if he had had one, might have saved Oliver Leese from the misjudgement which brought his highly distinguished career to an abrupt end. This book shows that his behaviour in the affair, as one would have expected from such a straightforward and honourable man, compares well with that of the others involved.

1

FATHER TO THE MAN

I suppose when you are in Pop and are Captain of your House,
you are more important than you ever are for the rest of your life.
                                                              Oliver Leese

Oliver William Hargreaves Leese was born on Saturday 27 October
1894. Japan was at war with China: a military report was published
from Hiroshima. In Moscow the Tsar Alexander III lay dying. In
Berlin the Chancellor Caprivi had tendered his resignation to the
thirty-five-year-old Kaiser. In the United States William McKinley
was occupied with his election campaign: under his presidency the
USA became a world power.[1] In Britain, all was well, and Queen
Victoria was holidaying at Balmoral.

Oliver Leese was a scion of the new aristocracy that had sprung up
during the Industrial Revolution and flowered in the Liberal England
of Gladstone, Richard Cobden and John Bright. One of Oliver's great
grandfathers was William Hargreaves[2] (1815–1874). Hargreaves's own
father owned a calico printing factory in Lancashire. The firm became
highly successful because of the sophistication of its machinery and
the beauty of its designs.

William Hargreaves, a semi-invalid, was educated at King's College,
Cambridge. He showed no direct interest in the family cotton business,
but devoted himself to politics, his circle of friends included Cobden,
and Bright. In 1859, John Bright stayed for six months as a house
guest with the Hargreaves family at Craven Hill Gardens, in order to
be near to Westminster, and afterwards remained in close touch with
William.[3]

---

[1] President McKinley was assassinated in 1901.
[2] The name is pronounced as though written Hargraves.
[3] I discovered 80 letters from Bright to Hargreaves while researching the present
biography. They total 35,000 words and chiefly span the years 1854–1878. The letters
are now in the British Library. Author.

Bright had an avuncular regard for William's daughter Constance, and when on a visit to family friends in Scotland, she became engaged to a young lawyer named Joseph Francis Leese, five years her senior, he teased William affectionately about the 'tragedy':

> What would you expect if she is allowed to go down into Scotland, that land of romance, without her mother to attend her!

The courtship resulted in a happy marriage. Constance became the mother of eight children and had her sixth child when she was twenty-eight.

William's nephew, Reginald (Regi) Hargreaves married at Westminster Abbey, in September 1880, Alice Liddell – the Alice for whom Charles Lutwidge Dodgson (Lewis Carroll) wrote the immortal story of a Golden Afternoon. Oliver Leese was therefore a first cousin, twice removed, to Alice in Wonderland; or, at any rate, to her prototype. He was to acquire the casual adaptability to circumstances of the Alice that Lewis Carroll portrayed.

The Leeses were another cotton family. Joseph Leese of Dunham Massey, Cheshire (1815–1909), made and lost two fortunes in cotton; he did not die a rich man as he gave away a great deal of money and also financed Richard Cobden in his political campaigns.

Gertrude Leese, one of his grandchildren, remembered Joseph Leese as a man of rare charisma. She would see him walking up Lord Street, in Southport, in winter wrapped in a dark grey wool shawl with fringe; when warm weather came, in a well-cut, very light grey suit, a light grey hat and a flower in his buttonhole. He showered his nineteen grandchildren with sweets and sixpences. To Gertrude Leese 'he was one of those people whom merely to meet in the street cast a radiance over the whole day.'

Joseph's son, Joseph Francis (Joe) Leese (1845–1914) who married Mary Constance Hargreaves in 1867, was Olive Leese's grandfather. Joe Leese became Liberal Member of Parliament for Accrington and Recorder of Manchester. He was knighted in 1891, and in 1908 became a baronet. He was a good cricketer who played intermittently for Lancashire from 1865 to 1878.

Joe Leese's son, William Hargreaves (Bill) Leese (1868–1937), Oliver's father, was in the Winchester Eleven for two years. He read Law at Trinity Hall, Cambridge, and played cricket for the University without getting his Blue. William was called to the bar, and later joined the London solicitors firm of Freshfields, becoming eventually senior partner. He did a great deal of work for the Bank of England, where his father-in-law, Albert Sandeman, of Sandeman's port, was deputy Governor. William in 1893 had married Violet Mary Sandeman.

Her mother, Maria Carlotta, married to Albert Sandeman, was daughter of a Portuguese viscount.

William Leese had five brothers and two sisters. Four of the brothers – Vernon, Neville, Theodore, and Cecil – were Wykehamists.

Oliver was the first of William and Violet Leese's four children, the others being Betty, born 1899, Peter, born 1905, and Alexander, born 1909. The children were a quarter Portuguese, and Oliver's dark complexion and black hair was a legacy from his Portuguese grandmother; his father and uncles all had light hair.

Oliver's birth was duly recorded in *The Times*. He was born at St Ermin's in Westminster, and an enthusiastic godfather sent him a chamber pot – still extant – bearing the legend 'Welcome, little stranger'. Oliver's earliest recollection was that when he was about three, he went for a walk one Sunday morning with his father across Rotten Row. When his father decided that they would go home, Oliver, who was wearing his best white suit, staged a demonstration to register his disapproval, lay down in the mud and shouted his head off. This action evoked much sympathy from passers-by, and, later, parental retribution. Another of his childhood recollections was of the occasion when he was being taken in his pram to see the sovereign's escort pass by – this was at the time of the Diamond Jubilee in 1897. Oliver had with him his precious golliwog Angelina. In his excitement during the procession he dropped her and Angelina was irretrievably lost. He was later to describe the loss as 'the first and by no means the last serious reverse of my life!'

Oliver Leese spent his childhood in stirring times, when the British Empire was at its zenith. Punitive expeditions had gone to India and Africa. The Mahdi's legions were defeated at Omdurman. The Boer War roused violent emotions. As a child of five, Oliver heard the triumphant 'mafficking' in London on 17 May 1900, and 'Goodbye, Dolly Gray' was sung by Saturday night revellers, flown with patriotism and beer at twopence a pint:

Goodbye, Dolly, I must leave you,
Though it breaks my heart to go,
Something tells me I am needed,
On the field to face the foe.

Oliver's nanny would take him to see the changing of the Guard. His Sandeman grandmother doted on him and, according to one member of the family, 'spoilt him rotten'. She bought him infinite strawberry ices, mouth-watering meringues at Gunter's tea shop, and a magnificent battalion of toy soldiers that he drilled with enthusiasm, while

Edward VII was establishing the *Entente Cordiale*, or being furiously polite to his nephew the German Emperor.

Oliver's first school was run by a Mr Hatch, at 28 Alfred Place, Westminster. 'At the age of seven' he wrote[1], 'I left our house in Ovington Square each morning, escorted by a messenger boy, rather smaller, I fancy, than myself.' After a few terms at Alfred Place, Oliver went to Mr Gibbs's school in Sloane Street. This was a day school, largely for boys between the ages of seven and ten, patronised by the professional classes. Mr Gibbs, who founded the school, was a young man when Oliver attended as a pupil. He was still headmaster over twenty years later when Christopher Milne[2] was a scholar at Sloane Street, and what Christopher Milne wrote of Gibbs's school was probably just as applicable in Oliver Leese's time as it was over twenty years later.

Christopher Milne found Gibbs a bridge between kindergarten and prep school, between plasticine and raffia on the one hand, and Latin declensions and simultaneous equations on the other; between childhood and boyhood, between the nursery world and his Nanny and the drawing room world of his parents. There were lantern lectures every Tuesday afternoon. He learnt 'Lars Porsena of Cluseum' and 'I stood tiptoe upon a little hill' and read *The Heroes of Asgard* and *Great Expectations*, learnt *mensa* and *amo*, the dates of George I and the shape of North America. In Oliver's time the curriculum would have been very much the same.

When Oliver was nine he was sent to Ludgrove, a school founded in 1893 in New Barnet by Arthur Dunn, the brilliant amateur soccer player whose name is commemorated in The Arthur Dunn Cup.

'I well remember my sister Betty', wrote Oliver, 'who was then about four years of age, standing on the doorstep weeping bitterly, and saying "Thank goodness he's going to school".'

Ludgrove was at that time one of a score of schools that specialised in preparing boys for Eton. The writer, Shane Leslie, who went to Ludgrove half a dozen years before Oliver, had vivid memories of Ludgrove's founder:

Arthur Dunn taught us to play football as honourably as the game of life, to recite the Kings of Judah and Israel, to love God and to hate Harrow. He died in his prime as the result of football strain – a bright and lovable memory, touching muscular Christainity at its highest. Yet most of his boys were doomed to die younger than he. To have been a schoolboy in

---

[1] Memoirs.
[2] Son of A. A. Milne and prototype of Christopher Robin, Mr Christopher Milne describes Gibbs's school in his autobiographical work *The Enchanted Places*.

the nineties was to have become fodder for the war flames of the next century.[1]

When Oliver went to Ludgrove, the school was run by G. O. Smith, who got a cricket blue for Oxford, but was probably better known as the England and Corinthians centre forward.

'He had a very strong team of masters,' wrote Leese, 'many of whom were Oxford blues and internationals, and as a result of this we were taught our cricket, our soccer, and Eton fives extremely well. There was, too, one master, Bunco Brown, whom I remember best as drinking daily a tankard of beer for lunch in a green Lovat suit. He was the one master who used to make us work. We were up to him when we got into the top form. If we didn't work he used to pull our hair and kick us on the shins; I have the deepest feeling of gratitude to him, because he was one of the few people in my life who made me learn how to concentrate and work.'[2]

The ten-year-old Oliver's end of term arrangements for December 1904, printed for the school, survive among his personalia: 'The 9.37 which starts from Barnet, and to which special carriages are attached is the most convenient train for those who have no particular connection to make. Servants are sent only by the 8.50 and 9.37 trains to Kings Cross terminus. Arrangements can be made for them to see boys off from other stations in London. Full particulars, and journey money, should be sent direct to Mr Smith at least six days before the end of Term.'

In the Lent term 1906 Oliver won the Division III mathematics prize. This was a beautiful bound copy of W. E. Henley's anthology of poetry for boys, *Lyra Heroica*, one of the best collections of verse for the young ever to be published. It was the first of several prizes he won at Ludgrove; with its stirring poems of action and patriotism and gentler verses of Wordsworth and Herrick, it was probably the one he cherished most.

His school friends at this time included Tim Nugent[3] and Robert Bridgeman[4]: the three were to remain life long friends. One of Oliver's letters of this period has survived. At the age of eleven he was already

[1] *The End of a Chapter.* By Shane Leslie (Constable).
[2] Memoirs.
[3] First Baron Nugent (1895–1973). Served in Irish Guards in 1914–18 war (MC). Lt Col Comptroller Lord Chamberlain's Dept, 1936–60. A Permanent Lord-in-Waiting to the Queen, 1960–73.
[4] Second Viscount Bridgeman of Leigh (1896–1982). Served with distinction at Dunkirk. Director General Home Guard and Territorial Army, 1941–44.

showing potential for writing his dispatches and a keen mind for logistics:

Dear Mummy and Daddy,

We played St David's [Reigate] away and they beat us 54–24. They went in first and we got them out very quickly. Then we went in. Their bowling was not better than the 2nd game bowling here, but as our XI are accustomed to fast and more difficult bowling they tried to poke it except a few people and got out.

Our XI was Eastwood ma (cap) Cornwallis Bailey Forster Carnegie ma Nesbitt mi Parker Dunne Swynne Hoare ma Nugent ma. On the Tuesday when the XI rested before the day they went to Reigate and the Wed the remnants of the first game played the best 16 in the 2nd game. We got them out for 31. Then we went in and hit at very nearly everything. I made 14. Then they went in again and we got them out with 2 men short. I made 5 against the 1st XI and for the 2nd XI. There was a masters match v the free foresters. They beat us 140–103. Will you send me 2 pots of honey and some brilliantine and some devonshire cream. Corbet and Monckton [later Lord Monckton] were caned for ragging in dormitory. At half term I was top in the exams and 2nd by 13 marks in classics. 3rd in Maths 3rd in History and nearly bottom in the rest. Hope all are well. Oliver.

The staff match against the Free Foresters was a regular fixture: an indication of the cricketing strength of the masters' team is that they had regular fixtures with the Free Foresters, Oxford University Authentics and the Butterflies. The school first eleven matches were normally confined to home and away fixtures with other prep schools, but a regular event in the boys' fixture list was a match against a House of Commons eleven: a number of the boys were sons or grandsons of MPs.

On July 21, 1906 the House of Commons team defeated the boys 144 – 112. Sir Joseph Leese, MP, made 13, and his son William, Oliver's father, co-opted, if not coerced, into the side, scored 7.

In 1907 Oliver was in the top division, coming sixth in the Final Order of Bunco Brown's form. He was top of the school in English History and 16th out of 16 with 28 marks out of 150 in the music examination. But he *was* learning the piano. He was batting more successfully in the cricket field for the first eleven, his best effort being an innings of 49 not out that saved the game in the local Derby against Stanmore, a school that sent most of its pupils at Harrow. Altogether Ludgrove won 8 and drew 4 matches, for the first time having an unbeaten record on the cricket field. Oliver, scoring 113 runs for 8 times out, is described as having 'batted well at times'. He also won the fives cup with Tim Nugent.

The Michaelmas term of 1907 was Oliver's last at Ludgrove. Now just over thirteen, he finished third in the school, and astonishingly won the music prize. A note about leaving boys states that Oliver Leese was placed in Upper IV at Eton as the result of the entrance examination taken in November. 'Throughout the term Leese's work has been quite as good as if not superior to that of many Ludgrove boys who have previously taken Remove.'

It is to be inferred that Oliver went to Eton more-or-less as a second string. His father was a Wykehamist, and had rather taken for granted that Oliver would go to Winchester. William Leese, however, was a little vague about entering his son, and when he started to make enquiries discovered that there were no vacancies for the required term; so Oliver went to Eton.

Oliver Leese took to Eton, the most paradoxical of schools, as a duck takes to water. The Duke of Wellington loathed Eton, Gladstone loved it, Shelley abhorred it: to Oliver it was a delightful club where you met your friends and involved yourself fully in everything that was going on. Was there ever a school more exquisitely civilised, more violently barbaric, more arrogantly philistine, more devotedly academic? – where committed scholarship aroused scorn, where a false quantity evoked horror – where boys had been known to quote Homer in the middle of a fist fight.

At Eton masters were beaks, new boys were scugs, scholars were tugs, to work hard was to sap. A term was a Half, and three Halves made a year.[1]

Oliver Leese was at Eton from the Lent half 1908 until the end of the Summer Half, 1914. As a new boy, age thirteen, he was tall for his age, well-built, dark-haired, normally wearing the cheerful, half-mocking smile he had acquired from his mother. Tim Nugent and Robert Bridgeman were again among his contemporaries, so too was the young Harold Macmillan. He was fag during his first year to John Crowder, a benevolent fagmaster. Later, as Sir John Ellenborough Crowder, he was a much respected Conservative MP for nearly thirty years. As a fag a good deal of Oliver's free time would be spent in doing odd jobs for his fagmaster, including cooking buttered eggs, at which he became adept, and toasting crumpets with the long toasting forks then fashionable at Eton.

Once again Oliver had a games playing headmaster. Edward Lyttelton (1854–1942), headmaster from 1905 until 1916, was a member of the famous scholar cricketer Lyttelton family. Seven brothers had represented the school at cricket. Edward Lyttelton had captained

---

[1] The word 'Half' at Eton has been kept on since ancient times, when there was only one long break in the school year.

Eton in 1874, and in 1878 was captain of a Cambridge side that won all their matches, and defeated the Australian touring team. He was sometimes considered to be more of a cricketer than a scholar. He gained second class honours in classics at Trinity College, Cambridge, but when he became Headmaster of Eton, after fifteen years as Master of Haileybury, his acceptance by members of the staff was somewhat cautious. A new broom is distrusted at the best of times.

The sway of classics at the school had been secure in the time of Lyttelton's famous predecessor, Edmond Warre, scholar, oarsman, virtual founder of the Eton OTC, but Lyttelton undoubtedly had disturbing ideas on the subject – he had even written a book entitled *Must we learn Latin Verse?* He had advanced views on sex education; his liberal ideas were also evident in the speakers invited to give lectures at the school – Norman Angell, for instance, was invited in 1912, to give a talk on *War and Peace*.

One day in July 1911 Oliver got into trouble with Lyttelton and later in the same day merited his praise:

> My first cricket colour came to me in a rather curious way at Eton. When I was sixteen I was on the fringe of my Lower Club Colour, and one day towards the end of the Summer Half I was caught cribbing and was very rightly beaten by Ted Lyttelton, the Headmaster. In the afternoon we were playing a house match, and when I had made thirty or forty the Headmaster suddenly appeared and came out and umpired. He brought me a lot of luck that day, and I went on to get 140 runs, and as a result of that I got my Lower Club. At the end of my innings the Headmaster came up to me and said 'Well done, my boy, if I hadn't beaten you this morning, you would never have done so much good.'[1]

As a junior, Oliver transgressed quite often, chiefly through failing to control his natural ebullience. Once, when the Eight were at Henley, he and some other boys were caught by a member of Pop bathing off rafts, and were duly beaten. Efforts were made both at home in North Mimms, where the family were now living, and at Eton to canalise Oliver's activities, and he soon settled down. At home there was the cricket club at Presdales, of which Tim Nugent was a keen member. Oliver also joined the Boy Scouts. His father, Bill Leese, was a Scout Commissioner, and Oliver took an active part in the flourishing troop at North Mimms.

In 1909, at the age of fourteen, he joined the Officers Training Corps, which at Eton was taken more seriously than at many public schools, though parades were regarded as a welcome change from academic work. In December 1909 he was given a licence to ride a

[1] Memoirs.

motor cycle, his sponsor was his housemaster, P. V. Broke, whom Oliver found 'a most charming man . . . most understanding; and he always stood up for us when we were in difficulty and trouble.'[1] Oliver had evidently talked both his father and his housemaster into letting him have a motor cycle: there was not much motor traffic on the roads in 1909.

In 1911 George V was to inspect a grand parade of Scouts in Windsor Park. Bill Leese was taking his troop, and Oliver, now an assistant scoutmaster, got Lyttelton's permission to go out for the day with them, Lyttelton adding that, of course he must attend early school. The only way Oliver could do this was to appear in class wearing his Scout uniform: he was the first Etonian to do so, and this was one of the earliest occasions of his eccentricity in dress provoking the amusement of his friends.

He was enjoying life at Eton to the full. The games fields attracted him more than the classrooms but he was getting on well enough with his work. In 1911 he took the School Certificate, obtaining passes in five subjects – Greek, French, Elementary Mathematics, English, English History and Geography, this last being only one subject. In December of the same year he added Latin and Scripture to his list of passes.

In November 1912 he successfully took the Certificate A Examination in the Officers Training Corps. It is evident from the examination papers that neither the War Office nor Oliver Leese and his fellow candidates were oblivious to what the future might have in store. Among the problems facing the candidates was the following:

'You have used up your supporting squad and have now only twenty men left in your trench. You see fresh troops of the enemy advance across the brook with bayonets fixed, they reach the firing line, and the whole pushes on towards the line of the trenches. What orders do you give?'

Eton was not a school that paid undue regard to form orders. But you were expected to work, and Oliver did not always feel like it. On a scrap of paper, probably torn out of a school exercise book, is a pencilled note: 'Leese. Again not known. Without notes. I am not satisfied with him.' Illegible initials follow. On the bottom right hand side of the scrap of paper his housemaster has written 'Nor I! P.V.B.', and on the left at the bottom his tutor C. H. Blakiston initialled the note in red pencil. Oliver would have taken the note to his housemaster and afterwards to his tutor, so that they would both be aware of his sins of omission. The second note is more specific: 'O. W. H. Leese,

---

[1] Memoirs.

unpunctual. Articles of Religion 1–15 inclusive, October 7 1913
C.W.A.' This time only C. H. Blakiston initialled the note.

'Sunday Questions' were scripture essays set to ensure that boys
were well occupied on Sundays, though, according to Shane Leslie,
these tributes to the Sabbath were often written late in the day, after
illicit smoking and catapulting of rabbits in Windsor Great Park. Two
of Oliver's answers, written on the large sheets of lined paper that
Etonians called 'Sunday Q bumf', still survive. In the first of these he
answered a series of questions connected with Saul, on four pages of
paper. The work itself is of a good academic standard, but the
presentation, written in a brilliant profusion of inks in which red, blue,
green and yellow predominate, elicited the sour comment: 'Absurd
colours. Don't do it again.' The second effort consists chiefly of
paragraphs on the story of David and Goliath, and a well composed
account of the life of St Luke. In an ill-advised moment the master
concerned had asked the form to draw a picture of Goliath. Seventeen-
year-old Oliver had done one of David as well for good measure, but
the resulting illustrations would have evoked censorious tut-tutting
from most eight-year-olds. The comment 'A poor picture' was a fine
piece of understatement.

Eton has produced better poets than Oliver Leese. Some verses on
Gideon evoked the criticism 'Not very successful, I fear'. Words were
beyond the history master who read Oliver's poem on the battle of
Marathon – only a couple of despairing squiggles in blue pencil show
that he had attempted to express an opinion. Doubtless feeling the
effects of the previous week's Wall Game, Oliver produced what was
possibly the worst sonnet ever written at Eton. The subject set was
that of 'Our Founder' (Henry VI). Evidently composed in the Shakes-
pearean sonnet form, Oliver's effort concluded:

> In spite the fact you died with faulty mind,
> We trust the Angels be toward thee kind.

In the Michaelmas of 1913 Oliver went up into the Sixth form, where
there were twenty boys, 'More because of my old age than for any
other reason'.[1] Nonetheless he was putting much time and energy into
his various school and out-of-school activities.

He thrived on his games, representing Eton at four kinds of football
– the wall game, the field game, rugger and soccer. For the St Andrew's
Day set-to at the Wall (Collegers v Oppidans) of 1912, Oliver was
twelfth man for the Oppidans.

'The Wall Game was always fun' wrote Oliver, 'and I had a reputation for

[1] Memoirs.

being a bit rough; but there were others who were much the same. There was one master, A. M. Goodhart by name, a most charming man who was a brilliant music master, with whom I crossed swords more than once at the Wall Game. Eventually he complained to my tutor saying that I really had been abnormally rough. My tutor was splendid and anted up on my behalf, adding that he didn't really see how anybody could possibly be rougher than Goodhart. So Goodhart and I shook hands and had another fight together next time.'[1]

In the Summer Half of 1913 he was in the 2nd XI, and made 68 against an I Zingari team that included Lord Harris. In the same Half he went with his tutor C. H. Blakiston, and two unnamed school friends, to attend the opening of the Eton Boys Club by Lord Roberts,[2] who became the Club's first President.

Oliver had an immense regard for C. H. Blakiston, who eventually left Eton to become Headmaster of Lancing. When he died in 1949, it was Leese who wrote his obituary for the Eton Chronicle. He had a great admiration for P. V. Broke, his housemaster; enjoyed his tussles at the wall with A. M. Goodhart; and he liked talking and playing cricket with E. C. Austen Leigh (The Flea), one of Eton's legendary characters.

A master who had the highest possible regard for Oliver's talents was A. B. Ramsay (The Ram), who tutored Harold Macmillan when the latter was seventeen and not well enough to attend school. A. B. Ramsay, as Mr Lamb, was one of the chief characters in Shane Leslie's novel, *The Oppidan*, which depicts the school at the turn of the century. Shane Leslie paints a portrait of a brilliant classicist, wise, gentle, meticulous, and possessing spiritual grace. Ramsay was one of the first to see in Leese a person of no ordinary ability, and after the second war was to offer him the mastership of Magdalene College, Cambridge.

At the beginning of the Michaelmas Half, Oliver was made a member of 'Pop', the name given to the self-electing Eton Society, which dates from 1811. Originally an informal debating society – Gladstone had been a member in the 1820's – 'Pop' had become an exclusive club for 'bloods' and athletes.

'Pops', wrote Shane Leslie in *The Oppidan*, 'were the athletic oligarchy who ruled the School under the symbol of their knotted canes, tied with light blue ribbon into the form of *fasces*. They alone enjoyed the privilege of wearing coloured waistcoats and flowers in their coats. But in their lowly name they bore the mark of a lost intellectual origin when they met over a *Popina* or cook-shop for intellectual discussion and debate.

[1] Memoirs.
[2] Field Marshal Lord Roberts – General 'Bobs', an Old Etonian.

Harold Macmillan[1] considered 'Pop' similar in many ways to Vincent's Club (for Blues and Half Blues at Oxford), though, he recalled, 'you didn't have to be an athlete for election to 'Pop' – Look at Ronnie Knox, who never played any game apart from chess.' Membership of 'Pop' was limited to thirty, and Oliver's fellow members included Tim Nugent, Victor Cazalet[2] and Oliver Stanley[3].

Oliver became a member of the Scientific Society; membership limited to twenty-four; in addition members of the staff could attend. He gave a lecture on the Boy Scout movement; sociology evidently coming under the aegis of the Society: other lectures, such as 'Recent Controversies on the Origins of Life', and 'Invisible Radiation' were more obviously of a scientific nature.

Oliver played for the Oppidans versus the Collegers in the last of the St Andrew's Day Wall Games before the War, although, St Andrew's Day in 1913 being on a Sunday, the Wall Game was played on Saturday, 29 November.

The Eton Chronicle, published on the day of the game, gave all its coverage to the event. The chronicler wrote of Oliver 'O. W. Leese, 13st. 3 lb. (1st wall). Has a good knowledge of the game and is very keen. Can hold well and plays a hard game. Does not mind pain.' A photograph in *The Times* and other London papers showed the Oppidan Walls[4] Leese, Napier and Paravicini – proudly wearing thick sweaters, corduory trousers, knitted scrum caps and scarves twined nonchalantly round the neck and falling knee length.

The day before the game, Oliver, in company with the rest of the Oppidan team, was invited to breakfast at 'Tap' – the Tap Inn, Eton High Street, the only licensed premises in the town to which Etonians were legally admitted – by G. D. Pape and N. Prinsep, who gave the invitations in their capacity as Keepers of the Wall. The breakfast menu was of the frivolous *genre* that had flourished among sporting circles in Edwardian England, the courses including porridge *au boue de muraille* and beef and brawn à Para, an obvious reference to the thirteen-stone Oppidan, de Paravicini.

This is how a contemporary journalist set the scene for the 1913 game:

A beautiful brick wall, a hundred yards in length and ten or twelve feet in height, a strip of green turf divided from the adjoining meadow by a narrow groove indented down its length, some ten yards away, two lines drawn

[1] Interview 13.11.1979.
[2] Victor Cazalet (1896–1943) Conservative MP and Liaison Officer to General Sikorski.
[3] Oliver Stanley (1896–1950) Conservative MP. Held several Cabinet appointments 1935–45.
[4] They would have been the equivalent of front row forwards in Rugby Football.

transversely in chalk at either end, a glorious elm tree, the patriarch of centuries, and an iron-studded door, and there you have the arena of the Wall Game.

The Collegers had won twenty-six of these encounters, the Oppidans twenty-five, and there had been twenty-two ties. This particular match drew more spectators than usual, shouting gleefully for the Oppidans was the thirteen-year-old Etonian Prince Henry, later the Duke of Gloucester.

The game started according to tradition at 12.30 p.m., the clock striking one being the signal for half-time. After ten minutes' play Prinsep kicked the ball into the Slough Road. The Collegers attacked dangerously after the restart. However, Oliver fell on the ball, and, despite terrific charging, remained there for the next twenty minutes and twenty seconds until the clock struck for half-time.

It was usual to restart immediately after half-time, but on this occasion the players largely involved were so exhausted that the game was delayed for four minutes. Nothing definite resulted in the second half and a fiercely contested game ended in a tie. This was Leese's match: by his obstinacy in falling on the ball when the Oppidans were in trouble, he had saved his side. The bully or loose scrum resulting from his fall was the second longest in the history of the Wall Game.

Oliver's tutor, Cuthbert Blakiston, celebrated the occasion by producing a sonnet, which began:

> It really would amuse the garden cat
> To see our Olly playing at the wall.
> It is so funny when he holds the ball
> And keeps the crowd off with his haunches fat.

In the Summer Half of 1914 Oliver was much involved in the Fourth of June celebrations in honour of Eton's royal benefactor, George III; and, now in the first eleven, he distinguished himself especially in the match against Eton Ramblers, scoring 69 in Eton's first innings.

The Band of the Life Guards performed on this day of days when Eton was *en fête*. They had some evocative light music in their repertoire – the 'Spring Song', 'Light Cavalry', 'The Blue Danube', and – to become immortalised only too soon by André Maurois – the 'Destiny Valse', beloved of Colonel Bramble.

The display of fireworks by C. T. Brock and Co., Pyrotechnicists by Appointment to H.M. the King, was an exuberant affair: The Lattice of Scintillating Jewels, special colossal fire portraits of H.M. King George the Fifth and Queen Mary; special colossal pictorial device representing a naval duel between super-dreadnoughts. Thun-

derbolt bombardments by huge batteries of special Roman Candles
. . . explosions of Cobras, Silver Snakes, Scorpions, etc., etc.

During the golden summer of 1914 Oliver's main interest was
cricket. However, he didn't do very well in the penultimate match
against Winchester – played, according to *Wisden* 'in almost tropical
heat'. G. S. Rawstorne, the Eton captain, left him out for the final
match of the season, against Harrow, which was always played at
Lord's, and he went to the game as twelfth man. 'It was the first real
knock I had in my life' he wrote.[1] In those days the Eton and Harrow
match was a national event, and, in the two-day match of 1914, more
than 40,000 spectators watched Eton win their fifth successive victory
against Harrow.

In July 1914, time was running out for Europe. The Etonian Shane
Leslie sensed the end of a chapter in the continent's history.

As for Oliver Leese, he had spent six and a half glorious years at
Eton and he was ready for whatever the future might bring. He had
loved sharpening his wits in discussion with his contemporaries and
with members of the staff. He had learnt something about the internal
combustion engine. The OTC, the Boy Scout Movement, and the
Eton Mission had taught him a good deal that would be of value in
the world outside the classroom.

At the end of the Lent Half the Musical Society had given a concert
which ended with the school song *Vale*, sung by a trio, each singing
one verse – Tim Nugent, Oliver and Rawstorne. Oliver preserved his
copy of the score, with the words 'Don't hurry' pencilled at the top.
He had sung the second verse, which would have echoed in his mind
as the last days of pre-war Eton slipped by:

> Old Eton places, old Eton faces,
> Though we be parted far away,
> Seen ever clearly, loved ever dearly,
> Shall then be with us as today:
> Each house familiar, each smooth meadow,
> Each bend of river, each old tree.
> Hearts growing older, love never colder,
> Never forgotten shalt thou be.

[1] Memoirs.

2

DISTINGUISHED SERVICE

One imagined that it would be all over by Christmas.
                                                              Oliver Leese

Oliver's intention, after leaving Eton, had been to go to France for a year or so, learn to speak French fluently, then return to England, and become 'something in the City'. The assassination at Sarajevo changed all that.

He was with the Eton OTC as a cadet officer in the camp at Mytchett, run by the Brigade of Guards, when war broke out.[1]

> A great friend of mine in my house [Broke's] Nigel Sutton, told me that his father was Colonel of the Coldstream and suggested that I should come and see him. I was very glad to do so and together we went to the RHQ in Birdcage Walk; and it was on that day that I made one of the happiest decisions of my life – to apply for a commission in the Coldstream Guards.
>
> The Regimental Lieutenant Colonel very kindly told me that he would take me on the special reserve of the Coldstream Guards and that he would let me know when I should report to Windsor.[2]

Nothing happened for a week or so. Oliver, with typical impatience, persuaded his father to see the Colonel and consequently was ordered to report to Windsor. When he got there he found that the Regiment had very few officers in training as reinforcements to go out to France. The training consisted mostly of drill and musketry; they did one or two tactical exercises, but there was no time for field training.

During this period Oliver visited Eton whenever he could and early in the Michaelmas Half played for an Old Etonian side against the school in the wall game. Impatient to go to the front, fearful that the

---

[1] His grandfather, Joseph Leese, had died on 29 July 1914. Oliver's father therefore had become the second baronet, and Oliver heir to the baronetcy.
[2] Memoirs.

war would be over before the end of September, there was still much of the schoolboy in the young soldier. In a letter to his parents on Wednesday 2 September (the eighth day of the Retreat from Mons), written from Victoria Barracks, Windsor, he requested the following items:

> 2 pr white flannel trousers, 3 white cricket shirts, the large XI sash, Rambler sash and white silk scarf with field colours on it. 2 stiff white shirts. Grey homburg hat. Straw hat. Umbrella. That large knife. Aquascutum – any white silk collars. XXII tie. Panama. Tennis racquet. Field Service regulations – Infantry training (little red handbook)[1] Those large photos of Johnnie, George, etc., in a big envelope in my cupboard. 2 pairs light blue socks – 4 pairs those green or brown socks Granny gave me. A big list, I'm afraid. I don't get my uniform until I'm gazetted.[2]

After five weeks' training in the Coldstream Guards, Oliver and three others – Beauchamp, Gell, Legge, were sent for to the Orderly Room. To their great joy they were to go to France within two or three days.

The emotive patriotism in the Leese circle was a microcosm of what was going on throughout Britain. True to the Leese motto, *Vita cara, carior libertas* – life is dear, liberty dearer – Oliver was determined to go to France the second he heard that war had been declared. Granny Sandeman, who 'spoilt him rotten' didn't want to lose him, but she thought he ought to go. To Bill – now Sir William Leese – she wrote on 9 October, 'he is doing what every English youth and man must do and therefore he could not have done otherwise.' 'You may well be proud of him' wrote the Vicar of North Mimms – the Leeses were his parishioners – adding with unconscious irony 'it is nothing less than wonderful that he should be considered ready to go after such a short time.'

'I'm off to France on Monday' wrote Oliver to Granny Sandeman in an undated letter from Victoria Barracks, Windsor, 'and I hope we shall meet again later, when I've done my little bit with the best regiment in the world.'

On Monday, 12 October, Oliver and his three friends set sail, evidently for St Nazaire. 'We all admire his courage and pluck' wrote Granny Sandeman to her daughter Violet (Oliver's mother), on 13 October. 'You would not have wished him to have done otherwise, though he is very young to leave you all'.

---

[1] Siegfried Sassoon was mystified by this manual, which was chiefly based on Boer War experience. It was eventually superseded by an excellent 32-page Manual on the Employment of Platoon.

[2] He was gazetted 2nd Lieutenant 15.9.1914, in the Special Reserve of Officers. Subsequently [15.5.1915] he was gazetted as 2nd Lieutenant in Land Forces.

The next news of Oliver came in a letter headed St Nazaire, dated Friday 16 October, written by 2nd Lieutenant Legge.[1]

Yesterday afternoon Oliver Leese and I went for a walk along the cliffs and back along the shore: quite lovely; little rocky promontories jutting out and white villas with mimosa beginning to bud and then at the end a sentry with fixed bayonet over the bathing place, and Seaforth and R[ifle] Brigade doing musketry on the cliff while the destroyers dashed up and down in front of us. Well, we got home, O.L. and I, pretty low spirited at Synge going up before us, simply on account of seniority, and sat down to dinner in our tent, five of us, off fried bacon [fried by Harry Gell over a candle], marmalade and cheese, and wine of the country bought from a camp hawker – white 80C., red 70C. After dinner we played bridge by the light of two candles stuck in dead wine bottles, and as we played, Rap! on the tent. 'Officers of the 3rd Coldstreams!' A line orderly – open went the tent. '2nd Lieutenants Leese and Legge' – Oliver and I gripped each other – 'To hold themselves in readiness to proceed to the front with the draft at any hour of the day or night.'

Down went the cards, and out into the pouring rain to call the roll of men. (It is done every two hours between Reveille and Lights Out, when you are standing by for active service), and so to bed.

Harry Gell was called at four: we slept on the bare ground and like tops: we dressed him in full armour and sent him, Synge and Beauchamp off. We go any time between 6 pm and 6 am with a draft, humanly speaking –

Well, that's the news.

Leese and Legge soon got their orders to move, though they were not together for long. The war was to be a far different affair from anything Leese had imagined, but he was neither worried by the stark horror nor by the vast amount that, as a young subaltern, he had to learn.

'Little did we realise', he wrote, 'how long the war would go on and how singularly unfitted we were to command a platoon.'[2] He and his three friends had done virtually no platoon training at all. Leese himself felt a certain 'spurious confidence' because he had been a cadet officer at Eton. He had got to France just in time to join the Third Battalion on the way up to Ypres after the heavy fighting on the Aisne. He joined his Company just before they were to go through Ypres, and was allowed to ride an old grey Flemish cart horse at the rear of the Company part of the way through the ancient town, which was as yet unscarred by war.

That night they bivouacked on the far side of the town and next

[1] Part of Legge's letter, presumably to his parents, was copied and sent to Oliver's parents.
[2] Memoirs.

morning took up a position in some open fields near St Julian and started to dig in. They were support company to their battalion, which had moved into the line to await the new German thrust towards Ypres. They stayed there all morning and in the afternoon the Germans got their range and shelled them with shrapnel.

'Almost at once' wrote Oliver, 'I was hit in the back, but not before I had seen a very large officer blown several feet in the air and then down again, quite unhurt with a whole mass of swedes, in the field around us.[1]

Oliver was wounded on 20 October, 1914. He was sent back to a casualty clearing station near Wimereux, where, luckily for himself, he fainted after walking up two or three storeys of the hotel in which the hospital was situated. If he had not fainted, the piece of shrapnel, which was actually sticking into his spine, might have gone in deeper and caused him permanent damage.

The following day Oliver and the other casualties were sent home by hospital ship, but were diverted to Ireland, as no further hospital beds were available in England. They were taken to Cork, where little or no preparations had been made. There were no stretchers so they were carried out in blankets.

Oliver was looking a little flushed, so a thoughtful civilian got a siphon of soda water from the refreshment room, and squirted it in his face. Once he was in hospital he was looked after properly and a surgeon named Townsend took the piece of shrapnel out of his spine. Leese made light of his wound, but it was a severe one, and he was left with a slight stoop for the remainder of his life.

The realities of war were dawning on military and civilians alike. 'I hope that Oliver's wound will not be a trouble to him, or to you,' wrote a family friend, 'and that it will heal without pain and much discomfort. I think he had a merciful escape – others in the same battle are gone.'

Long before the wound had healed up he was allowed to go back to England and to recuperate at his parents' home in North Mimms. 'It was a perfect way to do it', he reflected, 'but one cannot imagine being allowed to do this in the later days of the war.'[2]

After a few days he moved from his parents' home to Eton, where he stayed as a guest of C. H. Blakiston. The Eton move was the result of his joining the training battalion of the Coldstream Guards at Windsor. Travelling was thus minimal, and Oliver found himself in the Alice in Wonderland situation of life at Eton and in the Coldstream Guards at the same time.

[1] Ibid.
[2] Memoirs.

I'm really getting on well as regards my health [he wrote to his parents in an undated letter about this time. Barely twenty, he was still addressing them as 'My dear Mummy and Daddy']. Dempster[1] is rubbing my back daily and says I'm getting along well.

Only doing musketry on the square and so don't have to get tired. We went to dinner with P V B[roke] on Thursday and had a most amusing time – the Flea being there in great form. Last night we dined with the Head. C H B[lakiston] looks after me like a child.

Oliver, therefore, having played against the school at the beginning of the half, and watched the first round of the house matches, had been out to France, got wounded, got back again, convalesced – and now he was able to see the final of the house matches.

He was invited to Broke's, his old house at Eton, for the end of half entertainment in which a mixture of music and drama was presented. The drama included a production of Conan Doyle's one act play, *Waterloo*, in which Corporal Gregory Brewster, 67 years after the battle, recounts his achievements in the defence of Hougoumont.[2]

Oliver's second journey out to France was with the 2nd Bn Coldstream Guards, commanded by Colonel Pereira:

I never think I made a very good start with the Battalion, because the very night I joined them in the tobacco factory in Bethune, we had a very gay night in the Mess. In the course of this evening one or two of us who had just joined the Battalion were handed a tumbler containing every form of liquor poured out in layers and for all the world looking like a Neapolitan ice. I had come out pretty well straight from Eton, and this was about my first really good night out. I could not have enjoyed it more and in the course of it I was ragging round the room with Budget Loyd[3] who was then commanding No 2 Company . . . I stepped on the floor which was by this time pretty slippery, and I sprained my ankle. The next morning the doctor said I could not get up – the Battalion was going into the line that day, and he added I certainly could not go into the trenches. Later in the morning the C.O. came to see me, and as it was my first day with the Battalion, he rather naturally didn't seem all that pleased about it. Anyhow I managed to go up that evening and have a look at the line, but I wasn't allowed to go into the trenches for two or three days.[4]

When he did go into the trenches, it was as a platoon commander. For

---

[1] Dempster was the school masseur. Patrick Strong, the College Archivist, writes 'O.E.s will remember him and his daughters.'
[2] Officers and men of the Coldstream Guards played a major part in the epic defence of the Farm at Hougoumont during the battle of Waterloo.
[3] Major General H. C. Loyd. So nicknamed because he joined the Regiment on Budget Day, 1911.
[4] Memoirs.

several months during the spring and summer of 1915 they held the
line round Givenchy and the Guinchy brickstacks, and as the ground
was very waterlogged most of the defences were breastworks built up
above ground level. Hence they used a great many sandbags and
became very practised in building this type of defences. Sometimes
their defences were very close to the German ones, and there were
times especially on the brickstacks when it was quite easy to throw a
hand grenade into the German trenches. They felt safer when very
close up to the enemy because under these circumstances it was difficult
for the Germans to shell them without endangering the safety of their
own trenches.

In July 1915 he was wounded for the second time, receiving slight
multiple wounds in the face, but remained on duty.

'Just a line to say how sorry we are to hear that Olly is wounded again',
wrote Cuthbert Blakiston to Violet Leese, on 22 July, 1915, 'and how
much we hope it is only slight, if so it will be a great relief for you to have
him home to nurse awhile. Please don't bother to write – but if a p.c. could
let us know we'd be so grateful.'

While platoon commander in this area Leese had with him a bunch of
NCO's he thought the world of: Sgt 'Tipper' Davies, Sgt Groombridge,
Cpl Hollyhead from Stourbridge and Cpl Penderel from Wolverhampton. Oliver did much to promote a spirit of camaraderie within his
platoon. During periods of intensive shelling he organised impromptu
concerts in which he and the NCO's played leading parts, on penny
whistles and in which Sgt Groombridge excelled. The strains of 'Who's
your lady friend' and the army's new marching song 'Tipperary' were
effective answers to the enemy's aggression, and penny whistles, as
the Army had discovered during the retreat from Mons, were very
good for a soldier's morale.

There was a fine spring and summer of 1915. Oliver chiefly remembered the period as being an excellent one for making friends:

During the long periods at night, when you were on duty in the trenches
and you had nothing else to do except talk to the four or five sentries who
were on watch on the platoon front during the same time that you were on
duty. I don't suppose that ever afterwards officers had the same chance
really to get to know their men; until in this second war one had the same
small groups who lived and fed and slept together by their vehicles,
particularly in the artillery, in the tank units and in the armoured
cars.[1]

[1] Memoirs.

In September 1915, there were rumours of a big battle: this was the battle of Loos. During the initial stages they held the line. It was their first operation as a Guards Division, and for the first time they saw on their transport vehicles the eye which was to be the symbol of the Guards Division in the first war, and which Oliver was to use again when they formed the Guards Armoured Division in the second war.

At the start of the battle (September 25 1915), they were in reserve, and watched the other brigades in their division carry out a magnificent attack across open country. 'One of the last model textbook attacks of their day. The Brigade deployed over open country and advanced in battle formation in perfect array under heavy shrapnel fire for several thousands of yards. It was a most impressive sight, and owing to their discipline and perfect extension the battalions did not suffer unduly from the enemy fire.'[1] On 3 October 1915 Oliver was promoted Lieutenant (antedated to 30.9.15). On 27 October he was twenty-one: his mother's gift of a silver whisky flask was to save his life, in an unexpected manner, before his next birthday.

Towards the middle of the summer of 1916 there were rumours of big attacks down in the south, and of heavy casualties. The rumours, only too well founded, referred to the battle of the Somme. Hearing, while on Paris leave, of an intended offensive, Oliver 'commandeered' a vehicle so that he could get back in time to his battalion. In the event, Leese was wounded on 15 September: the next day his Commanding Officer received a signal to return him to Paris to face a court of inquiry in connexion with the missing vehicle. The Commanding Officer replied that Oliver had just been killed, and no further action was taken.

To go back in time for a fortnight: Oliver, having returned by unorthodox means, was made sniping and intelligence officer of the battalion, and lived at Battalion HQ. There were ten men in his section, all tough and excellent shots. Because of their appalling behaviour out of the line he christened them 'the Lambs'. He found them a splendid team to command. At the beginning of September they moved into the reserve in the undulating country round the Somme.

'While we were waiting to go into the line', wrote Oliver, 'we woke up one morning to see all round us some enormous objects covered by tarpaulins. We had no idea what these were, and it was not till some days later that we knew that they were tanks waiting to be used in their first battle. It was a thrilling moment, and we were full of expectation as to what they would achieve. The Guards Division was detailed to carry out its attack near Guinchy on the 15th September 1916, and we were to be supported by these tanks. It was to be the first tank battle in history.'[2]

[1] Ibid.
[2] Memoirs.

On the night before his battalion went into battle, Oliver was sent ahead of the Brigade to reconnoitre in front of the position they were to occupy. He was told to go to Guinchy railway station. Eventually he found a few bricks and two feet of steel girders – all that was left.

With regard to the attack itself the official cyclostyled report on the operations of 1st Guards Brigade, August–September 1916, says that zero hour was on 15 September at 6.20 a.m. and that the situation up to this hour was perfectly normal. The assembly march was carried out without a hitch, and units were all in position by 1 a.m. on 15 September. Arrangements to give the men hot tea and a meat sandwich before the attack started were outweighed by the necessity for keeping down the number of lights and fires. By 5.30 a.m. the leading Infantry went forward and the barrage started. The two leading Coldstream battalions came under terrific fire and several Coldstream officers were killed before they had gone a hundred yards.

Tanks went into action for the first time in history. Charles Carrington, who fought as a subaltern in the battle of the Somme, sums up:

> Thirty-six started; some were ditched, some broke down; some were shot up; eleven crossed the front line; and four or five made a useful contribution to the battle . . . How fortunate it was that their inadequacy was revealed before a large order was placed for them. Nevertheless, four days later Haig asked the War Office for a thousand tanks of better design, and when, a year later, the Mark IV tanks arrived with many modifications, we at last had a war-winning weapon.[1]

It was on this same day, 15 September, that Oliver won his DSO. The citation reads:

> For conspicuous gallantry in action. He led the assault against a strongly held part of the enemy's line, which was stopping the whole attack. He personally accounted for many of the enemy and enabled the attack to proceed. He was wounded during the fight.[2]

Oliver led his platoon at 6.20 a.m. in an attack on the enemy trenches. After a few minutes he was shot in the stomach by a German officer, the bullet piercing his whisky flask – his twenty-first birthday present from his mother. The flask was nearly full of whisky, the bullet piercing it on both sides; as a result, Oliver, as he was afterwards told, instead of being shot through the heart, was wounded in the stomach.

Close behind Oliver was Cpl Alma (Jack) Lambert – one of the

[1] *Soldier from the Wars returning.* By Charles Carrington, Hutchinson 1964.
[2] Another officer who won the DSO on the Somme on 15 September 1916 was Captain (later Field Marshal) Harold Alexander of the Irish Guards.

'Lambs', he weighed eighteen stone – who immediately shot and killed the German officer. He then carried Leese on his shoulders for about 150 yards; it was probably during this time that the whisky flask fell to the ground, remaining in the mud of the battlefield for another four years.[1] Leese, dazed and losing blood rapidly, was still able to do some quick thinking. He had, within the previous few days, heard a talk from the medical officer, saying that if you were wounded in the stomach, your best chance was to get back quickly. Seeing Cpl Sainsbury taking back some German prisoners, he stopped them, and told them to collect a stretcher and take him back. This they did, Cpl Sainsbury feeling pretty certain that the young Lieutenant Leese hadn't long to live. Cpl Lambert meanwhile went back to the German officer, and went through the contents of his pockets in case they contained anything of military importance. He also appropriated the German's Iron Cross and Luger pistol, and retained as a souvenir a postcard, on one side of which was the officer's photograph, on the other side the written message:

A little picture of me in Turkish khaki uniform. The crescent I received at the beginning of January for bravery in action.

There was no signature or address of intended recipient. The German officer was probably a regular, who had returned to the Western Front after acting for some months as an adviser to the Turkish Army.[2]

A few hours after he had been wounded, Oliver was taken down by train to No 2 Red Cross Hospital at Rouen, and after a few weeks was sent to England, and Lady Ridley's hospital in Carlton House Terrace, which he found 'a superbly run hospital . . . the sisters and nurses were charming, and while we were convalescing we had a glorious view right over St James's Park.'[3]

Cpl Lambert had kept the Luger for several months until he was on leave in England, when he visited Oliver at Carlton House Terrace, and they discussed the details of the attack in which he was wounded. Finally Lambert handed the Luger over to Oliver with the remark 'There you are, that's the b- that shot you!'

A number of NCO's and men wrote both to Oliver himself and to his parents: thus L/Sgt Carter to Oliver's parents (20 September)

[1] The flask now bears the embossed statement, on the opposite side to the original birthday inscription: 'Lost on being wounded by Ginchy, September 15, 1916, afterwards found by Gunner J. A. Gore RFA, and returned to OWHL on October 14 1920.'
[2] I am indebted to Mr Michael Willis of the Imperial War Museum for this information. Author.
[3] Memoirs.

We deeply feel the loss of our officer Mr. Leese, who acted so brave and
gentlemanly . . . he was our best friend and through him we had many
privileges making our life happier and enjoying more freedom which we
had not known before. He spared no effort for our welfare.

'His men thought so much about him as he did about them' wrote Pte
T. Rodgers (29 September). On 24 October Cpl Lambert wrote
thanking Leese's parents for a parcel, ending his letter with wry
humour – 'I hope to remain, your obedient servant.'

Oliver's first letter home after being wounded, addressed from No 2
Red Cross Hospital, Rouen, ran as follows:

5/10/16

My dearest M & D

Many thanks for several letters of before and after the Great Adventure,
also a delightful surprise parcel of scents, etc. I don't think I've ever
enjoyed a parcel so much before. My name is on the list for Blighty and I
either cross tonight or tomorrow, that is unless the conveys are off like the
end of last week. I'm very well prepared for the journey, having collected
me an air ring and chocolates. The Commanding Officer wrote . . . saying
that all he had with him was six ensigns. So the old 2nd Bn has come a
cropper at last. I'd always hoped its luck would follow it to the end.

Oliver was a patient at Carlton House Terrace by the second week in
October. 'I hope Oliver reached London safely' wrote a family friend
on 10 October who was nursing in the Rouen hospital, 'and was not
too tired after the journey, and that he managed to get into the right
hospital!' Granny Sandeman also wrote on 10 October: 'May he long
live to continue to distinguish himself in everything that is good and
right. I feel certain that he will do.' Cpl Sainsbury had his own definite
ideas. 'I will be pleased to see him walking about again, but not to go
out yonder, for he has done enough.' Oliver pencilled a note to Granny
Sandeman on his 22nd birthday, 27 October, 'I'm going on very well
and hope to be out of bed in two or three weeks.'

With the announcement in November of Oliver's DSO there were
many congratulatory letters to the family. There were frequent visits
from members of the fair sex. Sir William Leese himself marked the
occasion with a gift to his wife of a brooch.

It was in the form of a Coldstream Star made of diamonds, sapphires
and rubies set in gold, and was made from Leese family jewellery. The
brooch remained in the family's possession until 1983, when it was
presented by the Coldstream Guards Officers Dining Club, the *Nulli
Secundus* Club, to Her Majesty the Queen, as Colonel-in-Chief of the
Coldstream Guards, to commemorate the 200th anniversary of the
formation of the Club.

On 15 November Oliver was sufficiently convalescent to be able to attend the Investiture at Buckingham Palace when George V pinned on his DSO ribbon. He had evidently been allowed out of bed specially for the Investiture, as when Lance Sergeant Sainsbury (newly promoted) visited him on 21 November, Oliver was in bed. Writing on 22 November to Violet Leese, Sainsbury recalled:

I was very pleased to have had the chance of helping your son and if all officers was like him or half so good and brave there would be no men hanging back from the Army . . . I went to see him yesterday and I thought of seeing him walking about but I was disappointed but I know that he will pull through now but I did not think so when I picked him up on the battlefield and I wish him and yourself all the best in the world.

Recuperation took a full six months.

'As was the case with most wounds in the first war,' wrote Leese, 'mine took a long time to heal, because like every other big wound it went gangrenous. How very different the situation was in the last war with all the M and B and penicillin. I do however often wonder whether complete recovery was not perhaps quicker in the first war due to the fact that the wound healed slowly.'[1]

Oliver missed his platoon, and he and his parents sent them welfare parcels. Some fifty letters from the trenches to Oliver's parents survive, expressing concern for his well being, and thanks for gifts of cigarettes, tobacco, cake, chocolates, and the socks made in Violet's knitting parties.

The battle of the Somme petered out, the casualties immense. For Oliver the war in Flanders was over. Discharged in March 1917, he had two months' convalescence at home, and at last was pronounced fit for service in England.

On 12 May, 1917, he was sent to the Household Brigade Officer Cadet Battalion at Bushey, where he was given a platoon to train. There were 30–40 cadets in each platoon, the platoon officer looked after them during the whole of their course, and taught them every subject including drill, musketry and tactical training. There was a great deal to do in the preparation of lectures, and Oliver found the work taught him how to concentrate and to get his facts across – that having to teach was the best way of learning. Duff Cooper and Gerald du Maurier were among those who passed through Oliver's hands, and also the two younger brothers of Air Marshal Elmhurst, who remembered his ability and enthusiasm as a teacher, and his stress on discipline.

[1] Memoirs.

The year 1917 saw the entry of the United States into the war and the breakdown of the Russian Army followed by the Communist revolution. Tanks were used for the first time on a large scale in the brief triumph at Cambrai (20 November 1917).

Germany launched her final offensive in March 1918 in the hope of winning the war before the effect of American participation could make itself felt. There were anxious weeks ahead, but by July it was evident that Hindenburg and Ludendorff had failed in their final throw.

Just before the war ended, Leese was passed fit for overseas service. He returned to his regiment – and was posted to Budget Loyd's battalion at Aldershot. It consisted mostly of miners who had been in a reserved occupation and were released for the last phases of the war. In the event they never went abroad, but Oliver found them 'magnificent men who would have done extremely well.'

3

TEACHING AND LEARNING

You learned at Staff College how to work.
Oliver Leese

The war over, the Coldstream battalions returned to England. Leese was posted to the Second Battalion at Windsor: he soon became Assistant Adjutant and was responsible for musketry training. In March – April 1919, he attended a rifle instructor's course at the School of Musketry in Hythe, passing as Distinguished; and from 5 to 23 May he attended a drill course at the London District School of Instruction at Wellington Barracks and passed the examination in drill in command of a company on parade. Most of the working hours of the summer he spent on the ranges at Wraysbury. He could arrange his own programme, and, by starting early, was able to get most of his work done in the mornings.

There was a wonderful summer in 1919: it was the first year of dances and parties after the years of mud and blood and shellfire, and twenty-four-year-old Oliver Leese received a great many invitations. There was Army cricket to be played at Windsor. As for going to London, one or two officers had motor cars, but the great majority went up and down by train. Sometimes Oliver would go to two or three dances a night, returning to Windsor by train, and having great difficulty in not over-sleeping at Slough: one awful day he woke up in Reading.

Towards the end of the summer, Colonel Charlie Grant, who had just taken over command of the Third Battalion, asked Leese if he would go to him as his Adjutant. This challenge was a turning point in his career. If he did become Adjutant it would mean that he would have to take soldiering really seriously, work for the Staff College and make a career of the Army. Although he had taken a regular commission in 1915, he had not at the time intended to stay on in the Army.

After much hard thought following Charlie Grant's offer Leese decided that the Army was his métier, he therefore replied that he would be delighted to join the Battalion at Wimbledon, where it was part of a Guards Brigade which at that time was quartered in temporary huts on Wimbledon Common.

Charlie Grant had had a distinguished war career, and it was said affectionately of him that he had forgotten all he knew of peacetime soldiering. He left a good deal of the running of the battalion to Leese. At CO's orders the latter would write the appropriate punishment in large clear red ink, 'President' Grant leaning sideways so that he could read what was written.

Soon after joining the battalion Leese had reverted to the rank of subaltern. This he much enjoyed: it was easier as a subaltern to be friends with your team of subalterns, to look after the younger ones and to do things with them. When there was no training on, most company commanders went on leave, and Leese virtually ran the battalion for several months.

Leese found Wimbledon Common a ghastly place for a battalion just after their return from active service, and, as a result, discipline was poor. Soon afterwards the battalion was ordered to move up to Wellington Barracks and he found this a great opportunity to get the discipline, drill and turnout back to peacetime standard; he wrote that 'When the King's Guard mounted at St James Palace, we came under the eagle eye of the Duke of Connaught, who never let any slip on King's Guard go by.'[1]

Leese was enjoying life to the full, in the summer going to all the dances and parties with his fellow subalterns; in the winter time there were 'Drones Club' escapades in the West End of London. One of his friends, Major Guy Burges, recalls dinners at the Floriana before going on to some night club such as Bretts or the '43'. One Christmas Eve at the Floriana, he remembers 'Horatio Bottomley was dining at the next table, and Tom Bevan dancing a *pas de seul* on our table, while Oliver was shouting amid streamers abounding "Speech, Bumley, speech!"'[2]

Back on parade, life was serious enough. The men returning from active service were anxious to be demobilised so that they could get jobs, and they resented undergoing, with raw recruits, the blancoing and guard mounting of peacetime soldiering.

Leese spent almost two and a half years as Adjutant of the battalion, and he was then offered the post of Adjutant of the OTC at Eton.

---

[1] Memoirs.
[2] Letter to author (16.9.79).

He was quick to accept an opportunity that suited him admirably, as it would enable him to 'swot' for Staff College in his spare time.

Shortly before taking up his post, in a last Drone Club fling, he incurred the displeasure of the Metropolitan Police. He resourcefully gave his name as Charles Bagot to the officer on duty at Vine Street police station, and was released on surety of two pounds, later paying a small fine. He kept the receipt for £2 in the same file that recorded his school certificate credits at Eton and his DSO award for valour on the Somme.

At Eton he had a charming little house all to himself in the High Street. He took with him his old soldier servant George Ball, who had had thirty years in the Army and had been with him some time. George Ball's wife was a good cook and they ran an excellent menage in the High Street.

One or two houses at Eton didn't take the Corps seriously. Bummy Wells' house was one of these, although Bummy Wells himself was a great friend of Leese. On one Cert. A day, as usual, several officers came down from the Brigade of Guards to do the judging. Leese had a hunch that something would go wrong with this house, so told Sgt Major Aplin, who had been many years with the Corps, to keep an eye on this particular squad. Aplin was called away to the telephone, and when he returned, to his amazement he saw that the odd numbers in the front rank and the even numbers in the rear rank were wearing blue spectacles and scarlet puttees. The young officer examining the squad was somewhat at a loss, and told Aplin that when the squad had numbered, they had called out Ace, King, Queen, Knave and so on. Aplin sized up the situation, marched the squad off and dismissed them. The question next day was what to do. Leese's solution was to transfer the section sergeant, who had been too easy-going to veto the frivolity, and promote the ring leader from lance corporal to sergeant, putting him in charge of the section.

One of the officer cadets during Leese's regime at Eton was Quintin Hogg (Lord Hailsham). He remembers Leese well as Adjutant

and much enjoyed our relationship. His earthy language and his war record greatly endeared themselves, and were a breath of fresh air in the cloistered atmosphere of the school, and his instructions were in pleasant and startling contrast to the approach of the academic teachers. The sand table exercises over which he presided for Candidates for 'Cert. A' were virtually my only military training of an academic character before commanding a platoon in world war two. As a distinguished Coldstream Officer he gave a marvellous lecture, illustrated by a sand table, on the battle of Waterloo with special reference to the defence of Hougoumont Farm. His lectures on VD, lice, smelly feet and unwashed socks left nothing to the imagination, and when applied to riflemen, proved of great practical value.[1]

The novelist, Anthony Powell, is another Old Etonian who remembers the Adjutant:

He put a lot of energy into it while at the same time being an agreeable and popular adjutant. He used to yell: 'Rip those faces away' at the command 'Eyes right – eyes front' in a thunderous voice. I remember that on his first parade, instead of wearing khaki like the previous adjutant [a Rifleman, they went alternately with the Brigade], Leese turned up in a Guards frock coat and sword. The Company I was in paraded in Cannon Yard, and everyone cheered and banged their rifles on the ground. Leese let out a deafening 'Stop that!' and I must say the applause was immediately quelled. He also used to turn up at the annual parade on a grey horse instead of on foot. I rather think he looked after one of the Eton houses for some weeks when the housemaster was ill. One had the impression that although in one sense (deliberately) a stage guardee in another Leese was an extremely shrewd and approachable chap.[2]

During this time Leese used to run OTC camps, either at Tidworth or Mytchett. There was a good deal of organisation needed; and Leese's work did not escape General Sir Cecil Romer who sent him a congratulatory letter. When Lt Colonel Wright resigned as commander of the Eton OTC, in a special order of the day he wrote 'the Adjutant, by his untiring energy, enthusiasm and organising ability has stimulated the activity of the Corps in every direction, and has greatly improved the standard of "Cert. 'A" classes both in numbers and quality.'

From Eton Leese returned to regimental duty in 1925. He was with his Regiment in May 1926, at the beginning of the General Strike, and they went up to Victoria Park:

Our particular job was to protect some of the meat supplies of London and we humped many of the frozen carcases onto lorries and a very tough and very heavy job we found it. We arrived in steel helmets and battledress and we were received with a good deal of booing and shouting from the women of the adjacent streets, who within a few minutes of our arrival marched down the street in fours with tin jerries on their heads. This made our day. We all laughed, soldiers, strikers and women, and within a day or so our troops were playing the most ardent games of soccer against the strikers in Victoria Park.[3]

[1] Letter to author (3.6.80).
[2] Letter to author (1.7.80).
[3] Memoirs.

In July, Leese heard that he had passed into Staff College with flying colours, together with his friend of Ludgrove and Eton days, Robert Bridgeman. He soon got wind of the fact that two students shared a groom and an orderly, so he suggested to Bridgeman that they should join forces, and this they did.

On 21 January 1927, he was formally admitted as a Staff College student at Camberley. Montgomery, Dick O'Connor, Henry Pownall and Budget Loyd were among the instructors. Alexander, 'Bimbo' Dempsey and Douglas Wimberley were students in the senior division. Among the sixty in Leese's junior division, apart from Robert Bridgeman, were Philip Christison and 'Chink' Dorman-Smith; in the senior division the following year were Philip Gregson-Ellis, John Harding and Dick McCreery, with all of whom he was to come in contact later.

Leese was to write of his two years at Staff College in terms of great enthusiasm:

> You were presented with almost every known military problem in the many syndicates and schemes with which you were confronted . . . you came away with complete confidence that no matter what problem might face you, either in peace or war, you would always be able to find a solution.
>
> You learned, too, at Staff College, how to work. You were only given a limited time to get your exercise finished, and you knew that you had got to get it done in that time; you therefore learnt very quickly how to organise your work and how best to get it done in time, so that you were ready for whatever problem which might next be shot at you.[1]

Leese and Bridgeman were in a party of about twenty who were bachelors and who lived in the Mess. Another of the twenty was Lt Colonel B. L. Montgomery: Leese got to know him very well during the two years course, and liked him immensely.

In 1928 Leese ran the cricket and the Staff College had an enjoyable and successful season, Budget Loyd doing very well as a batsman and wicket keeper, Capt HRLG Alexander (Alex) turning out occasionally and Leese himself was successful as a batsman.

In 1927 he had made a hit as Captain Bonehead in the Staff College pantomime. The following year his part was specially written for him by the author, 'Chink' Dorman-Smith. In *Getting the Bird*, chronicling the activities of two nations, Bellaria and Pacifica, Leese brought the house down as Charon, a vulgar boatman.

After the show, when still in his costume, he was approached by the CIGS (Lord Milne), who asked him if he would like to become his Personal Assistant. Leese, who had heard that he might have the

---

[1] Memoirs.

opportunity of becoming Brigade Major in the 1st Guards Brigade at Aldershot, believing that his fortune lay in command rather than on the staff, politely turned the offer down.

Following Staff College Leese went once more to the Battalion. In a short time his wish was fulfilled: he was appointed Brigade Major to the 1st Guards Brigade on 11 November 1929 and on 30 November was promoted to the rank of Major. The Brigade was commanded by Brigadier 'Boy' Sergison-Brooke,[1] who had a magnificent first war record, and was to become one of Leese's greatest friends. It is said that Sergison-Brooke was the only person that Leese was ever slightly afraid of.

Life was active and exciting. There were tremendous mock battles with the Infantry Brigade in the other division commanded by Archie Wavell. There was the Aldershot Tattoo. Whilst Brigade Major at Aldershot, Leese had a great deal to do with the running of the Tattoo. One year they put on a pageant of Boadicea: one of Boadicea's daughters complicated matters by wearing horn-rimmed spectacles. Another year Queen Elizabeth at the time of the Armada was doing well until the Commander-in-Chief's wife noticed that Queen Elizabeth had a dirty neck: the matter was repaired with flour and paste. The Tattoos were great fun, and Leese learnt a lot from the training they gave him in staff work.

After two years with the 1st Guards Brigade, Leese went to London District Headquarters as Deputy Assistant Quartermaster General (chief administrative officer), the appointment being effective from 22 February, 1932. Leese found it 'quite tricky' serving two masters, but was lucky in who those masters were – General Pompey Howard of Eastern Command and General Alby Cator of London District. Cator had been in the Scots Guards and was 'one of the great Brigade characters of the first war.'[2]

Leese was with Cator at a time when the economic depression was at its worst. The hunger marchers were about to march on London and there were rumours of possible troubles in the police.

> The Major General (as we always described the General Officer Command-ing the Brigade of Guards) was only allowed to put one staff officer completely in the picture and he decided that I should be his staff officer; and in consequence I had to remain within one hour of the telephone day and night until the crisis ended – in fact whenever I went out of my office or my flat in London I had to leave a telephone number to ensure that I could be got at immediately.

[1] He was a cousin to Lord Alanbrooke.
[2] Major General Albemarle Bertie Edward Cator (1877–1932). Nine times mentioned in despatches in the 1914–18 war.

All, however, ended well. The hunger marchers came to London, the police behaved as usual in their exemplary manner, all passed off smoothly, my sentence of permanent confinement to barracks in London ended.[1]

[1] Memoirs.

4

A MARRIAGE HAS BEEN ARRANGED

Perhaps the most interesting thing we saw was a shop full of gas masks.

Margaret Leese, on a visit to Brussels, 19 May 1936

Margaret Alice, daughter of Cuthbert and Hilda Leicester-Warren, of Tabley House, Knutsford, Cheshire, was born on Wednesday 26 July 1905.

The Warrens were soldiers and statesmen in Angevin times. On appropriate occasions the local press related with enthusiasm that the estate and the family were traced back to the Conquest: a de Warenne had married William I's daughter Algiva.

William Leycester, the antiquarian, had a baronetcy granted him by Charles II in 1660 for loyalty to the Royalist cause. Leycester's grandson, Lord de Tabley, founded the Leicester galleries, and, for that matter, the Cheshire Yeomanry. He numbered J. W. M. Turner among his friends. He engaged John Carr of York to build Tabley House, and invited Turner to stay as a guest and to paint the house. Margaret's father, Cuthbert Leicester-Warren (1877–1954) was second son of Sir Baldwyn Leighton, Bt., and Eleanor, daughter of Leicester, second Baron de Tabley. Cuthbert changed his name from Leighton to Leicester-Warren, by Royal Licence in 1898. He married Hilda Davenport, daughter of a Shropshire landowner.

Margaret – to family and close friends she was always Margie – was educated at home, by her father and by governesses. She was a devout Christian and an apt pupil; she painted with competence and read widely; she soon developed a gift for writing fluently, although her orthography was always joyously unpredictable. As a thirteen-year-old in 1918 she had written in her diary: 'Nov. 9. Fine. Kiasor abdicated.'

In 1926 the portrait painter, Philip de Laszlo, saw her and was dazzled by her starry loveliness. Could he paint her? He would ask no fee. Margaret, accompanied by Crowe, her lady's maid – a Norfolk girl of Margaret's age – had six sittings in de Laszlo's studio. The finished portrait shows a lovely girl, light-haired, with plaits wound round her head.

The visits to de Laszlo sparked off her desire to write about painters, and in 1927 the Medici Society published two books by her, each of about 40,000 words, on the great Italian and the great British painters, in which she set out to portray the artists as people as well as discussing their works. Intended for the young, they are also absorbing reading for adults.

The even tenor of her life in the 1920's and early 1930's can be gathered from her diary. There was regular church going, and, as for secular matters, there were hunt balls, though she rode very little, theatrical parties, and holidays at Juan les Pins. Princess Mary was an occasional visitor at Tabley.

A regular visitor to Tabley House about this time was young Edmund Bacon, a contemporary at Eton with Margie's younger brother John. Edmund would go in the spring for the theatricals. There would be a fortnight's rehearsing and then the play would be performed for three days. He remembered Margie as 'a lovely creature . . . a brilliant actress, especially in drawing room comedy. Hilda would be fully occupied in the role of hostess; Cuthbert was the stage manager and lighting expert; John, who was handicapped by a stammer, assisted behind the stage.'

Another family friend, John Green-Wilkinson, was later to serve on Leese's staff. He was at Tabley as a youngster in 1927 when he remembered Margie's parents asking her to perform 'her dance' –

> which she must have learned at some finishing school. To see such a beautiful girl perform such a graceful and evocative dance has left a lasting impression on me even to this day.

John Green-Wilkinson remembers the Leicester-Warrens as indefatigable hosts, spending hours working out plans for their guests – timetables for theatrical rehearsals with Major Beith's (Ian Hay's) instructions, a golf competition on their nine-hole private course, or a battle of the Scout game played in the woods. They were a close-knit family, Cuthbert Leicester-Warren chiefly occupied in looking after the estate. Edmund Bacon felt that Cuthbert's delicate constitution prevented him achieving higher things.

It was John Leicester-Warren who was responsible for Leese being invited to Margie's 'coming out' ball. This was in 1925, when Leese was Adjutant at Eton, and John a sergeant in the OTC, and this was the first time that they met. Afterwards they met from time to time in London and at Tabley. Oliver Leese was a house guest on the occasion of John's twenty-first birthday festivities at Tabley on 28 September 1928, when the celebrations evoked the Victorian age. There were presentations to the young master – John was now an undergraduate at Magdalen College, Oxford – from the servants and tenantry; lunch was served in the gallery of the hall to the tenant farmers; later there was tea in a marquee specially erected for the occasion.

To begin with Margie was one of many girl friends. One story is that eventually she said 'Oliver, if you don't ask, I am going away shortly and you will never see me again,' and that this brought him to his senses. What is more likely is that the Leicester-Warrens considered nobody was good enough for their daughter, least of all a relatively penniless Guards Officer. They wanted a big matrimonial fish.

Margie had her own ideas.

'She is sad' Philip de Laszlo once observed. 'I want to paint her again when she is happy.'

Eventually, at a house party at Minsterley, near Shrewsbury, the home of Oliver's friend Robert Bridgeman, who had married Mary Bingley in 1930, they became engaged. Oliver now approached Cuthbert Leicester-Warren, in the traditional manner, to seek his daughter's hand in marriage. Cuthbert did not show undisguised enthusiasm, and replied that he was not going to have his daughter living in squalor. The Leese family at that time had an address at Cadogan Gardens, living in a house with six servants. This apparently was not enough. What else had Oliver to offer besides his Army pay? Oliver smiled blandly. 'Well, sir,' he replied, 'I'm going to be a great man.'

Reluctantly and somewhat ungraciously Cuthbert Leicester-Warren gave way. At first there was only the most provisional of understandings in the eyes of Margaret's parents. When he attended church at Tabley, Oliver was not allowed to share a pew with Margaret, but had to sit behind her; during introductions after the service, he was passed off as the architect. Eventually, on 2 August, 1932, the engagement was announced in *The Times*: 'A marriage has been arranged between Major Oliver Leese, Coldstream Guards, eldest son of Sir William and Lady Leese, and Margaret, only daughter of Mr. and Mrs. Leicester-Warren of Tabley House, Cheshire.'

The forthcoming wedding was a popular one, and gossip writers would occasionally find Oliver and Margaret in such delectable places as Quaglino's. Now that Margaret's parents were reconciled to the marriage, arrangements were soon enthusiastically in hand. On Wednesday, 18 January 1933 Margaret and Oliver were married in the private chapel at Tabley House, on a day when the nearby woods were white with untrodden snow. The chapel had been made from the stones of the original fourteenth century house, and this was the first wedding there for seventy years. A hundred and twenty guests attended the chapel service – it was relayed to a marquee outside, where a further five hundred guests were accommodated: Cuthbert Leicester-Warren was an amateur wireless enthusiast, and he was able to relay the ceremony to the guests in the marquee – the first radio wedding in history.

The honeymoon, subsidised by the bridegroom's father, was spent in Paris and Madeira. In Paris they stayed at the *George V*. They lunched at *Le Vert Galant*, dined at *La Cremaillère* and *Casanova*; they went to see Josephine Baker at the *Casino*.

They wandered about in byroads and alleys, and watched the world go by from cafés such as the *Dome* and *Le Coupole* and from more obscure but cosy bistros that attracted them. They dashed about Paris in Oliver's old Ford 'Albertine'. From Paris they went to Funchal, Madeira, staying at Reid's Hotel, famous for its atmosphere of Victorian comfort. They went shopping in the famous carts drawn by small oxen, buying fruit and trinkets, visiting the botanical gardens and admiring the Flemish paintings in the Museum. They tried their luck at the casino; they attended 'a tragi-comic bull fight'.

They were invited on board HMS *Dorsetshire* – anchored off Funchal – for a party, and, in reply to Margie's letter of thanks, the captain wrote with becoming gallantry (9.2.33.) 'As to thanking me – well – as we may never meet again I can say it – but it's the ship who should thank *you* for coming on board as we all agreed we had never thought it possible for anyone so lovely to exist and you just brought joy to us all.'

They returned from Madeira on the 13,000 ton *Balmoral Castle*, one of the veterans of the Union Castle Line, and moved into their flat at 20 Wilton Place, two minutes' walk from the Berkeley Hotel. The house itself was a relatively small one, narrow, four storeys high, shaped like a lump of sugar. But they had a nonpareil of a house in the country. Hilda Leicester-Warren had given her daughter Lower Hall, Worfield, a lovely black and white sixteenth century building next door to the church. Lower Hall was the Dower House to Davenport, half a mile away, and it had been in the possession of Hilda Leicester-Warren, who was a Davenport before her marriage. Although it was necessary to live in London a good deal of the time in connexion with Oliver's work, Lower Hall was the house that they loved above all, partly for itself, partly for its garden, partly for its idyllic setting in Worfield.

Oliver now resumed his work as chief administrative officer London District. Alby Cator, commanding London District, had died suddenly. He had been an extremely popular commander and Leese was severely reprimanded by the War Office for arranging for him to be given a gun salute in London and also a firing party at his own home in Cirencester.

London District was now taken over by Charles Grant, whom Leese had previously served under as adjutant of the 3rd Battalian Coldstream Guards in 1920–1922, when the latter was the Commanding Officer.

Soon after their return from the honeymoon, the Leeses attended court at Buckingham Palace, the occasion took place at 9.30 p.m., 12 May 1933; the ladies wearing court dress with feathers and trains, the gentlemen full court dress. Crowe remembered Margie's dress, resplendent with sequins, shining brilliantly each time that she moved.

One of the first tasks allotted to Leese on his return from his honeymoon was to organise a mammoth review of the Territorial Army by George V. This entailed a great deal of work, in which Captain (General Sir Frank) Simpson was his chief assistant. 'We upset a lot of people, but that couldn't be helped' wrote General Simpson later. They got hold of sand and gravel for the troops to march on: this was to be in Hyde Park. A powder room for Queen Mary became an important item on the agenda. A few hours before the review was due to commence heavy rain set in. It was soon obvious that the affair would be a disaster, and so all was cancelled at the last minute. Leese's arrangements for the review were described as 'masterly' but there was never any possibility of an indoor parade for so many thousands: General Simpson recalled that Leese stood up for him about any difficulties that arose.

As a result of his efforts – unavailing though they were – Leese was promoted Brevet Lieutenant Colonel[1] – 'the youngest of the lot' – a friend in the War Office commented. Charlie Grant wrote 'I hope this promotion will mean your rising very high.' Budget Loyd wrote 'I *am* glad you got your brevet. It is grand, and never was one better deserved . . . Everyone said your efforts over the Review were masterly.' Another friend wrote 'The War Office seem at times to have moments of real intelligence. I couldn't have made a better choice myself.'

Leese finished at London District on 11 November 1933, and then went back as second in command to Colonel John Wynne Finch in the 3rd Battalion. In November and December 1933 he managed a two months' leave, driving in *Albertine* with Margie through Flanders to Italy.

Margaret kept a travel diary of the tour. They visited the battlefield of Loos. Later, at Guinchy

---

[1] A sign that the 'powers that be' had their eye on him. Jane's Dictionary of Military Terms, compiled by Brigadier P. H. C. Hayward, gives this definition: 'BREVET: as a reward for distinguished service, an officer may be awarded brevet rank above that for which he is paid. This confers seniority in the Army but not within his regiment.'

We saw plainly the sunken road and the orchard out of which Oliver had gone the morning of the 15th [September 1916] and we saw whereabouts the trench he had taken lay, and Delville Wood where he was taken back wounded by the German prisoners. It is all there as he had expected it – only now there stood buildings and the land had covered its nakedness in green.

In Italy they visited Bondo:

Floors inlaid with different kinds of wood like the one at Davenport.

They visited Venice, Bologna, Padua – 'I feel like the *Good Companions* on the road.'

Leese's efforts to speak Italian at this time were more courageous than successful. On one occasion, according to Margie, he asked for breakfast in his best Italian, and was answered by the housemaid '*No parlo Inglese!*' Asked how many children his sister had, he mistook the question for how old she was, and promptly replied '34'.

In Rome Margie picked up an anecdote from an Embassy official, concerning an occasion when Baldwin, then Prime Minister, was staying with his wife at Aix:

Austen Chamberlain arranged for Briand and Stresemann to come over from Geneva to see Baldwin. But Lucy sat there knitting all the time and persuaded them to their bitter indignation to help her with crosswords – no mention of business was possible. Everyone was furious.

The Leeses met Pirandello and admired Raphael ceilings. They spent a day in San Marino, 'a queer little country left forgotten and alone.' They returned via Paris, where they went to a show. 'Mistinguett hides her years well,' recorded Margie. On 28 December they were back home in their yellow drawing room at 20 Wilton Place.

In February 1934 they went out to Tangiers. On the way out there in a Dutch boat they heard of fighting in the ante-Atlas Mountains in Morocco. This seemed too good an opportunity to miss, so Oliver made arrangements for them to go via Rabat to Marrakesh, where they witnessed a Tarquibah, which was a ceremony of submission to the French by a dissident tribe: 'It was a most imposing ceremony. The dissident tribesmen were drawn up inside the walls of the Kasbah and around them were the men belonging to the tribes loyal to the French. There were no French soldiers present. Just the General and a few staff officers.[1] A bull was brought in and its head cut off with one movement of a vast sword, as a gesture of submission to the French:

[1] Memoirs.

When this was over we sat down to have tea with the loyal Kaid, in whose Kasbah the ceremony had taken place. A sheep had been killed specially for the occasion. It was brought in and the sheep's eye was presented on a platter, like John the Baptist's head, to the French General, General Hure. He had a great sense of humour. Without any demur, he took the eye and presented it to my wife. She was also quite unperturbed and without batting an eyelid she swallowed the eye! and in the General's estimation became at least 'Madame la Général'.[1]

Leese's next appointment was at the War Office, where he was G2 from 7 April 1934 to 1 October 1936. He was in the Operations department that was responsible for the Dominions and the Colonies; his immediate superior was Tom Hutton, and others he met in the Operations department were John Kennedy, later to become Assistant CIGS when Leese commanded Eighth Army, 'Pug' Ismay and General John Dill. Leese admired Dill immensely, and would cut corners by lying in wait for him in the passage and then discussing his problems with him.

In December 1934 – January 1935 Oliver and Margie visited Italy and Sicily, again taking the little Ford, *Albertine*. They saw Botticelli's *Primavera* and the chapel where Giotto worked. In Sicily they went to Taormina, where they were saluted wherever they went – 'The car,' wrote Margie, 'not ourselves, aroused interest.' They spent time in Messina – which Margie found 'a strange, ugly place', Agrigento and Palermo. Two years previously Oliver had shown her where he had fought in the first war; now, in Sicily, he was astonishingly, and unwittingly, taking her to key points where he would be fighting in eight years' time.

Early in 1935 Leese was given an assignment after his own heart; he was to act as Liaison Officer in work connected with South Africa, African colonies and the War Office: he would be dealing with Empire troops not coming under the War Ministry. Dill allowed Leese to take Margie with him, she paying her own fare. They sailed on the *Armadale Castle*, 22 February 1935, keeping in training with deck tennis, deck quoits and bucket quoits – games always popular in the Union Castle Line's repertoire.

Arrived in South Africa, they were invited by Lord Clarendon (the Governor-General of South Africa) and his wife to a dinner party at Rondebosch on 12 March 1935.

'I think,' wrote Leese, 'I was about the first person in the War Office who was allowed to travel by air, by sea or by motor, according to which means of transport appeared the most suitable for the particular mission on which one was engaged . . .

[1] Memoirs. Leese had whispered to her 'imagine it's just a large oyster, Margie.'

My mission in South Africa included what eventually turned out to be the very agreeable task of getting to know Mr. Pirow, who was then Defence Minister. He somewhat complicated the start of my journey by sending a signal to the War Office to the effect that he was delighted I should visit South Africa, but that on no account would he visit me personally. So when I arrived in South Africa my task seemed a difficult one to set about.'[1]

It so happened that the Earl of Clarendon's son, George Hyde, had been a cadet officer at Eton when Leese was Adjutant, and they were good friends. George Hyde was going out rabbit shooting with Pirow the following Sunday on Robben Island,[2] and suggested that Leese came too, adding that once they were together in a boat, it would be difficult not to speak at all. In the event Pirow chatted most amiably. Later, they had several conversations in Capetown, Pirow eventually saying that he hoped Leese would be the British Military Representative at the opening cermonies of the capital, Lusaka, in Northern Rhodesia, to which he was going a month or two later.[3]

The Leeses travelled into the Transvaal and stayed as the guests of Myles Bourke in Pretoria. There were pleasant social events to attend in Pretoria and Johannesburg, and it was to prove of inestimable value to Leese that while in South Africa, he met military figures such as Dan Pienaar, Frank Theron, and Everard Poole, who were all to serve under him in the second world war. They travelled to Kenya, Basutoland and Zululand, where Leese met Empire Troops who were to do sterling service under his command in the Middle East, Italy and Burma.

On 11 May there was a visit to the 1st Bn the Rhodesia Regiment; and to Northern Rhodesia (now Zambia) from 28 May to 3 June for the formal opening of the new capital, Lusaka. They returned to Rhodesia and were among the 450 guests at the Government House Ball given in Salisbury by the Governor and Lady Stanley. There was 'a lovely drive in Nyasaland by coach'; time spent in Blantyre and Zomba. On 22 June they sailed away in a small government steamer to Zanzibar.

'This is a dear little place – the first one where he wouldn't mind coming to be Governor – O and I have decided!'

Later in the summer of 1935 they had a holiday in Italy, at the time that the Abyssinian crisis was reaching boiling point. Most of the time

---

[1] Memoirs.
[2] Once a leper settlement, and now a place of confinement for political prisoners.
[3] Later Pirow was to visit Germany and meet Hitler. Returning to South Africa he gradually fell from power.

they spent in Venice. Margie recorded that 'The Fascist march, 'Giovanezza' was played when *Il Duce*'s son-in-law, Count Ciano, arrived as the guest of honour' at the Venice Film Festival.

'Even a wet Venice is beautiful' she wrote. 'We did enjoy our stay there – and all and everyone we spoke to were charming, courteous and not one mentioned Abyssinia, though they talked of *Il Duce* and his reforms.'

They were back in England at the end of August, and on 3 October Italian forces invaded Abyssinia, 'in the interests of peace' as Mussolini claimed.

The invasion of Abyssinia marked the beginning of the era of triumph for the dictators. Hitler, to whom complete authority had been handed over by an ageing Hindenburg, had been Führer of Germany since 30 January 1933. At first few in England saw the menace that he imposed, but he soon showed his hand. Repudiating the Versailles Treaty, he embarked on a rearmament programme, and Germany left the League of Nations. The limited form of sanctions imposed on Italy had little effect as a deterrent, and Hitler took advantage of the democracies' weak handling of the situation: in March 1936 German troops marched into the Rhineland. To many, a second holocaust now seemed inevitable.

In May 1936 Oliver and Margaret had a brief holiday in the Low Countries – The Hague, Delft, Haarlem, Amsterdam, Middelburg, Walcheren, Blankenburg, Bruges. On 18 May Margie recorded

We passed by the village of St Julian in the fields above which Oliver had been wounded the first time.

They went to the battlefield of Waterloo, where Oliver explained the part that the Coldstreams had played in the defence of Hougoumont. Of Brussels itself Margie wrote 'Perhaps the most interesting thing we saw was a shop full of gas masks.'

In the autumn Leese was appointed to command the First Battalion Coldstream Guards. He held the command from 1 October 1936 to 28 September 1938.[1] Leese found that discipline was slack, and was determined to get his troops ready for whatever task should confront them. It was a fruitful struggle: as he summed it up 'they did very well in 1940.'

On 17 January 1937 Sir William Leese died: father and son had always been very close. Oliver Leese now succeeded to the title as third baronet.

---

[1] In 1937 the Battalion moved from Victoria Barracks, Windsor to Wellington Barracks, London, and to Chelsea Barracks in September 1938.

The battalion took part in the Coronation of George VI and formed the escort for the Trooping of the Colour. Leese was in attendance on Queen Elizabeth on the balcony of the Horse Guards, from which she watched the parade:

> The two princesses were with her and I shall always remember the joyous scream with which Princess Margaret greeted the magnificent figure of RSM Brittain as he passed the saluting base in all his glory.[1]

During this period the Battalion received their first mechanical transport. Liddell Hart[2] told Leese that 'we' – presumably himself and Hore Belisha, the Secretary of State for War – had been discussing him with regard to a future appointment at the Staff College. Leese, who wanted to stay with his battalion, told Liddell Hart that he was blissfully happy where he was, and had no ambition or desire to go to the Staff College. A few weeks later when he saw that Monty Stopford[3] had gone as Chief Instructor to Camberley he thought all was well.

When the mechanical transport arrived Leese was able to bring the standards of battalion training much more into line with what was required in modern war conditions. They needed a good anti-tank weapon. The Boyes rifle he felt 'a wicked weapon' for modern warfare. He felt that the army was inadequately equipped and trained to meet a heavy tank attack.

The Leeses spent September and October 1937 in Germany and Central Europe. Ostensibly on leave, Leese wanted to find out what he could and generally to get the 'feel' of Nazi Germany. On the surface things seemed pleasant enough. They visited Koblenz, Aachen – 'where young boys chat affably' – recorded Margie, Munich, Dresden – 'It's a lovely city, Dresden, full of light and order' – and Nuremberg. There was a discordant note outside Mittenwald, where a large sign proclaimed 'Jews are not wanted in this village'.

In 1938 Leese tried with his battalion a carefully planned experiment in amphibious warfare. He got the blessing of Boy Brooke and the little money available from his training grant. Friends commanding other battalions lent him vehicles and drivers. All this was in preparation for the 'Circus' to go to the North of England. General Bartholomew, commanding Northern Command, cooperated and arranged an exercise for the battalion in Yorkshire 'on our arrival up there'.

Leese's idea was for part of the battalion to go up by land, part by

---

[1] Memoirs.
[2] Captain Basil Liddell Hart, military historian, and for a period, *eminence grise* at the War Office.
[3] General Sir Montague Stopford.

sea and part by air. The project by land offered no problems. The air
transport was difficult, but he managed to get two small aeroplanes to
take his Adjutant and himself and one troop carrying aircraft to take
a platoon – and he managed to embark a platoon on a ship sailing from
London to Hull.

The programme worked well and all three detachments met according to plan on the Yorkshire training area. The exercise in Yorkshire
was cancelled as they were swamped out by rain, but the administrative
side in moving them up there had been accomplished and they had all
learnt something about the cooperation of the three services. The first
exercise at amphibious warfare had been achieved. On the return
journey, in a recruiting drive, they paraded by companies in full dress,
visiting industrial towns in the North and Midlands.

Having returned to Wellington Barracks, Leese tried out a local
defence exercise to see what equipment they had in case of enemy air
attack. He found they had virtually none, so asked for money to
tighten up defences. He was offered £25! In another defence exercise
Leese hijacked a passenger train that was going to Colchester, taking
the 'enemy' by surprise and capturing their HQ. There were com-
plaints that this sort of thing wasn't cricket. Leese felt that the next
war wouldn't be cricket, either.

In 1938 Oliver and Margaret, who had sold their flat in Wilton Place,
went down to Shropshire, as they had planned to make alterations to
Lower Hall. They put in electric wiring, central heating and hot water
– things they could never have done after the war. Just as they were
finishing the alterations to the Lower Hall, the blow fell. 'The Staff
College had reared its ugly head again' wrote Leese, 'and I was selected
to go as Chief Instructor – this time to Quetta.'[1]

---

[1] Memoirs.

5

LETTERS FROM QUETTA

It stuck out a mile that the attack [on Singapore] would come overland.

Oliver Leese, September 1938

Quetta, capital of Baluchistan, a village of mud huts in the 1830's, was a place of strategic importance at the high noon of the British Empire. In 1876, when Disraeli was Prime Minister, Victoria had been made Empress of India, to make it 15 – all with Germany, whose Kaiser had been proclaimed German Emperor in 1871, after the Franco–Prussian war; but at this period the competition with Germany was as nothing compared with the great game Britain had waged with Russia.

Britain was determined to maintain king pin positions in South East Asia. Many of the moves in the Great Game were made in the area near the North-West frontier of India. The Russians, according to British intelligence at the time, might well attack India from Afghanistan through the Bolan pass rather than the Khyber Pass. Quetta lay forty miles to the North of the Bolan pass and on the same road, and Quetta, therefore was leased from Baluchistan by the British in 1876, and in 1878 Quetta was used as a jumping off ground for the start of the second Afghan War.

Some thirty years later (1908) Kitchener initiated the foundation of a Staff College at Quetta, as the Indian Army equivalent of Camberley. It was as Chief Instructor (G1) at the Staff College that Leese went out in September 1938; Margie was allowed to accompany him, but once again she had to pay her own fare. She was to describe the journey a few months later in an article for the Staff College Magazine:

'We were sitting in the KLM office in Horseferry Road,' wrote ML, 'waiting for a bus to take us to Croydon. Farewells were over. People had looked at us sadly and murmured "Quetta? Oh yes, earthquakes." Then with a gleam of knowingness "Have you read *The Rains Came*?"[1]

[1] Louis Bromfield's best-selling novel, *The Rains Came*, published in 1938, was obviously based on the Quetta earthquake of 31 May, 1935.

'There had been the hectic months of trying to get Afghan and Persian visas. The Afghans, less suspicious, had granted them a fortnight ago, but the ink on those from Iran was scarcely dry – and then only after £10 worth of Foreign Office telegrams . . . We rattled through the closeness of stuffy London streets. Several friends at Croydon grasped our hands and were separated from us to the terraces where we saw them grow small and speck-like as our aeroplane rose.

'That day the clouds literally hung over Europe and we could see very little of the country beneath us. We lunched on the Pest aerodrome. It was chilly and misty and one could see nothing of the city and river. Belgrade was sunny and hot; Athens was hot, and we were made hotter by the idiotic Greek Customs – however, all was compensated for by the sight of the Parthenon by moonlight . . .

'Next morning we were at Alexandria by 8. It was a thrill being in the East again, even to the sight of a camel and a palm tree.'

At Baghdad the temperature was 115°. Here they were picked up by a German aeroplane, twenty-four hours late. They reached Tehran, where they stayed for a week at the British Legation, and went for 'a marvellous drive over the hills towards the Caspian Sea', but owing to the crisis could not go any long journeys from the Legation.

Eventually they left, the only passengers in a plane for Kabul, with a German crew of four 'two of whom were merely boys'. Shortly after crossing the Hindu Kush at 16,000 feet, the pilot went badly off course – whether by accident or design – before they reached their immediate destination. Margie was enthralled by 'the fascinating Kabul with its great covered bazaars, its Russian china, guns, embroidered coats, its myriad different types of people, to see the remnants of Amanullah's dream of westernization in the empty modern palaces,[1] to hear of the present dictatorial regime of Hashmin, the King's uncle, and his two brothers.'

There followed a two-day car journey to India 'over a road which rather resembled a river bed.' Leese was not disappointed with his first sight of the Khyber Pass:

The narrow steep gorges, the winding road, the forts above, the sentries and scouts, the camel convoys, and to add to all these symbols of yesterday, our modern motor car, and an aeroplane which happened to fly over just as we were passing.[2]

They reached Quetta at the end of September, and soon settled

---

[1] Amanullah, King of Afghanistan [1926–29] endeavoured to introduce reforms along Western lines, supported by his Queen, Suriya, an ardent feminist. Amanullah and Suriya were highly popular during their visit to England on their European tour in 1928. Amanullah was forced to abdicate in January 1929.

[2] Memoirs.

down in their bungalow at 2 Hunter Road. Oliver was promoted Brevet-Colonel on his arrival 28 September 1938. This happened to be one day before the signing of the Munich agreement by Hitler and Chamberlain.

Leese was not optimistic about peace in Europe or indeed about peace in South East Asia. Soon after their arrival in Quetta, the Commandant, General Brodie Haig, took the senior team of students off to Singapore for their final exercise. Their problem had been the defence of Singapore and they all thought the existing defences were laid out on a totally unsound basis, in that they were designed to repel a Japanese attack by sea whereas 'it stuck out a mile' that the attack would come overland.

Margie's letters home during their first six months at Quetta have evidently not survived, there are however two or three early letters from Oliver to Cuthbert Leicester-Warren, the first of which was written on 15 October 1938.

M. is settling in wonderfully well. She runs the Indian servants with complete ease and already has a grasp of 'housekeeping Urdu'. We have a *munshi* [interpreter] to teach us. I've concentrated on the garden – half of which is still only a stony patch of Baluchistan. [The house] might be a packet worse, and it has the great advantage of H and C and plugs that really pull! It takes a lot of getting into the place, as 'today' means very little and 'time' literally nothing – and this applies to many Europeans; just as much as it does to Indians. Furthermore all standards are pretty low – I can quite see it, after a glimpse of the heat in the plains of Baghdad and Lahore. I'll write more of the Staff College later. Suffice it now to say that they work mostly under very great difficulties, and so you cannot make any apt comparison to Camberley.

Montgomery, Chief Instuctor at Quetta in 1934, had emphasised to students the near certainty of a second world war, and told them the four golden rules to remember: 1) Morale means everything, 2) Simplify the problem, 3) Pick a good team of subordinates, then stick to and trust them, 4) Make yourself know what you want, then have the courage and determination to get it.

When Oliver Leese arrived, courses were of a year's duration, and tended to be infantry orientated. Leese had more up-to-date ideas: 'We were soon able to start a study on the employment of armoured forces in desert type of country. I remember how our first efforts were laughed almost to scorn by some officer instructors and students. But the vision of men like Horace Birks[1] and Tony Scott, together with

[1] Major General H. L. Birks. He commanded a tank at Cambrai in 1917. In 1941 he played an important part in the battle of Beda Fomm.

able students such as Dick Hull and Pete Pyman, enabled us to lay on exercises which helped us to think out the new problems of armoured warfare and to create situations which turned out later to be very akin to the conditions of warfare in the Western Desert.'

On 7 December 1938 Oliver wrote to Cuthbert Leicester-Warren describing the rebuilding of Quetta, following the earthquake of 1935.

> The whole place is now in process of reconstruction. Those who still live in the old houses of these parts, which did not fall, have to go out and sleep in *Wana* huts,[1] with mud walls and a tent roof. In the town itself reconstruction now goes apace. Many gallant shop keepers have got new shops up, e.g. Hereawell, the local Fortnum and Mason. All houses are concrete and have to pass the official test . . .
>
> The military cantonment is partially finished. All are single storied except the G.O.C.'s house and Officers' Messes. In the Staff College area there are a few quake proof houses finished – all single storied and made of cement and concrete. The rest live in the old bungalows and sleep in *Wana* huts. We work in the old Staff College – a new one is being built. The whole of Quetta is like a great garden city. Houses have gardens of ¼ acre to 1 acre – we have about 2 acres. But you have to go into purdah if you don't want to live in the street, hence the chittail – a kind of woven flax fence, we've put all round our garden, in which we have a few trees – we're lucky in this, as few new gardens have – though the old gardens have lovely hedges, trees and grass. We've built a most remarkable rabbit netting pen for our seedlings, to keep out the jackals – our friends are uncertain if it's for chickens, rabbits or tiger.

Leese's immediate subordinate at Quetta was Major Tony Scott,[2] who, with his wife Helena ('Tina') became great friends of the Leeses.

Tony Scott had served in France as a nineteen-year-old in 1918 and later in the King's African Rifles. After a year at the Staff College, Camberley, 1934–35, he had been posted to India, and was a staff officer, RA, in Western Command at Karachi when he was posted as GSO2 Instructor to Quetta in 1938.

> 'The first exercise at Quetta for which I was responsible,' wrote Major-General O'Carroll Scott,[3] 'was "the set piece battle". This exercise had been blessed, if not partially written, by the recently departed GSO 1, Col. Bernard Montgomery, and concerned the deployment of the Artillery, the 'logistics' of the dumping of ammunition; the break in; the breakthrough and the break out. With hindsight that exercise could well have been a rehearsal for El Alamein . . . I did try to add a final "problem", the blowing

---

[1] Wana is the name of a place: a Brigade camp in tribal territory in Waziristan where Wana huts were first used.
[2] Later Major General O'Carroll Scott (1899–1980).
[3] Communication to author, November 1980.

of a bridge on the line of retreat of the defeated enemy by a parachute drop. But the Sapper G80 1 said my scheme was impractical [1938] so the project was dropped: but I felt that the newly arrived GSO 1, Colonel Sir Oliver Leese, was on my side. Shortly after that exercise Oliver Leese asked me round to his bungalow to have a drink. As he was pouring out one for me and Margaret Leese was engaging me in chat, he called across the room, "Ever heard of Extensive Warfare, Tony?"

'Well, I hadn't. The expression stemmed, apparently, from the brain of the DMT India, Brigadier "Gertie" Tuker.[1]

'"I suppose he means" I said "warfare in Asia or Africa, where the country is immense and the troops few: by contrast to Intensive Warfare in Europe where the troops are shoulder to shoulder from Switzerland to the sea" "That's about it" answered Oliver, and added, "We will study the programme here at Quetta, and you, Tony, will be in charge."

'I worked: how I worked. But I never felt frustrated. Always I had behind me Gertie Tuker in Delhi and Oliver Leese on the spot to argue out points and cheer me on.'

A preliminary scheme on the study of movement by mechanical transport went off well; the study of Extensive Warfare demanded thought:

Alexander the Great and Genghis Khan had practised it. The Somaliland Camel Corps practised it. We in the K.A.R. practised it. The Indian Army practised it on the Frontier, though they called it Mountain or Frontier Warfare. In essence the problem was that one had to be prepared to be attacked (or oneself attack) from any direction, front, flanks or rear. Therefore when moving as an army, a division or even a battalion, one moved basically in a hollow square and *laagered* in a hollow square. Scouts far out in all directions, front and flanks, covering the fighting troops with the commissariat protected in the middle. In the K.A.R. that is more or less how we moved: in Somaliland they had wide ranging mounted patrols on ponies or camels with the Admin tucked away in the centre. In India flanking hills were piquetted while the main force and the baggage moved up the valley between. The problem therefore resolved itself into how to replace mules, camels and marching troops by armoured cars, tanks and MT.

In fact my greatest problem was how to carry my fellow instructors with me. Luckily our tank expert, Horace Birks, and our airman, Pug Ledger, were both marvellously helpful, and of course we were ever helped and encouraged (we never needed driving) by our leader, Oliver Leese.

We studied Extensive Warfare in all its aspects; advance to contact; battle; break through; break out; pursuit; defence and withdrawal. Many of our exercises were done 'on the ground' in the countryside round Quetta; some were conducted 'indoors' on maps or models.

---

[1] Major General Sir Francis Tuker.

When war broke out Oliver returned to the UK, and was destined to
practise the art of Extensive Warfare as Commander XXX Corps in the
desert. I met him again in the Arakan when he was GOC-in-C ALFSEA
and I was commanding an Infantry brigade. On seeing me he immediately
came across, and, holding out his hand, 'Well, Tony, we certainly taught
the right things when we studied Extensive Warfare at Quetta.'

Leese and Scott were fortunate in having a very bright intake of
students for the 1939 course. Dick Hull and his wife Antoinette lived
next door to the Leeses. Hull was to serve under Leese in Italy,
commanding 1st Armoured Division, and eventually become CIGS.
'Pete' Pyman[1] was another student. In his autobiography, Pyman
wrote:

The Quetta course was both exacting and stimulating. The G1 or Second
in Command at that time was the British Guardsman, Oliver Leese. At the
time the Tank Corps, or Regiment as it became that year, was not
universally popular. Oliver Leese, although a confirmed infantryman himself, would have none of this. He had lately commanded a mechanised
infantry battalion and had far too good a grasp of tactics not to understand
the value of Armour.[2]

Several hundred pages of Margie's letters to her parents have survived,
sometimes written, sometimes typed, generally on the official notepaper with the Quetta owl surmounted by a crown and perching on
crossed swords with the ribboned motto *Tam Marte quam Minerva* on
the top left hand side of each page.

Her letters from Quetta are not confined to news and gossip. She
has the painter's eye for colour, scenery, detail. She shows an absorbed
interest, lively and compassionate, in everyone she meets. She writes
with understanding and warmth, flavoured with the occasional pungent
remark, but always on the surface or under the surface is the joyous
effervescent gaiety of the lovely girl de Laszlo painted and Oliver Leese
adored.

The first letter, in May 1939, deals with the camp at Ziarat, a holiday
centre developed for the use of military and civilians. Oliver and
Margaret tended to go there at weekends, Oliver often taking his work
with him:

We arrived yesterday evening, found our advance party had made everything nice. We have a super camp, which even you would I think approve.
Comfortable easy chairs, 6 servants, silver! There are lots of attractive small

[1] Later General Sir Harold Pyman. In 1961 he became C-in-C, Allied Forces, Northern
Europe.
[2] *Call to Arms*. Harold Pyman [Lee Coopers].

birds and wildflowers and yesterday I saw some lovely blue butterflies . . .

There are all kinds of people in the mountains here, driven out of their own country centuries ago, and still keeping to themselves. There are two Persian villages, and, though they've been 300 years here, and some are quite wealthy, keep all their characteristics and language and customs and arts – they decorate their houses with Persian paintings . . .

[Oliver] has had 53 papers on international affairs to correct this week and has 53 reports to write next, so is occupied but interested.

To her father she wrote, in an undated letter, giving details of a typical day:

Oliver went off at 7 a.m. on a scheme. Breakfast. Household duties. 10.30 lecture on carpets.

11.45 Mrs. Haig [the commandant's wife] and Mrs. Abbott returned for a talk – ostensibly to see the garden.

1 p.m. Antoinette Hull's mother to lunch as I know was all alone next door. A daughter arrived. 2 p.m. the Munshi [to give M. a lesson in Hindustani]. 3 p.m. arrival of our camp furniture. 3.15 hairdresser, wash set and cut. 4.45 man about chittail which has blown down. Have written a lot of notes asking a dinner party of the English clerks at the Staff College.

Sat. [20 May] afternoon we raced. In the evening the Lancashire Fusiliers had a big cocktail party. Sunday we got up early for our Whitsun Communion – as we weren't here last Sunday – and we did a variety of things and in the evening we had 21 people to dinner followed by about 30 in afterwards, and we had a repetition of our cabaret with a few differences. That all went very well, the dinner party people especially. We had about 6 Indians and lots of students we hadn't had before. *Now everyone has dined!*

It was possibly at this party that a minor catastrophe occurred:

'They [the Leeses] decided to paint their dining room chairs gold' wrote Field Marshal Hull,[1] 'but did not leave long enough for the last 2 to dry. You can imagine the results on D.J. and a wife's best party frock!'

'We have a bevy of parties,' continued ML 'before our long leave on June 7 for a week. The Secretary of the Red X or rather St. John's here is one of the type of woman I most detest. I'm sure she was head girl of St. Winifred's or somewhere and she has never grown up.'

One of the 'bevy of parties' was the Agent Governor General's Ball[2] for the King's birthday, about which Margaret wrote to her mother on Tuesday 6 June, the day before setting off with Oliver for their week's leave at Ziarat.

[1] Letter to author, 21.2.81.
[2] The AGG was the King's representative in Baluchistan.

The dance was really lovely to look at, and we enjoyed it enormously. We danced under some chinar trees all lit with bulbs above us – on two big floors. The garden was floodlit . . . the most beautiful trees and flowering shrubs. There were marquees with supper (champagne flowing) two bands that played more or less continuously – no encores. The AGG is a priceless person. He hates entertaining but when he does he does it properly, but at 2 a.m. it stopped. Everyone wore uniform and best dresses – so they looked very nice. About 500 people I think from all over Baluchistan.

The next day, 7 June, they went to Ziarat. On 10 June Oliver wrote to Cuthbert Leicester-Warren:

We have just come up here for our week's summer break, which is designed to avoid the 'friction' consequent on a 14 week hot weather term. As a matter of fact we've been lucky – and the hot weather has only just started, and 'heat' in Quetta is really about the same as a hill station in the rest of India, as we always get cool nights up here it is delicious – juniper trees all round and at night we have an oil stove – M. is running the camp as if she had lived in camp all her life! and we consequently are very comfortable.

M. looked quite lovely for the AGG's ball – she wore her new gold dress – and everyone said how chic and beautiful she was. She has made a great name for herself as a hostess of amusing parties in Quetta and the world flock to her parties. She has made a point of learning to understand the Indian point of view – and the few well-to-do Indians in Quetta appreciate it so much.

We have had rather an interesting term, dealing with the employment of mechanised forces in countries like Italian East Africa, and I have enjoyed working out the various problems of mobility, air and administration.

We are busily thinking out our trip to Kashmir in August . . . M. will have told you all about our Afghan trip. It was most interesting. I had a talk with the Prime Minister, the King's Uncle, who runs the country and is the Ataturk of Afghanistan – a most charming cultured man – very pro-English and most anxious to promote good relations between us and Afghanistan. It seems so much to both countries' advantage, for it would help us immensely to have a peaceful NW Frontier in war, and to avoid the dangers of German and Italian influence in Afghanistan, totalitarian money spent there would mean instant ruin, as their army is not yet strong enough to compete with the Pathan tribes, if they combined, and many still think of Amanullah as the rightful King, especially his own tribe the Durans.

On Saturday, 1 July, Margie wrote from Ziarat:

We got here last night and went for a heavenly walk up among the hills, which are very like Bavaria, with lovely snow, green, grassy glades and open patches, and then more rocky pathways and lovely views. Our only difficulty is to avoid constant invitations from people we are seeing every day . . . I can be charitable for five days in the week but I do love the quiet we get up here – or as much as we can get it . . .

Oliver and I are having a beano tonight trying out the champagne cup [for Margaret's birthday party on 26 July] . . .

We have a polo tournament this evening. Lovely papers continually arrive – we shall never get so many when we get home again – now we have your *Tatler*, *Punch*, *Times* and all the fashion papers – Lady Leese's *Bystander*. Aunt B's *Apollo* and *Connoisseur*, Lady L's *John of London Book Review*, *Country Life*. They start with us, go up to Ziarat to wives up there because they've been ill, finishing at Married Families and Home for Soldiers! . . .

Oliver brings all his 'homework' [to Ziarat] and the summer hols start on the evening of Aug. 11th for Kashmir for a month – we really are very lucky – as long as Hitler doesn't start 'Hitlering' again about then.

Friday 7 July. You don't know how often we talk of the L.H. [Lower Hall at Worfield] and what a lovely and wonderful background it is to our lives and so much to look forward to in the future.

Saturday 8 July. Tomorrow we return for No. 3 term . . . I am sending you some yellow asphodel seeds, but I'm rather afraid they only like very high places. They don't want too much wet.

Monday 10 July. We had a wonderful run back [from Ziarat] last night across the fields of yellow asphodel with all the great mountains with their lovely blue shadows across them. The gardent [at Quetta] had come out even more in 24 hours – larkspur, antirrhinum, Sweet Williams, pansies, roses galore – lovely roses, Persian rosebushes, forget-me-nots, aubretia, sweet peas. Sunflowers do grow marvellously here, so we have planted a lot. Hollyhocks too grow really wild.[1]

Margie wrote about everything in the Quetta social scene – people, parties, picnics – depicting evocatively the cantonment life in the last days of the British Raj:

You'd laugh if you saw the retinue that go with us [to Ziarat] where in England one soldier servant would do everything! We take 4 servants, find one up there – and a gardener who is making some beds in the site! I can't tell you what a blessing our Ford van is out here.

She got people to lecture to the wives on Sikhs, Islam, etc., much to the surprise of the commandant's wife:

[1] Brigadier Neville Chesshyre writes: 'Quetta gardens were dependent upon an ingenious irrigation system. The Cantonment was sited on a long slope with Staff College at the top, down towards the town. Water was channelled from the Hanna River to the top of the slope and then distributed by a network of channels of ever decreasing size down to individual gardens. The sluices to these were opened according to a time table for a few minutes each day. This was a moment of feverish activity on the part of the *malis* [gardeners] who through their own networks of smaller and smaller mud channels, set out to distribute the water while it still flowed to whichever parts of their gardens needed it.'

She's a dear, but she's not at all interested in India except the English life. The Haigs belong to the India of 40 years ago. They have masses and masses of servants, none very efficient and they alternate between being wildly kind to them and bullying them. But Mrs. H. does talk Urdu beautifully, including the slang. She was born in India and has been here more or less all her life.

War is often in the background and sometimes in the foreground of their thoughts:

Some friends think war imminent, chiefly on Stephen King-Hall's letter, I think. There may be a method in it all, but it certainly carries the greatest and most depressing weight out here. He seems to be the Jeremiah of the British Empire.[1]

In less serious vein she let fly at her bête noire, the 'effort, St Swithin's' hockey-playing girl-woman:

Certain types I find difficult – the very boisterous: mercifully we haven't many – and the serious, rather priggish games players. The latter completely finish me, I am all for games played well, and in moderation, and of course among one's friends. It's a good thing to have people of all kinds, but I find the schoolgirl woman practically impossible.

Often there are glimpses of Oliver – sending messages to the Leicester-Warrens, working on a syllabus, correcting written work, going out on schemes:

'Tonight we have 15 dining. Poor Oliver went out at 6.30 a.m. and won't get back till tea.'
    'Oliver is here, too, engrossed in maps and programmes.'
    'We heard from Budget Loyd that they wanted Oliver to succeed him in the 1st Gds Brigade, but that the War Office, he gathered, had said he couldn't leave the Staff College, so soon . . . it's nice to know he's wanted both ends. *I certainly think it is vital to modernise the education here and to get the army ready – it is about Lord Roberts' time at present! You can't think what you're up against in prejudice and lack of imagination and energy.*[2]

There is a reference to the 1939 Eton v Harrow match. 'Thank goodness we were in India.' Harrow had won for the first time since 1908.

26 July was the day of Margaret's birthday dance. She had found

---

[1] Commander Stephen King-Hall. Famous for his wireless talks on Children's Hour, and as a BBC commentator on current affairs, as well as for his Newsletter which was sent by post to subscribers.
[2] Author's italics.

that it would be possible to do an excellent supper at the cost of 1/6 a head. The band would be thirty shillings, and even with the lighting, champagne cup and a couple of conjurers, the cost of a party for 200 guests would not be exorbitant. Excitement danced over the pages in her letter written home on 27 July:

> O and I dined here alone as we couldn't run a dinner as well and didn't want to leave the house. The dance was the greatest success – it really *did* go well. It looked lovely – the garden floodlit by fairy lights – looked really spacious, and the ball room and white *dhurry* [sort of carpet] stretched across the lawn, the size of a big tennis court, with strings of pink lights across it – very becoming. Chairs all over the garden with small lights on tables. The Cabaret was 1st a man/a conjurer with the mango tree and various very good turns, and the second another man, who did a very good handcuff trick, and then was nailed into a box, and got out, etc. Both short turns, but very well done and slick – proper blackouts, etc. We had *no* bar, a complete innovation here, but we had whiskeys and lemonades taken out on trays during the cabaret – and we had a champagne cup at supper – not a single youth was the slightest bit tight – but everyone was quite cheerful. We had 190 people – all our friends (all Staff College, of course) and anyone who had entertained us of all creeds – and everyone found friends and it just went. We also had a sit down supper, which wasn't done even at the A.G.G.'s!

Margaret sent home a copy of the invitation, of the supper menu and a dance programme. It was a good supper for 1/6 a head: cold consommé, salmon mayonnaise, chicken in aspic mousse, asperge au jambon, potato salad, Russian salad, ice pudding, jelly, coffee. They danced a mélange of foxtrots and waltzes: 'Blue Danube', 'Mexicali Rose', 'The Way You Look Tonight'. After the second cabaret there were three dances: 'Umbrella Man', 'Goodnight Angel' and 'Wine, Women and Song'. Finally 'John Peel' and 'God Save the King Emperor'.

Soon came the long wished for Kashmir holiday – flawed by thoughts of the war clouds over Europe: On 14 August Margaret wrote from Ledras Hotel, Srinagar, describing the journey to Kashmir, first by train, and then by car, when

> We got to Jammu, on the borders of the Kashmir state we started climbing, and out of the desert plains rose into greenness, *lovely* country, wild and wooded with deep gorges and rushing streams. The town, which is built on a river, is *very* picturesque, like a Dutch town, only very Eastern. In the city it is pure medieval, rather too much so, and the people look so terribly poor and miserable. It must have been like the European towns of the fourteenth century – I saw water being thrown from the top windows! One day there'll be a terrible bust up here – for the country must be *very*

rich, and the workpeople do the most lovely work for practically nothing. The rich Kashmiri brahmins take all the cash, and the ruling family are very weak . . .

Now we are going up the river by car to the Shalimar Gardens . . .

Aug. 16. Camp. Sind Valley. Kashmir. This is a most beautiful valley with sloping hills covered in fir trees and very green rice and corn fields running up into them, full of poplar and chinar trees. The flowers are beautiful, the back of the river is covered in white pinks! The colouring of everything is of a dreamland – a veritable fairy country. I only wish people were better off. It makes me understand the French Revolution. I've never seen such poverty. They aren't made for it somehow, like the burly Afghans, who laugh it off. We met a lot of old Tibetans this morning bringing down their wild ponies.

Aug. 20. Yesterday we caught about 27 trout between us. A good many we put back, but kept all over 10 inches. We are called at 7 a.m. with our tea, have a delicious bath which is open one side on to a little tiny stream, where two kingfishers live. We have breakfast of pink trout at 8 under our trees. We go out fishing about 8.45 – go up by car and walk back. As a rule we have lunch in Camp about 2 p.m. again under our trees, as otherwise it makes a very long day. Then we read, write and sleep until 5 p.m., and then go to the deep pools for the evening rise until after sunset, then home to hot baths within 3 minutes of our arrival, and a very good dinner in our sitting room tent . . . We sleep in our camp beds at the entrance of a tent which has a kind of canopy, so we really sleep out with the stars overhead, and we hear the rushing of our river below . . . At the moment two hoopoes are pecking about under the trees. There are a lot of camels which have just been chased out of the camp. A very holy man with long hair has just passed down the way with two satellites – and two very English people have ridden by on ponies!

On 25 August two acquaintances greeted them, bursting with the news of Germany's non-aggression pact with Russia,[1] and on 1 September, when German troops marched into Poland, they knew the worst. They returned to Quetta via Simla and Delhi. On 12 September Margie wrote to her family in reply to their first war letter:

I can well imagine the calmness and cheerfulness of all the country. No news much here. Prices go up on all imported things, but mercifully everything vital can be had in the country. We are economising in the garden, unwanted servants and drink.

15 Sept. 23rd anniversary of Oliver's DSO. Only last summer a little piece of shrapnel came out of his backbone. What a life it is! [This refers to the wounds of 20 October 1914].

[1] It had been signed by Ribbentrop and Molotov on 22 August, 1939.

9 Oct. Tell Old Nan I remember doing treasure bags in the last war, also hundreds of swabs. I don't think I was very patriotic. I remember hating it . . . I wish war was easy for us now!

16 Oct. O. is longing to hear 'Hanging dirty washing on the Siegfried Line' and he never has yet.

A proposed visit to *George and Margaret* by the Quetta dramatic society. Margaret thinks it hardly suitable for amateurs, especially as 'one of the Brigadiers' wives taking part is a most terribly proper (very nice) but staid lady. I suppose she is either carried away by artistic temperament or has such a pure mind that it doesn't convey the same to her.' Margie herself had thought it wisest 'to have rather hidden my own trend that way'.

Meanwhile, now that war was declared, the question of Oliver's future employment arose. On 20 October he wrote to Cuthbert Leicester-Warren, setting out the possibilities:

1 To stay on temporarily as commandant, dealing with the 4 and 5 month courses, compared with the 12 months courses before the war.
2 To go back to Europe at once.
3 To be sent either to or with British or Indian troops in Near, Middle or Far East.
4 To go elsewhere in India.

Oliver himself was anxious to go to Europe as quickly as possible and hoped to remain with Margie until sent to a battle front.

As for India 'I think that the possible Russian and Japanese threats to India herself, are gradually showing all classes in the country where their future freedom really lies.' He believed that Congress as a whole would combine with Government to win the war, and then settle India's political future.

In undated letters about this time ML wrote 'We have forbidden drink parties for the war. One of Hitler's better effects.' Of Unity Mitford 'This one was a longlegged hobbledehoy creature when I saw them as children, not nearly so attractive then as either the younger or the elder.'[1] In a letter to her father (17 November) she expressed her feelings about British treatment of Indians:

I know the kindest people whom, when I have been out shopping with them, or to a party where Indians are, I have simply hated for their beastly

---

[1] Unity Mitford, daughter of Lord Redesdale, and friend of Hitler. On war being declared, she shot herself with a revolver. She was sent back from Berlin to England.

rudeness. It makes me feel sick. It's always the Army, too, hardly ever the
political people. I know lots of people here feel the same as I do, and
gradually it's dying out, but alas too late as usual.

On 26 November Oliver wrote to Cuthbert Leicester-Warren a letter
which concluded with a summary of the political and military situation
in India:

> The Congress is, I think, made out a good deal worse than it really is.
> Gandhi is still the great influence in the country, although Bose and his
> extremists shout loudly otherwise.[1] He is the nearest thing to a saint, in
> the opinion of Indians of all creeds, and ultimately it is his views that count
> . . . a vast amount of the country is out to help in every way in the war,
> and I believe that even Congress are now seeing that they've gone about
> things in the wrong way to achieve even a small modification of their
> aims . . .
>
> It's interesting to see the old Russian menace coming up again, and I
> think it will do a lot to steady down the extremist opinion in this country.
> There are as yet practically no Indians of the Army capable of rising to
> very high ranks, and it's impossible to see India defending herself without
> British assistance against even the frontier tribesmen, let alone Afghanistan
> or Russia, and if we went I don't think it would take long for Baluchistan,
> Sind and Karachi to become part of an Afghanistan with whom were
> incorporated the bulk of the frontier tribes.

The 1939 course ended in November.

> 'We are in the midst of goodbyes,' wrote Margie, 'as all the students, plus
> families, depart in the next fortnight. It's very sad, as they've been such a
> nice lot of people and one has just got to know them.'

As had been provisionally arranged, they spent Christmas 1939 at
Bombay, as guests of Roger Lumley, Governor of Bombay. On Boxing
Day the party travelled to Mysore. They rode on elephants in the
reserved jungle, tracking bison, and on their last day hunted crocodile
from a coracle. Margaret described it while travelling on the train from
Mysore to Hyderabad (4.1.40.) 'Quite one of the most exciting things
I have ever done. You see the red eye of the croc shining in the
distance, and you get up very silently and shoot with the rifle which
has a torch – like they do tiger at night . . . the brute always slid under
as we got up. I think there has been a lot of poaching lately.'

[1] Subhas Chandra Bose. Cambridge-educated Bengali, who lost patience with Gandhi's
non-violence movement, and formed unsuccessful Indian National Army supporting
the Japanese. Bose was killed in an aeroplane crash in August 1945, when about to
seek his fortune with Russia.

7 Jan. Hyderabad. [The Nawab's] palace is quite surprising as one steps through the walls of the city into a complete kind of Renaissance looking house, with huge rooms and 36 courtyards and a fountain on which swim 2 black swans. The whole place is like a lumber room of wonderful Regency chairs, 'petit point' all sitting covered in a heap, good pictures, bad pre-Raphaelites, 100's of shot guns, walking sticks, collections of every kind of things. I think the toy collections were the best arranged of the lot. Our luncheon party consisted of some 30 people at least, English and Indian, and the menu was: caviar; soup; fish; cutlets; goose, pilao of chicken and curry; plum pudding; Indian sweet; cheese; fruit; coffee.

By now, the wires were humming with rumours of posting to England.

16 Jan. 1940. By this time if there is anything definite you will have got the telegram. Oliver is so excited and says he feels as if he has come out of prison! Although I am longing to see you all again I would have liked a few more months here with Oliver as Comdt. It was a good and interesting job, and I would have had lots to do too, but as Oliver says, not when there is a war on.

18 Jan. 1940 [7th Anniversary]. We heard late last night we are coming home definitely, so telegram is just going off to you.

25 Jan. Oliver is in the process of handing over to the new G1. It's been a bit of a business sorting out who was to run what, and what was to be run, till the next Comdt's wife arrives in the spring. In consequence of everyone trying to help, and I am sure kindly meant, but no tact or understanding, there was a most laughable muddle, which took me far more time and bother to sort, and which made me lose my temper for the first and I trust the last time in Quetta! I have never seen people so surprised! But I hope they will remember it when the next woman comes.

5 Feb. I simply can't understand America. I think I have more hatred for their righteous smugness than for the Germans even. How they would have abused us if we hadn't fought for the Poles . . . All the new arrivals have come and they seem a nice collection of young things. Very keen and cheerful. There is altogether less grumbling this year.

On 6 February, bearing in mind that careless talk cost lives, Margie announced obliquely the news of their homecoming. 'Today we start off on our tour and we are going to spend a few days with Roger.[1] We hope to see Knowles[2] and of course Cuthbert and Hilda some time about the first or second week in March. It will be lovely seeing them again.'

[1] Viscount Lumley, Governor of Bombay. Later Earl of Scarborough.
[2] Knowles was Hilda Leicester-Warren's lady's maid.

After a journey by boat from Karachi, they arrived in Bombay, where, on 15 February, Margaret wrote from Government House:

> We got here just in time to get off and dress and go to a big luncheon party H.E. was giving at the Race Course before the big race meeting of All India – like our Derby . . . An amusing luncheon including the Maharanee of Cooch Behar (the famous beauty) and her son. It was a very good race and I backed Steel Helmet, which won, which I thought was a lucky omen.

An undated note written by Margaret reads:

> Kabul society must be very difficult now. The belligerents (ourselves, French, Germans) who of course individually pre-war were quite good friends – have now decided to bow when they meet but not shake hands! It's of course impossible in Kabul not to meet.

6

A TOWN LIKE ARRAS

God heard the embattled nations sing and shout:
Gott strafe England *and* God save the King*!*
God this, God that and God the other thing:
'My God,' said God, 'I've got my work cut out!'

J. C. Squire

If all goes wrong with the French, things will be difficult for the
BEF. But it does not necessarily mean that we lose the war.
Oliver Leese 19 May, 1940

Oliver Leese's desire to be back in time for the fighting in Europe was soon gratified. Germany had overrun Poland in September 1939. The Russo–Finnish war lasted from 30 November 1939 to 13 March 1940. There had been initial Finnish successes: France and Britain made efforts to help Finland, and Britain nearly got herself involved in war with Russia as well as with Germany.

In April 1940, both Britain and Germany, in their own strategic interests, were preparing to invade Norway. Germany forestalled Britain by less than twenty-four hours; Hitler's intuition in using the insignificant German navy, in face of British sea power, proved supremely successful, and, on 9 April, the Germans made successful landings at Oslo, Bergen, Narvik and Trondheim. The War Office, prompted by Winston Churchill (First Lord of the Admiralty) now made haphazard arrangements for British troops to expel the Germans.

Oliver Leese had been on leave at Worfield, enjoying with Margie for a few days the delights of Lower Hall. During this time, he was nearly sent first to France, and second to Trondheim:

On the outbreak of hostilities in Norway, I was told to go up to London, taking clothes suitable for cold weather. I went straight to the War Office, where, after the barest preliminaries, I was told 'to capture Trondheim' on Friday. It was then Tuesday.[1] [9 April].

[1] Memoirs.

Leese was to be given command of the 32nd Guards Brigade for the assignment, he was told not to fuss, and to see General Sergison Brooke. The latter expressed the opinion that 'if anyone told him to capture any place with a brigade that had no signal section, and which had not as yet finished its platoon training, he would tell them to go to hell.'[1] Leese did so, politely, and asked if he could train them as an independent reserve brigade to go anywhere they were required. The plan was accepted, and they went to Camberley, with Anthony Head as brigade major.[2] For the next two weeks, in addition to normal training, Leese studied the situation at Narvik with General Guy Williams, of Eastern Command. This was in case it should be thought necessary to send them out there on a mission in which Williams might have had to decide on his own whether to take over from the existing commander. To Leese's relief and probably to that of General Williams, nothing came of this curious mission.

The Norwegian campaign fizzled out ingloriously. Tempers rose high in the House of Commons. Chamberlain, who on 4 April had declared 'Hitler has missed the bus', was now himself pressed to resign. 'In God's name go!' said L. S. Amery,[3] and, in the afternoon of 10 May, Churchill became Prime Minister. This may have seemed ironical to Neville Chamberlain, as it was Churchill rather than he who was responsible for the mismanagement of the Norwegian campaign; however, Churchill's intransigence towards Germany was doubtless a major factor.

Less than twenty-four hours earlier, on the night of 9–10 May, Hitler's armies moved into France and Belgium. The battle of France had begun, and on J 1 (Jour Un) the British Army started towards the front after 9 long months of waiting.

Oliver Leese related that on the morning of 10 May he was called by his servant Jack Lamb with a cup of tea. 'He said quite as a matter of course that it was a lovely day, adding as an afterthought that the Germans had invaded Belgium.'[4] Lamb had served under Leese as a Coldstream Guardsman, had joined him again on Leese's return from Quetta and was to remain with him throughout the war.

Later in the morning of 10 May, Leese received a signal instructing him to join the BEF as deputy Chief of Staff to General Henry Pownall, Lord Gort being Commander-in-Chief, and Leese went to France on the same ship as Colonel Herbert Lumsden, soon to make history with

[1] Ibid.
[2] First Viscount Head (1906–1983) Guards Armoured Division 1941–42 (GSO2). Secretary of State for War 1951–1956. Minister of Defence, Oct. 1956–Jan. 1957.
[3] L. S. Amery, Conservative MP and Cabinet Minister.
[4] Memoirs.

his 12th Lancers armoured car regiment, and to fight with Leese in the battle of Alamein.

It did not need exceptional intelligence to realise that the fate of the free world was in the balance. The best thing was to get on with the job and to count your blessings: Gort had some admirable senior commanders in the BEF. Alanbrooke, as Corps Commander, already had a great reputation, as did Alexander, 'Budget' Loyd and Montgomery among the divisional commanders.

Leese reached GHQ at Arras on the evening of Friday, 10 May, to find that Lord Gort and General Pownall had gone forward to Tac HQ near Brussels, and had left behind Philip Gregson-Ellis, a schoolfriend of Leese, to hand over to him. Robert Bridgeman was also at Arras as G1 (Staff Duties). Leese was replacing General Witts, who had returned to England a fortnight before. Witts had spoken French with more enthusiasm than accuracy, especially when talking to French Generals. Robert Bridgeman, who had gained distinction in an interpreter's course at the Staff College, felt that England was in danger every time Witts spoke French, not only because of what he thought he had said, but also because of what he thought had been said to him. Bridgeman, feeling that Witts should have a fluent linguist with him, had been instrumental in arranging for Ulick Verney to come over to GHQ in March 1940, where, with the rank of Captain, he acted as Personal Assistant to Witts. He was now to act in the same capacity for Leese, and was to serve under him in Italy and Burma.

Ulick Verney, who held a Commission in the Kings Royal Rifle Corps, was an Etonian who had been contemporary in Lubbock's house with Prince Leopold, now Leopold III King of the Belgians. In 1942, during a brief period of leave, he wrote his own account of life at GHQ from March until the end of May 1940. For much of the time during the last three weeks of May he was closely in touch with Leese.

This is Verney's description of Gort, during the last days of the 'phoney war':

> The Commander-in-Chief nether smoked nor drank, though he sometimes ate humbugs out of a striped tin. He disliked changing for dinner, even after a long wet day in the field; he insisted, even at Arras, on using a small, bare office with an ordinary white wood trestle table: he would have much preferred to sleep always on the floor.

Sometimes Verney saw him with the troops:

> Watching their training or looking round the defence lines along the Belgian frontier, striding along, looking like a keeper, with his hat on the back of his head.
> Here then, was a simple, hardworking Head Quarters, strikingly differ-

ent from that of Sir John French in 1914, without pomp, luxury or gaiety.
There were no slackers, no gilded ADCs, only Generals and Colonels wore
red tabs, puttees were commoner than field boots. Gort himself, Henry
Pownall, the great Quartermaster General Lindsell, and the Director of
Military Intelligence, Mason MacFarlane, all were strong personalities:
Philip Gregson-Ellis and Robert Bridgeman, the principal G. Staff Officers,
were interesting and brilliant in different ways: and my own master, the
DCGS, Oliver Leese, who arrived on the eve of the battle to relieve Freddie
Witts, was a scintillating and forceful character. It was a team of diverse
and remarkable personalities; and in the event their performance was up
to expectations.

GHQ had moved from the village of Habarcq to Arras in December
1939. Gort and his principal officers lived in the town, but the whole
of GHQ numbered 2400 of all ranks and covered an area of 80 square
miles.

The Commander-in-Chief's offices, ours of G Operations and some of
Military Intelligence were in the vast Grand Palais in the centre of Arras,
a fabulous, part medieval building, with a Bishop's Palace, a church and
municipal offices in other parts of it. All round were little angular, narrow
medieval streets, pavés of course; and many of their houses had been taken
over for messes, or offices, or billets; and surprisingly British phrases
would come out of their little white-curtained windows! . . .

Ulick Verney, like many of the HQ Staff, became singularly attracted
to Arras:

Once the proud capital of Flanders, many times besieged: the ancient clock
would strike eight with its cracked and tinny voice, and the farm carts
would rumble round the pavé: and the women in black shawls would be
chattering, as they set out the market stalls.

Leese himself had a sensitive feeling for his surroundings, though on
arrival in France his immediate interest was in morale. His first letter
to Margaret, Friday, 10 May, ran:

I'm glad to be here on the first day of the war proper and see the incredibly
good spirit that is everywhere. The will to win and confidence in victory
out here puts very definitely in its right perspective the shoddy performance
of parliament. We had a good journey and no bombs. A calm sea, a motor
met me. Here I found Rob and Philip [Robert Bridgeman and Philip
Gregson-Ellis] very well. Philip is handing over to me. It's very interesting
though a bit of a mouthful to grasp in a few hours.
    Ulick Verney is my Personal Assistant. We have a small mess but quite
a good one. We've a French chef. I've a good room, with a large double
bed!! Also hot and cold water basin. Lamb got settled in very well, and

he's put out all your photographs. I seem to have a very large staff to control. I hope I can do it allright. I've not yet seen Henry Pownall, as he's away, but I hope to see him tomorrow.

On his first evening at Arras, Leese had had a long chat with Philip Gregson-Ellis, and asked him about the state of the French army. Gregson-Ellis said that the French army was very good and well commanded mostly by professors from the Staff College.[1] Leese, who had just left a Staff College, didn't feel the same sense of optimism. There was an enormous amount of detail for him to assimilate: in the brief time that there was to relax, he was all the more appreciative of the surroundings of a civilised Mess.

'Round the corner,' wrote Verney, 'in a prosperous banker's house, was our Senior "A" Mess, whose members were our senior staff officers and which I ran, among my other jobs. It held good but not comfortable furniture of the French Landseer period: a little bar in the hall, an anteroom opening into a dining room, and four good bedrooms upstairs. It was not luxurious but it was clean, and warm, and we just fitted in the twenty-five who belonged to it; and gradually it acquired a certain charm, like a Scottish shooting lodge where one is happy, but will not be staying long.

'You would come in out of the quiet little streets into a buzz of friendly gossip at meal times. There'd be four or five people chatting round the bar over a Habarcq horror – in memory of our last HQ, or over the popular quarter bottle of champagne, at Frs 6 each; and inside people would be sitting about or going into lunch. Everyone knew everyone and asked about friends, and gossiped, and felt very much better.'

Leese wrote to Margie next on Saturday 11 May:

I sent my letter of yesterday home by Boy Browning[1], so I expect you got it fairly soon. We've had a busy day today. Tomorrow I lose Philip and have to take over myself, but luckily, now the war is on Rob also comes to me, and he naturally knows everything, and virtually runs the B.E.F. So I'm very lucky. I found Rusty Eastwood[2] today and also Bulgy Thorne.[3] Days are long, but it's a very interesting time, and one has been very lucky to get into it at the start. Our Mess is definitely good and we've a good champagne and an excellent claret, so that's all to the good.

Boy Browning was the first of Leese's letter carriers during the war. Leese quickly became adept at entrusting letters he had written to

[1] Lieutenant General Sir Frederick Browning (1896–1965). Boy Browning was married to Daphne du Maurier the novelist. Leese was to see a good deal of Browning later in the war, when the latter became Mountbatten's Chief of Staff.
[2] Lieutenant General Sir Ralph Eastwood (1890–1959).
[3] General Sir Andrew Thorne (1885–1970). Commanded 48 division, 1940.

Margaret to officers returning to England, thus accelerating the post. He maintained the practice throughout the war.

Leese was hoping to meet Gort and Pownall on 12 May but Gort was away and Pownall at a hastily convened meeting with King Leopold of the Belgians, his chief of staff Overstraten, Daladier (the French Defence Minster), General Georges and General Billotte, Co-ordinator of the Northern Allied Armies. The main result of this meeting was that it was agreed that General Georges should act as co-ordinator to the French, British and Belgian armies.

On 13 May Margie wrote from Worfield:

Your first letter arrived this morning, which was very good, and I was surprised and thrilled to get it. I was so glad you had got a good room, and everything sounds splendid. Oh it's so lovely here today. The woods are just coming out into bluebells. I'm sitting in the garden and the blossom is out and the birds are singing . . . I can send out quite a lot of asparagus at the end of this week. I will tell Fortnum to send some Kummel and chocolate. But just let me know anything you want. It's wonderful to know that the spirit out there is so different to the scenes that changed the Cabinet [ML was referring to the attacks on Chamberlain in the House of Commons and the replacement of Chamberlain by Churchill as Prime Minister.]

On 13 May the Germans crossed the Meuse at Monthermé. Corap's 9th Army and Huntziger's 2nd Army, completely inadequate for the mighty task of repelling the armoured columns of Guderian and Rommel, fell back in disorder and the panzers burst through. On the same day, probably after meeting Pownall, Leese went on a mission to the French with Rusty Eastwood. They took with them Ulick Verney, to act, when necessary, as interpreter.

'Caught about midnight,' wrote Verney, 'in an air raid in a town some 50 miles from Arras, we suddenly found ourselves charged by a French heavy supply column, doing a good 25 miles per hour without lights – a horrifying moment! For the last ten miles homewards, a beacon had shone ominously: and when we drove into Arras about two in the morning, the winding main street was still burning fiercely, and aged, whiskered gendarmes were combing the streets with their long rifles and bayonets, like figures in an 'Illustration' of 1870, searching for the twenty parachutists which rumour had sprinkled down.'

Having returned safely in the small hours, Oliver wrote to Margie a very spirited letter at about 3 o'clock in the morning of 14 May:

A very short line as it's almost daylight and I've just got back and we start again early. There's not much that I can tell you at the moment.

Our new allies have been very like the Portuguese in the last war – entirely shattered by the low flying air attack, followed, as in Poland, by the armoured formations. I'm sure we will give a better account of ourselves, and that it will be allright when the troops are accustomed to the new techniques. The effect is moral, much more than deadly, in its number of casualties . . .

One is of course influenced by the local situation on our front from the sea to Switzerland, but somehow I believe this is a decisive battle. If it were the British alone, I would have no worries, though I would like to murder the politicians, who have left us short of aircraft, guns and equipment. I met No. 1 [Gort] tonight, who was charming. They bombed the town you may think I'm near this evening [Arras] before I come back, and I leave it tomorrow. Only this news in case you were worried.

By 'our new allies' Leese is referring to Holland and Belgium. He would have been less scathing had he realised at the time the immense *strafing* they had suffered. The Dutch air force had been virtually wiped out on the first day of the offensive; and Belgian morale had suffered severe psychological damage when the 'impregnable' fortress of Eben Emach, completed in 1935, and considered the strongest in the world, was captured through the brilliant deployment of airborne troops, nor could her army withstand the panzer divisions. Following the bombing of Rotterdam, Holland surrendered at 2230 hours on 14 May. The officers at Gort's Headquarters had by now been moved down into the medieval cellars:

'Months before,' wrote Verney, 'our cells had been prepared with lights, chairs and tables, and neatly painted labels on each door: "C-in-C", "DCGS", "G1 Ops", and so on. But while the others had used their cells on schemes and so had dried them out, no-one had occupied Oliver Leese's, which I shared – perhaps for hundreds of years! So the water streamed down the walls, and either papers were wet to the touch, or else, when stoves were brought in, the atmosphere became unbearable. And rheumatism, if a minor horror of war, spoils the temper.'

14 May, ML to OL.

The cottage is now prepared for the evacuees if they ever come. It's such a glorious day and the garden looks lovely and full of promise. I am sitting on our future veranda writing – perhaps I ought to be getting on with the packing, but it's nearly finished and it's so lovely . . . I wish the evacuees would start arriving and one would feel one was doing something. Tomorrow I go to Tabley by a good train to Alderley Edge. It's horrid leaving here, but I shall try and get back soon – at the same time I don't think it would be easy to stay on alone here just now, and better for one to do something rather hectic.

On the morning of 14 May, having completed his letter to Margie and
indulged in the luxury of two hours' sleep, Leese set off to form
Advanced HQ at Renaix, some ninety miles away and well forward
into Belgium.

> 'He and I went ahead in his larger Humber,' write Verney, 'with Lamb,
> his stoic Coldstream servant and Colliton his driver, a quiet Aberdonian,
> who had driven Freddie Witts and also his predecessor, Gen. Philip Neame
> VC, since the BEF came out. While the last DCGS liked to go 35, Oliver
> Leese hated doing less than 70; and it was lucky I had trained Colliton
> to speed, on the quiet, in previous months. All concerned were much
> embarrassed by being given lilies of the valley by "laughing girls" as the
> poet says, on crossing the frontier into Belgium, and I think Oliver and I
> expressed some doubt if such happy sentiment would last.'

Renaix was a manufacturing town the size of Watford, with a lovely,
rectangular *place* with gardens and a fountain in the middle, and with
a perfect classic little Hotel de Ville.

On 15 May Ulick Verney went as interpreter with General Rusty
Eastwood to meet General Billotte. Verney had met Billotte a few
weeks earlier and found him impressive, but on this day, when the
panzer divisions were streaming through the forty mile gap left by the
2nd and 9th French armies, 'he seemed different, a little shrunken,
tired and worn. But he greeted us all with the chilling warmth of a
French official welcome, and listened with distant pleasure to Lord
Gort's respectful message.'

They left their new commander with a feeling of distinct unease.
Back at Renaix they found that command had passed to the Command
Post at Lennik St Quentin, a few miles from Brussels.

> 'The new Command Post' wrote Verney 'was charming: 1750 was the date
> between the intertwined initials of its owners, over the portico. It was of
> the period, formal, stucco, in pale tints, with green shutters, a gravel drive
> and a 'table cloth' of lawn in the front. And inside, all polished floors,
> ormolu clocks, silken hangings, pastel-tinted rugs, and pictures after
> Greuze.'

Major Jackie Crawshay (Gort's ADC) gave Leese and Verney a welcome
lunch with champagne: it was a quarter past four and they had
breakfasted at 7.30 that morning. Gort instructed Leese and Verney
to stay the night. They were lent bedding, and the two slept in the
passage outside the C-in-C's room. It was a memorable night, as they
had five whole hours' sleep, from 10.30 to 3.30! In the night someone

stepped on Verney. He called out sharply 'Who's that?' A booming voice answered 'The Commander-in-Chief!'

15 May, Tabley. ML to OL:

I had a good journey here 1 hr 55 mins! Everyone quite cheerful. Been Altrincham this morning and this afternoon to see 3 old ladies . . . Darling I do *so* love you more and more – and look forward passionately to returning to our little house! How lovely and peaceful it is – I am longing to see you again. Tomorrow I get my hair done and hope to return resplendent and very tidy.

At Renaix Leese found that there was no doubt about the seriousness of the situation:

'All through the morning of the 16th the temperature rose,' wrote Verney. 'News came in by telephone and wireless, by despatch riders, motor contact officers, liaison officers and it was all bad. While the BEF was in contact all along the time, and our 3rd Division [commanded by Major General B. L. Montgomery] in fierce fighting in Louvain, the Germans were hammering at our right, on to the 9th French Army. (Orders were actually found, about now, telling German troops to turn off a sector of British line and attack the French or Belgians rather than our men) . . . Corap's Army, clearly, had begun to crack up. The Germans had broken clean through to a depth of 40 miles, on a front of 7 or 8 miles.'

On the same day, 16 May, Churchill, in response to an urgent telephone call from Reynaud, flew to Paris for discussions. He was accompanied by Dill and Ismay. The party arrived at the Quai D'Orsay at 17.30 for a meeting that was attended by Reynaud,[1] Daladier,[2] Gamelin[3] and various others. Gamelin had produced a map about two yards square, with a black line showing the Allied front. In this line, Churchill was quick to notice, was a small but sinister bulge at Sedan.

After Gamelin had explained the situation for five minutes, there was 'a considerable silence'. Churchill then asked where was the strategic reserve. Gamelin replied that there was no strategic reserve.

Later that evening Churchill took Ismay[4] with him to call on Reynaud at his flat. He managed to inspire him a little, promised him the ten more fighter squadrons that the French had so urgently desired, and flew back to England the next morning.

Early on 16 May, Leese, taking Ulick Verney with him, visited

[1] Prime Minister.
[2] Defence Minister.
[3] Supreme Commander, French Land Forces.
[4] General Sir H. L. (Baron) Ismay. Churchill's Senior Staff Officer.

Billotte, to discuss some new question which had arisen. Leese wrote:

> [Billotte] was despondent over rolls and butter and coffee, which we had about 6 in a café, chilled to be bone. The brunt of the German attack was falling on Corap's 9th French Army below Namur, twenty miles to our right: and the native troops were demoralised under the dive bombing, of which they had never been warned.[1]

16 May, Tabley. ML to OL.

> I do hope you are getting my letters by now. I gather that General Eastwood also hadn't got his wife's. It's difficult to judge anything from here, but I wonder if the tide is turning or only a lull in the storm.

On the night of 16 May the BEF moved back to the line of the river Senne, the first of three natural defensive lines which run across Belgium. This is how Ulick Verney remembered it all:

> Inside the great chamber the main offices were emptying fast. A few officers stood, silent, reflecting, waiting: clerks were collecting last papers, orderlies were collecting each other. All the furniture was gone, except for one chair, one table, and on it the last telephone. Here the C-in-C was sitting, talking to the War Office in Whitehall, telling the Director of Military Operations our news. The line was evidently a bad one and his harsh, booming voice echoed round the great room. In the far corner the night orderly was lying back on a pile of blankets, his jacket off, his eyes half-closed, his hand behind his head. He was whistling the song of the day – if not precisely of the moment – 'Tomorrow is a lovely day.'

On 17 May the news coming into the newly established headquarters in 'the square, ugly chateau outside the village of Wahagnies' had become even more serious. An agreed withdrawal on three successive nights was to bring the BEF back on to the River Escaut (Scheldt) and it brought all the Allied forces north of the gap back onto a new line. The move was executed on the orders of General Georges: 'These being in fact almost the only orders he ever delivered to us', wrote Leese.[2] This move was inadequate, for the BEF rear HQ at Arras had to be protected. However, as one of the senior officers said years later 'in a town like Arras it is possible to have the defences well in hand.'

On arrival at Wahagnies – the procedure was to be repeated each time they moved headquarters – Gort and his staff were quickly operating in their new accommodation. Gort and Pownall had a small

---

[1] Memoirs.
[2] Memoirs.

'office' each on the ground floor; a large main room housed Leese, Gregson-Ellis and other G Ops people; and in the outer G Ops room the G.3's worked – David Meynell, Robin Gairdner, Geordie Gordon-Lennox and others. Here were set up the main operation maps, with the grim advancing flags of the Germans: and the 'In' and 'Out' message boards, their flimsy sheets bearing the same gloomy tidings. Whatever orders were made to the contrary, this room was often thronged with visitors, crowding round the maps, discussing the messages and vehemently disturbing the work of the luckless G.3's, who while capable enough of ejecting a visiting subaltern, found it harder to be firm with Administrative Generals or Brigadiers.

One of the luckless junior officers was Captain George Gordon-Lennox:

We G.3's were green as grass. We had no personal experience of war and knew even less about the workings of a Higher Headquarters. And so events as they unfolded during those hectic weeks in May 1940 left indelible imprints in our minds, not least the arrival and departure of Senior Officers. Oliver Leese's arrival as DCGS to Sir Henry Pownall during the retreat from the Dyle certainly made its mark. His huge, slightly stooping figure swept into our office with an air of smooth authority which filled us with confidence. He knew most of us and behaved as if we were all engaged in a really rather important exercise at Aldershot.

Until Lord Gort's Headquarters was split in two I saw a lot of him as I and another GSO3 were in charge of the Op Maps and had to register every signal that entered or left the Headquarters.

His grasp of the everchanging scene was extraordinarily quick and as the picture became increasingly depressing his tireless energy and sense of humour never deserted him. On one occasion when he decided to take a couple of hours rest he told me not to wake him unless a signal of urgent importance arrived. Of course it did, and reluctantly I was obliged to wake him up. Without a groan or rebuke he swung his long legs onto the floor and was instantly in top gear.

We junior staff officers soon came to realise how brilliantly the BEF and its revered Commander were being served by that remarkable team of senior general staff officers led by Oliver Leese and his two highly professional GSO I's, Philip Gregson-Ellis and Robert Bridgeman. Their skill and quickness of mind and their ability to read the battle from the increasingly confused information that poured into GHQ was an experience that none of us will forget. They always seemed to know what to do![1]

17 May, Tabley. ML to OL.

I got your letter of Monday [13 May] and was so very glad to get it. Thank

[1] Letter to author from Major General Sir George Gordon-Lennox, 23.11.1979.

you darling so so much – but you do know that just a service p.c. when you are tired is all that I would want. Though I love your letters more than all the world and they carry me through the days . . . Worfield is making great preparations if Wolverhampton get bombed! The excitement there is intense. I was glad to hear about the bombs [over Arras]. It came on the wireless last night, and made my heart jump in my mouth and stay there for hours although I knew it was over two days [ago].

. . . I am going into the local hospital in the quartermaster's department to learn all I can.

18 May. OL to ML.

I so hope you are allright. Have not yet had a letter but your parcels arrived from Fortnums. They are excellent. Will you thank your parents so much. We have had a pretty hectic time since I wrote. We moved forward and have lived in every conceivable kind of place and so far have managed to hide ourselves.

We just work all the time but I've managed to get a few hours sleep most nights. All the kit, large and small, has just worked out very well. The hairbrush, etc. case. Your flask, the brew bag, are excellent and save endless trouble.

The BEF advance was a triumph of planning and organisation. Road discipline was first class. We suffered practically nothing from the air. The troops fought extremely well on the Dyle, and we lost no ground. Since then we've successfully withdrawn and with an increase of fighters have so far not suffered much from the inevitable congestion of refugees and military traffic on the roads. The refugees are the most pathetic sights. It might be 'The Flight from Egypt'. The rich ones in motorcars have passed – now it is walkers, prams, bicycles, carts with horses, cows and dogs pulling them. One endless stream of misery – old women, cripples, babies in arms – but far too many young men, who should be fighting. The disturbing event so far is the bad handling and morale of one or two French divisions, who have crumpled before the air and tank attacks, and have given up water obstacles almost without a shot. We trust they will soon make a stand, but it's been a poor show so far on many parts of the French front. The one shining spot was the behaviour of the French mechanised cavalry . . .

The British morale is very high – the C-in-C is magnificent, an example of resolution, calmness and determination to all. This is a happy and efficient HQ, and it is grand to have Rusty Eastwood to work with. Henry Pownall is quite excellent – calm, far-seeing and sensible, and Philip [Gregson-Ellis] is extremely able, while Rob Bridgeman with our rear party has been a tower of knowledge, common sense and efficiency.

I hope to get you this by King's Messenger.

On 17 May GHQ had been moved to the unattractive straggling town of Wahagnies (known to the troops as 'Wee Haggie'), forty-five miles west of Renaix. Despite the guardedly optimistic note of his

letter to Margie, Leese probably saw better than anyone at GHQ what
was the probable outcome of the battle. The situations reports spoke
for themselves. On 18 May he had prepared a blueprint for evacuation
to Dunkirk by hollow square, with 50 Division providing a flank guard
along the Bassée Canal, which he read to Gort, Pownall and other
senior officers about midnight on 18–19 May.

What Leese had planned was in essence an example of the Extensive
Warfare he had been practising in Quetta with Tony Scott. Gort was
not however in an independent position and Leese's plan could not be
accepted.[1] The most Gort felt himself able to do in the matter was to
allow Leese on 19 May to explore with the Admiralty the likely Naval
requirements in the event of an evacuation, but the C-in-C did little
in the way of preparation for such an eventuality.

The relentless sunshine of Hitler's weather continued to pour down
on the refugees as they plodded along the roads. 'All about them',
wrote Verney, 'was this aspect of a tragedy enacted countless times
down the centuries.' It was now necessary to travel long journeys by
night owing to the streams of refugees. The defence of Arras had been
organised under General Petre (Petre Force). At one stage Leese
discovered to his amazement and delight 15,000 to 20,000 officers and
men sitting by the roadside. They had been sent as reinforcements.

As a result of a telephone call to the War Office from General
Pownall (19 May), General Sir Edmund Ironside, the CIGS, got a
meeting of the War Cabinet – Churchill, Chamberlain, Attlee, Halifax,
Greenwood, arranged for 4.30 p.m. on the same day.

Gamelin, of whom so much had been expected, was relieved of
his command and superseded by the 73-year-old General Maxime
Weygand, brought from retirement in Syria, arriving on 20 May with
remarkable panache to 'round up the panzers' as he termed it, and
thereby to save France.

On 19 May and 20 May ML wrote to OL, chiefly giving home news
and expressing her mounting concern for Oliver's safety. On 19 May,
OL wrote two letters to ML, the first on a sheet of blank paper, eight
inches by three, written in pencil on both sides:

> Just a line to say I'm very well. We are still going back and hoping against
> hope that the French will recover. If not, it all looks pretty gloomy. Even
> the Poles seem to have done better than the French. If all goes wrong with
> the French, things will be difficult for the BEF. But it does not necessarily
> mean that we lose the war.

The second letter, marked 'later' and dated 19 May, was written

[1] Nigel Hamilton [*Monty, the Making of a General (1887–1942)*] writes: Had Gort been
able to act unequivocally on Leese's outline plan, an orderly, well-administered
evacuation could have been effected instead of the near débâcle that actually followed.

on the official headed notepaper – GENERAL HEADQUARTERS
BRITISH EXPEDITIONARY FORCE printed in red block capitals
– that Leese had been using since arriving at Arras:

> A day I shall never forget. I had ½ hour's sleep last night! This morning
> things looked terribly glum and it looked like another Namsos.[1] Now the
> French seem to be taking a pull, and we are helping. If only we can stem
> this one rush, on which all is staked, we shall win . . .

Significant evidence of the pace of life and the lack of sleep is found
in the fact that both of these letters are dated Monday. There is no
doubt that they were written on 19 May, which was Sunday – a day
of national intercession in France, in which a special service, attended
by all the French Cabinet, was held in Notre Dame.

By 20 May Gort had split his HQ, as the BEF was virtually
fighting two separate battles. On the Eastern flank the three corps were
hard-pressed all along the line; while on the Southern and Western
flanks, Petre Force and Pol Force were holding off ever-increasing
bodies of the enemy. Robert Bridgeman ran the latter war, Philip
Gregson-Ellis the former, and Ulick Verney recounted that one would
throw the other a message across the table, saying politely 'Your war,
I think.' Leese would sometimes be working with either or both of
them; later, when all three were acting separately, Lord Bridgeman
has told the present author that, owing to the three knowing one
another well at Eton, each could gain a very good idea as to how the
other two would react under given circumstances, and would make
their own decisions accordingly.[2]

On 20 May Ironside conferred with Gort at Wahagnies, and tried
to gain his support for the Weygand plan for an attack in the direction
of Amiens. Gort, who was determined to preserve the BEF and who
felt that the French would never mount an attack, would not agree to
the project, even though it had Churchill's optimistic backing. Ironside, in a thoroughly bad temper, asked if he could take Pownall with
him on a visit to Billotte and Blanchard, commanding the French 1st
Army, at Lens. On arrival at Lens, Ironside asked Billotte what he
was going to do about the situation, and pulled him by the tunic. The
panzer legions meanwhile were surging on at an amazing speed.
Guderian's tanks entered Amiens, Corap's 9th Army had disintegrated
opposite Sedan and German forces were swinging towards the sea.

20 May. Tabley. Cuthbert Leicester-Warren to Oliver:

Witts came to lunch yesterday; quite pleasant but rather shy; ought not to

---

[1] A reference to the disastrous evacuation (April 1940) in the Norwegian Campaign.
[2] Interview. 17 August 1979.

be at his age, but I suppose it was the presence of Lord Lieut. and chief policeman which intimidated him . . . If you are in want of mutton for a change would you like Tabley sheep packed up and sent? Or better perhaps a blue Cheshire cheese? That might be more acceptable.

On 21 May Gort succeeded in getting the French to join him in a limited counter attack to relieve the pressure on Arras. Either by accident or design, he was unable to attend a conference with Weygand at Ypres.

21 May, Tabley. ML to OL.

It's awful, this anziety [sic] but I feel that it will pass like so many other appalling moments in England's history – *Stickez the Lilywhites*![1] – I am even glad now that we aren't at Quetta.

In a second letter from Tabley on 21 May ML wrote:

R.E. [Rusty Eastwood, who had just come back from France] just telephoned to say he'd left you in good health and spirits – 'in great form' and gave me your messages. I also got your dear Saturday letter [18 May] so I have been much elated.

On 22 May Leese went to Vimy Ridge to represent Lord Gort at a meeting to discuss whether the counter attack could be continued, taking with him Ulick Verney.

'We left Wahagnies at 1.30 in the dark of an ice-cold early morning,' wrote Verney, 'shivering and unfriendly after half-an-hour's sleep; and a three hours' drive brought us to General Franklyn's[2] temporary headquarters in Vimy village a full hour and a half before the conference was due to start! However, we did not like to disturb our hosts, who had had a bad time recently, and so waited chilled to the bone until the party assembled. Gen. Franklyn ran it, quietly and firmly, sitting at a writing table in the middle, while the dozen or so officers sat round on benches, and schoolroom chairs: we were all full of sleep and kept nodding and slipping forwards: and the illusion of an unusually Early School at Eton was heightened when Monty Stopford (commanding one of the brigades) saw me scribbling furiously to keep awake and said, in a stage whisper 'Writing your home letter or what, Ulick?' Suddenly the telephone went dead and I was sent up to the local exchange in the village to get it going again. The early morning stars were twinkling above the white road, the air was fresh, smelling of a country village: a cock was crowing; in the distance was a low mutter of guns. At the exchange the girls were shutting up and leaving, for – as they observed

[1] The Lilywhites: nickname given to the Coldstream Guards.
[2] General Sir Harold Franklyn, commanding 5th Division.

with a logic I could hardly refute – it was time to go; but there was one
youngish man there who was persuaded to remain, at least for an hour,
until our conference was over.'

Wed 22 May. Tabley. ML to OL.

Your letter, the lovely long one, arrived this morning though later ones of
Sat came first. [Oliver wrote twice on Sunday 19 May, but it is possible
that he wrote other notes on Saturday 18 May which have not survived] –
it was lovely to get and will carry me through the day. I am so sorry about
mine as I've written nearly every day, but hope you will have them by
now. Your letter has given me a vivid picture – those poor refugees.
Anyway, mon brave, one feels it is a war against all the worst cruelties of
the evil creatures who have no mercy. Now for another Agincourt – or
Armada – or Waterloo – oh God grant it may be so . . .

The country house near Premesques, where Advanced HQ was situated
from 22 to 25 May, was a two-storied, formal, early eighteenth century
building. A wide paved terrace gave on to a formal garden, french
windows opening on to sunlit lawns: meadows and woodland surrounded it; and in the park was a murky trout pool, which Leese
would have found very tantalising. It is unlikely that he ever had time
to do any fishing, but he had a fishing rod with him, probably brought
over from England.

On the afternoon of 22 May Leese got out for a short walk in the
sunshine with Verney, and while they were looking at the trout pool
Verney asked Leese if he could see any hope for the BEF under the
Weygand Plan.

This plan (sometimes called the Ironside Plan) involved a large
scale counter-attack by the French and the BEF. The chances of a
French commander being able to launch a counter-attack of any size
seemed remote; while the BEF, possessing little armour and no air
support, would have to turn its back on the enemy, advance away
from such bases as remained, and with food, ammunition and
petrol running steadily down. Further, if the Belgians gave way,
the Germans would be able to cut off the BEF's line of retreat to the
sea.

Leese thought that there was no chance for such a plan. He added,
that next day at Gort's request, General Sir John Dill was flying out.
Dill had just been appointed CIGS in place of Ironside, and every
effort would be made to persuade him of the impracticability of such
a plan at such a time.

As at Vincennes the week before, so now at Premesques, the burning
of documents began, and did in fact continue for three or four days.
Verney felt that 'there is no more gloomy occupation than burning

secret documents, letters and in the end shirts and bits of uniform in a wood under a drizzle.'

Dill's visit on 23 May lasted only a few hours, but he was quick to understand the situation and gave Gort his backing. The same day (0730 hrs) Gort gave the order for Arras to be evacuated. Ulick Verney recalled that

> about this time: Robert Bridgeman was working on a map board, and seeing me watching, handed it to me. It needed no explanation. On the talc which covered a large-scale map there were only eight or ten lines in red chalk. They framed a strip of land running in from the sea, some 60 miles deep and 20 miles wide: and across it horizontally ran four or five parallel lines, each 10 or 15 miles nearer the sea. Never was a historic operation of war illustrated as simply and expressively as in this picture of the narrow corridor along which the BEF must pass on its way to the sea and back to England. The C-in-C had actually asked HM Government two days earlier to allow him to prepare such a plan for use in emergency and leave had been given.

24 May. OL to ML.

> Today is the big decision. It is really beyond us to decide. Whatever it is, I hope we shall maintain the traditions of the Army. We are unbeaten, though in an almost impossible position, owing to the French break. Perhaps I shall see you in a day or two now. Bridgers and I wrote a very long order last night. It is great fun doing things together again. Hitler is lucky to get all this fine weather. Boy Munster[1] takes this.

24 May. Tabley. ML to OL.

> Thank goodness the Mosley gang have been taken up – but I wonder what you'll think of Maule Ramsay[2] being sent to Brixton Prison. We haven't heard the accusations yet. It's awful to think of treachery in high places, but there is no doubt there is.

24 May. Tabley. ML to OL. [2nd letter]:

> I am becoming Assis. Quartermaster to the Red X detachment here, and am going to do some hospital training as soon as it can be arranged . . . I will order you some more chocolates from Fortnums and also tell them to send Lamb a parcel.

On 25 May GHQ moved to the little Flemish town of Houtkirk, the

[1] Fifth Earl of Munster, ADC to Gort. He left the beaches on 29 May with Pownall, arriving in London on the morning of 30 May, and reported to Churchill while the latter was having his bath.
[2] Maule Ramsay. Eton, Coldstream Guards. Severely wounded 1916. Member of HM Body Guard for Scotland. MP(U) Peebles 1931–45. Detained at Brixton Prison 23 May 1940 until 26 September 1944.

journey over roads crowded with undisciplined convoys. Houtkirk was just one long street, two rows of little white houses, with painted green doors and window frames. Two old ladies in black mob caps edged with white offered beds and said the British officers must have every comfort they could provide; they did not realise they were offering hospitality to the British commander-in-chief and his staff – on their way back to the coast.

25 May. OL to ML [written on a sheet of scrap paper].

All well. Have just had Gen. Dill out. We so enjoyed seeing him. He gives one confidence and hope. We are all well and cheerful and full of hope that we'll bring this off. Maybe the Boche will once again overrun himself.

25 May. Tabley. ML to OL.

Just one word. I don't know quite what to say except I am thinking and thinking of you, and love you more than all the world.

On 26 May there was a second Service of Intercession at Notre Dame. There was also a similar service at Westminster Abbey. 'The English are loth to expose their feelings' wrote Churchill, 'but in my stall in the Choir I could feel the pent-up, passionate emotion, and also the fear of the congregation, not of death or wounds or material loss, but of defeat and the final ruin of Britain.'

On the same day the evacuation fleet moved off to Dunkirk. *Operation Dynamo*, as it was code named, resulting from War Office–Admiralty discussions, had begun.[1]

After various informal conferences GHQ was moved from Houtkirk to La Panne early in the afternoon of 26 May:

'Lorries, guns, supply wagons, motor cycles,' wrote Verney, 'hopelessly, irretrievably congested, the block stretched before us for miles across the bleak Flanders fields.'

It was decided to go across country. They were held up by irrigation ditches; so they put valises in the ditches; the valises would have to be discarded shortly, anyway, so it didn't matter.

'After this' wrote Verney, 'superb map reading by Oliver brought us by devious tracks back on to the main road by one of the canal bridges, crowded with British and French soldiers, artillery, trucks and tanks. And so into the perimeter of Dunkirk.'

[1] The evacuation fleet was organised by Bertram Ramsay, Vice Admiral, Dover: he and his staff working in a room beneath Dover Castle. The room was known in WWI as the Dynamo Room, as it then housed an auxiliary lighting system. Hence the WW2 code name – *Operation Dynamo*.

The journey to the precincts had taken place in cold rain, and it was still pouring when they reached Dunkirk.

'The little watering place,' wrote Verney, 'where King Albert of the Belgians had his headquarters for a time during the last war, looked like some dingier Folkestone or lowlier Ramsgate on an "off day" . . .'

At last they found the Hotel in La Panne, five miles from Dunkirk, that was to be their new headquarters:

Like any hotel on the front at Ramsgate, and a great empty villa next door, which was magnificently termed the Summer Palace of the Queen of the Belgians. In these buildings GHQ respectively worked, slept and fed, the latter in the Queen's own servants' kitchen, and off her servants' crockery: the crowns thereon were smaller than upstairs, and in mere blue instead of gold paint.

Verney saw here the stage set for 'a new Gallipoli' in Northern France:

The long, rushy grass bowed in the wind across the hillocks: the dunes rolled untidily back to low, scrubby trees behind: the sands were bare, windswept, business-like almost: cold spring rain beat in our faces. Behind, in a belt between the dunes and the hotels were low bushes, dripping, dripping, on the thousands of British soldiers waiting in long, sodden, weary columns: out of sight of the sea, slightly covered from bombers, patiently waiting for orders . . . there was no boat, great or small, in sight.

On 27 May, the orderly withdrawal began. The BEF by this time had less than 3 days' rations left, 2½ days' petrol, 3½ days' ammunition. There was no bombing on 27 or 28 May: possibly because King Leopold III had asked for an armistice, and the Germans were reluctant to bomb a Belgian town at that moment. On 27 May Dill took over from Ironside as CIGS.

27 May. Tabley. ML to OL.

There were crowds and crowds in all the churches yesterday. The Chapel was packed and I went to Holy C. after it [ML was referring to the Chapel at Tabley where they were married]. I think of our L.H. [Lower Hall] and the garden and the view and all the people of the village which is our England, and it seemed like a lovely world all on its own.

On 28 May the Belgian Army surrendered. The surprise of Churchill and Gort on learning this news is in itself a little surprising. Leopold had telegraphed George VI on 25 May, saying that Belgian resistance could not go on much longer, and Gort and the War Office had received

seven messages from Belgian liaison contacts to the same effect on 26
and 27 May. The Belgian army had fought with great courage for
eighteen days, but there was now an open gap of twenty miles between
Ypres and the sea.

Leese's efforts during the last three days of May were prodigious by
any standards. In the maps room, at conferences, on the beaches – he
seemed to be everywhere: he said afterwards that he was kept going
by Ulick Verney 'who had an uncanny knack of finding me champagne
by day and night.'

'We did our level best,' wrote Leese, 'to persuade the French to evacuate
with us and to withdraw side by side with us and we offered them every
facility for evacuation. It would have saved us many casualties, if they
would have done this. I went to one conference where the French insisted
on fighting to the last "*avec les drapeaux.*" I was very tired and I argued
in very bad French for ages. It was of no avail, and finally I remember
saying it had nothing to do with their colours – all they had to do was to
fight and then come down to the ships.'[1]

Lt.-Colonel Frank Simpson[2] (Simbo) had been with GHQ since the
middle of May. He was given various assignments. One of them was
getting rid of 'useless officers' from Monty's 3rd Division, and giving
them innocuous escort duties. For a week he was living on a diet of
caviar and champagne. There was no time to cook normal meals. He
supervised the running together of trains to block the railway near
Arras and hold up German tanks.

About 28 May Simpson came across Leese who was acting for Gort
in the Bray Dunes area between La Panne and Dunkirk. Leese asked
him what he'd been doing. Simpson summarised.

The roads in this area where thousands of the BEF would be arriving
were cluttered with abandoned French military vehicles. If the roads
were not cleared the position of the BEF would be perilous. 'Simbo'
said Leese, 'you've got to do a lot more now. Go and clear the roads.'
Leese was in charge of the Dunkirk bridgehead – among other things.
The BEF would be coming down on to the bridgehead and the roads
had to be cleared quickly. This was done chiefly by pushing the French
trucks and other vehicles into the canal by the use of bulldozers.
Occasionally French officers had to be cajoled, or, in at least one case,
threatened with a revolver before agreeing to this treatment of their
equipment. About the same time Leese and Lamb smashed the former's staff car, a splendid Humber Snipe, with a crowbar.

---

[1] Memoirs.
[2] General Sir Frank Simpson. He said in later years that Leese was virtually responsible
for saving the BEF at Dunkirk.

There were a fleet of ambulances waiting, but no senior doctor about. 'Go and organise them' said Leese to Simpson, and the latter was able to do this.

29 May. OL to ML.

Just a line by Henry Pownall [as Gort's Chief of Staff he had been ordered back to England, so that he would not be taken prisoner]. We've got to the sea, and are busily embarking on the beaches. So far today the Boche has done us very little harm. But our troops are utterly exhausted, and I doubt if we can make the withdrawal of our rearguard. We are doing our best and are full of hope . The C in C is staying and I am to stay as his Chief of Staff. It's a proud moment, and I hope we'll bring it off. At peaceful moments the beach is rather like Blackpool! Little discipline and a good deal of chaos.

On Wednesday 29 May, after lunch, the lull at Dunkirk was shattered.

'Some of us were sitting,' wrote Verney, 'slacking for ten minutes, on a dune in the hot May sunshine: Oliver Leese, Colin Jardine [the Military Secretary], Colin McNabb, Philip Gregson-Ellis, Peter Burne – a XII Lancer who had been our liaison officer with General Prioux's shattered cavalry division, came up with a camera to take our photos; cameras were strictly forbidden in the BEF and it must have been the only one on the beach. I said 'You may think this is Blackpool beach, Peter – I do assure you it isn't.' Twelve dive bombers came over five minutes later: *plus d'illusions* . . .

That happened three times that sunny afternoon . . . The last attack of the day, out of the setting sun, above the purple banks of night, was a lovely sight: the silver lines of tracer bullets against the clouds: the swooping dark planes: and the hot excitement. We had all rushed out, and the C-in-C, capless as usual among us, to see the fun: rifles and Brens added to the din, and the cheer that went up when a tracer went right into a plane! That was the last day when embarkation by day-light could be effected: the risks had become too great, despite the need, which was most pressing.'

30 May. ML to OL.

This is just in case letters still go. I didn't write yesterday, but I thought I would just send you my best best love and tell you how the thought and prayer of every man and woman here are with the BEF.

30 May. OL to ML.

It is all made a little hard, watching so many people going home – but, as we've so often said 'C'est la guerre.' Our chances are being frittered away by the Navy – a wonderful day with low clouds, and now not a single ship working, and we've not got many days to waste. In fact none.

The whole place is full of panic – mostly French. A retreat is a terrible thing to see, and before long we'll have men fighting for boats and food. We have embarked many rearward services – but unless things go well, we shall lose all the good fighting troops – including several Brigade Battns. This waste of time is most distressing. I send this to you by Lamb, who will stay with you till you know whether or not I get back. I must say I dread the thought of Germany, but there it is – I'm afraid my letters are very depressing, but I've kept a cheerful face – and it's a great comfort to get it off one's chest . . . We've a good chance of a get-away at the end – but it won't be easy to get the C-in-C to leave.

Leese 'kept a cheerful face' in the midst of a thousand duties, chatting to waiting groups of soldiers, answering questions and giving encouragement. He sometimes went the rounds carrying a fishing rod: here on the beaches it proved an admirable defuser of tension.

On 27 May Captain W. G. Tennant, Chief Staff Officer to the First Sea Lord, had been sent to Dunkirk to take charge of the embarkation of troops and to speed up the evacuation. But troops did not always arrive where the ships were, and *vice versa*. On 29 May Rear Admiral Frederick Wake-Walker was sent to Dunkirk to take charge of everything afloat, while Tennant remained Senior Naval Officer on shore.

The situation was desperate when Wake-Walker arrived off Bray Dunes in the early hours of 30 May. Leese had already telephoned the War Office saying that the perimeter could only be held for a very short time. The War Office replied reassuringly, but nothing happened. At 12.45 p.m. Leese tried again; this time with Dill. Wake-Walker sent an officer to Dover to stress the urgency of the situation.

Eventually the small craft – the little ships – began to pour in; at 2000 hrs Wake-Walker arrived at GHQ to see Lord Gort and work out co-ordination plans. He was invited to stay for dinner. In the conference afterwards it was put to Wake-Walker that the Army had done everything possible: it was now up to the Navy to try a little harder.

Wake-Walker contended that any lack of success was not through want of trying. Leese said that the Army had marched enough; the ships should go where the men were. He then referred to 'the ineptitude of the Navy'. Wake-Walker, who had commanded the *Revenge*, replied with asperity that Leese had no business or justification to talk that way.

Lord Bridgeman remembered that at GHQ in La Panne on 31 May, they sat down to a brief lunch of cold ham. Then Gort gave final instructions. Alexander was to take over after Gort left for England.

The War Office was now sending furious messages ordering Gort to board the *Keith* and return at once!

'I had the responsibility to get Lord Gort on to his destroyer,' wrote Leese, 'and I set out along the beach from our villa at La Panne with a small convoy, Lord Gort and his ADC Jack Crawshay in one car and the remaining personnel – some 20 in all of GHQ – in four others. I had been in touch with the destroyer [the *Keith*] which was sent for him, and it was lying close in to the shore near another destroyer. No sooner had our little convoy started along the coast that what seemed to be every Stuka in the world started a really good hearty raid on the shipping lying off the coast. Bombs started falling on the beach and I got my small party out of their cars and on to the sand dunes . . . When things quietened down I reformed my party and looked for the C-in-C. To my sorrow I saw him, always a great yachtsman, in a small boat, rowing out to sea alone with his ADC like 2 men in a tub! But what was worse – he was on the way to the wrong destroyer.'[1]

Leese managed to sign to the right destroyer for boats. They eventually reached the *Keith* in the middle of another air raid and up to their necks in water.

I never realised before how difficult it was to climb up a rope ladder, out of a pitching boat, especially if you are desperately clutching two packs and a fishing rod.[2]

By this time Leese was soaked through and the only dry clothes he could find were a pair of blue pyjamas, so 'to save my life and hide my confusion', the Navy lent him a duffel coat. Raids continued all day, so he could not get a boat to go to the other destroyer [the *Hebe*] until after dark. In doing so, they nearly ran into another boat, and shouted 'in no mean terms' for it to get away. Leese had good cause to believe afterwards that this other boat contained Lord Gort, who had gone out to look for him.

Eventually Gort and Leese made contact on the right destroyer. They then set off for England in Speedboat MA/SB6, with a crew of three. Gort and Leese sat in the tiny cabin. Gort was dead tired and throughout the journey slept with his head on Leese's knee. Leese himself had never been so stiff, but remained perfectly still so that Gort could get some sleep. They landed at Dover in the early morning, where they were met by Budget Loyd,[3] who told Gort that he was to go straight to Mr Eden, the War Secretary. Leese recalled:

We travelled to London by train. Lord Gort was really very well dressed.

[1] Memoirs.
[2] Ibid.
[3] Leese's friend from WW1, and fellow Coldstreamer, 'Budget' Loyd, commanding 2 Division, had fainted during a conference on 16 May. He was invalided back to UK.

I had on my blue pyjamas and duffel coat and was still clutching my two
packs and a six piece fishing rod to which were added a pair of soaking
field boots, which I had taken off on the ship. We drove to the War Office
and we went up to the Secretary of State's room. The C-in-C gave his final
report of the situation at the bridgehead . . . I was far too sleepy to
remember much of the conversation and I even left behind my precious
fishing rod, which, later in the day was located for me.[1]

Meanwhile, Alexander remained in command at Dunkirk until 4 June,
when the last troops of the BEF were evacuated.

In after years Leese was fond of recounting the story told him in
the first place by Alexander himself. When he had returned from
Dunkirk, Alexander, as Gort had done three days earlier, reported to
the War Office. In Alexander's case it was to see Walter Monckton,[2]
then a Junior Minister. They had both played for Harrow in Fowler's
Match [1912] when Eton defeated them in a sensational finish by 9
runs. No sooner had they met than Alexander, who had been Harrow's
fast bowler, chipped Walter Monckton, the wicket keeper on that
occasion, about dropping a vital catch. They discussed the matter
with so much animation that Churchill's arrival passed unnoticed,
until the Prime Minister, whose displeasure had steadily been
mounting, upbraided them: 'Gentlemen, please talk about serious
matters.'

'We are, Sir,' replied Monckton, 'we're talking about cricket!'

France surrendered on 22 June. On 17 July the all-conquering
Germans held a thanksgiving service in Notre Dame; the Almighty,
having heard the pleas of France and Britain, now received the thanks
of Germany. Shortly afterwards a stern message from Keitel, German
Chief of Staff, intimated that no more thanksgiving services were to
be held in the future.

Altogether 338,000 soldiers, including 110,000 French, lived
to fight another day. Among the British were Alanbrooke,
Alexander, Montgomery, Leese, Horrocks and Lumsden. Gort
was never to command an army again. There were some who said
he would have been at his best as a divisional or even as a
regimental commander; but in the last torrid days of May he had
proved himself right when Weygand and Ironside and Churchill had
been wrong.

Oliver Leese believed that if Gort had been allowed to command a

---

[1] Memoirs.

[2] Walter Monckton [Viscount Monckton of Brenchley]. A close friend of Edward
VIII, and wrote his abdication speech. After the war, as Minister of Labour, he was
highly respected as a negotiator. Briefly Minister of Defence, but resigned before
Suez.

division in 1940, instead of being picked to command the BEF above
the heads of men like Alanbrooke and Dill, he might have graduated
to higher command, and become one of the most successful wartime
generals. As it was, wrote Leese:

> he was a great national figure, and when one went out to lunch with him
> in London, he was constantly saluted and accosted by the men in the street,
> rather like one imagined must have happened to the Iron Duke a hundred
> years before.[1]

[1] Memoirs.

7

GUARDS ARMOURED

You have taught us so much, fired us all with enthusiasm, and created a magnificent division.

Allan Adair to Oliver Leese, 11 September 1942

Leese stayed on during the next three or four weeks helping Lord Gort sort out his reports, leaving him finally when on 12 July, he was informed by Postal Telegram from the War Office that he had been appointed Commander, 29th Infantry Brigade.[1] To his great joy he heard that they were to be one of the few formations to receive priority in equipment and armament. They were to concentrate at Aldershot and then move to Sussex as a Reserve formation in General 'Bulgy' Thorne's 12 Corps.

He soon found out that the new equipment was not entirely an unmixed blessing. Under his command he had four regular battalions back from India – Royal Welch Fusiliers, Royal Scots Fusiliers, East Lancashire Regiment, Prince of Wales Volunteers. They were first class material, but had little or no training with modern weapons or equipment, in fact the Royal Scots Fusiliers were the only battalion who had any trained drivers of mechanical transport. The rest were expert on mules – 'but then' Leese commented, 'we had no mules!' What he did have, and was more than thankful to have, was a Field Regiment, Anti-Tank Battery, Field Company RE, Field Ambulance and RASC Company; the majority of the last named troops came from the one Infantry Brigade Group of the 51 Highland Division which had succeeded in escaping capture at St Valéry.

Leese met most of his command at their detraining station near Aldershot, and then asked General Alanbrooke, who had commanded 2 Corps at Dunkirk and was now C-in-C Home Forces, if he could have 14 days in which to train the Brigade before taking them to the

---

[1] At the same time he learnt that he had been awarded the CBE in connexion with his efforts at Dunkirk.

south coast. Alanbrooke said there was no time for that and that he must get off to Sussex at once. Leese then arranged with Brigadier Brocas Burrows to have a 'battle' with his armoured brigade; this proved highly successful, and the Brigade settled into Sussex.

Leese soon found that few of the units had any sense of battle reality, and their ideas of local protection was very vague. His reaction was immediate and effective. With a team of handpicked young officers, mostly from Brigade Headquarters, they set out on an appointed night and 'liberated' one weapon from almost every unit in the Brigade Group. Some were carried off and some were towed off. The following morning the captured equipment was paraded outside Brigade Headquarters and the COs were told that they could fetch them back. Leese reflected years afterwards, that never again would he have ventured by night near any of his units on a similar errand. Not that he needed to.

These were battle of Britain days. His nephew, Bill Drake, has schoolboy memories of Leese tearing about, training units to resist invasion. 'There was a ditch running through Sussex near the coast – he believed it would hold the Germans up for two minutes, and he had two tanks, which were kept in a garage in Steyning. We just hadn't got anything.'

Major James Carne,[1] as he then was, joined Leese's HQ as a GSO 3:

> He [Leese] appeared to me to be a superb leader. He had a tremendous grasp of detail and had imaginative ideas. He had a particularly strong personality and a forceful manner but his pleasant approach put men at their ease and then he could be a good listener. He was a demanding character but a most attractive one.

On one occasion, when they were stationed in Sussex, Major Carne inadvertently created an embarrassing situation for his Brigadier to deal with:

> We were billeted in a fine house with a good garden. In planning its defence I found it necessary to dig a trench across a rosebed in order to cover a sunken lane. A few days later the lady owner inspected her property and then vented her wrath on Sir Oliver, at the desecration of the rosebed. It was the persuasive charm of the Brigadier which made me compromise the defence of Britain, to save him from embarrassment!

[1] Lt.-Colonel James Carne was to win the VC as Battalion Commander of the Gloucesters, in April, 1951, at the battle of the Imjin River, in the Korean War. Later, as a prisoner of war, he carved a Celtic Cross of North Korean stone, using two nails and a primitive hammer. The cross is now in Gloucester Cathedral. Colonel Carne died on 19 April 1986 aged eighty.

Once, a demonstration of a tank ambush was to be laid on by one of
the battalions. Major Carne was told to produce an anti-tank sticky
bomb for the Brigadier's talk after the demonstration. Having tried
all the normal methods, without avail, of obtaining a sticky bomb,
Major Carne reported that there was no hope of being issued with
these bombs in the foreseeable future, suggesting as tactfully as possible
that the Brigadier should concentrate on the tactical employment of
weapons with which it was equipped:

> Suddenly I was in trouble. Coldly, he [Leese] ordered me to be at the
> demonstration with a sticky bomb. Nothing was said about my scalp, but
> I knew it was in danger! Eventually a bomb was borrowed from Peter
> Fleming[1] who was commanding a special unit miles away. His kindness
> was of course directed to the Brigadier but it was the GSO 3 who was most
> grateful.

Just before Christmas 1940 Leese was promoted to the command of
the local beach division, the West Sussex, taking over from General
Brocas Burrows, who had earlier taken part in the mock battle with
Leese's brigade; and in February 1941 he was sent to Essex to command
the 15th Scottish Division.

He had heard a great deal about the prowess of this division in the
first war, and motored off to Essex in great haste with Ulick Verney
and Cosmo Crawley from his Brigade Staff and his driver Colliton,
who had joined Leese in the BEF and whom Leese described as having
an uncanny eye for night driving.

They arrived at HQ just before dinner in an empty looking villa
near Chelmsford. Here, to his surprise, Leese was handed a knife,
fork, spoon and mess tin and was told it was for dinner. He blew his
top when he found an administrative state of affairs much in accord
with his knife, fork and spoon. He quickly sorted things out, and
found conditions in the units were much more satisfactory. He liked
the Jocks and soon had a deep rooted admiration for their soldierly
qualities.

> 'Leese's personal influence was immense,' wrote H. G. Martin. 'By day he
> would be up among the forward troops, all night he would be making his
> presence felt among the supply columns, travelling 40 or 50 miles behind
> (it seemed as though he never slept) and at the end of it all he would
> hold the attention of all officers for several hours at conferences, where,
> apparently with no notes, he would sum up and comment on the events
> that had occurred.'[2]

[1] Peter Fleming (1907–1971), author of *Brazilian Adventure*, commanded several
special units during WW2.
[2] Article on 15 Scottish Division in *Blackwood's Magazine* 1948.

They moved up to Suffolk to take over the coastal defences from Felixstowe to Lowestoft. Leese was to find the next months an everlasting balance of values between the construction of coast defences and tactical training. He himself felt that the success of the division, when called upon to fight, lay in the efficiency of its individual and collective basic training and in the morale which could be built up by battalion, brigade and divisional exercises in which the team spirit was all important. Never a man to be Maginot-minded, he was no believer in the ultimate value of fixed defences.

★

The formation of a Guards Armoured Division was the brainchild of General Alanbrooke, when, as C-in-C, Home Forces, in the late spring of 1941, he decided to change two infantry divisions to armour to resist invasion. Alanbrooke's cousin, General Sergison Brooke, commanding the Brigade of Guards, after consultation with King George VI, expressed himself in favour of the project. Sergison Brooke had tremendous faith in the ability of Leese to achieve great things, and it was he who told Leese he had been selected to form and command the division and to be responsible for its conversion from infantry to armour. Leese's reaction was 'What a marvellous command, and what a fascinating one to fashion, mould and train!'

Division HQ was formed at Leconfield House on 19 June 1941, early in July HQ was transferred to Weybridge, where it quickly became a hive of activity with lectures and discussions. In September, HQ moved again, this time to Redlynch near Wincanton, and the Division was concentrated in the Warminster–Shaftesbury–Wincanton area.

With the change in organisation came a change in numbers. The strength of an infantry battalion was 961 all ranks; in an armoured battalion it was 637. At that time an armoured division was composed of 2 armoured brigades, each of 3 armoured regiments or battalions and one motor battalion, and what was known as a support group of two artillery regiments, one anti-tank regiment and one light aircraft regiment; in addition, one lorryborne infantry battalion (in this case, the first battalion, Welsh Guards.)

The change from infantry to armour involved an enormous amount of work. Conversion courses were arranged for all Guardsmen from Commanding Officers to junior NCO instructors, in the three basic trades of driving and maintenance, wireless, and gunnery; the driving and wireless courses taking place at the Tank Corps depot at Bovington, the gunnery school a few miles away at Lulworth.

Tanks for training arrived very slowly and were generally second hand. The first tank that arrived fell sideways off the transporter.

However, a great deal could be done indoors with models, bits of machinery, diagrams and so on. Tanks often broke down – and thus provided experience for crews and fitters.

The troop leader had it brought home to him what his tasks were – simultaneously to direct his own driver and the other two tanks of his troop, to read the map, to observe the ground ahead, to look for targets, to direct the fire of the other two tanks, to direct and observe the fire of his own tank, to keep in touch by wireless with his squadron leader, and to brace himself at a speed of probably twenty miles an hour against the violence and shocks as his tank took the banks and ditches. Signposts were down: map reading was therefore an essential.[1]

Tank troop duties, tank maintenance, the work of an infantry brigade within an armoured division, intensive battle training – all the components that lead to an efficient armoured division were given dedicated attention by Leese and his two brigadiers Allan Adair and Billy Fox-Pitt. Leese, on his motor-bike, was ubiquitous.

The division began with Covenanter tanks – beautifully sprung, they were capable of travelling at more than thirty miles an hour, but they often broke down. Exercises took place as soon as possible, first with troops, then with squadrons and at last with battalions. By spring 1942 training was sufficiently advanced for firing the two-pounder gun and Besa sub-machine gun from the tank on the move, at the Royal Armoured Corps ranges at Linney Head in South Wales. Each troop was able to make full use of almost daily practice for three weeks.

Covenanters were succeeded by Crusaders and Churchills. In July the first divisional exercise with troops was held – *Cheddar*, followed by *Lilo*, *Pegasus* and *Sarum*. Troops were learning how to live, feed and sleep in field conditions. In August there were two more exercises, *Ebor* and *Redlynch*, each lasting two days, and followed by a period of maintenance and reorganisation.

General Allan Adair, who later commanded the Guards Armoured Division at Arnhem, has this to say about Leese:

> He had all the drive and energy which were essential if guardsmen were to master quickly the very different and difficult role of tank warfare. From the start, he would tackle his seniors and the War Department with constant demands for equipment, training staff, etc., and didn't mind how outspoken he was. In the result our change to tanks got going remarkably quickly.
>
> As far as the troops under him were concerned (I was commanding the

[1] At the time of Dunkirk, signposts throughout Britain were taken down in case of invasion, and were not replaced until the end of the war.

6th Guards Brigade at the time) he was constantly around – getting the best out of us with his humour and sense of fun – but if he didn't like something he could fly into a rage – and his language was unprintable!

When our first tanks arrived near Salisbury Plain, the large Guardsmen could scarcely get through the hole into the driver's seat, but by dint of various methods, and with him watching and encouraging, they speedily overcame their difficulty.

To show his attention to detail, the choice of a sign to paint on the vehicles of the Guards Armoured Division, was 'the ever open eye' – so Oliver assembled 20 trucks and got the famous artist Rex Whistler [later killed in the Welsh Guards] to paint different eyes on the back of each vehicle – winking, poached egg, glad eyes, etc. – a fascinating display: we finally chose the original first war eye.

I think Oliver was remarkably good in selecting his staff, and co-ordinating the various units under his command. He was quite definite in laying down what was wanted – we became a team and all of us would work for him. When he was promoted and I took over from him, he handed over to me a thoroughly well organised division.[1]

Lt.-Colonel Gerry Feilden[2] was Leese's administrative officer from the early days of the Guards Armoured Division. Feilden recollected that when they first worked together in Curzon Street, Leese kept two files, one headed *Formation of Division*, the other, *Leave*.

Leese and Feilden together made a splendid pair, and got through an enormous amount of work. If Leese occasionally 'blew his top', Feilden would be completely unconcerned. They had a tacit understanding that these outbursts were not to be taken seriously. On one occasion, Feilden went into the office 'with papers and things' to find Leese very annoyed about something that had gone wrong. When Feilden disagreed with some point Leese threw the telephone directory at him. It just missed his head and hit the wall. Later in the day Leese had toothache. He rang Feilden up and asked him the name of his dentist in Salisbury.

'Shan't tell you now!' replied Feilden.

Leese was liable to be casual, even eccentric, in his turnout. Once, Feilden reminded him to dress properly and wear field boots the next day, as he was going to inspect the Grenadier Guards:

Oliver didn't say anything. The next morning I motored to the office and happened to park my car opposite the loo. No sooner had I done so than the lavatory window opened, a field boot hurtled through the air and landed on the car bonnet. Then Oliver went out and inspected the Grenadier Guards. He was wearing khaki plus fours and stockings.

[1] Letter to author, 27.9.1979.
[2] Major General Sir Randle Feilden.

Feilden could be a practical joker in his own right. There was the case of a burnt out tank. Feilden, as quartermaster, sent a note to the effect that the Commanding Officer of the unit should make good the loss – a matter of £24,000. The officer concerned took the letter as genuine, paced agitatedly up and down the room, observing – among other things – 'No wonder the captain goes down with his ship.' He was kept in suspense for a couple of days, and was then undeceived.

On 10 September 1942 came news of Leese's posting to the Middle East. In *The Story of the Guards Armoured Division*,[1] this is what is written of Oliver Leese:

> He had laid the foundations very surely and above all had instilled that drive and enthusiasm which are the vital attributes of an Armoured Division. He had made an entity of it in a remarkably short space of time by sheer force of personality and was responsible for the gunners, sappers and members of the services feeling every bit as proud of belonging to it as were the Guardsmen themselves, no mean achievement in the circumstances. No point was ever too small for his attention and woe betide any officer or man who counted on being too unimportant for the notice of the divisional commander. None who were present would ever forget the brilliant way in which he would hold a conference of all officers after an exercise. Without a single note he would unerringly discuss every phase of the past 'battle', remembering every detail and referring to units and sub-units and even to individuals by name – occasionally to the consternation and embarrassment of certain of the audience.

[1] *The Story of the Guards Armoured Division.* Lord Rosse and E. R. Hill.

8

CORPS COMMANDER

*It's a wonderful privilege to be serving here – in what may well be
the turning point of this war and one of the decisive battles of
history.*

Oliver Leese, 19 October 1942

Oliver Leese was sitting on the wall of the terrace at Red Lynch,
enjoying the quiet of a lovely September afternoon and waiting for an
aeroplane to fly him down to Linney Head, where the Guards Armoured Division tanks were shooting, when an orderly came running
down the steps to tell him that the Military Secretary wished to speak
to him urgently on the telephone.

The news was that Leese had been appointed to command 30 Corps,
and to join Montgomery in Egypt, that Montgomery wanted him at
once, and when could he start? It was decided that he should leave
the following night (12 September). Accordingly he said farewell to
his staff officers, two of whom helped him to pack – "with a great deal
of noise and laughter well into the night'.[1]

The noise and laughter were for friendship's sake. Leese was well
aware of the responsibilities that lay ahead. It was his custom on
such occasions to ask Stanley Moore, a family friend who knew the
Leicester-Warrens well, and who was now an Army Chaplain, to come
over and celebrate Holy Communion:

'I was very closely connected with Oliver Leese,' wrote Prebendary Stanley
Moore, 'and went with him to 29th Ind. Brig., then to 15th Scottish, and
finally to Guards Armoured Div. Each time he was asked to take over
another command, a dispatch rider would arrive at wherever I happened
to be, asking for communion to be given to him and Lady Leese the next
morning at the house they had taken while he was commanding the

---

[1] Memoirs.

division. I always got there in time to start the service at 7.30. Afterwards
I breakfasted with them while the room filled with staff officers, etc.'[1]

After Communion, the Leeses went to Lyneham airport. Apart from
the Dunkirk period they had been able to live together nearly all the
time during the last three years. Now, the parting might be a long
one. They made their farewells and Margaret stood stiffly until the
aeroplane was out of sight.

As in all these high moments in Leese's career, a touch of farce was
not missing, and the plane's bomb rack was its only vacant space for
him as passenger when he flew alone with the crew in an operational
Liberator, fervently hoping that the pilot would not put his foot by
mistake on the bomb release. All went well except that the Liberator
developed engine trouble and they had to spend a short time in Gibraltar,
where General Mason MacFarlane the Governor was his host. The Liberator was overhauled, and Leese arrived in Cairo on 14 September.

*

After Dunkirk, British troops having been driven out of the mainland
of Europe, it was logical that they should then fight in the Middle East.
Britain had long realised the importance of the North African littoral:
British soldiers had been stationed in Egypt since 1882, when Sir Garnet
Wolseley had defeated the Khedive's forces in the battle of Tel el Kebir.
Now, more than ever, the Middle East was important, for without the
products of the Mosul oilfields Britain could not wage war.

Italians were installed in Libya, and Mussolini's new Roman legions
had invaded Abyssinia in 1935. France, Maginot-minded to the last,
had built the Mareth line to prevent an Italian invasion of Tunisia. A
head-on collision was inevitable when, in May 1940, Italy threw in her
lot with Germany following the collapse of France.

The Italians were defeated by Wavell's Western Desert Forces in
December 1940. In February 1941, Marshal Graziani saw his Army
of nine divisions utterly defeated at Beda Fomm, south of Benghazi,
by General Dick O'Connor, with a force of 14,000; thus the situation
was all Sir Garnet once again.

A small German force under General Erwin Rommel, who had
done very well commanding a Panzer Division in France, was hastily
dispatched to Tripoli to aid the Italians, and O'Connor now prepared
to march with his Western Desert Force to encircle Rommel's troops
before they had time to strike. Had they been able to do so, there
would have been no Rommel and no Montgomery in the Middle East,
and no fighting up and down the desert from 1940 to 1943. As it was,

[1] Letter to author 10.7.81.

the powers at Whitehall switched the main part of O'Connor's army in a vain effort to save Greece and Crete from German invasion. Rommel, therefore, was allowed to flourish, and the troops that could have been victorious in North Africa were sent to defeat and another Dunkirk in Greece.

The war in the Middle East continued with its ups and downs. Wavell's operation *Battleaxe* was not successful. Tobruk was invested. Wavell was sent to India as Viceroy; Auchinleck, his successor in the Middle East, the forces at his command now renamed the Eighth Army, advanced in operation *Crusader* on 18 November 1941, his intention to relieve the beleaguered garrison at Tobruk, recapture Cyrenaica and open the way to clearing the North African coast. He succeeded in all but the last of his aims.

Early in 1942 Singapore and Burma had fallen. The outlook for Britain and her Empire had never seemed gloomier. Auchinleck was pressed by Churchill to mount another offensive. Rommel watched the preparations and decided to forestall the Eighth Army. With an adroitly deceptive attack he captured Tobruk (21 June) and 30,000 prisoners, raced towards Alexandria, and was finally held up at El Alamein, where defences had been prepared by Wavell two years earlier.

In July, during a series of actions that came to be known as First Alamein, both sides fought themselves to a standstill, and Auchinleck sent a signal to the War Office that the Eighth Army would have to be on the defensive for a few weeks. On 3 August, Churchill and General Alanbrooke, who had succeeded Dill as CIGS, came out to Cairo to see what was going on. 'Strafer' Gott, who had been in the Desert War from its very start, was appointed GOC Eighth Army. He was killed almost immediately while flying to take up his appointment. It was next decided that General Alexander should take over from Auchinleck, and that Lt.-General Montgomery, GOC Southern Command in England, should command Eighth Army.

Alexander and Montgomery were due to take over their respective commands on 15 August. Montgomery seized the reins forty-eight hours early, and set about restoring morale. This he did, wonderfully, ubiquitously and with panache. There would be no withdrawal: Rommel would be hit for six.

In no time at all Montgomery restored the flagging spirits of Eighth Army, calling up the newly arrived 44 Division from the Delta and altering the dispositions of the forces he had inherited from Auchinleck, who had the possibility of a quick withdrawal in mind, to one that was effectively defensive. In the battle of Alam Halfa (31 August –7 September) Rommel was uncompromisingly stopped, and Montgomery continued his preparations for the decisive battle.

Leese was to command 30 Corps in what was intended to be the breakthrough at Alamein. This was indicative of the confidence that Montgomery had in him, as apart from the improvisations of the Dunkirk period his last experience of action had been as a platoon commander in the battle of the Somme.

During the next three years (September 1942–July 1945) Oliver Leese wrote over 600 letters to Margie.[1] Allowing for the periods September–December 1943 and October–November 1944, when he was with her, this means that he was writing to her about six times a week. Soldiers were not allowed to keep diaries during the war, though many of them did. Leese's letters home fulfilled the dual purpose of keeping a diary and writing to his wife. There was much, for security reasons, that he could not tell her; sometimes he was writing about a battle in which he was involved before the full details had come in. Nonetheless, the real Oliver Leese comes across in these letters, as he lived and planned and fought from day to day; his comments from the fields of battle bring those days strongly to life.

Most of his letters from the Middle East were written on the forces Air Mail letter cards that were used at the time. His first letter to Margie was dated 18 September:

> When I got to Cairo I had a good bath – Julian[2] came to breakfast and after seeing one or two people he took me on a hectic shopping expedition. As usual the luncheon interval intervened, but we got quite a lot, including two bush shirts, three pairs of shorts and a chamberpot, bath, etc . . . I found a ghastly ADC . . . he lasted literally 5 minutes, and I left Cairo 3 hours later with a nice boy called Bernard Bruce, in the Scots Guards, who has started me off well, and I am going to try Maurice Trew's brother, who is 42. For battle purposes I shall, I think, get a young Australian. I went up and stayed the night with O [Montgomery] who was charming to me – he is quite excellent out here, and has already done a world of good and the whole atmosphere is grand – and all the troops full of fight and confidence. I also saw Alex, who had especially asked for me; and was most awfully nice. I've also seen Jorrocks[3] and Herbert L[umsden]. It's very nice being with one's friends.

Leese had devised a simple code in writing to Margie about the senior British Generals, referring to them by the second letter of their surnames – hence O for Montgomery and L for Alexander, though sometimes he would write their names in full.

'Julian' was Brigadier Julian Gascoigne of the Grenadier Guards, who had been flown out to succeed Brigadier George Johnson as

[1] There may have been others, though not many, that failed to reach their destination through aircraft being brought down by enemy action.
[2] Major General Sir Julian Gascoigne.
[3] Lt.-General Sir Brian Horrocks.

commander of 201 Guards Brigade. Gascoigne was in the Eton OTC when Leese was adjutant, he had been Leese's staff captain in London District days, had been his brigade major in the months after Dunkirk, and had commanded a battalion in the Guards Armoured Division under Leese's command for a year. As a senior Guards Brigade officer he had come to welcome Leese. Julian Gascoigne's understanding, width of outlook and general feel for the situation, backed by a riotous sense of humour, made him the very person to tell Leese 'the form'.

Leese spent much of his first day with Montgomery, when he met his divisional commanders – and next he wanted, as thoroughly as could be managed in two or three days, to know something of the desert terrain.

Bernard Bruce, an old desert hand, step-brother of David Stirling, founder of the SAS, acted as his cicerone. He wrote of his first meeting with Leese:

I met Oliver first when we drove to Alamein from Cairo on 18 September 1942. He had been in Cairo about two days. I was a Scots Guards supplementary reserve, leaving our second battalion, where I had just been made Intelligence Officer, at the shortest notice. All I knew of General Oliver was his reputation as a powerful commander of the Guards Armoured Division training in England.

During our first few hours drive to the Western Desert, I think we made friends, and he listened to what I had to say about campaigning there for most of the past two years – as a regimental officer and on the staff of Brigade and Corps HQ. Arriving at XXX Corps, General Oliver took over command at once, most energetically and inspiringly.

Bernard Bruce remembered his decisiveness and air of authority – 'He had the whole bearing of a leader of men – the aura of command.'[1] Again –

With the troops General Oliver was marvellous, soon establishing easy and confident relations – for instance, driving through the lines of the 9th Australian Division, on a very hot September day, they were digging trenches, wearing little but shorts, boots and their wide hats – these they waved at the Corps Commander's pennanted car. 'Ah,' said General Oliver, 'I see we're on a waving basis' – and waved back.[2]

20 September. OL to ML.

I've a grand lot of people on the whole, though not as yet with whom I've any friends in common, but so long as there's plenty to do that does not

[1] Letter to author 2.3.80.
[2] Letter to author 2.3.80.

matter, and I see no sign of being idle or unoccupied! There is a great
spirit in the Corps. My BGS [Brigadier General Staff] is Walsh, a very
hardworking little man, who will do me well for the next two months,
while I settle in. My chief engineer is a South African [Colonel Ken Ray]
and often goes to Lake St Lucia to fish.

The slightly condescending attitude displayed towards Walsh in this
letter soon underwent a complete change. George Walsh – who was a
cousin to Clement Attlee – remained with Leese until the end of the
war, by which time he had become one of the best Chiefs of Staff to
have served in the British Army. Leese always got on well with Ken
Ray, the cheerful extrovert South African sapper, and the two became
close friends.

23 September. OL to ML.

A quiet moment in the caravan . . . – and so I'll hope to get you off a letter
by aircraft. A lovely breeze, and – as we used to say in Quetta – another lovely
day, which I'm glad to say I thoroughly enjoy. O came to see me today
– in very good heart and most helpful. I visited my Indians yesterday and
got on quite well with my Urdu. I shall always be glad we took that trouble
with the *Munshi* . . . You'd be amazed to see this country. Both sides cover
enormous areas of sand! Everyone lives in his vehicle or under a ground
sheet – or in the front line in a slit trench. Vehicles are all at least 200
yards apart and all you see is scattered vehicles, all camouflaged and dug
in – against shell or bomb splinters, and it is well nigh impossible to tell if
it is a HQ, a lorry unit, a workshop, a battalion etc. – Just going to try my
trousers on.

24 September. OL to ML.

I've got a jeep[1] – which I look grand in. Also there is my caravan and
baggage wagon. We all go out in the desert for a practice run – that is the
above + my wireless! I've had a quite excellent ADC in Bernard Bruce –
but he ought to go to the Long Range Desert work, where he is due, and
will be very good. [Leese subsequently recommended him for the Staff
College at Haifa.] I am going to inspect the local HQ Sqn this afternoon.
Discipline is not its strong point – sunbathing seems to have preference to
saluting! I shall get up a Drill Sgt from Julian.

28 September. OL to ML.

The desert is an incredible mixture. Occasionally lovely hard going and

[1] Jeep. General Purpose vehicle or G.P. Small 1¼ ton open-topped military car. First
used by the US Army in 1941, they had just arrived in Egypt. Designed as a small
light reconnaissance and command vehicle. Speed 65 mph. Four-wheel drive and high
ground clearance made it admirable for use in the desert. The last jeep went into
production in January 1986.

you can travel on a broad front – sometimes rock – but often very soft sand, in which you at all costs must keep the car going. I broke the springs on mine. I've got another lovely Ford – I've also an armoured open Ford, my jeep and my caravan! Warren is turning into quite a good clerk. I dictated to him in the open car, bumping over the desert. His pencil seemed to be playing splodge cricket! I saw L yesterday [Alexander]. I also had tea with O – and I go to see him again tomorrow. We are having a great search for an ADC . . .

The 'splodge cricket' effect of Warren's shorthand was because it was impossible to take anything down accurately with all the bumps on the journey. Leese said it had been alright in England. Warren pointed out tactfully that it was easier to drive in England than in the Western Desert, and Leese arranged that in future he would only dictate when the car was stationary.

29 September. OL to ML.

Bernard Bruce did some good buying. We've found some corduroy at last, and a *dhurzi* to make up some trousers. We've got sheets, towels, bath mats, thermos, soap – even a door mat! Also Eau de Cologne, so we are almost pansy!

3 October. OL to ML.

Just returned from a training night out in the desert with my Highlanders.

4 October. OL to ML.

John G-W [Green-Wilkinson] turned up today, looking very well and most cheerful . . . Will you remember to send me my hair wash periodically. Rather more often than necessary in case of sinkings. I went to Church today, a nice Chaplain . . . I thought so much of you . . . and our last service together in the drawing room with Moore.

7 October. OL to ML.

I had a night out training last night with the Australians. Their discipline with their own officers is first class. They always say 'Sir' and fairly get a shift on. With the likes of me, though, we conduct affairs on a waving basis!

10 October. OL to ML.

I asked Jorrocks last night to let me have John G-W as Liaison Officer. So I hope, if all is agreed, he will come this weekend. I had a great conference yesterday with my many and varied head men. I think it went well. It was very inspiring – and very wonderful to be dealing with such remarkable people.

John Green-Wilkinson – he had known OL and ML since the 1920s
– had arrived in Egypt at the end of 1941 with a Rifle Brigade battalion:

> The first I knew of his [Leese's] arrival was when I was invited to lunch
> at the HQ, no doubt to be looked over, since a fortnight later I was
> appointed a G3 Liaison Officer with the task of keeping General Oliver up
> to date with information, but also guiding him round the desert. He seemed
> keen to have young officers around him whom he knew and who had
> experience of the conditions out there. I knew little of him at the time, but
> I had heard how he had visited my parents in Windsor Forest while on an
> exercise with the Guards Armoured and had rather startled them by
> speaking to them by a radio linked to the telephone so that they had to use
> wireless procedure . . .

> One day he was driving his open staff car on the road from Alexandria to
> Cairo and I was sitting beside him. We caught up with a 3-ton lorry filled
> with Australians, but we could not overtake because the lorry was in the
> centre of the road and nothing would make them pull to the side to the
> great amusement of the Aussies in the back. General Oliver promptly drove
> on to the open desert and started to overtake at a considerable speed. At
> that moment I saw in front of us a large ditch at right angles to the road.
> Instead of jamming on his brakes as I would have done he accelerated and
> somehow we managed to jump the formidable ditch and success was ours
> when we passed the lorry.

Leese's conferences with Montgomery and with his divisional commanders were of paramount importance, but he had been wise in
getting experienced, intelligent desert soldiers to guide him round the
terrain. Antony Part,[1] his Corps Intelligence Officer, noticed how
ready he was to absorb information and to listen to suggestions.

There were interviews, appointments, conferences, talks with divisional commanders, chief gunners, sappers, experts on mine-lifting,
talks to officers, addresses to troops. He was in overall command of
five divisions and it was essential that rapport should exist between
himself and his highly experienced divisional commanders. That they
had accepted him so quickly was a tribute to his personality and
immediate control of the situation.

On 12 October, as a change from air mail letter cards, he wrote to
Margie a sixteen-page octavo letter, in which, among a host of topics,
he described his divisional commanders:

> My Generals are a most interesting collection. Morshead – a really tough
> little man – has done magnificently out here. Controls his Australians
> completely. He's absolutely firm with them. No sloppy sentimentality, but

[1] Sir Antony Part GCB MBE.

has, and quite rightly so, a terrific admiration for them, and looks after
them very well.

Next we have Dan Pienaar. Talks just as much as he did in Bloemfontein
[where OL and ML met him in 1935] – an average amount of rot, mixed
up with much common sense. Very nice to deal with.

Douglas Wimberley – mad keen – goes into the most minute details
about everything. His army has a fine spirit and will I feel sure live up to
their tremendous reputations of the last war.

Then there is Tuker[1], whom I also like and get on with very well. Alex
and Monty have been incredible in what they have done in the time. From
what I hear, and what one still finds traces of, things had slipped to a
pretty low state, largely because there was no settled policy and no one
therefore knew what to do – or what order was coming next.

Leese made no reference in the letter to Freyberg (2 New Zealand
Division), probably because Margie already knew about him.

Bernard Freyberg was a legendary figure. He was one of Rupert
Brooke's friends who had buried the poet at Skyros; in 1918 he had
won the VC at Beaumont Hamel. He was married in 1922; his friend
the playwright J. M. Barrie being best man. Once he had come within
a quarter of a mile of swimming the Channel. Now, at fifty-three, he
had experienced eight years of battlefield fighting. Churchill called
him the Salamander of the Empire, because he thrived in the flames,
and Freyberg himself once made the somewhat startling assertion that
'shelling doesn't hurt anyone'. He had an excellent relationship with
Leese, but was generally far from easy to handle. He didn't get
on with Horrocks, who had gone to the Middle East shortly after
Montgomery, to command 13 Corps; and he was difficult with
Montgomery.

Leslie Morshead (9 Australian Division), was every inch a general,
despite his slight build and mild expression. He had a sardonic, rasping
Australian sense of humour. His soldiers knew him as Ming the
Merciless, then simply as Ming. Dan Pienaar (1 South African Div-
ision) had made a name winning an immediate DSO in 1940. Francis
(Gertie) Tuker (4 Indian Division) was a vastly experienced Indian
Army officer. A man of many parts, he wrote several books on India,
and he had a flair for writing light verse. Douglas Wimberley (51
Highland Division) was 6 feet 3, lean and cheerful. He radiated sterling
common sense. He had known Leese since 1922 and had been at Staff
College with him. He was known to his Jocks as Tartan Tam.

With the exception of Wimberley, who, like Leese, was a 'new boy'
to the desert, the other divisional commanders were old desert hands.
Their knees were brown, they had sand in their shoes. They summed
Leese up – and they gave him their complete confidence.

[1] 'Gertie' Tuker (see Chapter 5) was now commanding 4 Indian Division.

Leese excelled at conducting a conference. This could be an extraordinarily difficult task, as the Commonwealth commanders were
responsible to their respective prime ministers, and given an assignment that seemed too difficult, could always appeal to their own
ministers. On one occasion, before Leese had taken over, and the
Commonwealth commanders were asking difficult questions, Wimberley was heard to observe jokingly, 'Well, if that's the form, and I get
anything to do that I don't agree with, I shall complain to the Secretary
of State for Scotland.'

Colonel Urquhart, of Wimberley's Staff, (as a Major General he was
later to lead the 1st Airborne Division at Arnhem) was highly impressed
with Leese's handling of a conference:

> 30 Corps then, was very much an international Corps, with divisions whose
> commanders were figures in their own right, some even with private lines
> back to their Prime Ministers . . . And the Highland Division, especially
> its commander, could be as difficult as any of the others!
>
> I was impressed more and more by OL during the desert days. He had
> a grip, which was not obsessive but firm and clear. He certainly gave me
> a feeling of confidence. Before Alamein, and subsequently, I used to
> attend his planning conferences with my General. OL soon sorted out the
> characteristics of the divisional commanders and treated each of them
> differently. This was particularly marked in the case of Freyberg – the NZ
> commander. At one conference OL discussed a certain course of action
> which Freyberg did not seem to like much – but no more was said. At the
> next meeting Freyberg brought the same course forward as a bright idea
> on his part – naturally this was acclaimed, welcomed, and quickly brought
> into the plan! As an onlooker, with merely staff responsibilities, I found
> the handling of these meetings masterly. George Walsh, the BGS of 30
> Corps, was a tower of strength and I found him easy to work with – as was
> most of the 30 Corps staff.[1]

13 October. OL to ML.

We have laid in a store of chocolate, whiskey, soap, toothpaste, torch
batteries . . . and our 'hall mark' the WPB!

16 October. OL to ML.

Thanks for birthday wishes [he would be forty-eight on 27 October] . . .
I've asked Julian for Ion Calvocoressi of the Scots Guards. I knew his uncle
well, and in fact was partly responsible for his coming to the Brigade. He
has done very well out here and has been wounded.[2] . . . I found a large
assembly of Australians round a mobile cinema, completely in the middle
of the desert. They were loving it – and it was jolly good. The screen

---

[1] Letter to author.
[2] Ion Calvocoressi won the Military Cross at First Alamein.

suspended and screened from the air between two lorries, and a 36mm projector. I'm just off for a conference with O. Julian, I hope, comes down to stay with me in a few days. It will be nice to see him.

17 October. OL to ML.

John G-W has arrived, very well and cheerful. O brought Lord Trenchard up to see me today. He was in very good heart – full of enthusiasm and talk, and very funny about the politicians . . . The six sheep [his sheepskin coat] is invaluable and I wear it most evenings going out to dinner, and today I went out in my grey corduroy trousers, my soldier's cardigan, the six sheep – in my jeep! On which I mount my flag – it's a grand sight. We have a wild boar as our sign.

19 October. OL to ML.

This letter will be much delayed, as I cannot send it off till the party begins! [written at the top of the page].

I expect you have all been wondering what we have been doing out here – and by the time you get this, I expect my birthday [27 October] will have passed, and I hope and believe we will be on the way to a great victory.

We have a terrific task as we have to do the breakthrough attack, in order to create the gaps for the Armour. It's a wonderful education to higher command; and I only pray and trust that I shall be up to it. It's a wonderful privilege to be serving here – in what may well be the turning point of this war and one of the decisive battles in history. I have over 90,000 men in the Corps – and so, if I never do anything else, I have had 'my day'! The troops are in magnificent heart and everyone is full of confidence. Walsh has done some incredibly good staff work, and his orders will be a model to posterity – I think we are making the best use of guns. Some 600 in number. The Boche is very strong. He has plenty of time to dig, mine and wire, and it will be a very hard battle. I don't think we can expect a spectacular success at first, but we shall wear him out in a dog fight, for which we have better powers of sustenance than him.

I have just inspected my tactical HQs Escort. 3 South African Armoured Cars and/or 3 Valentine Tanks. An Armoured Car for my wireless set to my own HQs – and two White scout cars [like we had at home] for any other two wireless sets – and 3 Liaison Officers each with a Carrier, a Jeep and a Wireless Set – so I trust we shall succeed in controlling the battle. John [Green-Wilkinson] comes as one of the LO's, and two other good chaps, Miles Smeeton in the Indian Army, and a wild Irishman, Paddy Crean. My new ADC, I hope, comes soon. I think his name will be Nigel Barne. He has just got a MC. I believe he is about 30 – has been out some time, and was a LO at Bde HQ, so knows a bit about the Staff . . . My caravan is now swinging wildly as several workers are hard at it, fixing a shelter, in which Warren can type . . .

This afternoon I gave a ¾ hour 'Pep' talk and explained the plan to all the officers of Corps HQ. Seemed to be well over 100 – Heaven knows where they all come from . . .

O gave a grand pep talk today to all my Lt Colonels and upwards, in a vast Shamiana[1] made of camouflage netting – about 200 chaps. He was superb. I shall have to stop soon, as the work on the caravan is swinging it so much that I shall soon feel sea sick. After several days dust and rain, it is gorgeous this afternoon and one can see for miles, and the desert resembles a vast mass of dark ant heaps, each a vehicle, dug in under a net, about 200 yds from the other . . .

It's now midnight, and I'm just having a peg before I go to bed, I've just returned from a tour in my Jeep with Miles Smeeton, watching some of the guns moving up. The concentration for the battle has been a wonderful piece of staff work. So far it is working well, and the driving of the New Zealanders was grand tonight – It's glorious moonlight and the tracks we have made and marked with signs and beacons of stones show up well – it's wonderful seeing it all gradually come into being. It's wonderful driving at night here – not even sidelights and not a light to be seen anywhere in the desert – except the Very lights from the front and the flashes of the guns, it's the most complete blackout.
    Tomorrow we move up the essential parts of our HQ – and from this caravan I'll continue the letter – with I hope the sea splashing at our door!

20 October (continuation of previous letter).

We have moved up, and the caravan is within 20 yds of the sea – and it is lovely hearing the waves – reminds me of the stream at Worfield.

For the majority the last few days before the battle were taken up with moving forward into position. Leese was happy with his dispositions when he wrote to Margie on 21 October: the great game of *Steps to London* was nearly complete:

O came to see me, after visiting all my divisional commanders. He said they all knew exactly what to do, were in excellent form and full of confidence. So that speaks well for our plan and orders. All our preliminary moves every night are running well. All the guns are in; and the infantry and tanks are gradually coming in – it's a great feat of concentration. All by night – and everyone concealed by day – dummy vehicles and tanks removed when the right ones come up. I went round some of the area today, and talked to a lot of troops, including some very old soldier medium gunners. Full of heart. I saw some of my Highlanders having their pep talk – their eyes full of fire. They are mad keen for their first battle, and go forward between the Australians and the New Zealanders, so they'll have no trouble on their flanks . . . Please God, our plan is sound. I believe

[1] Shamiana: a large tent without side covers or awnings.

it's good. Like every military operation, it needs a bit of luck. Anyhow, I'm going to have a bath tonight, as tomorrow I shall be out again all the early night, as there is a lot of final movement in progress – and one must start the battle clean! Herbert Lumsden came to lunch and then O and he and I had a talk. We were photographed as usual. It's like being a Hollywood star, and I don't suppose I feature any better out here than elsewhere. It's gorgeous here by the sea. One would spend pounds to come here in normal times.

On 22 October Brigadier Julian Gascoigne, in answer to a signal from Leese, arrived at the latter's headquarters.

'I was in Syria at the time' he told the present writer, 'and as soon as I got Oliver's signal I drove off, stopping on the way at GHQ Cairo. My old friend Brigadier George Davy, the Director Military Operations, said to me "You can't possibly join Oliver Leese! Monty's expressly forbidden army visitors to the area." [Monty had given the order on 6 October]. Anyway I said that Oliver had sent for me and that I was going. "Well," he said, "whatever you do, for heaven's sake don't let Monty see you!" So I arrived in the morning, we had a bit of a gossip, and as we went into the mess for lunch, the first person we came across was Monty.

'Monty glared at me.

"Well, what are you doing here?" he said.

I let Oliver answer for me.

"I thought it would be good for his education, General, to see from close quarters how a modern battle was fought."

"Oh!" said Monty, "Oh! Well, don't be a nuisance to the General. He's going to be very busy."

'It was during the next few days that I came to realise what a truly great man Oliver was. He had got five divisional commanders. All of them highly experienced. Just imagine it, Freyberg – exceptional commanders like that! I went round the divisions with him the evening I arrived. He was met by the div. commanders and, you know, no-one had any questions. On the eve of battle no-one had any worries at all. It had all been discussed; worked out to the minutest detail, with the div. commanders, with Monty, and so on. Oliver was absolutely incomparable.'

22 October. OL to ML.

I sent off two letters to you today, including the very long one, which was unsigned, as O came up to see me; and I gave it to his ADC to send off for me, and I had no time to sign it. Julian arrived with Gilly [Lord Guilford]. It is grand having them and I feel quite different. I took Julian out today and we visited Douglas Wimberley, and then went to the New Zealanders, and South Africans. We took the Grenadier Drill Sgt with us; and so we had a great Brigade party. Tomorrow we lunch with Bernard Freyberg. Tonight Julian and I went to see the infantry moving up. All going very smoothly, – it seemed just like the first movement exercise of the G.A.D.[1] Some shelling and lights in the distance, but a curiously cold-blooded atmosphere – and knowing that by this time tomorrow – everything, guns, mortars, machine guns– will be giving him hell. I saw John G-W tonight – very cheerful, and, I think, doing very well here. It seems funny to be writing this quickly in my caravan – and I suppose this is the last night's sleep for several days. It will be desperately interesting looking back on this battle – I believe we shall have a tremendous success, and that we shall, as a result, get control of North Africa, with all possibilities in the future of opportunities to seize Sicily, Crete, Corsica, etc., as bases from which to knock out Italy.

[1] Guards Armoured Division.

9

ALAMEIN

This battle will be argued for many years as to whether the cavalry might have got through as a result of our initial break.
Oliver Leese, 29 October 1942

On the first night of Alamein Oliver Leese wrote to Margaret:

23 October.

The most wonderful night. We have started – I went up to a nearby hill. At 20 minutes to 10 – we started with 600 guns on a front of about 7 miles. It was a wonderful sight seeing the flashes all round and the whole night was and now is like a roll of drumfire. We started on enemy batteries, and, as far as one can see, his retaliation has been checked. I do pray and trust that all goes well with the infantry. At the back of the guns one can see the giant flares being dropped to guide the bombers, and the red lights of the Bofors guns and vertical searchlights keep the troops on their right course. It is a wonderful moonlight night, and on all the tracks the Armoured Corps is moving up to go through. We think we have deceived him, and that he is expecting us to attack in the dark nights of November. I do hope this is right. At any rate he has not interfered with our concentrations and moves. If we have deceived him, it is a wonderful triumph of staff work. It is now 11 p.m. and I'm going to bed for a short spell, waiting very very anxious for news.

Oliver Leese's letter, piping hot from the battlefield, had been written, as usual, on an airmail lettercard – his writing desk a piece of hardboard on his knees. The letter had been commenced about an hour after the first barrage had started.

Soon the signals began to come in to 30 Corps Headquarters. The first three of them, all marked 2155 hrs, would have been received before Oliver Leese returned from watching the barrage:

51 Div on start line
2 NZ are off
1 SA Div are off –

and, Leese having just started his letter to Margaret, another message [2231] from Douglas Wimberley's 51 Highland Division:

> Troops well over start line. Transport going through gaps. Very little shelling.

Leese would have been in bed and asleep when the news came just before midnight that the Australians had cleared 1500 yards of minefield, and the South Africans reported that Bottle, Boat and Hat tracks had been constructed through forward minefields and marked.

In the early hours of 24 October promising signals were coming through. At 0340, 9 Australian Division reported tanks up with the infantry and having trouble with mines, and at 0448 a South African signal announced that tanks were going through with Botha Regiment riding on tanks. At 1035, Leese, who had slept little and who had already done a day's work, was reported as on his way to the New Zealand Division. At 1040, 30 Corps received a terse message from Morshead himself: 'Have been successful. Situation O.K.'

★

On 23 October, the day before the battle, Nigel Barne had arrived from Syria as ADC to Oliver Leese:

> Rather reluctantly I set off because I had only been in Syria a very few weeks and was thankful to be away from the desert where I had spent the last 9 months – and reluctantly for another reason. Captain OWH Leese had been Adjutant of the Eton OTC in the early 20's and had a fearsome reputation. Would I be able to cope? One need not have worried too much, but one had to be on the top line at all times.
>
> When I first arrived at HQ 30 Corps on 23 October I was surprised how calm everyone was. The reason was that the plan of the battle had been made and all was arranged. After dinner that evening we all went up on to a rise and watched the artillery barrage.

Michael Carver, a G1 at Alamein – he was later to become a Field Marshal – describes the situation during the last few hours before the guns of 30 Corps opened up:

> Most people read books or played cards, or just slept, almost all wrote letters, which many thought might be their last. For almost everyone, but particularly for the infantry divisions of 30 Corps due to take part in the assault, the 23rd was a long, trying day. The infantry had to spend it immobile and hidden, crowded in their slit trenches, which they could not leave even for natural purposes.[1]

---

[1] *El Alamein*. By Michael Carver (Batsford).

Artillery observers, watching from their sangars on 23 October, had been issued with stocking masks made of butter muslin, dipped in cold tea for camouflage, to keep the flies away. Flies were everywhere. The Two Types, immortalised by the cartoonist Jon, with their scarves and pullovers and sheepskin jackets, always carried their fly whisks. Desert sores, which never seemed to heal, had long been an occupational hazard.

★

Leese's task was to take and secure a bridgehead through the enemy minefields before dawn, to help Lumsden's tanks of 10 Corps to pass through and to exploit the break-in. The 'extensive warfare' he had practised at Quetta would be standing him in good stead.

> 'The bridgehead,' wrote Michael Carver, 'was to extend two miles north of Kidney Ridge, the responsibility of Morshead's Australians, through the east edge of it south-eastwards to the north-west end of Miteiriya Ridge, these two points marking the flanks of Wimberley's objectives. On his left Freyberg was to advance 1000 yards beyond the first three miles of the ridge, while Pienaar came up in line with him for the remaining three miles of it.'[1]

Leese's chief cause for anxiety was whether his troops would cover the necessary ground before the dawn. The most precious element of war is time, and there were Rommel's minefields, *The Devil's Gardens*, to contend with. The artillery barrage served its twofold purpose of giving the infantry opportunity to reach their final places and to subdue the enemy artillery: the infantry had a mile and a half to go – fifty minutes at a pace of a hundred yards in two minutes – before they encountered enemy minefields; so they moved forward, and hard behind them were the teams of sappers in their perilous trade of mine-lifting.[2]

The plan was that if certain objectives were captured by 0245 on 24 October, Lumsden's tanks would pass through the gaps and out into the unknown. Leese's 30 Corps achieved most of their objectives, but Lumsden's 10 Corps suffered much frustration. The armoured divisions had their own task forces to lift the mines and follow the 16-yards-wide tracks. Sun, Moon, Star, Bottle, Boat, Hat there were indicated with rough designs painted on half jerricans spaced at intervals along their respective routes. Difficulties in mine-clearing arose. In some cases the detector didn't work, in others the minefields were more heavily strewn than had been anticipated; Lumsden's armour, therefore, did not make the expected progress.

[1] *El Alamein*. Michael Carver (Batsford).
[2] Each division was responsible for its own mine-lifting.

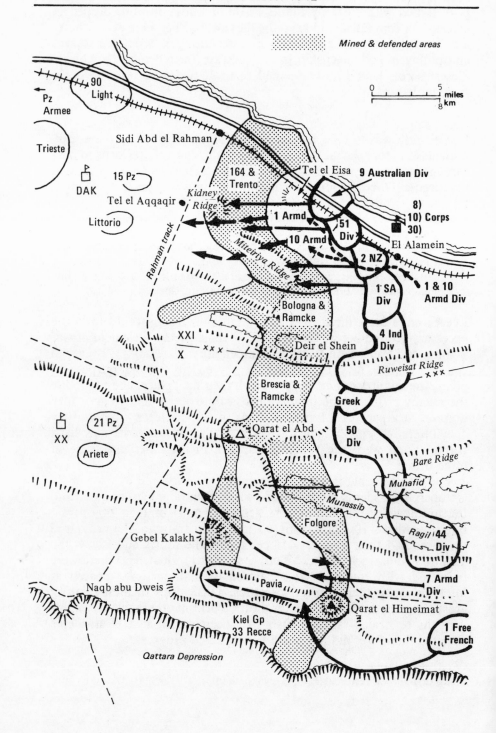

Mined & defended areas

0   5 miles
|--|--|--|--|--|--|
0   8 km

Pz
Armee

90
Light

Trieste

DAK   15 Pz

Littorio

Sidi Abd el Rahman

164 &
Trento

Tel el Aqqaqir   *Kidney
Ridge*

Tel el Eisa

9 Australian Div

1 Armd

51
Div

10 Armd

Miteirya Ridge

8)
10) Corps
30)

El Alamein

2 NZ

1 & 10
Armd Div

1 SA
Div

Rahman track

Bologna &
Ramcke

XXI
X   xxx

Deir el Shein

4 Ind
Div

Ruweisat Ridge   xxx

Brescia &
Ramcke

Greek

50
Div

Bare Ridge

21 Pz
XX

Ariete

Qarat el Abd

Muhafid

Munassib

Folgore

Gebel Kalakh

Ragil 44
Div

Naqb abu Dweis   Pavia

7 Armd
Div

Kiel Gp
33 Recce

Qarat el Himeimat

1 Free
French

Qattara Depression

24 October was a day of anxiety for the Eighth Army. Leese took Nigel Barne out with him early, strolling along the brilliant white sands – 'and met', wrote Barne, 'the great Monty, whose blue eyes pierced right through me when I was introduced.'

Shortly after first light, Wimberley, going in search of the forward elements of 51 Highland Division, was blown up in his jeep. He remembered sailing in the air, then lost consciousness, probably for a few seconds, and when he came to, he thought for a second or so that he was dead. However, he was commanding his division again within twenty-four hours; although two occupants of the jeep were killed.

Brigadier Julian Gascoigne, who was with Leese much of the day, observed his coolness and handling of 30 Corps in the mounting battle. 10 Corps, with Commanders frustrated and uncertain, were making little headway. Recommendations for the advance to be abandoned were made at 2.30 am, 25 October, by Lumsden to Major General Francis de Guingand, Montgomery's Chief of Staff. De Guingand, realising that this was the critical hour of the battle, summoned Leese and Lumsden to meet Montgomery at 0330 and then wakened Montgomery. It was an extraordinary conference at an extraordinary time. When Leese and Lumsden, both of them 6 feet 4, met Montgomery in his map lorry, the Army Commander was making up for his lack of inches by sitting on a high stool, studying the situation. He made it clear that the original plan should be carried out. The meeting over, he kept Lumsden behind, warning him that if he and his divisional commanders didn't proceed with the plan, they would be replaced. The attack went forward.

25 October. OL to ML.

30 Corps attack was a great success. We had casualties, but not so many as I had feared. We cleared practically all [the minefields], and I'm convinced the Armour could have gone through and exploited that critical time immediately, after a successful attack. But I'm afraid they've no stomach for a fight – and are not given the lead or have the will to succeed. Sometimes I feel quite ashamed to have been in armour. All my Infantry think nothing of them. The battle is, I think and hope, going well. We still have the initiative, and we have forced his tanks several times to attack us. Up to date we have held all the ground we have taken. I dined with O tonight. He is a first-class leader and very sound. Bernard Freyberg has been wonderful and did a grand effort when he personally led his armoured brigade out at night through minefields when all were rattled by the bombing and heavy gunfire on the gaps. The RAF have been splendid, and by day the enemy are unable to operate their bombers. They manage enough by night though!

It was a strange coincidence that Leese should write about having 'no stomach for the fight', on St Crispin's Day, 25 October, the anniversary of Agincourt. Montgomery would have remembered the anniversary, and a quotation from *Henry V* loomed large in his caravan; but it is doubtful whether Leese in his letter to Margie noticed that he was quoting Shakespeare, whose works he had probably only read under duress at Eton. With regard to Lumsden's unease, it could be emphasised that Freyberg, Morshead and Pienaar all doubted the feasibility of a breakthrough before the mines were cleared.

By 25 October Eighth Army had suffered significant casualties (6000), the brunt of them from 30 Corps. The Highland Division had suffered grievously, having lost 2100. Rommel, who had been on sick leave since 18 September, now returned to take over command of the Axis forces.

26 October saw the South Africans forced back under heavy fire. Montgomery issued new orders shortly after noon. Wimberley was to carry out mopping up operations; Morshead was to prepare for a further attack in the north; Leese's operations were to be minor ones to enable Lumsden to break out.

27 October saw confused and murderous action on Kidney Ridge. For Eighth Army the position was critical : on the other side of the hill it was worse. Rommel sensed the beginning of the end.

27 October. OL to ML.

It was a queer birthday today [his forty-eighth] but I've a great hope that, though there is a long way to go, we have turned the corner in our battle. It is a hard task as his initial positions were strong – and he was organised in great depth with masses of mines and strong screens of anti-tank guns. He has also damaged us a lot with medium and heavy artillery fire. Our Corps' initial effort was phenomenal. 5000 to 7000 yds penetration in the moonlight – in some places 5 or 6 minefields – each several hundred yards in depth. All over a featureless desert. Owing to the mass of mines it has been very difficult to get the Armour out, and when they get a start, the[y] find strong anti-tank gun screens, which the enemy has had time to put in. But today we managed to force a tank battle -- and the enemy lost a number of tanks, and up to date we have beaten off all enemy counter-attacks with our infantry, and anti-tank guns! If he goes on counter-attacking, it gives us our opportunity to destroy him – provided we can hold him – so we have got to an interesting stage in our battle.

Brigadier Julian Gascoigne, who acted through the battle as a sort of senior liaison officer, outlined some of Leese's movements during the course of the battle:

He would get into a car, and drive off, say, to HQ 51 Highland Division. Oliver would get out, and the Divisional Commander would greet him. 'Are you clear about today?' Oliver would ask. 'I'm not very happy about the minefields.' In half an hour's discussion they would go through the next 24 hours. Then to the New Zealand Division. After the formal stuff they would go into the mess for a drink. Then lunch. Then two more divisions. Generally, by afternoon or early evening he would have seen all the divisional commanders. Always the culminating thing was the discussion with Monty. [There would be present Monty, Leese, Walsh, Gascoigne, de Guingand, Bill Williams,[1] and one or two other members of Monty's staff]. Very interesting, those discussions. People spoke their minds and made their points, but everything was relaxed and harmonious.

On 28 October at 0800 hours Montgomery held a conference with Leese, Lumsden and their chiefs of staff, the main outcome of which was the decision to give up for the time trying to break through in the Kidney Ridge area, but to use the New Zealanders for backing up the Australians. Freyberg was told this at lunch, and the project was named *Supercharge*.

Sir Antony Part who was an Intelligence Officer [G 2] at 30 Corps HQ, has this to say about the change of plan:

After the initial German counter-attacks and the withdrawal of a number of 30 Corps troops into reserve, Montgomery's original intention was to organise a thrust by 9 Australian Division along the axis of the railway and the coast road.

Intelligence sources were soon able to point out that such an attack would run into particularly formidable German resistance as the most powerful bodies of German troops had by then been concentrated in that northern sector. On the other hand, an attack due westwards would be directed mainly at the Italians 'corseted' though they were by some good German troops. General Leese responded quickly to this information and advice, which reached him at about the same time as similar advice was being given to Montgomery by the Intelligence Staff at HQ 8th Army.

The plan of attack was soon altered and the breakthrough was achieved.[2]

The battle had now lasted nearly five days; Churchill was becoming restive and suggested to Alanbrooke that Montgomery was fighting a half-hearted battle. Rommel would not have agreed with this reading of the situation.

Fresh evidence suggested that Rommel had anticipated *Supercharge*. It was then decided that the New Zealand troops, instead of passing

[1] Major Edgar Williams, G2 (Intelligence). Now Sir Edgar (Bill) Williams. Secretary Rhodes Trust 1951–1980.
[2] Communication to author 11.2.81.

through the Australian division, as originally planned, should, on the night of 30 October, strike west, so as to bring them just east of the Rahman track, north of Tel el Aqqaqir. They were to be supported by all artillery available and reinforced by 51 and 152 Infantry Brigade and 23 Armoured Brigade. Leese was in control of this operation.

29 October was a very long day. The Australians were held up; Leese rang up at 4 am for details. The Australians were attacked by Stukas. Signals wanted to make gaps in minefields in order to put up overhead telegraphs. 51 Division was politely told it was impossible to supply them with 500 shovels and 250 picks. The Australians reported concentration of enemy tanks as an excellent bomb target. RAF could not accept the target – it was too late. The night was one of feverish preparation; the first for a long time in which no real attack was made.

29 October. OL to ML.

This battle will be argued for many years, as to whether the cavalry might have got through as a result of our initial break. We had deceived and surprised the enemy, and I feel there was a chance. All our infantry feel that. I have been very definite with Herbert [Lumsden], and I trust they really will make a big effort, if we can get another break-in. Bernard [Freyberg] is doing the break. So there is a grand chance. The enemy is beginning to feel our shelling, bombing and general pressure, but I think the battle is not yet over by a large margin yet. Gen Alex and Dick McCreery came to see me yesterday – very cheerful. They brought Mr. Casey the Minister for State, with them. I liked him.[1]

On the night of 30 October, Freyberg, aware of the fatigue of the infantry and of other practical difficulties, asked Leese for a 48 hour postponement of the attack. Leese referred the request to Montgomery, for the sake of propriety rather than of doubts in his own mind. Monty reluctantly agreed. At 0800 hours 31 October Monty held a conference in which zero hour for *Supercharge* was given at 0100 hours 2 November.

'We are having a hell of a dog fight,' wrote Leese on 1 November. There was fierce fighting in *Supercharge* on 2 November, and on 3 November the breakthrough seemed imminent. A battalion of Wimberley's 51 Highland Division was sent to an objective reputedly taken by the Armour. There had been a mistake.

'Worst of all' wrote Major General Wimberley years afterwards, 'thinking that it was an advance rather than an attack, the Gordons put a number of

---

[1] R. G. (Baron) Casey. Leese was to meet him, later, in South East Asia, when Casey was Governor of Bombay.

their Jocks onto tanks to be carried on them forward to the objective. I
saw these tanks later coming out of action, and they were covered with the
dead bodies of my Highlanders. It was an unpleasant sight and bad for any
troops' morale.'

'Surely it's not necessary to continue like this?' said Wimberley over
the telephone to Leese. The latter replied 'It surprises me that you of
all people should say this.' The Highlanders attacked again, and their
fallen countrymen were avenged.

On 3 November Intelligence reported clear indication of general
enemy withdrawal. Pursuit would commence forthwith. Rommel, the
Desert Fox, was turning his hand again to the laying of booby traps
as a form of delaying action. Discarded helmets and water bottles
could now be very dangerous: the occasional meretricious bar of
Cadbury's Milk Chocolate left lying invitingly on the desert sand was
best avoided.

3 November. OL to ML.

An extraordinary day. Our breakthrough attack on Sunday was magnificent. The Infantry did 400 yds behind a barrage – and my armour followed
it up another 2000 yds in the dark. It was not so difficult as our first night,
but it was a fine feat. The Armour then again failed to get out – but they
beat the enemy in a dog fight. Today we seemed almost ringed in again by
anti-tank guns – though we were easily through the minefields. Then it
suddenly became clear that we had beaten him, and that he was going
back.

It was a famous victory; by 5 November the Afrika Korps was in
retreat. Rommel had left 1000 guns and 450 of his 600 tanks on the
battlefield. Over 30,000 Axis troops, 10,000 of them German, were
taken prisoner. The Eighth Army, that had so long flattered only to
deceive, had now achieved glorious success. Its soldiers, from Putney
and Pitlochry, Tipperary and Treorchy, Athens and Alençon,
Adelaide, Otago, Calcutta and Pietermaritzburg had merged into
one of the immortal armies of history. The church bells in England,
silent since Dunkirk, burst into carillons of victory. 'This is not the
beginning of the end' said Churchill, 'it is the end of the beginning.'

10

ALAMEIN TO SFAX

*The GOC came over and had quite a long conversation with me,
talking about the military situation, and ending, as I well remember,
with the discussion of the value of a classical education.*
                              Brigadier Lorne Campbell, VC, DSO

*[Recollections of conversation with Lt. General Sir Oliver Leese,
in no-man's-land, on the coast road to Tripoli, January 1943].*

Alamein fought and won, Leese was feeling as relaxed as any general
could feel in the middle of a campaign, and sensed the exciting prospect
of victory in Africa. That he was happy in his command there was
no possible doubt: especially he was happy with Monty as Army
Commander. The two had much in common, much that was divergent.

They differed in that Monty was a roundhead; Leese, despite his
first name, a cavalier. Monty sought publicity: Leese shunned it.
Monty's interests were circumscribed; Leese's were wide.

As soldiers they shared similar beliefs. The morale of an army they
knew to be of supreme importance; welfare a contributory factor. As
games players, they believed in team spirit – in *esprit de corps*.

Their sartorial habits was eccentric, but for different reasons. Monty
wore funny hats so that his army would recognise him, and he
encouraged eccentricity of dress in the Eighth Army.[1] Leese, impecc-
ably clad when need be, preferred to wear clothes that were comfortable: e.g. – sheepskin coat, pullover, plusfours, stockings, shoes –
only the hat would be military.

Morale, they knew, was developed by informal talks at all levels: it
was also fostered by mail from home and by the availability of cigarettes. So they gave their pep talks, kept an eye on the post, and gave
out cigarettes and chocolate from the welfare truck.

---

[1] Monty wrote in his autobiography that he only gave one order relating to dress when
he was in North Africa. After passing a truck driver who was clad only in a top hat
he issued the command 'top hats will not be worn in the Eighth Army'.

During the five months from Alamein to Sfax, Monty and Leese were in daily touch with each other, their caravans 200 yards apart. They got to know one another well, to the point of telepathy: many of Leese's ideas became incorproated in the Army Commander's decisions. Leese was afterwards to say of his relationship with Monty that 'each knew how far he could go with t'other.'

Operation *Torch* had been mounted on 7 November, with an Anglo-American invasion of Algeria, under the command of the hitherto unknown General Eisenhower (he had been a Major in 1940) with General Kenneth Anderson commanding the small British First Army. Eisenhower's first efforts were hesitant and ineffective; but he was to grow immeasurably in stature.

Writing home to ML, Leese described his caravan, feeling 'a cross between a sheik and a gypsy queen.' On 13 November, he met Monty at Buq Buq. Up till now, 10 Corps (Horrocks) having made the breakthrough, were doing the pursuit, but as soon as 10 Corps had reached the Benghazi area, 30 Corps were to assume responsibility for the subsequent operations, Monty considering it likely that the enemy would stand in the Mersa Brega–Agheila line.

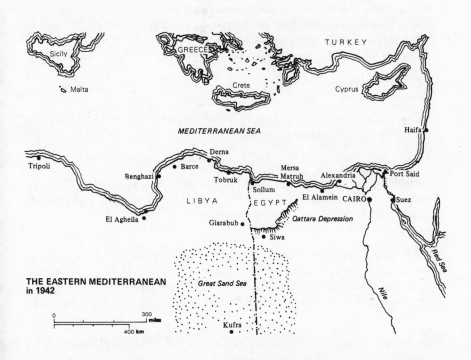

THE EASTERN MEDITERRANEAN
in 1942

18 November. OL to ML.

We have moved a lot since I last wrote. I have seen Mersa Matruh, Sidi
Barrani, Halfaya, Sollum, Bardia, El Adem – Tobruk, and it has been
very, very interesting to see what has happened before. Bardia is a charming
little Arab town, whole clusters of buildings with a minaret. Tobruk is a
fair-sized town – with some big buildings – quite a good-sized port, with
a mass of ships sunk, but still plenty of room. Most buildings gutted out
– large numbers of Basuto boys were released. They had been working as
prisoners. Now mostly tight on Chianti.

The Africa Korps had now reached the very strong Agheila position.
30 Corps had advanced 600 miles in a fortnight, so that Leese was
faced with a vast administrative problem. He had been moving about
in a little utility, seeing people:

We carried all our food with us – and also water – which is now like gold,
and has to come for miles. Now I've got my caravan back, I am quite close
to O as we are thinking out our next problems.

20 Nov. OL to ML.

Derna is a lovely little place – a small white township nestling in the side
of the hills, the houses mingled with palm trees, all backed by a small
harbour and the bright blue of the seas . . . Nigel [Barne] and I went to
see Cyrene. We got there as the light was going, with a wild red sunset –
I think it's the most wonderful sight I've seen – a vast ruined city of reddish
brown.

25 Nov.

I don't think the Arabs in Benghazi and Barce welcome us much – more
post-war complications I expect.

28 Nov.

In the midst of my jeep rides I went and looked at the excavations at Leptis
Magna – Greek and Roman – they are very lovely, especially some double
pillars on top of each other, and the baths.

On 30 November Leese heard that he had been awarded the CB for
Alamein. He was now preparing for the next venture beyond Benghazi.
There was a long supply line, and the priorities had to be sorted out.[1]
Nonetheless, Leese was optimistic: 'I have a hunch that he is beat and

---

[1] The German General von Ravenstein, captured at Sidi Rezegh in November 1941,
had described the desert as the tactician's paradise and the quartermaster's nightmare.

shall old-soldier him out of it.' He was anxious to push forward, and slept with his telephone by his pillow.

1 Dec. OL to ML.

I had a great afternoon yesterday looking at the enemy posts.[1] We had a lot of crawling to do: I was OK in my corduroy +4's. [Wimberley was wearing shorts]. HD – it's a remarkable division. Rather like the Brigade of Guards, in their knowledge of each other, but more inbred – like the Birkbecks, Barclays and Gurneys of Norfolk.

As you can imagine, the further we go, the smaller force we can maintain . . . But, who knows, everything may soon loosen up. It's very interesting and we have to be very careful here to be properly balanced – so as not to run the risk of being knocked off our perch by a sudden counter-thrust.

We are just removing a commode from the caravan, to turn it into a cupboard – who thought of a commode in a caravan in the East was a great man.

On 12 December reports indicated that the enemy was thinning out. The Italians, who had no transport, were being sent back first, and the Afrika Korps was taking over the line. By mid-December, 7 Armoured Division had made a brilliant advance, and the Afrika Korps withdrew towards Tripoli.

19 Dec. OL to ML.

I hope to send this off by David Stirling [the founder of the SAS] who looks glorious – rather like a beachcomber or an Apache. We have just heard that Dan Pienaar has been killed in an aeroplane on his way back to the Union. I am so very sorry. He did so well here.

On 24 December, Leese had a two hour conference with Monty. On Christmas Day he read the lesson (Luke 2, 1–14). He had used his drive and powers of organisation to see that the whole of 30 Corps got a good Christmas dinner:

Lovely turkeys, everyone making stuffing, pork sizzling in the ovens – lovely iced cakes, with *A Merry Christmas* written on them in fine icing. Fine pudding – I believe we are the only Corps to have got it all up – I gave my officers free lance to shoot anyone of any rank who tried to say them nay! I then went to Holy Communion very nicely done in a tent – I

---

[1] Wimberley's Highland Division had been having a difficult time with mines. The poet Keith Douglas, who was in the HD area at this time, referred, in *Alamein to Zem Zem*, to 'every kind of mine, booby trap and explosive charge in the most likely and unlikely places . . . The verges in the gaps on the road were mined with anti-personnel and vehicle mines, and mines were sown in the treads of vehicles, where other vehicles might be expected to follow in hope of being safe where someone else had gone.'

thought so very much of you – it was lovely as I felt we were together – just for those few short minutes.

On Christmas Day, Sirte was occupied by manoeuvre – a virtually bloodless victory.

26 December.

O came. 1st class conference. The difficult times are the long days of planning and reconnaissance, and in a queer way I feel that O values my judgement. History books afterwards are easy to write, but one's emotions at the time are very human.

29 December.

I am Governor of Tripolitania! but so far have very few subjects.

Leese spent Hogmanay with Douglas Wimberley.[1] There was dinner for twelve, to bagpipes at Wimberley's HQ in a sandbagged elephant shelter – twenty feet by ten feet. Afterwards they danced an eightsome reel, then went to a concert by the 'Balmorals', the stage a 'liberated' Italian trailer. Then they sang 'Auld Lang Syne', and 'God Save the King' and drank hot rum punch. Leese went to bed, and woke thinking he heard reveille – but it was the pipes still going strong at 4 am.

On 6 January he went for a day's tank ride with John Harding,[2] on reconnaissance. The same day two tanks arrived for Leese – 'So we shall now have a fine stable: 2 Grant tanks, 3 armoured cars, 2 White scout cars, 1 open car (armoured), 1 Ford utility, 1 jeep, 1 caravan, 1 baggage wagon.'

Tripoli was the next important target. Rommel had withdrawn from Mersa Brega and gone a long way back to his Buerat position. The Eighth Army were now faced with a no-man's-land as dangerous as it was extensive. David Stirling's SAS group and the Long Range Desert Group were providing invaluable information with regard to likely enemy intentions. Reconnaissance into no-man's-land would be undertaken by battalion commanders – and indeed by Leese himself.

Colonel Lorne Campbell, commanding 7 Argyll and Sutherland Highlanders of 154 Brigade, the Highland Division, whose battalion was sent forward to cover the front while preparations for the advance on Buerat were made, remembers an encounter with Oliver Leese:

[1] The Highlanders were then resting out of contact with the enemy.
[2] Major General Harding, commander of 7 Armoured Division, later to become Field Marshal Lord Harding of Petherton.

'My battalion,' wrote Brigadier Campbell, 'was on the coastal road, and I wanted to go ahead up the road and have a look at the ground over which we would probably have to advance. I did not much fancy the area as it was no-man's-land all the way and as a single vehicle travelling along the otherwise deserted road was likely to be an irresistible attraction for any fighter pilot looking for a target. A colonel had been killed the day before. It was quite a long drive and I drove pretty circumspectly, feeling distinctly isolated and vulnerable, till I came to a place from which one got a good view of the country ahead. There was a parking place there, and I drove my jeep into the sandhills on the other side, where it would be less conspicuous and got out and began looking round. I had only been there for a short time, feeling far from home and completely alone, when to my astonishment two or three cars, glittering with red cap bands, drove up behind me. They parked nose to tail in the parking place and out got the Corps Commander and several members of his staff, presumably also wanting to have a look at the ground. The GOC came over and had quite a long conversation with me, talking about the military situation, and ending, as I well remember, with a discussion of the value of a classical education. Shortly afterwards, the party got back into their cars, turned round and drove back home again. I soon followed them.'[1]

The advance towards Tripoli started at first light on 15 January 1943. Buerat was taken and the enemy gradually withdrew.

16 Jan. OL to ML.

An interesting day – and I think the decisive one of the battle. I don't think the enemy will stand up and fight for long this side of Tripoli. George [Walsh] is a first-class duty officer. His orders are really brilliant. He is very good on the blower and he is unperturbed.

17 Jan.

It is grand seeing all the vehicles and guns and tanks in serried ranks, about 100 to 200 yds apart, drawn up, in columns, as required for battle – might be the Tattoo at Aldershot any day!

7 Armoured Division (Harding) and New Zealand troops pursued the enemy. Wimberley pushed on towards Tripoli, with 51 Highland Division, which had been fighting, sometimes in platoon or company action, almost ever since the battle of Alamein: on 20 January Major General Harding was badly wounded while conducting operations from the top of his tank. Lieutenant-Colonel Michael Carver (Field Marshal Lord Carver) who was Harding's G1, informed Leese of the situation.

---

[1] Communication to author 7.3.81.

'Luckily,' wrote Leese, 'we managed to get a light aeroplane on to a forward strip and very uncomfortably we packed him into it. The days of casualty evacuation by air were still in their infancy, and we are lucky to have got an aeroplane at all.'[1]

The loss of Harding slowed up the operation through the desert route, which Leese described as 'sometimes the most glorious going, like Daytona Beach – then miles of soft sand – then large fields of high hummocks – then steep wadis and cliffs, full of great boulders.'

In their advance the Eighth Army used three widely separated routes. On the right was the Highland Division, on the coastal route, in the middle Monty himself with 22 Armoured Brigade, and on the left OL with 7 Armoured and NZ Divisions.

23 Jan. OL to ML.

At about 6 a.m. we heard that the 11th Hussars had entered Tripoli in their Armoured Cars. At 8 a.m. George [Walsh] and I set forth in our White Scout car, with Brigadier Lush[2] and Peter Acland, the Political Officer, with our Armoured Car escort – and met a variety of officers at the Benito Gate which we had laid down as our rendezvous. In the meantime our Highlanders and their tanks had entered the town by the coast route – and according to a pre-arranged plan had occupied the big square in the centre of the town. Everything was quiet in the city – many Italians and Arabs were standing about. All shops were shut. The harbour mouth was blocked by sunken ships and the quays and cranes and moles and warehouses badly damaged. Otherwise the town was intact, except for the results of our own bombing. I heard that O had arrived – and I went to meet him at the Benito Gate. He shook me warmly by the hand. It was a week since we had met – and it was a great moment.

O then spoke to all the Press, and their pansy crush who got tight staying in a hotel the first night in Tripoli, and were banished by O into a field! We all still live in caravans, tents and fields, etc. – and a good thing, too.

O then took me in his motor, followed by his tank, with 'Monty' emblazoned on it in large letters and we made a triumphal progress round Tripoli, with batteries of cinema and ordinary photographers taking photographs from jeeps. It was a glorious party – O and I then sat under a statue of an Alpini – in a garden on the waterfront, and ate our sandwich lunch!

We returned to a lovely almond blossom orchard, and gave out the orders for the next phase of the operations . . .

At the end of January, Ion Calvocoressi arrived to take over as ADC from Nigel Barne. His first important assignment as ADC was to make arrangements for an *alfresco* luncheon in Churchill's honour, when the

[1] Memoirs.
[2] See Chapter 19.

Prime Minister arrived in Tripoli on 4 February. This turned out to be an extremely hectic job. Calvocoressi had not only to provide food, drink and furniture for the occasion, but first of all he had to find a new site for luncheon, the position previously selected by a senior officer having been considered unsatisfactory. Owing to practical considerations, there was little choice, however he managed to find a suitable spot, got tables, food and wine from local hotels, and all was ready on time.

'The P.M. arrived,' wrote Leese, 'accompanied by Alanbrooke, and after a very moving drive round the desert types, he took his place at the saluting base. It was a thrilling moment. Nearly every man had a kilt, which had somehow come the journey from Alamein disguised as ammunition, bully beef or precious water: as Mr. Churchill said, the flower of British manhood was passing by and he was visibly moved.'[1]

'All went beautifully,' Ion Calvocoressi wrote in his war diary. 'Winston arrived and I met the car, and was introduced to him by General O. He said quite a few words and was very nice, and said he wanted his lunch badly. He also said 'We must have a photograph of this *alfresco* scene.' Lunch went very well, and in the middle of it he said this was the best day he had had since the war began.'

A good time was had by all, and Churchill had five well-diluted whiskies.

5 Feb. OL to ML.

It was fine and sunny and warm and a rainbow out to sea! I met the P.M. in the Square, with a group of officers whom I introduced. It was a wonderful moment – with the Square lined with tanks and armoured cars with their crews in front. Everyone was turned out incredibly well. Even I wore my best SD jacket, plus fours, stockings, Fortnum shoes and my Sam Browne belt.

It was a memorable moment with the P.M. and Bernard [Freyberg] met. Two great toughs, who are great friends. We had an excellent tea with them.

Most of the day I drove with the CIGS and Alex. Today we have settled in earnest to plan our next battle. We have some 500 miles to Tunis, while the 1st Army at one time only had 20 miles – it's a good bet. We will get there first.

Matters were not going well with Operation *Torch*, and General Anderson, commanding First Army, was not proving an inspiring leader; it was therefore decided that 30 Corps should assault the Mareth line as soon as possible. The chief difficulty was the administrative (logistic)

[1] Memoirs. The inspection and march past was of troops of the Highland Division.

situation. Owing to bomb damage Benghazi harbour was not much use, and it would be several weeks before Tripoli would be working effectively. It looked as though 30 Corps might have to tackle the Mareth line alone, instead of combining with 10 Corps. General Bobbie Erskine, who had taken over 7th Armoured Division after Harding had been wounded, meanwhile relentlessly drove back the enemy rearguards.

At the time of Churchill's review, Leese was asked by Monty to organise a two-day exercise for senior officers. This was scheduled for 15 and 16 February, and most of it was to take place in the theatre.

> 'Our object' wrote Leese, 'was to show the employment of Infantry in the Desert warfare attack, the employment of tanks in conjunction with guns and infantry and the employment of a division such as the New Zealand division in mobile outflanking movement.'[1]

Among the generals who descended on them was the American General George Patton, commanding the US Army in Tunisia. He stayed with Leese at his HQ, and Leese was fascinated by him. Monty began the conference by saying 'No smoking, gentlemen, please!' This maddened Patton, who was a chain-smoker. At intervals he got out a cigarette and Bedell Smith[2] made him put it away. Finally, Bedell Smith gave him some chewing gum. Patton's face was a study. Monty gave a brilliant two hours' lecture on warfare in general; on the way to lunch Leese asked Patton what he thought of the lecture. Patton, at last puffing happily at a cigarette, replied 'Well, I may be slow, and I may be stoopid, but it didn't mean a durn thing to me.'

16 Feb. OL to ML.

Our two [American generals] of last night thoroughly enjoyed coming. Lee – a general in England – and an extraordinary old man called Patten [sic], who had a mind like a sink. I should say very gallant, but with no idea about soldiering.[3] At lectures he alternately yawns and chews. He's a queer mixture. But the Americans are very much out to learn and co-operate, which is a good thing, and they were much impressed with our methods of teaching – so it has been well worthwhile.

19 Feb. OL to ML.

My own objective is [to] fit myself to command an Army – if I don't fail, I feel one day, I shall have to do so. Each step we take seems tremendous, but I feel that if I have to go one higher, it is a vast step, and I try and feel that I can learn to do it.

---

[1] Memoirs.
[2] General Water Bedell Smith. Chief of Staff to Eisenhower.
[3] Leese was by no means alone in this wrong opinion, which was shared by all the British generals at that time. He quickly changed his views.

20 Feb.

Here we are some 150 miles from Tripoli. Douglas [Wimberley] has just been in – very well – having been 140 miles today in a jeep. He was like a terrier – surrounded with Tommy guns and petrol cans – and straining at the leash. We turned the enemy out of Medenine today, and shall soon get a look at his Mareth line.

On 22 February, Major Sidney Kent arrived. Twenty-seven, educated at Wellington and Sandhurst, commissioned in the KOYLI, he was soon to become one of the youngest brigadiers in the British Army. As a G3 at Aandalsnes, in the unfortunate Norwegian campaign of April 1940, when capture by the enemy seemed imminent, he had had to destroy the troops' pay. He had gone to the Middle East with 44 Division, serving at Alamein as a G2. He was posted to Leese's HQ by the Military Secretary, though nobody at 30 Corps seemed to know anything about it. Both Leese and Sidney Kent were at first somewhat wary – 'We walked around each other' said the latter, years later. There were no real difficulties: Sidney Kent was quickly at home with the rest of the staff, and Leese was quick to see that the casual, relaxed manner of his new G2 hid a brilliant mind.

Just as 30 Corps was entering Medenine, Monty received an urgent signal from Alexander, who had arrived in Tunis to conduct land operations under Eisenhower, asking him to create a diversion, as the Germans were concentrating all their resources of armour against the Americans, and there was the likelihood of the British 1st Army getting into difficulties. Monty therefore ordered 30 Corps to push on as quickly as possible and gain contact with the Mareth line between the sea and the main road. 51 Division pressed on, protected by 7 Armoured Division. As Alexander had hoped, Rommel consequently pulled his armoured forces off the American front to counter-attack Eighth Army before they could break out into the plains of Tunisia. 30 Corps was now in a dangerous position: they were close up against the Mareth line with extremely weak forces, their left flank exposed to the German threat over the mountains. As reinforcements to the New Zealand division the Guards Brigade arrived 2800 miles from Syria, and 200 heavy tanks were brought from Tripoli on transporters.

About this time, Major Harry Llewellyn,[1] Army Headquarters, was sent for by Freddie de Guingand, Monty's Chief of Staff. 'I have had a word with Master [Monty] and General Leese,' said de Guingand. 'You are to collect your gear and proceed immediately to General

---

[1] As Colonel Llewellyn, he won a gold medal on Foxhunter in the 1952 Olympic Games.

Oliver Leese's Headquarters, to act there as the Army Liaison Officer and feed us with reports.'

Major Llewellyn was much tickled with Leese's genial Lord Emsworth manner, which suggested that the Libyan desert was merely an extension to Blandings Castle, and who gave him 'a charming reception as if I was a guest coming to stay for a weekend's shooting'.[1] George Walsh was less enthusiastic, considering an Army spy at Corps HQ unnecessary, but Sidney Kent and Victor Balfour[2] – another promising member of Leese's staff, who was a friend of Llewellyn from pre-war days – were extremely helpful. Llewellyn was able to exchange pleasantries from time to time with Ion Calvocoressi, who he felt had the flair to 'translate' his general to many people who might not understand him. He enjoyed his visits to 30 Corps HQ, 'as they always had a good supply of Groppi's chocolates.'[3]

5 Mar. OL to ML.

This is the most extraordinary day I feel that I have ever spent – it seems quite certain that the enemy will attack us with over 150 tanks tomorrow morning. Today everything is unnaturally quiet – the lull before the storm . . .

I am sending this back by a pilot who is flying home tomorrow. I hope you will get it quickly. Colliton [his driver] is very bothered about his wife. She is to have another baby. There is no water laid on to the house and she has to carry it all. They have been on the council list for a better house for 6 years, but are always passed over. I enclose addresses. Can you deal with the situation? He'll be very grateful. In addition to the above the roof leaks and the bottom houses have been condemned.

It is indicative of Leese's character that the plight of Colliton's wife should so exercise his mind that he took immediate action, with an important battle only hours ahead. On receiving the letter, ML made the journey to Scotland, spurring the local council into action. The child was stillborn, and ML arranged for Mrs Colliton to go on holiday and then to be with Crowe at Tabley until her new home was available.

On 5 March, Ion Calvocoressi wrote in his diary 'The Army Commander says that if the Germans do not attack at 6 am tomorrow-morning, he'll eat his hat.' On 6 March he recorded that the German attack started at 6 am.

[1] Communication from Colonel Llewellyn.
[2] Later General Sir Victor FitzGeorge-Balfour.
[3] Groppi's was a Cairo café famous for its mouth-watering teas and confectionery. There are frequent references to Groppi's in Olivia Manning's *Levant Trilogy*. It was also where Kenneth Widmerpool first met Pamela Flitton, in Anthony Powell's novel *The Military Philosophers*.

The battle of Medenine was fought on 6 March 1943. Monty described it later as the model of a one-day battle. Rommel attacked with three Panzer divisions, 90 Light Division and some Italians.

'We beat off every attack,' wrote Leese, 'with our six pounders against his tanks and with vast artillery concentrations . . . Rommel is now pulling out and racing back northwards having wasted a lot of tanks and petrol.'

Monty's 'intuition' about a 6 am attack could have been the result of a message from *Ultra*. He would not have known about this intelligence organisation based on Bletchley Park, and may have considered it came from dissident officers working within the German Army, but there was no doubt in his mind that these particular messages were reliable – hence his hypothetical hat-eating. Following the victory at Medenine, Leese recounted, a thanksgiving service was held 'in the yellow flower meadow outside my caravan.'

Monty and Leese were now preparing for the next battle. The Mareth line, 22 miles long, extending from the Matmato Hills to the sea, was a series of defence works constructed on Maginot line principles shortly before the war by the French, as a barrier against an Italian invasion of Tunisia from Tripolitania. Success would mean the beginning of the end in North Africa. Rommel had gone on sick leave on 9 March, never to return to the desert. He had handed over his command to General von Arnim.

15 Mar. OL to ML.

We had an incredible evening. Winston sent out to O a release of *Desert Victory* by air, and Jorrocks, George [Walsh], Ion [Calvocoressi] and I went and dined with O – and then we all joined about 1000 men in a hollow and saw the film *en plein air*. It was very wonderful, with the background of the thunder of our guns in the start of the battle for Tunis. I thought the part dealing with the battle of Alamein was great – particularly the tense moment before the barrage opened.

19 Mar. OL to ML.

The most damnable thing has happened – in fact the one thing I was trying to avoid. The Guards Brigade has suffered very bad casualties. We have been facing up to the Mareth line during the last few days – and this necessitated a series of small advances and attacks, carried out by the Highland and 50th Divisions. All went very well, with relatively small casualties, except the Guards Brigade, where the Grenadiers lost 30 officers and 300 men, I think, and the Coldstream about half that number.

They had experienced Sappers with them, who cleared gaps well for them, but their whole technique was not yet good enough to compete with the situation – which was a slightly different one to those we had previously encountered. If I had thought they would have come up against minefields on this scale, they would have tackled it differently – it's easy to be wise now.

One can think of a hundred things one might have done differently. I blame myself very much, I had thought it would be an easy blooding for them – and I gave them 250 guns to themselves, and experienced sappers, and an experienced General and Staff to run their show. The Grenadiers did magnificently. Although their attack failed I believe that by holding the German Infantry in that area – they will play a dominating part in the coming battle.

Leese was writing before all the facts had emerged, and because of this he had not been able to present the entire picture. He was of course fully occupied at the time in running the Corps battle.

201 Guards Brigade, for the battle, was under command 7 Armoured Division (General 'Bobby' Erskine). General W. G. F. Jackson, writing thirty years later, saw the Mareth battle in perspective:

Time for reconnaissance was short, and the few patrols, which could be sent out in the time available, reported no mines. The artillery programme was more than adequate, Montgomery jokingly saying 'It is going to be a party and when I give a party it is always a good one.' The trouble was that there were a number of uninvited and undesirable guests present. The position was far from lightly held . . . heavily mined by anti-personnel as well as anti-tank mines . . . It is to the great credit of the two Guards battalions – 3rd Coldstream and 6th Grenadiers – that they took most of their objectives. They were too weak by then to hold them. Over 38 officers and 500 men were lost, many to anti-personnel mines as they tried to rush the minefields.[1]

It is typical of Leese that when affairs prospered he would give the credit to others, so, if matters went wrong, he would put all the blame upon himself. Monty did not consider himself blameless in this affair, and indeed wrote apologising for his misjudgment to Brigadier Gascoigne, commanding 201 Guards Brigade.

Operation *Torch* was not proving successful. In accordance with a decision taken at Casablanca, Alexander was to exercise tactical command of the battle in Tunisia as soon as English Eighth Army had crossed the Tunisian frontier, and Eisenhower had told him to take over on 20 February. Alexander was highly critical of Anderson's handling of 1 Army, and wrote to Monty asking if Leese could be spared from 30 Corps to replace Anderson. Monty replied characteristically (17 March 1943):

[1] *The North African Campaign 1940–43.* W. G. F. Jackson (Batsford).

My dear Alex,

Your wire re Oliver Leese. He has been through a very thorough training here and has learnt his stuff well. I think he is quite fit to take command of First Army. I hope you will agree that Oliver cannot be spared from here just at the moment. If *Pugilist* [Mareth offensive] is a success it may well mean the beginning of the end of the war in N. Africa, the task of 30 Corps is very important, and it would prejudice the whole affair if Oliver was taken away at this juncture.

Monty wrote again on 29 March releasing Leese, but Alexander had by that time changed his mind, and was virtually commanding First Army himself.

It is interesting to conjecture what destiny would have had in store for Leese had he taken over First Army. Almost certainly he would have gone back to England and later commanded an Army in France. Monty for instance considered Leese far abler than Miles Dempsey, who was to command the Second Army in France.

20 Mar. OL to ML.

O and I are together as usual for the battle – our caravans within a couple of hundred yards so that we can make our decisions at once. He and Jorrocks have just been over to see me.

On 22 March, 50 Division captured the five forts nicknamed Betty, Mary, Sally, Susan and Jane – very complex forts, consisting of a warren of trench systems, covered approaches and pillboxes. The enemy were able to open fire behind Eighth Army troops where mopping up had not been complete. After heavy fighting on the afternoon of 22nd, the Germans recaptured a considerable part of the bridgehead, just taken by 50 Division.

'I have little doubt' wrote Leese, 'the counter-attack would have been stopped if we had had 6-pdrs across in reasonable numbers. It was most unfortunate that the towhooks to drag them had not been placed on the Valentine tanks. I understood that they had been put on and this just shows how you cannot check up too thoroughly in every detail.'

During the early hours of 23 March, Leese went to see Monty and tell him the bridgehead had been lost. This and the second night of Alamein were the only times Leese had had to waken Monty during all their fighting together.[1] He told Leese to return in a few hours.

[1] De Guingand wakened Monty during Alamein, but it was in connexion with a 30 Corps problem.

What happened next is described by Monty's biographer, Nigel Hamilton. Monty ordered Leese's 30 Corps attack to be closed down, and Horrocks, using his 10 Corps headquarters and 1st Armoured Division to take command of the left hook towards El Hamma. Leese, abashed, but not without grace, smiled at Horrocks and said 'Off you go, Jorrocks, and win the battle.'[1]

Leese ordered 4 Indian Division, supported by 7 Armoured Division up into the hills, and Horrocks joined Freyberg at El Hamma. The enemy line was then heavily attacked by air and artillery with the setting sun behind. What resulted was the triumph of flexibility. The frontal attack had not made the breakthrough: the outflanking attack under Freyberg, achieved success.

The enemy became disorganised and started to pull out of Mareth. 'We've done it again,' wrote Leese to ML, 'and the enemy has evacuated his famous Mareth line.'

On 29 March he wrote some furious comments to ML, which, though no doubt containing more than a grain of truth, he would have expected her to take with more than a grain of salt:

> If the BBC reporters seem to be able to give away our movements they do so wholeheartedly. I quite frankly loathe the Press and the BBC. I don't think they have any ideals except their own mercenary attempts to prove themselves . . . This American and 1st Army racket seem to have no control of anything. They concentrate on dress. We find fighting a more urgent necessity. I want to get on to Sfax as they say there are good cafés there!

> 30 Mar. OL to ML.

> Just returned from my dinner with Eisenhower. I liked him. He is full of life – outspoken – all out to be friendly, and above all to win the war. He is, I think, too, pleased to meet the Eigth Army. He never stopped talking at dinner, and, like all the Yanks, put things in the most entertaining way. At a first meeting I was impressed with him as a man. As a commander we have yet to see.

The enemy had now taken up a very strong position along the general line of Wadi Akarit. Leese was given again the reinforcements out of the NZ division and told to plan a breakthrough attack. He had now two difficulties to face – lifting mines on a moonlight night, and getting sufficient ammunition dumped for the attack. He got the ammunition dumped, and minelifting was delayed until first light.

In the one-day battle of Akarit (6 April), Leese gained the initiative

---

[1] *Monty, Master of the Battlefield 1942–1944*, by Nigel Hamilton. Hamish Hamilton.

by starting the attack in pitch darkness. The 51 Highland Division formed two of the brigades to attack at right angles to one another in total darkness, and the 4 Indian Division climbed in the black night to attack in the hills.

'It was a hard day's fighting' wrote Major General Wimberley, 'and in it HD had heavy casualties, but we held on to most of our objectives we had taken, despite heavy German counter-attacks . . . I remember meeting Oliver on the top of Roumana Ridge (which we captured) the day after the battle and a few hours after the Germans retreated, and he congratulated HD and me, on a fine achievement of soldiering.'[1]

The attack had been a great success: many Italian prisoners even being taken without their boots on,[2] and 21 and 10 Panzer Divisions which were in touch with the Americans had no chance to come over and intervene. Twelve hundred prisoners were taken, and much equipment captured.

In this battle, Colonel Lorne Campbell, who a few weeks previously had discussed the value of a classical education with his Corps Commander in no-man's-land, gained the Victoria Cross, repelling a German counter-attack in the evening after attacking unceasingly for twelve hours during the day.

30 Corps now moved swiftly. On 8 April the 11 Hussars entered Sfax, and an official entry into the town was arranged for the following morning. Leese arranged for a reception on the racecourse, at the end of which he drove Monty round, so that the crowd and Monty could enjoy themselves. Several people tried to kiss Monty, and one lady handed her baby to Leese to enable her to embrace Monty, leaving Leese holding the baby:

'Mindful of my wife watching a film of this parade,' wrote Leese, 'I had the presence of mind to drive the car with my knees and to hand back the baby to its distributor with the words in excellent French: "*Madame, c'est à vous.*"'[3]

Lieutenant-Colonel Michael Carver, as GSO1, 7 Armoured Division, knew Leese best during the period from mid-January to mid-April 1943, when Eighth Army advanced from Buerat to Sfax:

I always found him refreshingly down to earth and full of common sense – in contrast to the mercurial showiness of his fellow corps commander,

---

[1] Letter to author 24.1.81.
[2] Major General Wimberley recollected that no Germans were captured in this manner.
[3] Memoirs.

Brian Horrocks. He was vigorous, tough, determined and consistent. His good humour, illustrated by his familiar snort and guffaw, was seldom absent.

I much preferred dealing with him to being subordinate to Horrocks. It is interesting that at that period he was clearly Monty's favourite corps commander.[1]

Leese's next task was to help in the planning of Sicily.

[1] Letter to author 7.11.80.

11

SICILY

I must own that it is a great thing to have plenty to do.
Oliver Leese, 16th August 1943

In January 1943, Churchill and Roosevelt, together with their Chiefs of Staff, met at Casablanca, to settle future aims. At this conference demands for 'Unconditional Surrender' were formulated, plans were made for the reconquest of Burma – and for the invasion of Sicily.

In coming to the decision to move against Sicily – preferred to Sardinia – the Combined Chiefs of Staff listed three objects: to secure lines of communication in the Mediterranean; to divert German pressure from Russia; and to intensify the pressure on Italy. An outline plan for 'Operation *Husky*' was immediately produced. Invasion was to be carried out by forces coming from the eastern and western Mediterranean respectively. Eisenhower was to be Supreme Commander, and Alexander his Deputy, although Alexander was senior in rank and experience and the British were providing the larger part of the forces.

A special planning staff was formed, early in February, with its headquarters in Algeria, and other branches in London, Washington and Cairo.

An extraordinary ruse, to make the enemy believe that an invasion of Sardinia was being planned, met with almost total success. A dead body was washed ashore on the coast of Spain, purporting to be that of an English officer bearing a letter from Lt.-General Archie Nye, the Vice-Chief of the Imperial General Staff, to Alexander. The 'bait' consisting of veiled allusions to Sardinia, was swallowed hook, line and sinker by all the Axis top brass concerned, with the exception of Kesselring.

The planning staff for the invasion of Sicily held many conferences and there was much to-ing and fro-ing while the draft plan was on its travels. When Monty studied the plan in detail it was late in April, and having done so he called for numerous changes to it.

On 21 April, Monty sent for Leese and told him that an invasion of Sicily was planned for 10 July 1943. He gave his copy of the draft plan to Leese, instructing him to go through it with de Guingand in Cairo and to be ready to discuss it with Monty himself when he arrived there forty-eight hours later.

On studying the plan it was immediately apparent to both Leese and de Guingand that far too great dispersion was intended for both the American and the British Armies. About twenty landing points over a distance of more than 100 miles, they both considered, was asking for trouble; a greater concentration of forces was essential. Monty when he arrived agreed with them.

Monty decided to put forward an alternative plan at the forthcoming conference at Allied Forces HQ at Algiers. However he got a bad chill and was unable to attend the meeting. De Guingand started off to take his place, but had bad concussion in an air crash, so Leese deputised for Monty.

Oliver Leese was liable to see himself in Groucho Marx-like situations when he travelled on important journeys. This occasion proved no exception. He set off with Ion Calvocoressi on what he described as 'my first mission on that kind of high level'; adding typically 'we soon came down to earth'. The only greeting on their arrival at Algiers was a balloon barrage which took the pilot unawares, though he managed precariously to fly through it and effect a landing.

> 'When we did land,' wrote Leese, 'nobody met us, and so my first drive as the representative of the Army Commander was a lorry hop into Algiers. I went into the Conference Room to find a table surrounded with the flags of the Allied Nations, and a group of senior officers, all very well and correctly dressed. I had on my usual shirt and shorts and no medal ribbons.'[1]

Leese then put forward their case, to which Alexander immediately gave total support, the remainder wanted to hear Monty speak for himself before committing themselves. In any case Monty would be able to deal with supplementary questions which would be beyond Leese's brief as a corps commander. Tedder[2] and Cunningham[3] were both opposed to the scheme Leese advocated, Tedder in particular saying that it would leave several German airfields without being dealt with.

A day or two later another conference was held and this time Monty

---

[1] Memoirs.
[2] Air Marshal Tedder, Air C-in-C North Africa.
[3] Admiral of the Fleet Sir Andrew Cunningham.

took Leese with him to Algiers. Leese was intrigued to see Monty buttonhole Eisenhower's Chief of Staff, Bedell Smith, in the lavatory shortly before the conference began, and 'sell' him the whole plan in a few minutes. Smith supported Monty in the conference and all was well.

The main change in the plan, finally approved on 13 May, was that Patton's invasion targets were switched from near Palermo to the south-east of Sicily close to Monty's army, and both armies' landing points would be more tightly massed. The object of the invasion was to land in Sicily, occupy Messina and dominate the Straits in order to carry the fighting into Italy and knock Italy out of the war. It was essential for the landing to be carried out with fighter cover; and, as the fighters were based in Tunis and Malta, the landings would have to be carried out in the south-east or south-west corner of the island. The new plans for the invasion stood a reasonable chance of sucess, but Monty and Leese felt that they left a lot to be desired.

'It is difficult to balance patiently,' OL wrote to ML on 1.5.43, 'one's own knowledge of what really happens in war with plans made out in London, Washington and Algiers, very often by people who have never seen war. I always try to remember one's forward companies in the minefields, in the anti-tank obstacles, following the barrage in the moonlight, digging like hell so as to be able to take the mortaring and shelling that will come at dawn, standing steadfast with tanks all round them, serving their anti-tank guns under heavy fire in the massed tank attack and always cheerful and mad keen for the next venture.'

During the weeks immediately prior to the invasion, Leese had an enormous daily workload. Monty had gone to England for a few weeks and accordingly Leese was temporarily in command of Eighth Army. He was also, of course, commanding 30 Corps, which, for the purposes of the Sicily Campaign, consisted of 1 Canadian Division (Major General Simonds), 51 Highland Division (Major General Wimberley), 231 Infantry Brigade (Brigadier Urquhart). In addition he was keeping an eye on 51 Highland Division training in Tunisia and controlling personally that of 231 Infantry Brigade in the Suez Canal zone. Roy Urquhart, who had been Wimberley's G1 in 51 Highland Division, became their Brigadier, so all ran smoothly.

Writing to ML, Leese referred to these undertakings, coming as they did on top of 7 months' fighting and high scale planning, with all the irritations of inter-services and inter-allied problems of Algiers.

It has been a great asset to have the knack to get on well with people, as I get these great visits to ships, etc., which makes so much difference. Also it has helped tremendously with relations generally out here, especially these last few weeks, when many a hand has been rather against O, partly jealousy, and partly because I think we did ride a bit roughshod over people. It was hard to avoid, however, during all the long advance – and so much that he said and did was designed primarily to keep up our terrific morale. People will not realise that he is the greatest soldier of our age and that he had won very great victories and that they must be ready to forgive certain foibles.

On 13 May, Leese visited the Combined Ops training centre. He changed the Brigadier and brought in 30 officers to teach the troops. Like Monty, he was not over-optimistic about the invasion, though he confided his thoughts to ML alone. 'The chances of bringing this off are none too good' he wrote on 9 June. 'I'd like to shoot the ★★★ who chose this plan – and send his head on a pitcher back to Mountbatten and his useless racket.'

Miscellaneous news for ML: he had lunch with Victor Cazalet[1] 'who was very amusing, with gossip from England.' John Green-Wilkinson was now a Major – 'he has never looked back since the day that we lost him at a *thé dansant* in Sfax.' Once, on the road to Bizerta OL and his driver 'suddenly saw an aeroplane driving along the road towards [us]. It saw us, taxied, and went into a gate, and waited for us to pass!' He arranged for monthly food parcels from South Africa, not only for ML, but also for the wives of three of his drivers.

2 July. OL to ML.

Tomorrow I hope to see my master of the 1940 venture for a few days. It will be interesting to see his parish. [He was going to Malta, where Gort was Governor].

4 July.

I am dining with the Field Marshal tonight. He has a brace of very pleasant palaces, and with a glorious garden – part of it rather like our Quetta garden, with masses of zinnias, like we grew them there, hollyhocks and marigolds, and then very nice orange groves, all in a big walled garden, covered with bougainvillaea!

6 July.

We land tactically loaded, so that each ship contains men or vehicles of several different units, so as to ensure on landing that infantry, guns, tanks, engineers, anti-tank guns etc. are available in the best proportions for the particular task. Each ship is therefore given a special serial number. Every

---

[1] Conservative MP and Political Liaison Officer to General Sikorski, Prime Minister of Polish Government in Exile. He was killed with Sikorski on 4 July 1943, when the Liberator bomber in which they were travelling crashed at Gibraltar.

unit is then sent to concentration areas near the port. From here movement control staff call them forward into assembly areas, where all the vehicles are waterproofed, and each serial number is collected together – thence they are sent down to the fort, to load on the big or little personnel or vehicle craft for which they are allotted.

This morning I had to go down a rope ladder to get into my pinnace, but I achieved it successfully, and even with a modicum of grace. I'm glad to say we were able to return to a gangway.

As usual in our battles *everyone* knows the Allied Army, Corps, Divisional, Brigade, Bn, Coy, Platoon plan – the higher ones very roughly and the lower in corresponding detail.

As you will by now know, the Americans land on our left – commanded by our old Tripoli visitor 'Chewing Gum' [General Patton] – as you know I cannot see much in him – but I hear he has a good Corps Commander in Bradley, whom I look forward to meeting.

Leese had changed his mind about Patton by the end of the campaign.

General Sir Victor FitzGeorge-Balfour, at this period Leese's G1(Ops), who was responsible for the planning and execution of the Sicily campaign, including the crossing to Reggio de Calabria, found Leese a wonderful person to work for, and has a particularly vivid recollection of him shortly before the Sicily D-Day:

I remember in Malta just before the Sicily invasion his skill at dispelling an appalling atmosphere of gloom over the prospects of success which had arisen – incredibly uncharacteristically – from Monty's pre-D-Day peptalk.

The landings on the beaches of Sicily took place in the early hours of the morning of 10 July 1943. In command of the naval force was Admiral Cunningham, and a total of 3000 ships were used to ensure the timely and safe arrival of the assault forces at their beaches, and provide cover while the troops disembarked.

The covering force included the British battleships *Nelson*, *Rodney*, *Warspite* and *Valiant*, the *Howe* and *King George V* covered the eastbound convoys. The British Eastern Naval Task force, under command of Admiral Sir Bertram Ramsay, was responsible for landing the Eighth Army. This was divided into three forces under Rear Admirals Troubridge, McGrigor and Vian. The perfect timing of this colossal naval enterprise owed much to the planning and direction of Admiral Sir Andrew Cunningham: this assault on the beaches of Sicily, by eight divisions simultaneously, was greater than that in Normandy during the famous D-Day landing on 6 June 1944.

The Security of Operation *Husky* was of an amazing standard: all were closely familiar with details of the particular beach on which they would land; but very few were trusted with the knowledge of *where* the beach might be. The British landings were to be on a forty mile

stretch of coast on the south-east corner of Sicily, the Americans on a
forty mile stretch of the south coast, there being a twenty mile gap
between Patton's Seventh and Monty's Eighth Army.

The Armada set forth, Leese sailing for Sfax on the evening of 8
July with George Walsh and a small tactical HQ of 30 Corps in HMS
Largs, the HQ ship of the 51 Highland Division, whose infantry assault
troops came out of the harbour in their LCTs (Landing Craft Tanks).
Rear Admiral McGrigor, immensely popular with Eighth Army per-
sonnel, flew his flag in HMS *Largs*.

During the day before the landing there was a high sea and a heavy
swell, which, if it continued, might prevent the landing craft being
lowered into the sea. Admiral Cunningham, as Naval C-in-C, had a
difficult decision to make. A postponed landing would lose the value
of surprise; a sea that was too rough could well cause tragedy. Cunningham's decision to go ahead was a brave one, and it proved right. All
went remarkably smoothly.[1]

About midnight the convoy approached the shore. Leese had been
anxious, if possible, to avoid landing in the dark on heavily mined
beaches, and was relieved when his recommendation for 30 Corps to
scramble on the smaller beaches, that were probably not protected,
had been accepted.

Lieutenant Ian Weston Smith (Scots Guards) who fought in the
Sicily campaign, and was later taken prisoner at Salerno, wrote, while
a PoW in Germany, an account of the Sicily campaign which he read
to his fellow prisoners. The first landings had taken place at 3.45
am, and during the course of the day, 150,000 Allied troops had
disembarked:

> 'By ten am,' he wrote, 'the sea off the Pachino peninsula [Leese's desti-
> nation] was almost gay – landing craft and warships stretched in all
> directions, imperturbed by even an occasional enemy aircraft, and Generals
> Montgomery and Leese with Admiral Mountbatten stood watching vehicles
> disembark from landing craft with only the sight of the odd "waterproofed"
> truck sinking like a stone to ruffle the calm. The weather was as fine as
> one could wish for a regatta.'

There were eight Italian and two German divisions on the island. Of
the Italian there were four coastal and four field divisions, the coastal
troops being handicapped by their coastal defence guns, made by
Vickers in 1905. The field divisions were considerably better, and the
backbone of the island's defence was supplied by the reconstituted
Hermann Goering division and the 29th Infantry Division. Hitler

---

[1] Eisenhower had a similar problem to face over D-Day, and took a similar course of
action.

had offered Mussolini further reinforcements, but the latter, whose position was already precarious, declined the offer as acceptance would make his own difficulties more apparent.

Altogether there were in Sicily about 200,000 Italian and 32,000 German troops plus 30,000 Luftwaffe ground staff. There was a difference of opinion between Marshal Kesselring and the Italian General Guzzoni as to the best use of the two German Panzer divisions. In the end it was agreed that one should defend Palermo and the other be prepared for Allied landings in the east or south-east.

Just ahead of 30 Corps an airborne landing took place towards Syracuse which was captured on D-Day, and consequently every searchlight in the island was turned on, and there was one on the Pachino Peninsula. Fortunately, it never moved from the vertical position – presumably searching all the time for aircraft. As it was located just behind the water the whole Corps could easily check their landings – which proved a complete surprise and enemy officers were captured in their pyjamas.

Monty was soon signalling Leese to press on. He needn't have worried:

> 'With the exception of the Americans,' wrote Ian Weston Smith, 'who had already met some German resistance, all troops started a rapid advance inland. The speed of their advance was limited only by a certain sense of caution and very limited transport as extremely few vehicles are landed with the assault flight. General Leese himself entered Spaccaforno and Modica driving in a jeep ahead of the Canadian division.'

The next day they drove inland and on 12 July captured an Italian general: 'a nice man' wrote OL to ML, 'we had him to dine with us –

> and we are sending a wire to his wife. But he has no stomach for the battle . . . Mountbatten is kindly taking this back and sending you a telegram.'

So far, the invasion was going well. Monty realised that, if Catania were taken quickly, there was a chance that the campaign would be over in a few days and a battle of attrition avoided.

An airborne attack to capture the Primosole bridge over the river Sineto (on the outskirts of Catania) failed, as many of the paratroopers were dropped in the wrong places, and Catania, instead of falling on 14 July, was not taken for another month.[1] The first phase of the

---

[1] Nigel Hamilton in *Monty: Master of the Battlefield*, points out that the assault on Catania was a forerunner of the famous *Bridge Too Far* attack at Arnhem in September 1944.

campaign, the landings and the advance in the Catanian plain occupied the first eleven days. The British forces had cleared the whole south-eastern part of the island by 12 July. On 14 July the Highland Division eventually captured Vizzini, but the race for Catania was off. Advances had often to be made on a 1-tank front; this did much to discount Allied armoured superiority, though Leese's man-oeuvres twelve months previously, in the Somerset lanes, stood him in good stead.

★

General FitzGeorge-Balfour recalls that Leese was 'a rather impetuous, impatient and not very good driver', and about this time he had what was literally a narrow squeeze:

> The ADCs and I were quite used to it [his driving] and I suppose had placid dispositions – not so George Walsh, luckily he seldom travelled around with OL. Once, near Lentini, they went together to a conference at Army HQ; the roads were narrow and flanked by drystone wall; OL was driving too fast and too adventurously and got squeezed between a wall and a 3-tonner. Luckily no one hurt but the car a bit bent but not undrivable. George Walsh very angry.

14 July. OL to ML.

> In one town they threw bombs and shot at our troops. I'm now going to take hostages, and I shall shoot them if we have any more nonsense.

The killing of hostages is as old as war itself. The Romans did it, the Germans did it, the victorious Allies regarded and treated it as a war crime. As it happened, Leese did not shoot hostages, nor did he take any. The cause of his anger, according to General Balfour, was probably German snipers detached from their regiments. Leese probably an-nounced in the hearing of a few officers that he was going to take hostages, and indeed he wrote to ML to that effect. He certainly did not follow up his threat.[1]

By now the civilians in Sicily were giving obvious signs of welcome to the Allied armies.

> 'Once the first shock was over,' wrote Ian Weston Smith, 'and when they realised that invasion meant the end of bombing and probably of privation,

---

[1] Monty published an order in Sicily, that German paratroops operating in civilian dress behind the lines, if captured, were to be treated as spies and shot. But when one paratroop was captured, he rescinded the order and said they were to be treated as prisoners of war. *Monty: Master of the Battlefield 1942–1944*, by Nigel Hamilton (Hamish Hamilton).

the Sicilians heartily welcomed their liberators, declared they were anti-fascist and always had been, and gave generously of eggs and what little wine the Germans had left them. Later, of course, the commercial habit reasserted itself, prices rose, and with them the old North African trick of selling tea brewed up to five times.'

18 July. OL to ML.

We have a first-class liaison in progress with the Americans . . . I went to see General Bradley, commanding their Corps – I liked him very much.

Even so, there were problems; as Omar Bradley outlined in his memoirs, *A Soldier's Story*. He had sent a brusque note to Leese when the latter had side-stepped the town of Enna, leaving the American flank exposed. Bradley soon regretted his curt note when Leese sent him prompt and profuse apologies, together with two bottles of Scotch: Leese had assumed that his staff had notified Bradley of the intended move.

There was a good deal of touchiness concerning the use of roads. There was one viable road (Highway 124) available for the main weight of American and British vehicles, and an arrangement for sharing was made accordingly. It was soon reported that Patton's Americans were using the road all the time irrespective of agreements, and, at a time when co-operation between the two allies was of vital importance, the two army commanders Patton and Montgomery sulked in their respective tents.[1] It was to Patton's advantage to avoid discussion, nor was Montgomery likely to ask favours of a man who had yawned throughout his lecture on Alamein.

Leese wrote to ML [20 July]

We have not handled one or two situations very well with the Americans and Patton is a bit het up . . . O is sometimes a bit impatient and hasty with others, and L as in our last party simply does not step in and control the issue at critical moments.

In connexion with the first part of Leese's observation, Nigel Hamilton's comment is relevant:

General Leese was astute enough to recognise what Monty did not, that by treating the Seventh Army as a poor relation Monty might well irk the Americans to moving in the opposite direction – westwards – and thus lose the chance of the Americans guarding Leese's flank.[2]

The difference of opinion with the Americans that had blown up

[1] In fact Monty had his caravan and Patton a most imposing palace in Agrigento.
[2] *Monty: Master of the Battlefield 1942–1944*, by Nigel Hamilton (Hamish Hamilton).

concerned the use of the Caltagironi–Enna road. Freddie de Guingand
visited Leese to ask him if he could do anything about it. Leese
accordingly visited Bradley, who was willing to help but had not the
authority to do so. 'You will have to see the Army Commander'
said Bradley. Leese had always got on well with Patton, and he
could now see that the latter's flaunting of ivory-handled pistols,
his profanity and histrionics, were his own peculiar methods of
impressing his personality and getting the best out of his troops,
and realised that Patton was not only a gallant soldier but also a
great general.

Leese went with Ion Calvocoressi on 21 July to Patton's Army HQ
in Agrigento, and stayed the night, as this was well out of Leese's
Corps area. Difficulties concerning the use of roads were soon settled
and there were no more traffic problems. Leese had done what Alexander had failed to achieve. He afterwards received a mild rebuke from
Monty for going outside his area, which was the Army Commander's
method of saying he understood what Leese had been about, and
thanking him for clearing up the situation.

Strongly increased German resistance forced 30 Corps, reinforced
now by 78 Division, to continue the attack round the west side of
Etna. Patton's Seventh Army advanced with little opposition to reach
Palermo on 22 July.

28 July. OL to ML.

They [the Americans] are all out to co-operate so as to win through
quickly. They must have advertisement for their Press and Patton relies on
'histrionic play acting' to impress his troops. It is all a technique. However,
it works. He is personally a very brave man, and has infused a real fighting
spirit in his troops.

On 25 July Mussolini was deposed as the result of a *coup d'état* in Italy,
but resistance in Sicily was bolstered by stubborn enemy defensive
tactics. The advance along the steep narrow lanes was held up by
demolitions, lava and the effect of 30 Corps bombing.

7 Aug. OL to ML.

I am very fond of Bradley, who is a very nice man, and a good soldier. We
get on very well – and we tied up a lot of liaison and artillery details
between us. These visits make all the difference. We had lunch with him,
and ate peanut butter. I prefer cow's!

12 August.

We have moved to the other side of Etna, and I had my first view of

Taormina – I wonder if we shall destroy it all . . . The flowers here are good, bougainvillaea, asters, hibericus, oleanders and that yellow creeper we used to see in India.

13 Aug.

We captured Randazzo and we made good progress on the coast towards Taormina.

14 August.

We are delayed by every form of blown road, destroyed bridges, mines, demolished houses, etc.

30 Corps had to advance up the Corniche road from Taormina to Messina. There were several places where the enemy could block the road very seriously by demolition if given time to do so. As a result Leese was given the opportunity of organising an amphibious landing, something on similar lines to his own pilot scheme of air, land and sea warfare, which he carried out in 1937.

For this he was given No 2 Commando, which had operated in Norway and at St Nazaire. Leese got in touch with Admiral McGrigor who was operating with 30 Corps again; and was told that a small force of all arms could be concentrated and put ashore at Augusta and Catania within 48 hours. Leese then appointed Brigadier Currie of the 4th Light Armoured Brigade as Commander.[1] Currie's command consisted of No 2 Commando, a squadron of his own tanks from the 4th County of London Yeomanry, a troop of anti-tank guns, a troop of self propelled artillery, howitzers, signals, Naval Forward Observation Officers and two platoons of sappers. Leese arranged for this force to be ready to land either at Ali in the North, or at any suitable beach between Ali and Taormina, required by General Kirkman, whom Leese had provided with a number of landing craft.

50 Division entered Taormina, but to the north of Taormina progress was difficult, owing to a landslide caused by the heavy gunfire of the Royal Navy, so it was decided to use Brigadier Currie's troops of 40 Royal Marine Commando to effect a landing, which they did on 15/16 August at Scaletta, eight miles south of Messina. Patton was doing more-or-less the same thing at Spadefora, twenty-five miles away, on the north of the island. The Axis troops were now pulling out of Sicily.

16 Aug. OL to ML.

We have had a vast amount to operate and plan lately. I must own that it is a great thing to have plenty to do.

[1] Brigadier Currie was killed later in the war.

17 Aug.

Tonight the Sicilian campaign is finished. I am delighted that the Americans got to Messina first. They have fought magnificently.

On the day that the campaign ended Monty announced that the Eighth Army's next task would be to assault the toe of Italy.

A link with the victorious days of the desert campaign was broken: Wimberley was to return to England to take over the Staff College at Camberley. He had fought with Oliver Leese in eight battles, five actions and six engagements during the ten months they had been together, and the Eighth Army would not be quite the same without his courageous, cheerful and untiring presence.

22 Aug. OL to ML. A reference to the combined operation:

When we flew up to Catterick that time with the 1st Bn. That circus was a try out and prelude to all these moves and the first one we ever did of its kind in England, and yet they cheese-spared [sic] over the money – in the same way as they did over the air raid precautions. I wonder if we shall be as stupid again.

The landing in Sicily was the first opposed landing with intent to secure a bridgehead made by the Allies during the war. Many lessons were learnt to be put into practice on the D-Day landings in 1944.

It had been an arduous and difficult campaign, in which defence had been so much less difficult than attack. In Kesselring's well-organised withdrawal across the Straits, nearly 40,000 German troops and 60,000 Italian were evacuated.[1] Many Italians surrendered; 5500 Germans were captured and a few thousand were killed. Allied casualties amounted to 22,800.

Of the Allied generals, Alexander was vague when he should have been decisive; Eisenhower was hesitant; Monty, pessimistic in Malta, was too impetuous at Primosole; Patton was cantankerous. As for Leese, he put his best foot forward as a general, and never put a foot wrong as a diplomat.

On 26 August Leese made an assessment of more than normal interest in his letter to ML:

The news of Mountbatten's command [Supreme Allied Commander, South East Asia] came in this morning. This will shake some of the old sea dogs. It may be a very good one – as he has more experience than most

[1] *History of the Second World War*, B. H. Liddell Hart (Cassell).

in combined operations. He is very forceful and appears overbearingly conceited. It all depends on his balance and judgement. I would say that if he has good people with him and not sycophants, it should go well.

★

Leese himself, having returned to England was soon to face the challenge of Commanding the Eighth Army in Italy.

12

ARMY COMMANDER

The British soldier can stand up to anything except the British War Office.

George Bernard Shaw

The old 8th Army camaraderie of the road is spreading to the Poles, Italians and Canadians. In fact it is a pleasure to drive about the 8th Army area and see the very high morale.
Oliver Leese to Major General John Kennedy, 16 April 1944

On arrival in England Leese settled 30 Corps HQ near Newmarket. A much-needed month's leave was spent with Margie.

'He has been fighting continuously since Alamein,' wrote Monty to Alan-brooke on 29 September 1943, 'except for the short interval between the end of the War in Africa and the beginning of *Husky* – and that interval was very hard work in planning *Husky*. He began to get irritable with his staff and difficult with them after Sicily was over . . . you would not think it, but he is of a nervous disposition and temperament – and there have been times when his staff found him very difficult. This continuous fighting is a great strain for a Corps Commander who has of necessity to deal with certain things in considerable detail and thus to have a firm grip on the tactical battle. A good rest of 2 to 3 weeks will put him quite OK. He is a very valuable officer and has done splendidly as a Corps Cmd in my Army – he is easily the best I have.'[1]

After his leave with Margie they stayed at the Dorchester for six weeks where a suite was virtually transformed into his TAC HQ. They went to Tabley for Christmas and on Christmas Eve 1943, Leese had a telegram from the Military Secretary, ordering him to proceed as soon

[1] Quoted by Nigel Hamilton in *Monty, Master of the Battlefield 1942–1944* (Hamish Hamilton).

as possible to Italy and take over command of the Eighth Army from
Monty, who was appointed to command 21st Army Group in the
United Kingdom.

Leese then rang up Ion Calvocoressi on Christmas Eve, asking to
go and see General Simpson at the War Office, to get permission for
Leese to leave England a day or two later, because his clothes were at
the cleaners etc.

'I marched into the Chief of Staff's room,' wrote Ion Calvocoressi,[1] 'in fear
and trepidation, having never been there before, and Simbo's reply was
"Oliver has had plenty of leave, and anyway he must go on the 27th,
because if Monty gets to England before Oliver leaves, then Monty will
not allow him to go out to Italy as he will want him for the 2nd Army."'

On Boxing Day, Leese left London, having travelled there from
Tabley, for Cornwall, accompanied by George Walsh, once again his
Chief of Staff, Colonel Sidney Kent who was to be G1(Ops) at TAC
HQ, and Major Ulick Verney, who had rejoined him as Personal
Assistant. Ralph Warren, his secretary/clerk, and Lamb also went with
him.

Ulick Verney wrote of their departure:

On Friday 24 December, General Sir Oliver Leese, commanding 30 Corps
in East Anglia, was ordered to take over the Eighth Army in Italy and to
be ready to fly out about the 27th. The small staff to go out with him
were duly warned; an improvised Headquarters came into action at the
Dorchester, in the suite which already served as TAC HQ 30 Corps. These
rooms were a scene of cheerful activity, with hospitality to all and sometimes
sundry. ADCs operated at high speed, two telephones rang ceaselessly,
and business ranged from higher questions of strategy down to last minute
purchases of clothing.

The great day of departure, Tuesday 28th Dec., was a nice, typical, raw
December morning. Everyone assembled in good time, and the trifling
hold-up of an hour while the Air Ministry coped with an unfavourable
weather report was borne with equanimity.

They flew to Lyneham and then to Portreath aerodrome in Cornwall.

'The scene,' wrote Verney, 'round a woodfire in the centre of the Nissen
Hut, the Mess of the Aerodrome, was so like a theatrical reproduction of
an Airport Mess in war as to seem unreal. Australian, Canadian and Polish
pilots read magazines around the fire: WAAF waitresses were handing out
tea and drinks: a WAAF orderly changed the records on the gramophone

[1] Letter to author 19.10.82. General Simpson was then Director of Military Operations.

and put on the wireless at full blast, and there was a coming and going of
visitors, suspended like us between the old life and new.'

On the early morning of 29 December they were not able to land and
refuel at Gibraltar owing to bad weather, so they landed in Morocco
on an American airfield near Port Lyautey. They asked for breakfast.
The Americans, seeing Leese and George Walsh in their red hats,
mistook them for military police, conducted them to a vast GIs
cookhouse, and gave them breakfast with bacon, tomatoes and marmalade all on the same plate.

They spent the night at Algiers and flew on via Palermo to Naples,
where they needed an aeroplane to take them to Foggia. Owing to cloudy
weather no aircraft was forthcoming, and Leese was anxious to get across
to Foggia quickly so that he could see Monty before the latter left.

Fortunately, Leese saw a young RAF pilot walking across the
aerodrome. The latter was just going back to Foggia. He mentioned
casually that he had just come over for the day to buy a hat, and would
be delighted to take Leese and his party with him, as there was plenty
of room in his Wellington: accordingly he took them to Foggia and
then to Vasto. 'I said good-bye to our most charming and enterprising
pilot,' wrote Leese, 'whom I hope one day may read this account of a
most exciting night.'[1] Leese then motored on to Paglieto, where he
found Monty at his TAC HQ.

On 1 January OL wrote to ML saying that he and Monty had
gossiped well into the night and then he had seen Monty off in his
aeroplane, escorted by a squadron of Spitfires:

> He will, I am sure, do wonders with the British and American armies in
> England, and is already on first-class terms with Eisenhower – and will, I
> think, command the combined Armies in actual practice. He will make a
> clean sweep of the dead wood in England – and I expect demands from
> many people from here. I hope he will not bleed us too much. The War
> Office say they will defend us! but I don't fancy they will have any say in
> the matter. In the end, it will be between O and me – and we are very
> good friends. I'm all out to help, and I feel sure he will be reasonable.

Leese's assessment was to prove to be unduly optimistic.

The situation that Leese had inherited was not an enviable one. The
Eighth Army and the US Fifth Army under Mark Clark were spread
across the width of Italy for a distance of a hundred miles. The
possibilities open to the Allies were to advance along the Adriatic
coast, and also through the seven mile gap of the Liri Valley, the
gateway to Rome, of which Monte Cassino, dominated by the fourteen

[1] Memoirs.

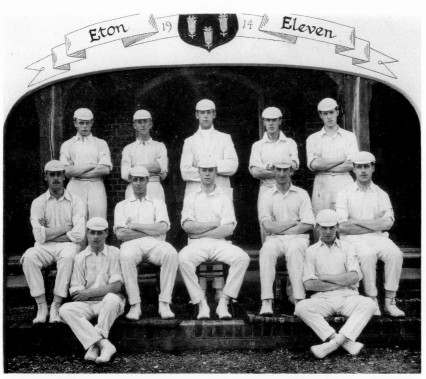

The Eton Eleven in 1914; Leese is in the centre of the back row.

The German officer who shot Leese.

Jack Lambert who shot the German officer and rescued Leese.

Leese with his Divisional Commanders, Morshead, Wimberley and Pienaar.

Leese with Ion Calvocoressi.

Luncheon, Tripoli, February 4, 1943. "We must have a photograph of this *alfresco* scene," said Churchill. Seated round the table: Alanbrooke, Randolph Churchill, Leese, Winston Churchill, Monty. Ion Calvocoressi is behind Monty.

Leese, Alexander and Mark Clark.

Leese, knighted on the battlefield by George VI.

Churchill's visit to the Italian front.

Photograph taken near Rimini, September 29, 1944, the day before Leese left the Eighth Army.

Myebon, Arakan: Generals Wood, Christison and Leese and Brigadier Kent.

Mountbatten, Slim and Leese.

"THANK YOU, SIR OLIVER."

The Two Types ride again. The cartoonist Jon celebrates the jubilee of Alamein, October 1967.

Oliver Leese and Margie at Worfield.

At Lord's with the Queen.

Leese standing by the de Laszlo portrait of Margie.

Frances Denby.

centuries old monastery of St Benedict, was a formidable gatepost, and Monte Maio the other.

On the left sector Mark Clark was preparing to launch an attack through the Liri Valley, while, so far as Eighth Army was concerned, the heavy fighting by the first Canadian Division in the ruins of Ortona was just finishing – this had been the latest effort to break through on the Adriatic coastline, and the front was quiet except for patrol activities.

5 Corps (Allfrey) held the right sector, and 13 Corps (Dempsey) the left centre. As Leese expected, Dempsey went off almost immediately to command 2nd Army in England. Before he left, Leese had a day with him, visiting forward troops in the snow. He replaced Dempsey with Lt.-General S. C. Kirkman, who had been Monty's chief gunner at Alamein, and had commanded 50th Division at Sicily. The appointment was to prove a great success. Leese possibly underestimated the ability of Lt.-General Charles Allfrey, although Monty found him slow and inclined to bellyache.

3 January 1944. OL to ML.

I have had a day of nothing but long interviews with my head gunner, sapper, etc., and all my heads of services, so I have learned a lot.

4 Jan.

I have asked for a man by name of Bastyan, who is very intelligent and experienced in Q – but has no war service. I hope he will be good. O will soon start asking for people – and so he will have the backing of the PM, he can get from anywhere whomsoever he wants. [Leese then referred to meeting a Polish General, who asked him if he could talk French.] Naturally I got cracking at once: it was a great success, as neither of us had the least idea what the other was saying. My French is now rusty, in addition to being rapid, inaccurate, short of words and colloquial. You would appreciate it.

6 Jan.

I am using the caravan trailer given me by Harry Broadhurst as my sitting room. It will be excellent, though at the moment the furniture resembles a rather low immoral sitting room in Bloomsbury. But David Butter has reached Main, and his first task has been to improve on this.

8 Jan.

O is skinning a lot of his people from here, but I don't [think] it will matter – so long as I can ensure that it does not impair the efficiency of the 8th Army. [This is the first specific sign of Leese's temporary disillusionment with Monty.]

9 Jan.

John G-W should be with us soon . . . He went sight-seeing to Jerusalem
– and he even went to a *thé dansant*! My Poles come to dinner tonight. It
will be a meal of incredible linguistic achievements. I tremble to think
what will happen.

On 10 January Ion Calvocoressi arrived from England – with some of
Leese's clothes that had been at the cleaners, and met Bastyan for the
first time, in Bari, the latter being on his way to take his appointment
as Leese's administrative officer. They shared a room in the transit
camp, on the way up to the Eighth Army.

'He was a delightful man. I liked him at once,' wrote Ion Calvocoressi, 'and both he and Walsh did a tremendous amount to make
Oliver's victories possible.'

'Dricky' Bastyan met Oliver Leese for the first time on 10 January
1944. This was how he described the occasion, years later, in a letter
to Ion Calvocoressi:

I was taken to his caravan by his M.A. [Ulick Verney] and was then
presented to him, the M.A. then leaving us alone. I was immediately
impressed by the General – by his stature – by his cheerful greeting and
by his firm handshake. He said – 'Things are rather bogged down at present
and we must get moving again. The Chief of Staff will put you in the
picture, so go and see him. I know nothing of you personally and hope all
will go well. I should know within a month.' I finished my drink quickly,
said 'good night, Sir' and stepped out of the caravan into a bitter cold
evening and went to the Chief of Staff.

12 Jan. OL to ML.

Saw the Editor of *8th Army News* . . . rather a nice boy really – I trust I
shall have no difficulty with the paper. In most ways it is first-class for the
troops, who much appreciate it, and it does good to morale. We distributed
about a hundred thousand cigarettes today.

22 Jan.

I am having a big problem with Canadian commanders. Harry Crerar[1] is
here and of course knows nothing of military matters in the field, but is
presumably the commander designate of the 8th Army.
    I have since heard that the CIGS has ruled that Guy Simonds is
to go home, so I have to teach Crerar for a time, and then change to
another totally inexperienced commander. Like everything else it
will pan out all right – but one has been completely let in by O – who

---

[1] Lt.-Gen. H. D. G. Crerar (1888–1965), later to command 1st Canadian Army in
North West Europe.

shelved the necessity to teach Crerar, and now runs in behind the skirts of the CIGS, and refuses to take him as Army Commander till I've held the baby – as far as I'm concerned, over all this O has been 4 letters!

The Eighth Army had finally ground to a halt after brilliant victories and lightning advances in fourteen months from Alamein to the river Sangro. The weather was filthy, cold, depressing, the ground deep with mud. The phrase 'Sunny Italy' taxed even the British soldiers' sense of humour.

'The massive Apennines' wrote C. V. Harpur, 'were like a spine which held together the flesh and blood of the entire Italian campaign. From these spring great rivers and ravines running in parallel from the centre to the west. Nature could have provided no better defence system designed to hold off any invader moving either way on a north-west axis.'[1]

The Apennines are about 800 miles in length, in some places attaining a height of nearly 10,000 feet. C. V. Harpur listed fourteen rivers that the Allies needed to cross during the campaign: the Sangro, Volturno, Garigliano, Trigno, Moro, Liri, Rapido, Melfa, Sacco, Perscara, Chienti, Arno, Cesaro, Metauro.

Thus, whenever a river had been crossed, the sappers having coped with the difficulties in establishing bridges, there was always another river awaiting them with the Germans, having retired in good order, facing their opponents in excellent defensive positions yet again. The Germans had had plenty of time to establish their defensive lines: their dugouts frequently possessed every mod. con. including wallpaper. The terrain in general, steep, muddy and wooded, was unsuitable for tanks. Leese quickly became aware of the importance of mules in the campaign.

General Alexander described the Italian campaign as 'a long slogging match'. The challenge it presented, through the long grim grind, was the challenge of maintaining morale. Here Leese excelled. Even more difficult to surmount than the difficulties posed by the terrain and by the enemy were the efforts of the Allied politicians and the British War Office. The penchant for withdrawing troops at a time when more troops were needed was remarkable: at one period, when the Germans were moving 8 divisions *to* Italy, the Allies were withdrawing 7 divisions *from* Italy.

The Germans, for all their excellent defence system , were obviously handicapped by the Italian defection of September 1943, and Badoglio's declaration of war against Germany a month later.

Field Marshal Albert Kesselring, the German commander in Italy

---

[1] *The Impossible Victory*. Brian Harpur (Kimber).

– he had commanded the German forces in the Sicilian campaign –
had not only to cope with the allied forces but also with Italian partisans
working for the Allies. He was admirably fitted to contend with such
emergencies. Of the allied commanders, General Sir Henry Maitland
[Jumbo] Wilson had the sonorous title of Supreme Allied Commander
Mediterranean. He was metaphorically a shadowy figure, and it was
Alexander who was Commander-in-Chief of the Allied Forces in Italy.
To Gregory Blaxland, an officer who served with distinction in Italy,
Alexander's dress and casual elegance conveyed an air of Czarist
Russia.

Mark Clark, commanding the US Fifth Army, was to be Leese's
partner in the campaign. How they were to get on together was
obviously of much importance. Clark was about the same height as
Leese, but much thinner. He was avid for publicity; determined that
his army should have its rightful share of glory, desperately jealous of
the Eighth Army's achievements. One of the most promising of the
young American generals, he had no love for the Britishers, as he
called them, and was not likely to appreciate an Old Etonian with a
Drones Club sense of humour.

Leese had taken over from Monty an already legendary Army,[1]
which, after its successes in the Middle East, had lost its momentum,
and come to a standstill in the mud of the Italian winter. 'I am going
to play myself in!' he had said with his honking laugh to reporters
asking for a statement. He was certainly going in on a sticky wicket.
Now he was putting his own stamp on Eighth Army, building a team
which developed and thrived in the family atmosphere that he was
adept at creating.

Ulick Verney commented on Leese's immense height and breadth
of shoulder, his casual dress and appearance. He set a very high
standard in everything, 'except his own dress, which grows progress-
ively worse as he rises in rank.' He liked to have people round him
who had served him before. He practically never read a document.
Proposals brought to him had to be explained in a few simple words;
then he would accept or reject them. This gave him time to be with
his troops; getting to know his commanders; seeing for himself the
country and its conditions. As an army commander he quickly developed in patience, understanding and political foresight. To an
amazing extent he was without personal ambition and personal vanity.

About this time, Lieutenant John Stimpson of the 12th Lancers, an
old desert hand, tall and lean, 24-year-old son of a Norfolk farmer, joined
Leese's staff as a G3 (Liaison). Like Sidney Kent, he found that there
was no exclusionism, that he was immediately welcomed into the party.

---

[1] But without 30 Corps, 7 Armd Div., 50 and 51 Divs. – and no Australians.

He noticed that Walsh and Bastyan worked perfectly with Leese – outstanding staff officers with complete independence of mind.

Ion Calvocoressi had now been with Leese nearly a year. To him the Army Commander was approachable, informal and unorthodox, especially in dress. He did not suffer fools gladly, using strong and original language when provoked; but he had a keen sense of humour and schoolboy fun. To 'achieve' was his motto in life. He often sent his young staff officers on important missions, with absolute confidence – 'Never frig about on a low level!' he would tell them: 'What have you achieved today, boy?' he would ask when work was over for the day.

To David Butter, Leese was

The most wonderful person to work for and although we were always kept on our toes, we had such fun, and many laughs, and intensely interesting times as he always confided in us.

Graham Lampson, son of Sir Miles Lampson, British Ambassador to Egypt, (later Lord Killearn), who joined Leese's staff later in the campaign, spoke of

a simple outgoing manner, completely natural and outspoken, but totally sincere, and totally involved and interested in those he was talking to on whatever level. His favoured circle developed its own habits of thoughts, its own jokes, its own language: but he remained a good communicator with those outside also. For somebody who seemed immersed in the 'Sandhurst–London District' attitude to professional soldiering, he had a remarkable interest in and knowledge of aspects of Italian history and culture.

Oliver Leese would delight in selecting a mild idiosyncrasy in a person – or even inventing one – and once the fantasy had been developed it would never be forgotten. He loved to tell stories about his staff to visitors staying at his Headquarters. There was the famous *thé dansant* story involving John Green-Wilkinson who, after the liberation of Sfax, had been invited by some families to join their celebrations:

Out came the wine and a wind-up gramophone to which music they proceeded to dance and no doubt we joined in. When I rejoined General Oliver later in the afternoon he wanted to know where I had been. Unwisely, I mentioned the dancing, so with his usual 'snort' in place of a laugh, he announced that I had been to a *thé dansant*.

Here was a delicious fantasy – the ADC who bicycled off to seek a *thé dansant* on the battlefield: wherever John G-W went after that –

Jerusalem, Windsor, Rangoon, it was always, according to Leese, in search of a *thé dansant*.

On one occasion, at dinner in the Mess, David Butter announced that Tommy Trinder was coming out to entertain the troops.

'Oh, yes,' said Leese, his eyes gleaming, 'and what does Tommy Trinder do?'

'Well, he says "You lucky people!"'

'He says *what*?'

'He says "You lucky people"'

'Does he now? Does he? He says, "You lucky people!" How very interesting!'

For the rest of the evening, and not infrequently for the remainder of his time in Italy, David Butter would be addressed and referred to as Trinder by Oliver Leese. Leese himself once said to Lord Tweedsmuir, eldest son of John Buchan, who joined Eighth Army staff as a liaison officer, concerning the leg-pulling in the Mess: 'It helps me to unwind when the work is finished for the day.'

A journalist's eye view comes from Warwick Charlton, Editor of *Eighth Army News*:

> He has no nickname, and his character does not lend itself to one. He told me he realised the immense task before him – that of following in the footsteps of Montgomery. He set about his job quietly. 'I don't like advertisement – that is, personal advertisement' he told me, 'but I realise it is important in modern war, when the whole nation is under fire. It is part of the war effort to let the soldier and his folk at home know who is leading them.'
>
> With all his toughness he was a little afraid of cameras . . . When he spoke he invariably tucked his stick under his left arm,[1] had his hands in his trouser pockers, and rested his left heel on the ground, toe pointing upward as if his legs were too long. His gestures are broad and sweeping. Apparent casualness is deceptive. He gives orders quietly, but they have to be carried out to the letter.

Leese's Eighth Army now consisted of two Corps ready for action, 5 Corps (Allfrey) and 13 Corps (Kirkman). A Canadian Corps, untrained for modern warfare, had been 'wished on' Leese by the CIGS. Even the normally equable Alexander sent an acid telegram to Alanbrooke, asking to be consulted over such matters in the future. He considered Leese would have enough to do without training Harry Crerar and his troops at such a time. The vanguard of a fourth Corps – Anders' Poles – had just arrived.

Leese had been deprived of 5th British Division on arrival, and also

---

[1] In fact he hardly ever had a stick.

had to hand over the NZ Division to Alexander: they were replaced by 4 Indian Division. 78 Division was holding the left of the Eighth Army line.

There were four Corps in Mark Clark's Fifth Army – 2 US, 1 French (Gen. Juin) and 1 British. Horrocks, wounded three weeks before at Salerno, had been succeeded by Lt.-General Richard McCreery as commander of 10 Corps. All told, Clark had eleven divisions ready for the coming battle.

Kesselring's policy was to halt the Allies on the Gustav line of which Cassino was the main stronghold. By mid-January, 1944, he had twenty-one divisions under his command opposed to Alexander's eighteen. Kesselring's skill at improvisation would soon be put to the test, especially as Alexander was now receiving vital information from Ultra.

On 17 January Leese staged a diversionary attack to help Mark Clark, entrusting it to the Canadians who over confidently referred to it as 'the Arielli show'. The 'show' which was under Allfrey's command, was not successful. Several senior Canadian officers lost their jobs after the battle.

20 Jan. OL to ML. (on the subject of publicity).

One wants at all costs to avoid this Monty fetish. How very silly of him to go again in his battledress to the Royal Box. The sad fact is that there is no need whatsoever for him to do this – and it merely alienates so many people.

21 Jan.

Bimbo [Dempsey] went off today.I shall miss him dreadfully. Kirkie comes up to see me tomorrow. I do hope he will do well . . . I think he is the most efficient of them all. Guy Simonds also went home today.I shall miss him. I just can't help feeling sore, as I've got the sticky end every way. All the promises of Archie Nye meant just as much as a bit of paper! While O got it his way out here – and now gets it again at home. But somehow, we'll do the lot in, and the 8th Army will, as before, lead the world. It is better to do so against all odds – and the easy path is no proper road to success and victory.

Tommy Trinder arrived. He is doing a first-class bit of work. He goes round by himself in a jeep, talking and telling stories to the troops. Today he visited gun positions. Then he visited our chaps, had tea with us, and I saw him on my return. If only more stars would come out here it would do a world of good. Ion heard that Leslie Henson was in the Middle East, so we at once telegraphed and have got him and his party especially over to the 8th Army – which is good.

I think Bastyan, my new Q, will make a great success.

Alexander had already told Leese of the Anzio project, and had warned him that in addition to McCreery's 10 Corps, and the 1st and 5th Divisions, which were to take part in the Anzio landing, he might have to lose even more divisions to the Fifth Army. This did not make matters easier for Leese. Many of his divisions were already needing a rest after the heavy fighting up Italy; and he realised that in three or four months he would have to fight his first big offensive battle.

He had three problems. First, much-needed divisions were to be transferred to Mark Clark's American Fifth Army. Second, Monty, with the backing of Churchill and Alanbrooke, was 'skinning the Eighth Army' with continuous demands for outstanding senior officers. Third, he had an inexperienced Canadian Corps to cope with. Leese felt that Monty had shelved the task of teaching the senior Canadian commanders and had to do it himself. Guy Simonds, the one outstanding Canadian general, had been called to England within a fortnight of Leese's arrival in Italy. Leese had written to Major General John Kennedy, Assistant CIGS about his problems, and the latter replied on 27 January:

> I realise only too well the burden that had been imposed upon you for the moment by the numerous changes in command and Staff. But I hope the changes have now come to an end. As I told you in my last letter, we will support you in any objection you may make to further changes. It is all the more important that you should be left undisturbed, as there is so much to be done in the way of getting your various formations into fighting trim.

In the early morning of 22 January, Major General Lucas's 6th US Corps landed on the beaches of Anzio. Churchill described the enterprise as 'hurling a wildcat on the shore'. Lucas, rather than pushing ahead for the Alban hills – and for the next thirty-six hours there was little opposition – spent three days digging in; the element of surprise was lost, and the wildcat had become a stranded whale. Mark Clark's own attempt to break through the Fifth Army towards Frosinone was also unsuccessful after three weeks of arduous effort.

On 26 January, the day of his long talk with Alex, Leese went with George Walsh to see Mark Clark. Leese's first impressions were good. They found him in his caravan 'Young and alive and very friendly. We liked him. It is a pity he had not been taught by O, but he is a character, and I think we will work well side by side.'

Leese was to have an aeroplane. 'With that and the two small whizzers,' he told Margie, 'we shall be allright.'

28 Jan. OL to ML.

David [Butter] and I motored up today in the open car. It is a nice little

Humber. Very easy to drive. Monty had it all the way from Alamein – so it is a great warrior.

He was pleased with his conference room:

A lovely desk, polished table 8 ft × 2½ ft, which folds up by its legs collapsing under it. Excellent folding chairs, up against the walls. Linoleum on the floor and very good red and brown curtains.

31 Jan.

Conference room 'looking like a Victorian sitting room in Bedford Square. The boys were very worried that they couldn't find an aspidistra.'

On 1 February he visited a Gurkha battalion, where his Urdu was taxed to the core, but he felt he was improving. 'I think that even a few words please them.' Kirkie had very much become one of the party: 'I am really welding together a completely new team into the 8th Army spirit.' The same day Major General John Kennedy wrote again to Leese from the War Office, among other things about the Anzio landings:

The results of the 5th Army operations have been extremely disappointing so far. No doubt the difficulties were great, but at this distance it seemed hard to understand why the Germans were given so much time to bring up reinforcements and adjust their dispositions before a heavy blow could be struck.

Apologising for a disjointed letter, Kennedy wrote that he had been interrupted twice: 'Once by General Monty who asked me to send you his love.' Kennedy, who had worked himself to the point of breakdown at the War Office, was at last going on leave for a few days salmon fishing, adding, that while he was away 'Simbo will open your letters.'

On 3 February, Lt.-General E. L. M. Burns took over the Canadian Corps in the place of Guy Simonds. On 5 February he met the Poles and referred to the language problem. It was a weakness that before long he would turn into a strength.

On 7 February, Leese took Ion Calvocoressi with him to Naples.

'It was hell,' Calvocoressi recorded in his diary, 'snowing all the time and when we got into the hills we suddenly came upon a stretch of vehicles, almost 4 miles long, all stuck. This was about 3 o'clock, and I suppose we covered about 2 miles in the next 4 hours, by dint of the General and myself walking up and down the road organizing things, and getting the frequently bogged [down] vehicles towed out by a bulldozer or dug out . . . We fell down lots of times.'

On 11 February Leese met Anders for the first time, and wrote to
ML:

> They hate the Russians even more than the Germans. It is really very bad
> for them, as they have so little future either way. His [Anders'] wife is in
> Poland and he never hears of or from her. To make things really go with
> a swing my *8th Army News* published a post-war Russian map of its
> republics after the war – with no mention of Poland at all . . . I've sent
> some very scathing messages to Charlton.

General Wladyslaw Anders was two years older than Oliver Leese: his
experience as a fighting soldier was comparable to that of Freyberg.
In the first world war he served with distinction in the Russian Imperial
Army. When Hitler invaded Poland in 1939 he was in command of a
Polish cavalry brigade: he had soon found himself fighting both
Germans and Russians. Wounded and captured by the Red Army,
Anders was kept in indescribable conditions in Lvov, later he was
transferred to the Lubianka prison in Moscow. Following the German
invasion of Russia he was released and given the opportunity to form
a Polish army from the soldiers and civilians who had been imprisoned
by the Russians. Anders led his exiles into Persia, where he formed
an army of 75,000: his troops were now ready to fight in Italy.

Anders' ADC, Prince Eugene Lubomirski, was a landowner from
the Lvov area. Following the Russian invasion of Poland, he was
imprisoned as 'potentially dissident' and sentenced to seven years'
imprisonment. On being released from the Lubianka prison, he demanded – and got – from Beria's ADC, a ticket for *Swan Lake*, before
leaving Russia for ever.

After a prickly start to their relationship, Leese and Anders got on
excellently, and Lubomirski, who spoke fluent English and had a
delightfully warped sense of humour, was always on hand if an
interpreter was needed. Leese and Anders spoke to one another chiefly
in French – and this became of unexpected importance.

The American attack on Cassino having petered out early in February, Alexander gave orders for the New Zealanders and the 4th Indian
Division to take up the torch. Major General F. S. (Gerty) Tuker was
wounded, so the brunt of the responsibility went to the New Zealand
war horse, Freyberg. Tuker and Freyberg had been in favour of
bombing Cassino monastery from the air as a military necessity. Mark
Clark inclined to feel that, even if reduced to a heap of rubble, the
monastery would still remain an obstacle, but left the agonizing
decision to Alexander, who decided (12 February) to go ahead with
the bombing, considering that bricks and mortar, however venerable,
cannot be weighed against flesh and blood. Warning leaflets were
dropped, and the bombing began on 15 February. The Indian Division

had been ill-supplied with ammunition, Baad's 90th Panzer Grenadier Division performed meritoriously and Freyberg's efforts failed to command success, so the second battle of Cassino petered out.

On 24 February Ion Calvocoressi wrote in his diary:

General stayed in all day planning. Big things are afoot. [He had been told something of the forthcoming Operation *Diadem* in which the Eighth Army was to move westward.]

25 Feb. OL to ML.

Yes, there are moments when I feel I could wring O's neck. It was a very different game to serve under him, but to serve parallel he certainly does not inspire affection. But still, so long as he wins his battles, it will finish the war the quicker.

We had a great study day on tanks today run by Kirkie in our opera house. It was great fun, produced as a play.

On 28 February Leese attended a conference, run by Alexander, with Harding and Mark Clark, at Caserta Palace. Operation *Diadem* was unfolded. Leese was to smash through the Gustav and Hitler lines, 'and set his armoured might rolling along the corridor of the Liri Valley, with mobility at last restored by the drying sun.'[1] This was to involve transferring the greater part of the Eighth Army up to eighty miles from the east to the west of Italy, without the Germans' knowledge. Leese was delighted at the idea, Clark, cast for a supporting role, was less enthusiastic.

1 March was a day of conference for Leese. After breakfast Kirkman visited him at Main HQ for an hour's discussion on future operations. Then Anders came, with Lubomirski. The discussion was held in French, but there were long interpretations in English and Polish by Lubomirski over technical problems.

By 9 March it had rained continuously for five weeks. On 11 March they were at last on the move, and 'one of the greatest hoaxes in military history' as Warwick Charlton described it, was completed in less than a fortnight. On 13 March Leese set up his little camp in a peaceful glade near Venafro. It didn't remain peaceful for long.

On 15 March the third battle for Cassino started, (Operation *Dickens*) with the New Zealand attack supported by some wildly inaccurate American bombing.

'The General and John Stimpson and Sidney [Kent] went out early to see the bombing of Cassino,' wrote Ion Calvocoressi. 'About 10.30, when we were doing accounts in our penthouse, there was a whistle of bombs

---

[1] *Alexander's Generals*, by Gregory Blaxland. William Kimber.

followed by terrific explosions. David [Butter] flung himself on the ground, and I leapt under the desk. The blast was immense and blew my money all over the place . . . We came out to see desolation. Two caravans upside down, the other 3 badly battered. The chaos caused by 6 × 2000 lb bombs was immense. It was absolutely heart-breaking . . . I felt bitter against the American Liberators, especially when they tried to do it again about ½ hour later.'

When Leese himself returned and saw the chaos he observed urbanely to Ulick Verney, 'Ah, I see our American friends have called.' He then rang up Mark Clark, enquiring, 'Tell me, as a matter of interest, is there anything we've done to offend you recently?' Mark Clark duly apologised and all was well. 'During the bombing of Cassino yesterday,' he wrote to ML on 16 March, 'some aircraft read their maps very wrong and they decanted 10 bombs into Tac – mercifully we only had 4 men wounded . . . All the caravans were damaged – in fact this seemed to be the main target area.' By next day there was an overall improvement, although TAC HQ now possessed only 4 teacups.

On 19 March, Harold Macmillan arrived to talk Polish politics. Churchill had appointed Macmillan Resident Minister, Mediterranean – a position he filled with great distinction, and which set him towards the top rungs of the political ladder – in December 1942. The post carried cabinet rank but Macmillan was not a member of the Army Council. His work involved, among other matters, acting as political adviser to the Allied generals. He had been contemporary with Leese at Eton, but it was in Italy that he really got to know Leese, and was soon to appreciate his ability as a general.

After his talk with Macmillan OL wrote to ML:

I am sorry for them [the Poles]. It is difficult for these men as they mostly come from East Poland. I feel the best that they can do is to settle down and fight here and keep out of politics, and then try to settle things amicably with Russia – when we have beaten the Germans. I also saw Mark Clark – his nice little chief of staff Gruenther. I think I can work with Clark. He thinks that I am a b-y fool. He will have a great awakening.[1]

On 24 March, the third battle of Cassino became bogged down. The wounded 'Gertie' Tuker was going home. 'I shall miss him but he is tired out at the moment. We are sending off the aeroplane with more

[1] Ion Calvocoressi writes: 'Oliver encouraged people to think he was a B.F. and in this way led them on!'

tired officers to Algiers and Gibraltar. I hope they will bring back some sherry.'[1]

27 March. OL to ML.

This new army is terrific, with all nationalities and new troops – some from 1st Army and some from 5th Army – I pray and hope that I can weld it all into the old Eighth Army spirit and framework.

On 30 March, Calvocoressi was out with Leese and Freyberg, and recorded in his diary:

Visited 1st Gds Bde and then went to all sorts of view points, in the most exposed positions, to look at Cassino, the Monastery and Monte Cairo. The monastery is an amazing sight . . . perched on the tip of sheer, cave-ridden cliffs. The approaches to Monte Cairo across the plain, and in full view, are now the most desolate battlefield I have seen. Stunted trees, ruined houses, dead and smelling mules, knocked-out tanks and vehicles, shell-holes and mines. Very grim.

The weather, and Leese's spirits, were now both very much brighter. 'The first real spring day' he wrote on 3 April.

On 7 April there was a 'State Lunch with Mark Clark. Photographer attends.' OL considered himself 'getting like the Garbo'.

Ulick has organised an excellent hut and bathroom for himself, which he believes to be for me. It is like the royal box at Drury Lane. It is known as Ulick's Fox Hole.

9 April.

Easter Service. After which we then had Communion, and I thought so much of you, and prayed so much for you, and for steadfastness, courage and wisdom in the terrific tasks ahead of us.

10 April.

The War Office estimated our requirements on 5 quiet winter months . . . .: I don't feel that I could be civil to the War Office or to O, and all I feel is 'Thank God we've got Worfield.'

---

[1] Ion Calvocoressi writes: 'The trips of tired officers, mostly to Cairo, is another example of Oliver's kindness. Whenever the Dakota [under US Captain Aldworth and his crew] was not wanted, Oliver had the idea of sending tired commanding officers for a week or so in Cairo. The plane took them with one of us boys, returned stocked up with sherry, chocolates, etc., and then go back to Cairo 10 days later with another group and another boy.'

13 April.

Luke Asquith arrived as G3 – 'quite young, was working for the bar when war began . . . I think he'll be an asset here. Speaks good French.'

14 April.

The blossom is glorious.

20 April. OL to ML.

I had 7,000 from all manner of line regiments there, the loud-speakers were good, and I sat them all down in front of me, and I spoke well. It's a difficult new technique – the mass harangue – but I shall learn from it, the men were keen and looked good, and I gave them a pep talk. Went to a Polish sand table exercise in a cellar, with artificial light, no ventilation and all smoking gaspers – it was an efficient show. An interpreter interpreted specially for me. I summed up at the end, and put over a few points, which I wanted to do – I then had tea with them – they will be good.

21 April.

Umberto.[1] Speaks English very well. Was very pleasant and interesting and out to help. We discussed our previous visits to Italy.

As the time for battle approached, Leese moved into top gear. On 23 April he discussed plans with General Kirkman (13 Corps) in the morning. Then he entertained Macmillan and several others to lunch. After lunch, more planning, this time with Dick McCreery (10 Corps). Next a talk with Alex; a conference with George Walsh; a conference with Dricky Bastyan; a talk with Chris Vokes, commanding 1 Canadian Division. Vokes had tremendous admiration for Leese, with four war correspondents; and finally a talk with a brigadier going home.

Activities in the next two or three days included watching a company crossing a river with boats, and enjoying a day on a Honey tank, seeing a tank exercise. He wrote of 'practising crossing obstacles in boats, rafts, ropeways, etc., – there seem to be nothing but rivers and ravines in Italy.' He came across a regular RAMC senior officer whom he referred to as 'all bumph and Old Boy'.

29 April. OL to ML.

Vast *Alfresco* lunch for over 60 including 20 generals – all nationalities, British, American, Poles, NZ, SA, Canadian – Ion did the lunch very well, they helped themselves in the hut and then took the food to tables and chairs under the trees outside.

[1] Son of Victor Emmanuel III and heir to the throne of Italy. After the war became King of Italy for a month, until Italy became a republic following a referendum.

13

CASSINO

'Our task was to break through these powerful defences [the GUSTAV and HITLER lines] frontally. We did this by a carefully prepared operation, for which we had plenty of time to rehearse. Everyone knew exactly what he had to do.'
Letter from Lieutenant General Sir Oliver Leese to General Bernard Montgomery, 11 June 1944

Now that he was to take over the main thrust in Operation *Diadem* with the object of penetrating the Gustav Line through the Liri Valley, it was evident it would fall on Leese's shoulders to fight the fourth battle of Cassino.

This would be his first major battle as an Army Commander. He was getting near the inevitable stage of 'having a baby' as he called it – the feeling of suppressed tension that developed as a battle drew near, that he had experienced as a Corps commander from Alamein to Sicily. But he was now vastly experienced, and, as he would be the first to admit, he had learnt a lot from Monty.

On 1 May he drove back from Alexander's HQ to Tac in the open car. 'It is great fun' he wrote to ML, 'as so many troops now know us and wave on their own – and even whistle to draw our attention to them! It would make some generals of old throw a fit. But in these modern days it is a wonderful tie of friendship.'

3 May.

I saw 8 bns [of Keightley's][1] some practising village fighting. They had taken over part of a partially mined town – turning out temporarily some 40 families – and were doing most realistic exercises.

On 7 May OL wrote to John Kennedy at the War Office:

I have been round the training of all the divisions: it is very satisfactory.

[1] General Sir Charles Keightley (1902–1974). Army Commander-in-Chief of the ill-fated Suez Operation of 1956. He carried out the military operation successfully despite 'the stream of confusing and contradictory instructions' from the Government.

Kirkie has organised his training in 13 Corps extremely well, and his 4 divisional commanders – Russell [8 Indian Division] Keightley [78 Infantry Division] Evelegh [6 Armoured Division] and Dudley Ward [4 Infantry Division] have got first rate shows running. Charles Keightley has done wonders with the morale in 78 Div. This is once again a great division.

8 May. OL to ML.

I got a very friendly letter from O! We now correspond again. It's a queer world.

From now on Leese and Monty were on the best of terms until Monty's death in 1976. Leese's admiration for him would have been seasoned by the happenings of the past four months.

10 May.

Another great day for talks – this morning with Charles Allfrey's[1] and Dick McCreery's Lt-Colonels – some 150 in all – in a lovely wooded glade in the hills, followed by an *alfresco* lunch. It was very well done, and I spoke well. I then came back and spoke to our 40 or 50 8th Army Pressmen. This went well, and they said it was the best briefing they had ever had. Tomorrow I speak to all my Canadian Lt Colonels after lunch – and tomorrow night – WE ATTACK.

It is our first big battle. In some ways rather like Alamein. As soon as the last 5th Army battle of Cassino failed, we took over the line down to the Liri Valley. We kept it secret in the Press, and the Boche was never quite sure what we were up to. It was a terrific task – we shifted the whole axis of the Army from North of the Apennines to the Naples plain. We took over all the British and Polish Divisions – with one or two exceptions. Our ration strength is over 300,000. It is an immense Army. George and Bastyan have been quite wonderful – and all is ready. Our troops are in great heart – all we want is fine weather and a bit of luck. It is a good simple concentrated plan with no frills, and we are all confident, and just waiting – which as always is a trying time. We have got everything well tied up with the French and the Americans and I am confident in the French who fight alongside us. Our Poles are on the right. They are mad keen, and I pray so much that they may achieve without too great casualties. Kirkie has been very good during the planning period, and I hope he will have a great success in his first battle.

10 May. 10 pm in the Mount Royal.

In 60 mins hell will be let loose, the whole way from Monte Cassino to the sea. At 11 pm, 11 May, over 2,000 guns will burst forth. There has been

---

[1] Since 11 March, Allfrey had been under HQ Allied Armies. In August he took command of British Troops Egypt, Lt.-Gen. Charles Keightley becoming GOC 5 Corps.

very little firing, and I hope very much we may get surprise. I think the
Boche is mainly expecting an attack from the sea, and with luck we may
get a tactical surprise . . .

Duncan Sandys is staying with us, and has gone up with Ulick and Luke
Asquith to see the start of the gunfire. I shall watch what I can from my
caravan. Just like Alamein.

I spoke to all the Canadian Lt Colonels this morning, and then after
lunch I spoke to 400 officers from Army HQs and my Army troops . . . I
then motored down towards Cassino in my jeep, and found all the chaps
in great heart. Bernard [Bruce] and Ion went round the divisions . . .[1] I
sent Kirkie a bottle of gin and a box of chocolates. George Walsh had a
great day – making a series of speeches to RAF and American pilots; and
to all the men at Main and also Rear Army HQs. Sidney [Kent] spoke to
all our men up here. And I hope that the whole Army will know what is
our task in the great spring offensive . . .

Lamb is all prepared to make tea all night. Like in the old 30 Corps
days, but I don't think there is much that I can do tonight on an Army
level – except go to sleep.

At 2300 hours, 11 May, the barrage started 'setting an arc of 30 miles
aglow with palpitating sheet lightning' wrote Gregory Blaxland.[2] John
Tweedsmuir remembers:

> There was a silence before the barrage started at 11 o'clock, and then we
> heard the most lovely nightingale song imaginable. Then the barrage
> started with heaven knows how many guns, then, over the noise of the
> guns, the nightingales sang even louder, so that you could hear their song
> above the barrage of the guns.

Soon the fog of war descended, and it was obvious to Leese that some
parts of the battle were not going right. As there was nothing he could
do he went to bed, and when he was called in the morning the situation
was still obscure.[3]

About midday the position was becoming clearer and Leese decided
to visit the commanders of the two assaulting corps. He went first to
General Kirkman (13 Corps), who was optimistic. 4th British Division
and 8th Indian Division had got across the river with their leading
battalions. On 8th Indian front the bridgehead had been pushed
forward several hundred yards. The assault troops of 4th British

---

[1] A good example of how OL trusted very young officers to go and see divisional
commanders.
[2] *Alexander's Generals*, by Gregory Blaxland. Kimber.
[3] Leese was briefed each morning at 0730 on the night's events, usually by Colonel
Sidney Kent, his G1 (Ops). In the evening the day's events would be discussed with
Walsh, Bastyan, Kent, together with administrative problems – petrol, oil, etc. – and
future planning.

Division were held up by minefields and by spandau and mortar fire. The situation was now made more difficult by the fact that the right flank of the Division was within 2000 yards of Cassino and Monastery Hill. Kirkman however was confident that they would get a bridgehead across during the night. Leese left him feeling assured of final victory, but he also had the impression that he would find the Polish Corps back on their start line.[1]

Shortly before all this had taken place, he had written to ML:

> There is a vast smoke screen like a yellow London fog, over the battlefield and drifting back to Tac. Duncan Sandys has just gone off with Ulick in a jeep to see what he can see . . . We have got across the river everywhere – and tanks and anti-tanks are now crossing, so we should be firm against counter-attack and will, I hope, be able to get on this afternoon or tonight. The Poles are fighting a hard battle very well – I shall have to ensure that Anders goes to bed tonight. I suspect he was up most of last night. L is coming to see me this morning, and I think I shall go out and see Anders and Kirkie this afternoon.

The Polish assault on the night of 11 May had been led by General Rudnicki. His was an unenviable task. The Carpathian Division had an unpleasant surprise: a minefield had been laid in March between Albaneta and the small pass at the head of Death Valley. Their attack was soon halted and German counter-attacks mounted. The Poles also met twice as many German battalions as had been anticipated, the Germans inflicting terrible slaughter with mortars and machine guns. Eventually, as Leese had feared, Anders had to order a complete withdrawal and the Poles retreated to their starting line. They had suffered nearly 4000 casualties.

On the afternoon of 12 May Leese was about to set off for Anders' HQ, when John Tweedsmuir arrived with news of the Polish attack – and of their casualties:

> 'When I saw him,' said Lord Tweedsmuir,[2] 'Oliver was in a field of cornflowers. He put out a hand as though to bring me to a halt, and said "Stop!" before I had the chance to tell him anything. He said "let's pick some cornflowers." We picked cornflowers until our arms were full. Then he said "Right! Now tell me about the casualties."'

On his way to the Polish HQ Leese met General McCreery who had come over to find out how things were going. Leese then went on to the Polish HQ, where he found Anders and his staff very distressed

---

[1] Memoirs.
[2] Interview 13.12.80.

because of their lack of success in their first battle. Leese calmed them down, and realising that owing to lack of reinforcements they could only carry out one more attack in the battle, told Anders to hang on to his present positions and be prepared to attack again in a few days' time. Anders had spent the night in his command post, with no sleep, so Leese told Lubomirski to see that he went to bed, and he went away feeling that all would be well.

It was typical of Anders that he ordered the Poles to attack again: and of Rudnicki and his troops that they were ready to do so. The Army Commander's attitude was also typical. Having heard the worst from John Tweedsmuir and having talked briefly with McCreery, he went straight to Anders at the appointed time and consoled him, explaining that far from affecting the overall plan adversely the Polish troops had faced a difficult situation with great valour, that they had learnt much from this first encounter and that the next attack would assuredly be successful. He told Anders not to launch his second assault until he (Leese) gave the signal, which, in the event, was in five days' time.

During the night of 12/13 May the 4th British Division advanced effectively under heavy close range fire. The whole outlook of the battle changed. The French captured Monte Maio (13 May) and drove on towards St Georgio on the Liri river. Leese decided to advance towards Pontecomo and ordered Burns to move his Canadians forward in that direction. Meanwhile seven bridges had been constructed on 13 Corps front, so that troops, guns and tanks were pouring across.

John Williams, a subaltern in an anti-tank battery, originally Worcestershire Yeomanry, which was parked in a mountain village near Cassino, remembers:

> Early in the battle who should honour our humble mess but the 8th Army Commander himself – Oliver Leese – who wished to see the trout hatchery at the source of the Volturno, which was in our area. Afterwards he was good enough to have a drink with us, explaining how the great battle was progressing, in the course of which he included the memorable sentence 'last night the French unleashed the Goums'.[1] The latter were, of course, mountain troops from North Africa, and shinned over the [to us] trackless mountains, to turn up behind the Germans, causing alarm and despondency.[2]

14 May.

We have got several bridges now across the Rapido, and plenty of tanks and have secured a reasonable bridgehead. The French on the left have

---

[1] Ion Calvocoressi remembers that they were 'not unlike the Gurkhas in their methods and inspiring the same apprehension!'
[2] Letter to author 11.6.81.

done splendidly. Our immediate problem is Cassino and the Monastery –
and then the Adolph [sic] Hitler line, which I suspect will be strong.

15 May.

We have strengthened up our bridgehead and got several bridges over the
river, and a nice lot of tanks across. The Boche is hanging on to the most
extraordinary places. I went up to see Anders this morning and I found
him in great heart.

16 May. Major General John Kennedy to OL.

Now *Diadem* has got going we are relieved of a great responsibility vis-à-vis
the Americans . . . The Germans will find it difficult now to free additional
divisions from Italy to meet *Overlord*, however slowly or fast the battle
moves, and your contribution to *Overlord* is therefore already a big one.

16 May. OL to ML.

A good day in our battle – and tomorrow we have another big attack,
which, with a bit of luck, may lead to the capture of Cassino and the
Monastery – it would be wonderful if this were to come off. This, together
with our crossing of the Rapido, would be a great start for the new 8th
Army. It is stiff fighting in the Liri Valley, as it is difficult country. He
has plenty of troops and it is difficult to outflank him.

We've been lucky so far in the weather, and this has made all the
difference – and I hope we can soon clear Cassino, so that we can use the
main road [Highway 6].

On 16 May 78 Division had attacked with infantry and tanks, advancing 3000 yards on Highway 6, so Leese decided, with Kirkman and
Anders, that on 17 May they would carry out a simultaneous advance
towards Highway 6 with the object of isolating the Germans in the
Monastery at Cassino.

One of the soldiers that Leese encountered on 17 May was a West
Indian REME mechanic, Derief Taylor, who was doing maintenance
work on a 25 pdr gun. He was the one black man in the Division, and
had been without sleep for several nights. Suddenly he felt a stick
pushed against his chest. He spun round: an officer, six feet four,
with black moustache and brown twinkling eyes, was regarding him
quizzically.

'Well, I hope you know what you're going,' said Leese, 'because I
don't. *Do* you know what you're doing?'

Derief Taylor, whose passion was cricket, decided to stonewall.

'Yes, sir.'

'Well, can I help?'

Derief Taylor's reply would not have won him a prize for diplomacy.

'No thank you, sir. This requires precision.'

Leese remained unperturbed.

'Well, at least I can get you a cup of tea. Where's the cookhouse?'

Derief, speechless, pointed the way. Leese strode off, returning with two mugs of tea. He stayed and chatted.

'I hope we'll get this lot knocked off by tomorrow,' he said, and continued his tour of the battlefield.

They were to meet again at Edgbaston in 1959; Leese as President of the Warwickshire Cricket Club, Derief Taylor as a famous cricket coach.

17 May. OL to ML.

We had a large attack this morning and we advanced our line some way, but so far we have not entered Cassino, though we have cut the highway behind the town . . . The Poles have fought again today, but they have not had a great success again, which is a pity. However their tails are very high and they may yet bring it off. Kirkie and his people on the other hand have done magnificently. I hope that Burns and his boys [1 Canadian Corps] will do as well.

On 19 May he wrote twice to ML, the first time obviously early in the morning:

The Germans gave out on the wireless that they had evacuated Cassino. In point of fact many are in the town and in the Monastery. We are right round behind them – and so I expect that many simply could not get out – and some undoubtedly would never get the orders to clear out, and they are so good, these Paratroops, that they would go on fighting to the last, unless they received orders to the contrary. In the meantime we are driving on towards the Adolph Hitler line – and with luck will gain control of it either today or tomorrow. It will be a great 8th Army triumph when we can say that Cassino and the Monastery is ours.

His second letter brought news of victory:

A great day, we have broken into the Gustav line and tonight our tanks are on the threshold of the A.H. Line.

Our British troops [4th British Division] entered Cassino and our Poles [12 Lancers] the Monastery – I visited Anders and we drank sweet champagne at 10 am. It was terrific. The success has made up for all their casualties – and the Polish flag flies proudly on the Monastery.

A victory and an advance are a great tonic. I thank God very much for allowing me a victory in my first Army battle.

In later years Leese wrote of the Poles who had fought under Anders:

They had dedicated themselves to the future of their country in this titanic struggle for Cassino. It was their first contribution to the 8th Army, and a magnificent one at that . . .[1]

13 Corps and the Canadians now drove on towards the Adolf Hitler line, and in the evening the line was penetrated in the area of Aquino.

19 May. OL to ML.

A disappointing day – all along the line we have come up against strong defences. Freyberg stayed to tea. I gave him a bottle of sherry and a box of Groppi chocolates.

I have just checked over the draft of my periodical letter to John Kennedy – I think it's a good thing to keep a demi-official channel for correspondence going with them.

21 May.

I went in to see Kirkie in a vineyard. Then up to our new site where we get a first class view of Monte Cairo, the Monastery Cassino and the Liri Valley. It is great to be on the move again.

Mark Clark has laid 4–1 against our crossing the Rapido. As they say at a private school 'Sucks to him!'.

22 May.

A day of waiting today, and tomorrow I hope and pray that the Canadians will break through the Adolf Hitler line – and then we shall have finished with organised lines for a bit – they are expensive to deal with. Anders came in to see me, and while he was here a telegram from L arrived to say that they had awarded him the CB. It was great fun. I gave him my ribbon. He was delighted.

. . . A site in a vineyard with a carpet of poppies and wild lupins. It seems strange to be looking out on Cassino and the Monastery. I hope we may soon move our HQ.

The last week in May brought varied news. On 23 May the Canadians under Burns broke through the Adolf Hitler line. On 24 May 'we built bridges within easy machine gun range – a very fine feat of arms. Alex received the Order of the Bath. In a grey bush shirt with red tabs – his cap with the very red greasy peak – breeches and brown rubber knee boots. He and Macmillan arrived for lunch.' 26 May, 'An hour in bed telephoning all the time this morning. Like Winston I just did not have time to get up and shave.' 28 May, a slow move towards Frosinone: 'So many of our troops are new to the Army, and green to mobile warfare . . . Anders came to tea. A long talk in 8th Army French.'

[1] Memoirs.

Eighth Army French was a child of Leese's fertile brain. During the weeks before Cassino he had been trying to 'get through' to Anders, who, after his previous experiences, he had found withdrawn and unforthcoming. They normally conversed in French, which Anders and Lubomirski spoke fluently, and which Leese spoke reasonably well though with a pronounced English accent. Once, when he wanted to use the phrase 'plenty of room' (for artillery) he said 'beaucoup de chambres' instead of 'beaucoup de place'. Anders burst out laughing and corrected him. This was enough for Leese. Following that occasion, in less serious moments, he communicated with Anders in French liberally spiced with schoolboy howlers. On important matters they conversed seriously in French, often with Ulick and Lubomirski present, but in casual conversation Leese exploited his new language; and in off duty moments he developed Eighth Army French with his ADCs.

On one occasion – it was probably on 17 May, when the Poles were being held up in their second attack, he visited Anders and, after the preliminary courtesies, said '*Mon Général, donnez vos soldats un coup dans la fourchette.*' Anders was for a while silent. Slowly a grin spread over his features. '*Oui, mon général,*' he replied, '*je comprends.*'

Most of the expressions in Eighth Army French were, of course, deliberate howlers – *nous sommes livres dans*; *coulez les haricots*; *n'ayez pas douleur d'estomac*; *il n' y a pas de mouches sur lui*; *juste le travail*; *bien je jamais!*

These frivolities achieved their object: Anders and his staff became more cheerful, more relaxed; the Polish Corps became an integral part of the Eighth Army.

30 May.

I hear that A.L. [Mark Clark] stated tonight on the wireless that he would get to Rome in 5 days. I understand that they have everything prepared for a 5th Army Triumph with A.L. as the Jeanne D'Arc of his era. Well, I only hope he can do it. It will save us a lot of trouble and lives – but if he can't, it will mean a big battle for us both – and then I shall race him to it. I hear from Ulick that each fortnight he sends home to his wife a pair of pants for auction. I told Ulick that you and Crowe had a very poor opinion of my pants and would be shaken to the Corps [sic] if I sent one of my 'sacrosanct' pairs of Holy Wolsey underwear back to you for sale to the Bucklow Rural District Council Works party.

30 May. [2nd letter].

We have a lovely site under oak trees, in a wheatfield – with a carpet of mauve aubretia, and a lovely view over the mountains.

1 June.

A.L. is making desperate efforts to get Rome on his own. I only hope he
will do so, and we can then go North on our own business – but I'm so
afraid he'll bungle it like Cassino – and then we shall have to clear it up. I
believe it would have been much better if he would wait for us to help –
but he is terrified that we might get to Rome first, which is the last thing
we now want to do. I only hope it will not warp his military decisions.

Mark Clark was obsessed by his ambition to capture Rome, and
determined to be the first general since the Byzantine Belisarius, who
entered Rome in AD 536, to capture the city.

Alexander's instructions were loosely framed, but there is no doubt
that the first priority was the pursuit of the retreating German 10th
Army and the consequent capture of many thousand prisoners who
would thus be unable to fight on the second front. The capture of
Rome itself was of no military importance.

Mark Clark's ambition, as Leese had feared, did warp his military
decision. The Americans took Rome and in so doing failed to achieve
the first priority, and Kesselring's troops, past masters at withdrawal
through unoccupied corridors, were able to escape to fight another
day.

It was not in Alexander's nature to keep a tight hold on his subordinates in the manner of Montgomery. As early as 28 May, Churchill had
warned Alex by telegram 'I would feel myself wanting in comradeship if
I did not let you know now, that the glory of this battle, already great,
will be measured not by the capture of Rome or juncture with the
bridgehead, but by the number of German divisions cut off.' This was
fully understood by Alexander: with the benefit of hindsight it is easy
enough to say that he should have kept Clark on a tighter rein.

The Americans entered Rome on 4 June, forty-eight hours before
the D-Day landings on the French coast. Leese immediately decided
to have a look at Rome, taking with him Sidney Kent and two others.
The plane – a Fairchild – took off from a small air strip. The aircraft
had a heavy load and there was a small runway with a hedge at the end.
The American pilot just cleared the hedge, and pilot and passengers had
a hair's-breadth escape from disaster.

Meanwhile, a Leese-inspired signal reached Alexander: 'Congratulations. How thoughtful of you to capture Rome on the Fourth of
June,' to which the Harrovian Alexander replied: 'Thank you. What
is the fourth of June?' Inwardly, Alexander was seething at the golden
opportunity that Mark Clark had preferred to miss. Not until twenty
years later, when his memoirs were published, did he reveal his sense
of grievance:

For some inexplicable reason General Clark's Anglo-American forces never reached their objective, though, according to my information later, there was nothing to prevent their being gained. Instead Mark Clark switched his point of attack . . . If he had succeeded in carrying out my plans, the disaster to the enemy would have been much greater, indeed most of the German forces South of Rome would have been disposed of.[1]

Field Marshal Lord Harding, Alexander's Chief of Staff at the time, wrote of the assault on Rome:

Alexander's style of command has frequently been criticised, but he did hold together, inspire and lead to victory the most conglomerate [nationality wise] army that any commander in history has ever had to handle. I doubt if keeping his commanders 'on a tighter rein' – especially Mark Clark – would have been equally successful.[2]

'There was no chance,' says Lord Harding, 'of completely encircling the German 10th Army, even if Mark Clark had carried out Alexander's intention about which he could not possibly have been in any doubt. If he had done what was expected of him it would in my opinion have made the German retreat more difficult, have inflicted greater casualties from air and ground attacks, increased their losses of material by forcing their retreating columns eastwards on to the more difficult mountain roads and tracks, and possibly have made it impossible for them to reform a cohesive front between Rome and Florence.[3]

The Americans certainly went to town on Rome, which was put out of bounds to the Eighth Army. A major on Kirkman's staff was held up at gunpoint by a white-helmeted military policeman, so was Major Sidney VC, of the Grenadier Guards.[4] Actions such as these were hardly likely to improve Anglo-American relations.

11 June. OL to ML.

I take them [the Press] into my confidence, and so far they have respected that, and put things out sensibly, and do not blare my own activities to the world.

14 June. OL to ML.

We are in Orvieto, Narmi and Terni. We have had to fight hard for them – and I am very pleased with the leading troops. I am very glad I made the thrust on the left bank of the Tiber. AL was tiresome about it. He is very rigid about boundaries.

[1] *The Alexander Memoirs.* Cassell.
[2] Communication to author, 1.4.83.
[3] Communication to author, 1.4.83.
[4] Now Lord de Lisle and Dudley, son-in-law of Field Marshal Viscount Gort.

Inter-Army boundaries and particularly allocation of bridges over the
Tiber caused Harding, as Alexander's Chief of Staff, more difficulties
than anything else in the Italian campaign. Leese was once asked to
compare Monty and Alex as generals to serve under. He replied 'Monty
would tell you exactly what he wanted, and if you slipped up in the
smallest detail he had no further use for you: Alex would give the very
vaguest of instructions, but if you were in difficulties he would always
back you up.'

Monty had written to congratulate Leese on Cassino, and Leese
replied (11 June), Monty having asked Leese for his opinion of the
battle as a whole.

The first phrase was to break through the winter line between M. Cairo and
the sea. The Eighth Army had to assault the powerful defences in the Liri
Valley – firstly, the Gustav Line: secondly, the Hitler Line. Both these positions were strong naturally, and had been fortified for several months by the
Germans. Our task was to break through these powerful defences frontally.
We did this by a carefully prepared operation, for which we had plenty of
time to rehearse. Everyone knew exactly what we had to do. We concentrated
the greatest weight of artillery fire and tanks. In fact, we carried out everything that you had taught us!!; and the Eighth Army went through the battle
with its own indomitable spirit. It was a difficult proposition and the fighting
was very tough, but, as you know, we succeeded.

The American effort from the bridgehead was extremely good; the troops
fought magnificently and with great dash. I think that General Alex timed
the move extremely well; and the proof of the pudding is in the eating . . .

'What a wonderful battle yours has been!' wrote John Kennedy on 16
June. 'Again a thousand congratulations.'

16 June. OL to ML.

There has just been a mass attack on a cherry tree – Sidney up the tree –
John Tweedsmuir on his jeep under the tree, with his servant balancing
David, standing on the top of the windscreen to reach a recalcitrant laden
bough – I directed and the troops cheered.

18 June.

Freyberg and Anders get on very well. At midnight they were patting each
other on the back, talking together in no known language.

On 18 June Field Marshal the Earl of Cavan wrote to Leese, thanking
him for his account of the battle of Cassino:

My dear Oliver,

I was thrilled with yours and the story of Rome. Most kind to find time.

We are under the pepperbox here – and our Chapel (WB) got it at service this a.m. I know no details. It's a silly business as it can't help Hitler's war effort nor delay ours except for loss of sleep. Some of the girls who work in London get a bit short of it, but put in an hour if they can when they get home. I'm thankful to be here now and not at N. Berwick . . . I disagree with the military critics of the Press who will write of yr show as 'secondary' – I think it is and will continue to be the *primary* threat to Germany and Austria. I don't think the Po will stop you – and once over that I can follow with personal knowledge every move . . . These are very wonderful days to be living in – the gradual unfolding of the immense Power of the Allied Nations – backed by the sense of Right.

The wonderful fortitude of the old ladies and few old boys who throng the churches and walk home through the showers of stuff coming down from the AA fire. As also all the working girls laughing and upright – a fine sight.

Meanwhile Parliament goes plugging on with Education – Building Plans – land acquisition and so on and just an occasional soul stirrer from Winston – all very English.

This letter was written on the day that the Guards Chapel at Wellington Barracks was hit by a V2 ('Doodlebug'). One hundred and nineteen people were killed and 102 severely injured. Cavan knew the north of Italy well because he had directed operations of the Italian Army in Northern Italy in 1918.

On 20 June Ion Calvocoressi returned from leave, to find 'the General in great form and looking much better than when I left.' Leese had just taken Perugia and moved up to Lake Trasimene.

20 June. OL to ML.

The Mount Royal is lovely tonight, with carnations, flocks [sic] and lovely madonna lilies. Chocolates which Ion brought back from Cairo, and lovely boxes of Groppi cakes and Turkish delight . . .

21 June a reference to his 'Kesselring' panama hat – presumably so named in celebration of Leese's recent victories. Of a conference arranged for 23 June he wrote 'I am not much looking forward to seeing AL and all his claque – but it has got to be done.'

On 22 June Ion Calvocoressi ate his lunch at the Colosseum. He was 'entertained' by an American loudspeaker blaring out 'GI Jive for the boys'. Leese was more fortunate: 'On the way back to the aeroplane Ulick, Sidney, John Stimpson and I went to see Orvieto Cathedral – you will remember it – black and white Byzantine inside – with more Norman and Gothic arches. Mural painting – Giotto and Fra Angelico – also some very queer frescoes of the Resurrection and Hell by Michael Angelo's teacher.'

23 June. OL to ML.

I wish we had Brad and CG [Patton] here – I can't make myself like AL. He is so entirely out for himself, and though he has a healthy respect for both myself and the 8th Army, he dislikes us both intensely.

He described a visit to the Sistine Chapel. He met Smuts and found him wonderful;[1] visited Perugia and had forgotten how lovely it was; received a Polish Corps badge from Anders; sent affectionate greetings to 'Old CG'.[2]

On 29 June, referring to the new HQ at Lake Trasimene, Ion Calvocoressi wrote 'General Oliver seems to love the new place.' It was probably the most attractive HQ during the campaign. It was Ion Calvocoressi's job to pick each new TAC HQ, which had to have a view:

The General would go out for the day, I would go ahead to find the spot and signal back to David [Butter] and the caravans where to meet me. Then, later, go and find the General.

On 7 July, Monty wrote to Leese from TAC HQ, 21 Army Group:

You chaps have done most terribly well in Italy, and this has helped us no end. I do hope they will not close down in Italy; when you have got a front that pays a really good dividend it is madness to close it down. I have given my views very forcibly to the CIGS. But pressure from America may be too much for him.

This prompted OL to comment on 10 July in a letter to ML

If only they [the Americans] had not done the South of France venture we would have been in Venice by now. I'm sure it was bad strategy.

Monty and Leese were referring to the controversial operation *Anvil*, later *Dragoon*, in which 7 divisions (3 American and 4 French) had been withdrawn from Alexander's forces, in order to support the Normandy invasion and to capture the port of Marseilles.

The operation was first advocated at the Quebec conference in August 1943. It was recommended by Roosevelt in the Tehran conference of November 1943; the idea was warmly supported by Stalin. Churchill strongly advocated what became known as the Vienna alternative, which was that the Allied armies should invade Istria, go through the Ljubljana gap and reach Vienna. Alexander, Harding,

---

[1] Smuts stayed a night at HQ and gave a fascinating after dinner talk on how he saw the world after the war.
[2] ML would have been in touch with Patton, as American officers were billeted at her parents' home, Tabley House.

Leese and Mark Clark all supported this. Had the Vienna alternative
been adopted and had it been successful, then British, French and
American troops would have occupied the Balkans before Soviet forces,
and history would have been written differently: on the other hand
the Allied armies might well have been bogged down in the Alpine
winter. As it was, American shortsightedness and Russian shrewdness
gave no chance to Churchill, and *Anvil* was given final endorsement
on 2 July.

9 July. OL to ML.

I have written to the Archbishop asking for another bishop to come out as
my guest! This must defeat the Army Chaplains department. I have 700
chaplains and they must have a bishop to conduct their religious activities
and give them spiritual guidance. Also no one can get confirmed. [The
Bishop of Lichfield had been out for a few weeks.]

On 14 July, Leese was invited by Juin to the *Quatorze Juillet* ceremony
in Siena. Sidney Kent and Ion Calvocoressi went with him. Leese was
escorted to a makeshift stand, at the bottom of the main square. Then
things went amiss, as he explained to ML:

Everyone waited – and about ½ hour late two motor cyclists drove into the
square at a terrific rate, followed by a jeep, and then a vast limousine with
an enormous American flag on one side and a great huge red flag with 3 stars
on the other. Out stepped Mark Clark, very like Mistinguett. Meanwhile
General Alex, who had been waiting till this eccentricity occurred, came
in next, and was welcomed by Clark and Juin. The 3 then went to the
centre of the Parade, and then they played the National Anthems. They
then inspected the Parade. No one took the slightest notice of me, except
photographers, who quite obviously came and photographed me . . . in the
crowd standing at the salute during the national anthems. This behaviour on
the top of their insolence in Rome, which they put out of bounds to me
and the 8th Army, and the fact that they never asked us to a single
ceremony in Rome, or ever mentioned the 8th Army in any speech – was
over the odds. It is bad for the 8th Army repute. So I walked out on them
in the middle – I sent a telegram to Juin saying I was sorry I had to leave
for operational reasons. But I trust the Americans noticed something.

Leese had undoubtedly been placed in an exceedingly embarrassing
position. Possibly Juin thought that by inviting the senior British
and senior American commander he had acted correctly – there was
certainly no ill will between him and Leese.

Mark Clark gradually mellowed; success brought a more mature
outlook; Leese came to respect him for his military ability and the two
kept in touch after the war. General Mark Clark wrote affectionately
of Leese in a letter to the present writer (29.1.80):

He was a fine officer, a good strategist and made friends easily. We got along beautifully and I admired his soldierly qualities and his battle leadership.[1]

On 15 July OL wrote to ML that he had made twelve speeches in the last twenty-four hours; that peaches were good for his voice; adding 'Old CG [Patton] must be having a great run round France.'

In a second letter to ML on 15 July OL wrote:

Ulick had a Fox Hole opening ceremony last night. I enclose the invitation to open his new caravan! Very well planned one. Too many drawers, though, and we will have opportunities to lose even more papers! We call it the Mobile Gas Chamber, partly because his official post is G2 Chemical Warfare! and partly because of what he usually talks . . . He gave a great party and everyone laughed a lot.

16 July. OL to ML.

A great day – we have entered Arezzo, and our tanks have passed through and crossed the Arno. It has been a very model little battle, and it has come off very well, according to plan.

20 July.

George [Walsh], Ken [Ray], Frank Siggers [Signals] and Donald [Prater – G1 Plans] came to lunch. Then Charles Keightley, Burns and Anders came, and we had a conference in 8th Army French. I suddenly realised that I was wearing my Kesselring straw hat whilst on the table was a flowered chintz parasol brought by Bernard [Freyberg]. The conference took place at a card table, on deck chairs outside the caravan, all in French – we thought that the Staff College could never have imagined such a conference. Lubomirski says that I have ruined Anders' French since Cassino.

On 21 July, Oliver Leese wrote that the Poles were very proud of the capture of Ancona. 'I met Piers Legh [Equerry to the King] – out on a visit. He comes to stay with me tomorrow night.' [This was to prepare for the King's visit a few days later.]

On 21 July, General John Kennedy wrote again:

I was very glad General Alex was here to plead his own case when we were reviewing the availability of forces to continue the battle in Italy. I am sure he realised we were strongly on his side and have done and will continue

---

[1] Mark Clark, in a letter to Lord Killearn (8.1.80), wrote: 'I'm so sorry to hear of the passing of Oliver Leese. He was a magnificent soldier and I valued his friendship. If you can contact any of his loved ones, tell them of my deep sorrow and deep admiration for him.'

to do our utmost to get him every man we can. [As Alanbrooke was often inveighing against Alex in his diary, Kennedy may have been trying to smooth things over and hoped that Leese would pass on the message.]

The letter ended in a lighter vein:

Did you hear how de Gaulle was advised to call on 84-year-old Pershing – 'Now General, tell me, how is my old friend Marshal Pétain?'

On 23 July, Leese visited the Polish troops, with whom he felt so involved. He wrote to ML that they were 'much younger and in many ways of finer physique than they were before the Cassino battle. So many [of] them bore the marks of their sufferings in prison in Russia. The new ones are deserters and prisoners from the Germany Army.'

14

KING'S GENERAL

*There is nothing harder in life than succeeding to a place held by
a very distinguished and successful man. When you succeeded
General Montgomery you found yourself in this traditionally difficult situation. I think you can be assured that you have carried on
and strengthened his work.*

Harold Macmillan to Lt-Gen Sir Oliver Leese,
20 September 1944

*Sir Oliver's racy informality, the clarity of his presentation, the
scope of his discourse, and his abounding confidence made an
impression that his audience were unlikely to forget.*

Canadian Official History

The visit of King George VI to the Eighth Army in Italy came as a
much needed fillip. The success of the Cassino campaign was quickly
forgotten by the public; there was brief excitement following the
capture of Rome, and then the Italian front was largely forgotten
during the blaze of publicity attending D-Day and the progress in
France of Operation *Overlord*.

The King, who had travelled under the pseudonym of General
Lyon, arrived at Alexander's HQ near Viterbo, overlooking Lake
Bolsena, on 24 July. It was a hot day, and an awning was necessary to
provide some shade for the King's caravan.

This is how Leese described George VI's visit:

27 July.

I have not written for two days as we have had the King with us. He
thoroughly enjoyed himself – was most cheerful – and the visit was the
greatest success. He loved his caravans with their glorious view, and was
most comfortable.

We were lucky, as the Indians fought a good little battle about 6 miles
away. He had a wonderful view, first from an OP [observation post] in
Arezzo and then from his bath, while the Grenadier band played just

behind his caravan. He was thrilled. Few Kings in these days can have watched a battle from his bath to the strains of martial music by his own guards. [OL was showing more enthusiasm than regard for syntax.] On 25th I went down to lunch with Alex and I was presented to the King, who was most charming and called me Oliver and could not have been nicer. We then took him by air in Jumbo's luxury aircraft all upholstered in blue leather and carpets. We went to Perugia and met Dick McCreery and motored through large numbers of cheering British and Indian Troops. He stopped several times and talked so nicely to officers and men.

He knighted Dick [McCreery] after tea. We then went to the OP and then here. Alex came to dinner and Dick.

Ion had laid on an excellent dinner. Whitebait from Lake Trasimene. Some of our own fat geese. A sweetcorn cob. Flowers and trails of green decorations all over the table, and huge baskets of oranges, plums and pears. He stayed talking till midnight – and enjoyed himself. [Leese had introduced him to Eighth Army French].

Next day was a long one. We started at 8.30 a.m. with Kirkie, and drove through many British, Indian, Canadian, NZ and SA troops, to say nothing of our Basuto boys who greeted him with loud 'WOOS'. He had a very long drive, but we sustained him with tea and sherry in the middle. [As no spoons were available, Ion Calvocoressi thoughtfully proffered a corkscrew, laughingly accepted, for the King to stir his tea.] He had two parades. At the first he gave two V.C.s, to Capt. Wakeford and to our friend Fusilier Jefferson. At the second he presented the VC to the Indian [Sepoy Kamal Ram] who won it on the Rapido. Vic Cowley, my pilot, then took him in my whizzer[1] to Siena, where we boarded Jumbo's aircraft once more. It was a great whizzer flight. 14 of them! We then flew to Castiglione, on Lake Trasimene, where I presented my Army HQ's brigadiers, and then we had a great parade of the Poles. 1000 of them. They were magnificent. Beautifully turned out and so proud and confident in themselves. They marched past, with that wonderful Prada goosestep – it was most impressive. In the morning the King knighted me at TAC. I knelt bareheaded with my right knee on a small stool. He touched me on both shoulders with his sword and then shook me by the hand. I put my hat on and saluted. It was wonderful to be knighted in the field, and I was very proud. A wonderful week for me.

When we came back in the evening it was nice and early, and he came and had a quiet tea under the trees in the cool. He enjoyed it as it had been a very hot day – and when passing troops he sat up on a cushion at the back of the motor so that all could see him well. He then had a bath and did some writing. Then some Brigade officers came in to meet him. Charles Haydon – Andrew Scott – Erich Gooch – George Burns. Bob Coats – Jocelyn Gurney – [Derek] Cardiff – John Nelson – who was Lascelles's Coy. Commander when he was captured – Leveson, whom the King specially asked to see. Sosnowski and Anders came to dinner. We had the Polish orchestra to play and also the Pipes of the Scots Guards. We made the band play 'Lili Marlene' – three times. It

[1] Auster two-seater liaison aircraft.

is now well known as my favourite tune. We also made Anders sing his folksong of Lwow – and the King and I sang the chorus in what we called Polish![1] He must have been enjoying himself to sing at dinner, and quite early during the soup. This morning I talked military matters to Anders and Erich Gooch, and then the King went off with Dickson for a day with DAF. I am glad to say that the battle made good progress while he was here, and we are within 8 miles of Florence . . . I drove the King practically all the time in the open Humber. It must be the first time any Army Commander has driven his King.

Oliver Leese's driving was not always plain sailing. Leslie Mavers, who was driver for Monty and then for Leese, wrote:

When he parked on a slope, we always had to find a rock or something to put under the rear wheel, so we could take the handbrake off. He had the habit of starting off with the brake on, realising something was wrong, releasing it and making the car leap forward. He did this in Italy when King George VI was sitting high up on the back. His feet went up in the air which nearly sent him head over heels over the back. His Majesty laughed and said 'Are you trying to kill me, Oliver?'[2]

The visit had been a great success. 'In my experience,' wrote Piers Legh to OL (30 July) 'I have never known the King enjoy a visit more than on this occasion.' On the same day, OL wrote to ML, 'We have also sent him a further glossary of Eighth Army French. He enjoyed that.'

During the first fortnight in August there was a variety of matters to write home about. Keightley, the new commander of 5 Corps 'is going to be a first class corps commander – young, keen and full of inspiration.' Ulick and Ion had taken Alex and Harding to see a number of paintings, including Botticelli's *Primavera*.[3]

'Florence is now an open city. I wish we could get on quicker.'

David Butter, who had developed a mild form of polio, had been succeeded as ADC by Graham Lampson. Leese had been lent a 'long, low, sleek, black open Fiat which Mussolini used to drive in for ceremonies and parades.'

Lt-General Sir George Gordon-Lennox remembers him about this time:

He sent for me in about July/August of 1944. He was sitting in a tin bath of about 2–3 inches of water in it with a drink in his hand. Having given me one he set himself the task of trying to persuade me that it was time I moved to

---

[1] The chorus had been written phonetically for them.
[2] Letter to author 26.2.81.
[3] They had been hidden from the Nazis in Sir Osbert Sitwell's house at Monteguffoni, South of Florence, and were leaning up against the walls in a barn.

another job – I had commanded my Battalion for nearly two years. He failed – and I continued on for another space![1]

It was early in August, while the Eighth Army was fighting on the outskirts of Florence, that Leese and Kirkman came to consider the possibility of a switch to the Adriatic. This was in fact the switch that was eventually carried out under the code name Operation *Olive*.

Leese wrote in his memoirs that it seemed both to him and to Kirkman that with their attenuated forces it might well be impossible to continue with the original plan of forcing a way through the mountains direct from Florence with the Eighth Army on the right and the Fifth Army on the left and then break out northward into the valley of the Po. The country between Florence and the Gothic line[2] was difficult, and it was doubtful whether, with the limited number of divisions available, it would be possible to carry out a successful frontal assault and afterwards have sufficient strength to exploit success. The battle should obviously be fought where Eighth Army's advantage of tanks, guns and aircraft could be exploited. It was therefore decided to transfer the main thrust to the sector along the Adriatic coast.

In a communication to the author, (3.12.81) General Sir Sidney Kirkman recalled that during his discussions with Leese they considered the possibility of this switch, quoting relevant entries from his diary:

3 Aug. Took the Army Commander up to an OP in Casciano but visibility was very poor and we saw little. Whilst there, discussed at some length future policy, after which he went off to see Alex.

7 Aug. Am not happy about plans particularly in view of the fact that the enemy has strengthened his forces on our immediate front, so rang up the Army Commander and talked in veiled terms and also wrote to him.

8 Aug. Flew to Siena aerodrome intending to put my views to the Army Commander for half an hour before John Harding arrived, but was asked to stay and put my views and ended up by staying for a long discussion and lunch. After much discussion I think we more or less brought John Harding round to our point of view.

10 Aug. Summons to TAC 8 Army now near Siena, to see the Army Commander and arrived just before Alex left. He took me aside and gave me the whole situation. The plan is entirely according to my suggestion, though not necessarily for that reason. The only snag, and I'm afraid it is perfectly logical is that 13 Corps will go under the command of 5 Army.

It would appear from General Kirkman's account that it was conse-

[1] Leese wanted him to command a Guards Brigade.
[2] Originally known as the Pisa–Rimini line.

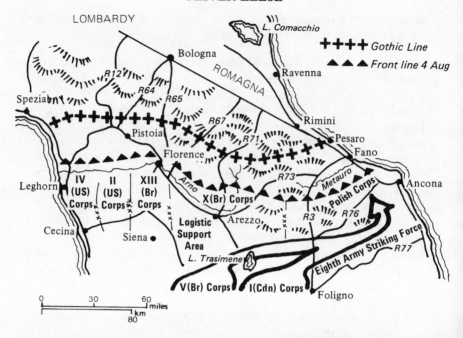

PLAN OLIVE suggested by Leese, 4 August 1944

---

quent upon his discussions with Leese that the latter advocated the
switch plan when he met Alex and Harding at Orvieto airfield, on 4
August.

> 'When the switch to the Adriatic was agreed,' wrote General Kirkman,
> 'Oliver Leese must have been delighted to be well separated from 5th Army
> and to get away from the inevitable wrangles and the unpleasant spirit of
> competition between the two armies, which was always encouraged by
> Mark Clark. I do not know if this was a factor influencing Oliver Leese's
> views; it was not a factor which I put forward.'[1]

It is unlikely that Leese would have been influenced by the prospect
of being eighty miles further away from Mark Clark, and Kirkman

---

[1] Communication to author, 3.12.81. In his biography of Mark Clark, Martin Blumenson states that Leese advocated that Kirkman should go under Clark and that Clark
thanked Leese warmly.

would have known it to be probable that, as commander of 13 Corps, he would himself be temporarily under Mark Clark's command, but he certainly appears to have put the long term strategy before his own personal likes and dislikes. It should be recorded however that Lord Harding does not agree 'that Oliver and more still Kirkman were entirely objective in putting forward their proposals.'

On 7 August, Leese wrote to Major General John Kennedy, explaining his reasons in favour of the switch; and on 12 August he wrote to Kennedy again, stressing that the US Fifth Army thrust from Florence, and the Eighth Army thrust along the Adriatic were coordinated. Alex, he said, had assured him that the transfer of 13 Corps to Fifth Army was a purely temporary measure.

Returning to the immediate future, he wrote that the idea was to give the impression during the next two weeks of an immense build-up, both American and British, in the Florence area; then, at a moment selected by Alex, after the launching of the Adriatic Ops., Fifth Army would launch the offensive from Florence.

The Adriatic thrust was to be the primary Army Group effort, but if the enemy weakened on the Florence front, that thrust was strong enough to assault the main line and advance in the direction of Bologna.

The plan was for the Poles to seize high ground north west of Pesaro; the Canadians to advance west of Pesaro, then strike north to Cattolica; 5 Corps were to attack the Gothic Line on the left of the Canadian Corps, then along the inland axis west of Rimini.

'This is a very worrying time for the Poles,' wrote Leese, 'owing to the many repercussions of the Russian advance into Poland . . . It is difficult to know what to believe. It is naturally, however, very worrying for the Poles. They hate the Russians. Their wives and families are in Poland now, and they are in constant dread of what may happen. On the other hand they are good soldiers and in this theatre are keen to defeat the Germans. So I hope all will be well.'

So the switch went forward and the mountain roads were thick with traffic.

On 17 August, OL informed ML that he had 'made 5 speeches and drank 6 glasses of lemonade'. The speeches were made at Folligno, to battalions of the 4 British Division. Lieutenant Cyril Golding of the 2/4 Hampshire Regiment, remembers him speaking to them in a large field:

The troops all liked him for his sincerity – well who wouldn't? He said the same kind of thing that was in the printed message – 'Swiftly and secretly once again, we have moved right across Italy an army of immense strength and striking power – to break the Gothic Line.

'Victory in the coming battles means the beginning of the end for the German armies in Italy.' Well, after all you've been through, that kind of thing doesn't half buck you up.[1]

Leese was staying for a day or two in the Grand Hotel, Rome, and on 18 August wrote to ML

[writing] in a vast sitting room – the Royal Suite with pile carpets, tapestry, painted furniture and vast mirrors. A great contrast to the caravans. Goering and Hitler were in this room. It is said to have microphones concealed all over it! When Hitler was here he had 700 police guards in the hotel. At a black market restaurant signed the vicitors' book: it was very interesting – Goering, Goebbels, Ciano, Kesselring, Funck and all their wives, headed by Frau Goering. It must have been an extraordinary racket.

On 21 August, in reply to a letter from OL, John Harding wrote:

The C-in-C and I are in full agreement with your conception of the plan, and it is my belief that 5th Army are now so too. I myself believe that your penetration into the Po Valley and subsequent pursuit may well prove to be one of the culminating decisive battles of the war, and I look forward with great confidence to a brilliant victory for the Eighth Army.

On 22 August, Patch's Seventh US Army landed in the South of France. This was the beginning of the controversial Operation *Anvil/Dragoon.*

Leese had more distinguished visitors to receive. The first of these was Alanbrooke, the CIGS, who noted in his diary for 23 August:

We then drove up to Oliver Leese's HQ when we had lunch and discussed his forthcoming offensive. Met Walsh his BGS[2] and also Batton [Bastyan] his Chief Q.

On 24 August, OL wrote to ML:

What wonderful news – Paris and Marseilles, and Roumania out of the war.

In the second letter he wrote:

As the whole world knows we have sent American and French divs. to this South of France venture – a venture which may or may not have been

---

[1] Interview 7.8.84.
[2] Major General Walsh was at this time Leese's Chief of Staff.

right. Only history can tell. Personally I think it was an American political decision to gain American limelight. They found the Press and photographs an irresistible attraction.

Meanwhile, Leese was still optimistic. 'Gentlemen, we march on Vienna!' he told his battalion commanders in an eve of battle address. 'See you on the Po' said Charles Keightley to the officers of 2nd Armoured Brigade.

On 25 August, the day the Gothic Line offensive opened, OL released the news to ML that 'a pansy colonel' had lost his (Leese's) woolly. He also referred to the fact that Mark Clark had not been given the Army Group in Southern France.

It is silly as he would have done it well. Both he and Juin are full of experience and energy – and yet they are passed over.

Leese was not the man to bear animosity for long.

Ion Calvocoressi's diary for 25 August refers to another distinguished visitor – Winston Churchill, who had spent three days at Alexander's HQ:

The General and I went down to Jesi airport to meet him . . . The PM arrived with General Alex at about 6 p.m. and a good crowd greeted him. We went on the long and dirty drive back to our HQ. He loved the view, the caravan, etc., and was very pleased that we were so near the front. We had dinner fairly late, and he was in terrific form (on whiskey, champagne and Kummel). He talked on all sorts of subjects, de Gaulle, Stalin and Molotov . . . Winston was all on our side re the absurd South of France invasion and said Marshall was very stubborn . . . The barrage started at midnight and he was thrilled by it, and sat up till after 1 a.m., watching the flashes and smoking his enormous cigars.

26 Aug.

Winston soon appeared [continued Calvocoressi]. He had a bottle of white wine for breakfast and champagne for lunch. Gen. Alex took him out all day, and he returned in the evening very tired, but thrilled, having seen every description of fighting.[1]

Dinner was even more interesting. He covered a wide range of topics [including] his new name for the Conservative Party after the war – the National Party, which he hoped Bevin would join.

26 Aug. OL to ML.

A terrific day. We launched our attack last night with 4 divs. It was an

---

[1] 'At last – the pleasant sound of musketry,' Churchill had observed earlier in the day.

almost complete surprise – and we are advancing strongly all along the line. I hope we shall be in contact with the Gothic Line tomorrow. The PM is still with us in great heart. In fact he is enjoying himself so much that I think he will stay a second night. John Stimpson has taken him out to see the battle with L. He is a wonderful man. He goes off in the open car regardless of the appalling dust . . . We had a lovely bathe on the way to meet him. He then asked to come back in the open car, and we got full of dust again. He thoroughly enjoyed his caravans and bath. We gave him just the same as the King. Conference room as sitting room. White cottage bedroom. A large bath in the pent house. He was in great form at dinner, where we sat on very late. He told us many stories and much of great interest. We then sat out – a glorious starlight night – and he was thrilled to see the barrage open. In some ways the flashes that rent the whole sky reminded me of Alamein. This morning a battery of camera men taking the PM, L and I with a map of the battle. Then he went off for the night.

Meanwhile the Crown Prince Umberto and 3 Italian officers came to lunch. I must admit I quite like him. He is very civil – and most interested in the Italian troops. I will send this back by the P.M. so I hope you will get it soon.

27 Aug.

Another great night with the PM who left us this morning. He was all the better for his visit – He went out with L yesterday and went well up to the front line, in fact on to ground shortly captured. Luckily he was not shelled or blown up on a mine! L showed him an infantry attack with tanks – done 1500 yards away. He had great welcome from the troops, and also from Italian civilians, whose village had been bombed, shelled and liberated that morning. He is very interested in our front and is all out to help us compete with this wholesale emasculation of our front, in order to start the South of France venture. We shall move on again tomorrow.

Major General B. M. Hoffmeister, commanding 5 Canadian Armoured Division, felt that Leese knew precisely 'what was going on':

During the battle . . . I received messages from him showing that he was following the battle in detail and adding encouragement when it was needed. It was somewhat unusual for a divisional commander to receive messages directly from the Army Commander, and appreciated very much indeed.

2 Sep. OL to ML.

We have broken the vaunted Gothic Line in 3 days – a great triumph, and all done by surprise. Secrecy – efficient movement, strength in concentration, simplicity in planning, speed and ruthlessness in execution. I hope to send this letter back by Attlee.[1] He spent last night with us. We all liked him – quite a sense of humour and all out to be friendly.

3 Sep.

We have moved forward; and are looking down direct on the Gothic Line.

5 Sep.

This campaign is a hard row to hoe. It is the most difficult country in Europe, and yet we always get troops and equipment taken away from us for elsewhere. We have done all our fighting on a very narrow margin of relative strengths – I suppose it is all the more satisfactory to achieve.

Things have not been easy with L and particularly A since I decided not to go on slogging opposite Florence. I am sure I was right, and we've been partially vindicated since we've broken into the Plains, and I think there is disappointment. They don't realise what we are up against and that it takes time.

To split open the German front in the drive to the River Po was the task of the 1st Armoured Division. It was commanded by thirty-seven-year-old Major General Richard Hull, who had been one of Leese's students at Quetta, and was later to become CIGS. He had 300 tanks – Shermans and Stuarts – to achieve the task.

On 3 September the River Foglia was crossed; an attack on San Savino (5–6 September) met with only moderate success. Leese was presented with a formidable problem – to pause and gather his army together for a further massive attack or to go forward with an exposed flank. He chose to pause: it was the right choice.

Alex called on Leese on 7 September, after a night of heavy rain. He agreed with Leese that several days were necessary in order to gain the impetus to attack the Coriano bridge and gain entry into the plain.

13 Sep. OL to ML.

1000 guns heralded the start of our new advance. Mr. Amery[2] was thrilled – a pleasant little bore, dapper with a lucid and clear brain for a pedagogue.

16 Sep.

We are in the middle of the hardest battle since Alamein and Cassino. [Ten divisions were facing them].

On 19 September he was able to write to ML 'We have forced the Gothic Line and started to break out into the Po Valley.'

[1] Attlee was a first cousin of George Walsh. Attlee as a Major in the South Lancashire Regiment during the Suvla evacuation [Gallipoli] would have been confronted with similar problems to those that Leese faced at Dunkirk.
[2] L. A. Amery (1873–1955). At this time Secretary of State for India and for Burma.

Harold Macmillan, acting in the vague yet nonetheless responsible capacity of Resident Minister Central Mediterranean, had seen a good deal of Leese since the latter had taken over command of the Eighth Army. In a conversation with the present writer (13.11.79) Macmillan said that Leese was an example of a certain type of brilliant Englishman who wore a mask of stupidity to cover an astute mind. 'Oliver,' said Macmillan, 'talked like a Wodehouse character in the Mess; but I quickly spotted the brilliant mind behind it all.'

At the end of a brief visit to TAC HQ, Macmillan wrote to Leese (20 September)

My dear Oliver,

I do not think I have ever enjoyed any two days as much as those which I spent with you. It was indeed good of you to give me so much of your time.

It was a wonderful experience to see the whole battle line and such a large number of formations of various armies and nationalities. You must be proud of the way in which they are all welded into a single team with a spirit of pride and mutual affection.

There is nothing harder in life than succeeding to a place held by a very distinguished and successful man. When you succeeded General Montgomery you found yourself in this traditionally difficult situation. I think you can be assured that you have carried on and strengthened his work. I do my best to preach to all I see here and with whom I communicate at home some account of what the armies in Italy have achieved. *But nobody who has not seen the ground can really appreciate the true story.*[1] Some day it will become part of military history and the campaign will rank very high both for the skill of the commanders and the valour of the troops. In that story Eighth Army will hold its true place.

23 Sep. OL to ML.

We took out Harold Macmillan in a cluster of jeeps to San Marino. It was the greatest fun. We went up along some of the most awful roads – passing masses of traffic. We saw parts of every division in the Army. We talked to many and waved to all: and everyone was in terrific heart.

Leese and Macmillan were given a Ruritanian reception in the fairytale kingdom of San Marino by the two Governors, who appeared, though never together, in tail coat and top hat. Macmillan said he thought they shared these articles between them.

24 Sep. OL to ML.

I took Harold Macmillan round the Gothic Line this morning. He did not

_____
[1] Author's italics.

in any way realise what we had been up against, so I am very glad he came.[1]

Macmillan himself wrote of Leese in his diary for 23 September:

He is indeed a very popular figure and I told him that he conducts the whole war like an election campaign. It is a remarkable contrast with the last war. Then a general was a remote Blimpish figure in white moustache, faultlessly tailored tunics, polished boots and spurs, emerging occasionally from a luxurious chateau and escorted as a rule in his large limousine Rolls by a troop of lancers. Nowadays an Army Commander is a youngish man, in shorts and open shirt, driving his own jeep, and waving and shouting his greetings to the troops, as he edges his way past guns, tanks, trucks, tank-carriers, etc., in the crowded and muddy roads, which the enemy may actually be shelling as he drives along.

28 September came the great news:

I am to be an Army Group Commander – a Commander in Chief – with a Union Jack! Starting in India, under Mountbatten, to Command the British Armies in the final fight against the Japanese. So we start and end the war in India. It's a wonderful command in war time, and I pray for strength and wisdom and guidance to carry it through.

Gen. Alex told me this morning on the beach. He was so nice about it, and said I was the only person. George is coming, also Sidney, Ulick, John Green-Wilkinson, John Stimpson, and old Lamb, who said that all said and done he might as well spend the war with me as anyone else.

Colliton, Bryant and others are being asked now. We shall come back to England by air this week – and I hope we may get a few weeks in England – oh, it will be lovely to see you again! . . . I am thinking of taking Dricky and Ken Ray. So the old firm will start forth together.

29 Sep.

It is amazing how everyone wants to come to India with us. It shows a very fine spirit in the sixth year of the war. We have well over 30 going with us now. We were alone last night and Ken [Ray] made a most touching little speech and they all rose and drank my health. I shall miss the friendship of the 8th Army.

Leese handed over to Dick McCreery on 1 October 1944. 'I am most grateful to you for having left me such a splendid machine,' wrote the latter, and it was now for McCreery to carry on where Leese had left off. The campaign was to continue until virtually the end of the war

[1] Macmillan's visit to the Gothic Line was made four days *after* he had already expressed awareness of the enormous difficulties encountered by Eighth Army.

in Europe; the Eighth Army ended its existence as such the day before the entry into Vienna, and was redesignated British Troops Austria. Mark Clark's assertion that the Eight Army always lagged behind the Fifth is hardly borne out by the Allies' losses during the Italian campaign: British Commonwealth 148,000, US 119,000, other nations 46,000.

*

The evidence is that Operation *Olive*, the switch to the Gothic Line, was fully justified.

'After all,' wrote General Kirkman, '5 Corps reached the Po Valley long before the 5th Army; the enemy was forced to split his forces, thus reducing the strength of his resistance at any one place. The point really was, could we have got through the mountains more quickly with a concentrated effort north of Florence? I doubt it, chiefly because in the mountains I fought in, it would have been impossible to use a greater concentration of troops; the roads and lines of communication were indequate, and, having got to the front, it was difficult to get wheels off the road, hence impossible to deploy all the divisional artillery, and for artillery regiments in action, and infantry battalions holding the front in frightful weather conditions, it was often necessary for their transport to be parked 40 miles in their rear, and of course tanks were useless.[1]

Oliver Leese, often his own severest critic, had no doubt about the success of the switch:

The 8th Army achievement was a great one. Firstly, to move an entire army across Italy secretly in two weeks and completely up to time; secondly, to gate-crash the powerful Gothic Line defences at very small expense and before the enemy was ready; thirdly, to defeat 11 German divisions in sustained battle and to break out into the plains of Lombardy.[2]

Two hundred and thirty miles in nine months does not compare with the 1500 miles in six months achieved by 30 Corps in the desert. However Leese was always fighting three enemies – the Axis forces, the weather, and the topography of the country.[3] It was a 'slogging match' that featured innumerable rivers, blown bridges, unscalable mountains; tracks not wide enough for private cars, let alone tanks; seas of mud; sloughs of spongy earth, everything to favour defence, nothing to help attack by armies often emasculated by Whitehall and Washington. Above all was the continual searing battle to maintain morale.

[1] Communication to author 3.12.81.
[2] Memoirs.
[3] Field Marshal Alanbrooke often spoke of these 'three enemies'.

'General Leese,' wrote Luke Asquith,[1] 'kept nearly all the good parts of Monty, almost the greatest of which was briefing everyone down to the lowest level before set battles. The preparation for these battles was meticulous and sometimes awe-inspiring, but the public light was shining more and more in other places. Monty himself had been brought to a very smart halt at the Sangro River, and it was not General Oliver's fault that progress up the mountainous Italian countryside was slow. I often was amazed, not that progress was so slow, but that it was as fast as it was, with an experienced German Army opposing in an ideal defensive country.

Monty took with him not only his personal staff, but all the front line senior staff officers – quite rightly of course. General Leese's staff nevertheless coped in the next few months with battles longer than Monty had yet faced, and coped extremely well.'

A last glimpse of Oliver Leese as Commander of Eighth Army comes from General Chris Vokes, commander of 1st Canadian Division, who first met him shortly before the invasion of Sicily:

I next saw him after he had assumed command of the 8th Army at the beginning of 1944. During December the 1st Cdn Div had occupied Ortona after a month-long struggle in the rain and mud of the Italian winter. Our casualties from battle and sickness had been very heavy and our morale was none too good. A visit from Sir Oliver soon put things right again. Every officer and man felt their spirits rise after meeting this remarkable British general.

We fought under his command in the Liri Valley in May and along the Adriatic coast to Rimini in August and September, and with considerable success.

In my opinion General Leese was the best British General I served under in World War II and they were all good.

It is relevant to recall that the British Generals Chris Vokes served under included Monty and Alexander.

---

[1] Communication to author. The Hon. Luke Asquith had joined OL's staff as G3 on 13.4.44.

15

THE FINEST FIGHTING SOLDIER

My great ambition was to get the finest fighting soldier in the British Army to take charge of the major British effort against Japan as soon as the war with Germany had reached a point at which such an officer could be spared.

Admiral Lord Louis Mountbatten
(*Letter to Lt General Sir Oliver Leese, 18 August 1944*)

Before dealing with Oliver Leese's achievements in South East Asia, it is necessary to say something of the war in the Far East from 1941 to 1944.

Japan had for several years been threatening aggression against America and the Western democracies, and entered the war when her aircraft attacked the American fleet at Pearl Harbor on 7 December 1941. The attack was similar in conception to that of the bombarding of the Russian fleet at Port Arthur in 1903, which marked the beginning of the Russo–Japanese war: in both cases Japan declared war following the act of aggression. The Japanese had undoubtedly learnt a thing or two from Nelson, who had destroyed the Danish fleet at Copenhagen when the two nations involved were not at war.

The results of Pearl Harbor were, first, that America was brought into the war; second, that Japan, having temporary command of the Pacific, embarked on a series of military exploits in the Far East, at the expense of Britain, the United States and China.

Hong Kong fell on Christmas Day, 1941, America lost the Philippines, the Japanese swarmed into Malaya, Burma and China. Leese's forebodings of 1938 were proved to be justified when the Japanese attacked Singapore from the land. General Percival's enforced surrender of the city, on Sunday 15 February 1942, was a devastating blow to the British Empire. General Alexander, sent to save Rangoon, narrowly escaped capture, and arrived just in time to order its evacuation. On 8 March, Rangoon fell to the Japanese, and British troops began the wearisome thousand mile retreat to India.

October 1942, with the relief of Stalingrad and the victory at Alamein, saw the end of the beginning of the Second World War. In the Far East the position became stabilised and the offensive passed to the Allies.

During the Quebec Conference of August 1943, Admiral Lord Louis Mountbatten was made Supreme Allied Commander in the Far East. General George Giffard commanded 11 Army Group, and the highly popular Lieutenant General (Uncle Bill) Slim, who had made a name for himself with his leadership and courage in the Burma retreat, became Commander of the newly-named Fourteenth Army. The victories at Kohima and Imphal in May and June 1944 made it clear that the Allies would soon be launching an offensive to reconquer Burma. Much had been done, but a great deal more remained to be done, and a general in overall command of the land forces, who would accelerate the drive to victory in the Far East, was urgently needed.

Mountbatten sacked the Army Group Commander, General Sir George Giffard. His dismissal during the battle of Imphal – there had been disagreement about the movement of reserve troops – was greatly regretted by Slim, who to some extent had played Monty to Giffard's Alexander. Grieved though he undoubtedly was, Slim apparently expected to be appointed as Giffard's successor, though none of those involved in selecting a successor, from Churchill and Alanbrooke down, considered him for the post. Meanwhile, Mountbatten, who had dismissed Giffard, had the embarrassing duty of asking him to stay on until a successor could be found, and this Giffard did with a good grace.

To many, including General Henry Pownall, Mountbatten's Chief of Staff, there was only one man for the job, and that was Oliver Leese. It was Pownall who pressed for his appointment. He had taught him at Camberley, and in the days of Dunkirk, when Pownall had been Gort's Chief of Staff, Leese had been Pownall's deputy. On leave in England in June, 1944, Pownall brought up the subject of Leese with Alanbrooke.

'I have not succeeded in getting a successor earmarked for Giffard' he wrote in his diary [29 June]. 'Oliver Leese, prime favourite, is with 8th Army, and the mainstay of the British side.' The only other possibility was Dick O'Connor, a friend of Leese from early days, and victor of Beda Fomm. He had been taken prisoner in the desert, escaped in Italy in 1943, and was now in top form.

Eventually – by mid-August – Alanbrooke accepted that Leese was the man for the job. No doubt the visit to Leese's HQ by Alanbrooke, on 23 August, and by Churchill two days later, was partly concerned with Leese's possible promotion, but it was not until 14 September that Alanbrooke considered Churchill in a sufficiently good mood to get a definite answer out of him. 'Saw Churchill in bed 9 a.m.' he wrote. 'He was in such a good humour that I tackled him about the transfer of Oliver Leese from Alexander to Dickie, and got him to agree.'

Mountbatten himself had been apprised a month before that Leese had been chosen for the job, and on 18 August had sent Leese a letter that was handed to him by Alanbrooke – but not until October 24:

My dear Oliver Leese

When the CIGS hands you this letter it will mean that he has offered you the job of Allied Military Commander of the land forces in South East Asia and that you have accepted.

I felt that I must write at once to say that my greatest ambition was to get the finest fighting soldier in the British Army to take charge of the major British effort against Japan as soon as the war with Germany had reached a point at which such an officer could be spared.

Ever since I met you with Monty in Italy[1] I have followed your doings with the greatest interest and have for months been hoping that it will be possible to get you to come out and take charge of the British, Indian, West African, East African, Ceylonese, American, Chinese and Dutch forces in South-East Asia. The CIGS will have told you that we have a thrilling programme of operations ahead of us, which only require aggressive and competent leadership on the military side to ensure resounding successes.

I visited Monty yesterday in Normandy to see whether he would release any of his highly trained staff officers, particularly on the Q side which is notoriously weak in India. He said he thought he could persuade Miles Graham to part with Jerry Feilden to come out as the new MGM if the new Allied Military C-in-C wanted him. He also thought he might be able to spare some more key staff officers in the coming weeks, as the war with Germany gradually comes to an end. If you want him or any other officer you will, no doubt, get in touch with him yourself.

Please rest assured of a sincere and hearty welcome at the South-East Asia Group of Headquarters in Kandy. The mere fact of your coming will put added heart into all our military forces.

Yours very sincerely,
Dickie Mountbatten.

Mountbatten had not only asked Monty for some of his highly trained staff officers, but had obviously told him of Leese's impending promotion, as in a letter to Leese of 21 August Monty had written:

[1] Mountbatten had met Leese during the preparations for the Sicily campaign, and later, during the crossing to the Pachino peninsula.

Dickie Mountbatten came to see me the other day. He is a most delightful person but I feel his knowledge of how to make war is not very great!! You ought to go out there as his Army C-in-C, and keep him on the rails!

News of the appointment, when it did come to Leese, would not have come altogether as a surprise. He spent most of October in England, partly on leave, mainly preparing for his work in the Far East. On 23 October, the second anniversary of Alamein, he had seven appointments in various rooms of the War Office.

On 24 October, he and Margie had lunch with the Churchills, the Prime Minister talking to him about Burma. Churchill emphasised the importance of taking any reasonable risks to bring the land operations in Burma to a speedy and successful conclusion. At 4 p.m. Leese had an audience with the King. There were interviews with CIGS, with Sir James Grigg, Secretary of State for War, and with Leo Amery, Secretary of State for India. On 25 October, he gave a talk in the morning at Eton, and, in the afternoon, at the Staff College, Camberley.

Leese set off for the Far East on 1 November, accompanied by Sidney Kent, his Brigadier Ops, Ulick Verney, Personal Assistant, John Stimpson, ADC, and John Green-Wilkinson, G3 Liaison, in his Eighth Army Dakota, later to be named Lilli Marlene, with its American crew. The first night he spent at Brussels with Monty, and next day lunched in Paris with Eisenhower, the Supreme Allied Commander – they had last met at Akarit on 6 March 1943. He stayed the night at Eisenhower's guest house in Versailles. Next evening he dined with General Schreiber in Malta.[1] On 4 November, Leese and his party went on to Cairo. The news of his appointment had been released and he wrote that he found it odd to have his name blazed abroad on the wireless. At dinner in Cairo he spent a somewhat unhappy evening with General Paget, whom Leese had much admired when he was commanding Guards Armoured Division and Paget was C-in-C Home Forces:

He kept on criticising the way in which General Monty and I used to take our Chief of Staff with us from one command to another. I tried to tell him that all we were trying to do was to form the most efficient staff possible, with a view to winning the battles. I am afraid our views were just diametrically opposed, and the evening finished rather sadly.[2]

The practice of commanders taking senior staff officers with them has

[1] Lt Gen Sir Edmund (Teddy) Schreiber (1890–1972). Commanded 5 Corps after Montgomery, 1941. Governor and Commander in Chief Malta, 1944–46.
[2] Memoirs.

long been a controversial one. Five years before Monty was born, Sir
Garnet Wolseley had incurred criticism for taking with him half a
dozen of his so-called Ashanti ring for the Tel el Kebir campaign.
Monty had done it in the Middle East; later he did it at Leese's
expense, when he whittled away Eighth Army officers for 21 Army
Group. Eisenhower took his own 'circus' with him to the UK when
he became Supreme Allied Commander after the Sicily campaign. And
now Leese, who had been angry with Monty, was taking his own
'circus', including half a dozen senior staff officers, to Burma.

On 6 November, Leese's party reached Karachi and on 7 November
they arrived at Willingdon Airport, New Delhi. Here they were met
by General Giffard and General Auchinleck, the C-in-C, India, and
the next four days were to be spent in taking over from Giffard.

On arrival at Delhi, Leese was entertained to lunch by the Auchin-
lecks:

> Lady Auchinleck asked almost at once if I hadn't got any medals. I just
> had a shirt and shorts on, like we used to wear in the desert. I laughed and
> said 'No.' I learned again the lesson, which I might well have remembered
> from Algiers – 'when in Rome do as the Romans do'.

He got on well with Auchinleck, with whom he had a long talk after
lunch, and stayed the night with Wavell at Viceroy House.[1] For the
next three days Leese was working at full stretch, becoming *au courant*
with matters in South East Asia. He very much liked Giffard, but
privately considered him too gentle for the post he occupied. 'He has
done very well here' he wrote to ML, 'and does not get the credit for
it. It has not always been easy, as he has had to keep ignorant and
excitable people's feet on the ground.'

On 8 and 9 November there were a host of meetings and interviews,
especially with staff officers and senior civil servants. On 10 November,
Leese left by air for Colombo, with Sidney Kent and John Stimpson.
They were met by General Pownall, who motored Leese to Kandy.

> 'Oliver Leese has arrived safely,' wrote Pownall on 18 November.
> 'Although Giffard has behaved very well of late, it is right that he should
> go and a younger man come. It was odd that it should fall to me to go
> down to Colombo to greet him, three hours in the car each way. He was
> one of my students at Camberley, and my deputy (as a Brigadier) in France.
> But that's all past, and a chief of staff should be present to welcome a new

---

[1] Leese had first met Field Marshal Earl Wavell when the latter was commanding an
Infantry Brigade (1929) and Leese had been appointed Brigade Major to Boy Brooke.
He was C-in-C, Middle East (1939–41), C-in-C, India (1941–43), and Viceroy of India
(1943–47).

commander in chief. Nor was the journey up wasted, for I gave him 3 hours of indoctrination, for which and for meeting him, he has written to thank me in the nicest possible terms. That is much to his credit for gratitude is not a common virtue.'[1]

Leese and Pownall drove together up the mountain road, through forests and jungle to Kandy. Most of what Pownall passed on to Leese would have been connected with the day-to-day running of affairs at Kandy; some of what he said would have contained oblique references for Leese to pick up. A staff officer of the first class, Pownall, who spoke Japanese, had an acute analytical mind. The three hours' indoctrination would have contained suggestions as how best to cope with Mountbatten's foibles.

'He is apt to leap before he looks,' Pownall wrote a few weeks later of Mountbatten. 'He is too impulsive by far, and putting the engine back on to the rails is pretty near a whole time job, at any rate it is so if combined with preventive action to avoid an impending derailment.[2]

Admiral Lord Louis Mountbatten had been Supreme Allied Commander at Kandy since October 1943. He was the son of Prince Louis of Battenberg, the German-born First Lord of the Admiralty who in 1914 had been forced to bow to the force of public opinion, resign his position and retire into private life.

Born on 25 June 1900, a great-grandson of Queen Victoria, christened Albert Victor Nicholas Louis Francis (Prince Louis of Battenberg) his name and title was changed to Lord Louis Mountbatten in 1917.[3] The young Mountbatten entered the Navy and served under Beatty as a midshipman from 1916 to 1918. After a brief period at Cambridge, he married the millionairess Edwina Ashley in 1922. The two became leading lights among the Bright Young Things of the 1920s, Charlie Chaplin and Noel Coward were among their friends. Back to the Navy, Mountbatten's habit of turning up at the docks in a Hispano Suiza did not endear him to less well-breeched naval officers, or indeed to the old sea dogs. He worked hard as a signals officer: a superb teacher, his instructional book on signals became the standard text book for the Navy.

In 1939 Mountbatten was promoted Captain and given command of HMS *Kelly*. The destroyer was damaged several times before being sunk in May 1941, during an action in which Mountbatten showed great personal bravery.

He was made Chief of Combined Operations in 1942, and was largely

---

[1] *Chief of Staff*. The Diary of General Sir Henry Pownall (Leo Cooper).
[2] *Chief of Staff*. The Diary of General Sir Henry Pownall (Leo Cooper).
[3] He became Lord Louis because his father was created Marquess of Milford Haven and he was the second son.

responsible for the planning and organisation of the Dieppe Raid of 19 August 1942. Many critics have laid the blame for the failure of the raid fairly, or unfairly, upon Mountbatten's shoulders.

It came as something of a surprise when at the Quebec Conference Mountbatten was made Supremo of South East Asia Command. Churchill, who seemed at times haunted by his involvement in the dismissal of Battenberg in 1914, argued strongly for his promotion, saying that Mountbatten was young and triphibious.

According to his biographer, Philip Ziegler, Mountbatten was at this stage of his life 'still impetuous, and occasionally imprudent, but years of working closely with susceptible and sometimes jealous senior officers had taught him the necessity for discretion.'[1] Another biographer, Richard Hough, felt that though he could nearly always find dedicated organizers to prepare his briefs, he also needed charmers and sycophants, and quoted one of Mountbatten's senior staff, who referred to 'handsome social chaps who could always be relied on to say "the champagne's over here, Dickie."'[2]

When they reached Kandy, Leese and his party went to King's Pavilion, where they were to stay the night. Here Leese met Mountbatten and they dined tête-à-tête. Dinner was a success: Mountbatten was charming and amusing. He invited Leese to go with him to a ball at the Officers Club, suggesting that he (Leese) took an ADC. Leese accepted the invitation, explained that he had not brought the appropriate clothes with him and said that John Stimpson would be the ADC to go. Mountbatten himself conveyed the news to Stimpson. Pointing a Supremo's finger in his direction he said: 'There's going to be a dance at the Officers Club which the general and I are attending. You will be going with your General.'

They all went to the Officers Club in a small Austin car with Supremo driving. As they went into the ballroom the band started to play 'Happy Birthday to you'. A very pretty Wren walked across the ballroom and kissed Mountbatten with *empressement*. Leese turned round to John Stimpson, his expression briefly registering amazement.

Dances at Supremo's Kandy HQ were very much the thing. Indian Army officers during this period, according to Major General O'Carroll Scott, were in the habit of referring to Kandy as Wimbledon – 'all balls and rackets'.

This is how Leese described the evening to ML:

U [Supremo] lives in a comfortable house, the old country seat of govern-

---

[1] *Mountbatten*, by Philip Ziegler (Collins).
[2] *Mountbatten, Hero of our time*, by Richard Hough (Weidenfeld and Nicolson).

ment. Big, high, cool rooms, but a house of reasonable size. I dined alone with him in a small room, an excellent dinner served by Ceylonese servants – smart and efficient in white duck suits. He speaks well and fluently, is always flitting from one subject to another. He never draws breath, but he is interesting and intelligent, gay and full of vitality and energy, and out above everything to win the war.

After dinner he took me to a dance given in the local hall by Harrison, the Chief Engineer, and a Brigadier, for their birthdays. About 40 people, the women all WRENs or Intelligence Officers, all in evening dress. It was an incredible contrast to our old life. They went to extreme pains to explain that it did not often happen! But I doubt that. It was gay and full of life – full enough of drink – and very odd. Most girls were U's and other secretaries, and they seemed to spend their time sitting on the arms of U and others' chairs. It all seemed a pity somehow, as it gives the Playboy atmosphere, in terrible contrast to those from the battle.

Although Leese thought the HQ more efficient than common report had it – he gave credit to Mountbatten for his team of scientists and for an excellent war room with good maps and everything in the gadget line, such as graphs, charts, talc, folding and sliding maps – he found the set-up at Kandy pretty astonishing. In his first letter to Alanbrooke from South East Asia, after referring pleasantly to the 'great welcome' that Mountbatten had given him he described his initial conference at HQ:

> To me Kandy is like a dream: It is so utterly different to General Alex's or Field Marshal Monty's Headquarters.[1]
> Business is conducted in vast conferences at which Professors and Officers of all ranks, employed in hitherto unknown assignments, vie with Commanders-in-Chief to express their views. But it seems to come out in the wash and as long as I am represented by a General Officer I need only go down there when really important decisions are taken. It takes me at least 14 hours each way, and I have plenty to do without that.[2]

Alanbrooke, replying, commented drily: 'Your description of Kandy was illuminating.' The CIGS had no great faith in Mountbatten. On

---

[1] Montgomery was promoted Field Marshal 1.9.44. Alexander was promoted Field Marshal in December 1944, but his promotion was backdated to the fall of Rome. Leese was writing in November when Monty was in fact a Field Marshal and Alexander a General.

[2] The VCIGS, Lt-General Archie Nye, described Mountbatten's morning conference at Kandy as being like a well-produced pantomime, with Mountbatten as the Principal Boy – 'various fairies floated in from the wings, dressed in Air Force coloured silk, signals in their hands from the Supreme Commander.' Nye to Major General Frank Simpson, quoted by Nigel Hamilton in *Monty The Field Marshal 1944–1976*. Hamish Hamilton.

16 November, he referred in his diary to Mountbatten's plans – 'which, as usual, are half-baked'. On 20 November, he recorded that 'After lunch Browning came to see me to be informed that he is to go as Chief of Staff to Mountbatten. He took it well, but I doubt whether in his heart of hearts he was thrilled.'

On 22 November, Giffard, now back in England, lunched as Alan-brooke's guest. The CIGS commented that Giffard had

> poured his heart out to me about his treatment by Dickie Mountbatten, and, as I thought, he was given a very raw deal. I blame Henry Pownall for a great deal of it. He should have been able to control Dickie better than he did. In any case I feel that most of the credit for the Burma success is due to Giffard.

On Saturday 11 November, the morning following the ball, Supremo took Leese to SEAC HQ, where he met Mountbatten's deputy, the American General 'Specs' Wheeler, and other senior officers. There was a farewell party for General Giffard, after which was the daily war meeting, and then Leese spent a couple of hours in conference with Major General Playfair[1] who was to be his chief staff officer in Kandy.

On 12 November, Leese assumed command of 11 Army Group and took the title of C-in-C, Allied Land Forces, South East Asia, or C-in-C ALFSEA. It seems surprising that Leese himself was not promoted, but remained Lieutenant General.

Leese settled down to sift and memorise the information gleaned from Mountbatten, Pownall, Giffard, Wheeler, Playfair and others. His immediate concerns were with operations *Capital* and *Romulus*. *Capital*, originally *Champion*, had been given the go-ahead at the Second (Anglo-American) Quebec Conference in September 1944; this was an offensive, now being mounted, towards Central Burma and the Irrawaddy. *Romulus*, to be mounted in December, was an operation to clear the Arakan of Japanese and to capture Akyab. *Capital* was to be followed, in 1945, by Operation *Dracula*, an amphibious attack on Rangoon.

Time involved in travelling was going to be one of Leese's problems. Air Command set up great difficulties. As C-in-C land forces he would be working with Air Marshal Garrod who was C-in-C all air forces in the theatre, and who had his HQ at Kandy.[2] In day-to-day work, as tactical commander of the ground forces fighting in Burma, Leese worked side by side with General Stratemeyer, who was under the command of Air Marshal Garrod.

[1] Major General I. S. O. Playfair (1894–1972). Decorated in WW1 he had been Director of Plans in the War Office, 1940–44.
[2] Garrod was a temporary replacement for Air Marshal Sir Trafford Leigh-Mallory, who had been killed in an air crash when flying to take up the appointment.

On 14 November, Leese left Kandy for his own HQ at Barrackpore, twenty miles from Calcutta. Leese, Sidney Kent and John Stimpson went by aeroplane from Colombo to Calcutta where Ulick Verney met them with a police jeep and cars. They stayed the night at Government House, and early next morning drove to Barrackpore, through streets packed with trams, buses, taxis, rickshaws, bullock carts, Army vehicles, and thronged with Indians in their white dhotis. Here, at Flagstaff House, Barrackpore, Leese settled into his new headquarters, and here, later in the morning, he met Slim and Christison.

He had asked them to meet him at Barrackpore on 15 November, to save him the extra time that would be necessary if he flew first to the Arakan (Christison) and then to Kohima (Slim).

'Rather indignantly they arrived,' wrote Leese, 'so I assured them that in future I would never call them back and never again did I do so.'[1]

Christison he knew well, but Slim he had only met once before, when Leese was Chief Instructor at Quetta.

'I got a good impression of Slim', he wrote to ML, 'though I think he bellyaches. He was slightly defensive about the Indian Army, the difficulties of Burma and the need to understand how to fight the Japs. I said how glad I was to come to his great 14th Army. He showed no signs of wanting to see me! But I feel somehow that all will be well. He is very proud of his Army, and well he may be. I think he is sound in his tactics.

Christie was in great heart. He gave me some gloriously scurrilous comments about my staff.

Afterwards Leese met General Stratemeyer, a bluff American who went everywhere with a dogwhip in his hand. He commanded all the American Air Forces in India and Burma. Leese and Stratemeyer got on well from the start. The two were to work very successfully together. The final successful outcome of the Burma campaign was in no small degree due to the excellent relationship between Leese and Stratemeyer.

Mountbatten now had a tidier command set-up. His chains of command to Fourteenth Army, 15 Corps, NCAC and the Chindits now all ran through C-in-C ALFSEA. There had been changes which had helped to improve relationships between the many headquarters that were so widely scattered and between commanders whose temperaments were equally diverse.

Major General Orde Wingate, leader of the Chindits, protégé of Churchill, had been killed in an air crash. Brilliantly daring at his best,

[1] Memoirs.

he had been at times impossible to handle. His successor was Major General W. D. A. (Joe) Lentaigne, a Gurkha Officer.

General Joseph Stilwell (Vinegar Joe) had been recalled. He had held several key positions. Northern Combat Area Command (NCAC) had been under his direct command; he had been chief of staff to the Chinese General Chiang Kai-Shek, and Deputy Supreme Commander, SEAC. He hated Britain and her Empire, delighted in making anti-British comments, and refused to work with Giffard.

He got on well with Mountbatten, however, to whom he once said 'I like you! You're the only Limey that wants to fight!' – a compliment that was modestly repeated from time to time by the Supreme Commander. Stilwell's recall, at Chiang Kai Shek's insistence, had resulted in three appointments – General 'Specs' Wheeler becoming Deputy Supreme Commander, General Dan Sultan taking over the NCAC forces, and the British General Lentaigne taking over the Chindits. Sultan's NCAC and Christison's 15 Corps in the Arakan, were now both under Leese's command; and, with Leese as overall land forces commander, Slim was able to concentrate on commanding his own Fourteenth Army.

Leese's Headquarters were at Barrackpore, where Giffard had wisely decided to move from Delhi, and Mountbatten had agreed to Leese

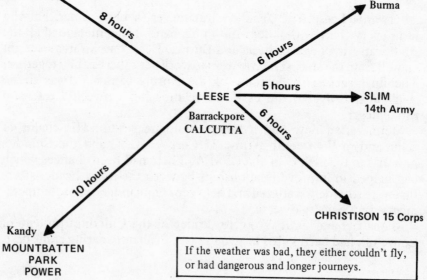

THE BATTLE FOR BURMA
Diagram to show Leese's journeys

AUCHINLECK
Delhi

8 hours

SULTAN(USA)
Burma

6 hours

5 hours

LEESE
Barrackpore
CALCUTTA

SLIM
14th Army

6 hours

10 hours

CHRISTISON 15 Corps

Kandy
MOUNTBATTEN
PARK
POWER

If the weather was bad, they either couldn't fly, or had dangerous and longer journeys.

having advance HQ at Barrackpore, provided main HQ was situated at Kandy. At this stage Kandy would have been an impossible site, as it was some miles across the sea from the nearest part of the front on which Leese's troops were fighting. Most of the work was done at Barrackpore where the bulk of the staff, including Walsh and Bastyan, was concentrated. A small section of the staff under General Playfair represented the Army viewpoint at the routine C-in-C conferences at Kandy.

The necessity of keeping in close touch with Stratemeyer, Christison in the Arakan, Slim and the Fourteenth Army in Central Burma, Sultan away on the Ledo, made Barrackpore the obvious choice. Even as it was, it took Leese 1500 miles flying to visit his three commanders. Further, by living at Barrackpore he could get to know his commanders and their troops, and visit the combined troops centre at Bombay and Cocanada – vital in view of the amphibious operations which were being carried out. Leese was able to visit Christison about twice a week and Slim at least once a week.

Leese had got his Tac HQ in as central a position as possible; nonetheless a high amount of time had to be spent literally on flying visits. It was an eight hour journey to Colombo plus three hours by car to Kandy; eight hours to visit Auchinleck in Delhi; six hours to Sultan (NCAC) in the Ledo, Burma; five hours to Imphal [Slim] and six hours to the Arakan (Christison). If the weather was bad, as it often was in the Monsoon, they either couldn't fly, or had dangerous, longer and uncomfortable journeys. A breakdown of Leese's flights in *Lilli Marlene* during the two months November and December 1944 reveals that he was flying during thirty-three of the sixty-one days, for a total of 211 hours, during which he travelled 36,000 miles.

17 Nov. OL to ML.

Yesterday and today have been days of conferences and meetings, trying to tie up a mass of things and get into the picture – and ginger up some of the people who enjoy saying 'No' and 'Can't'.

Ken Ray, his South African Chief Engineer, had arrived:

He replaced a real dud, who does not shave. What I should have done without my little staff I tremble to think. I went out to see the Auk yesterday. He helps one a great deal, and I like him. I shall stay with him when I return.

In his *Brief History of the Operations in Burma*, a 27-page booklet completed on 31 May 1945, Leese wrote that the first task assigned to him in his Directive was to protect the air route to China, to open the Burma Road via Myitkyina, Shamo and Wanting to Kunming, and to protect the airfield at Myitkyina. He was next to destroy the Japanese Army in Burma. In conference at Kandy, Mountbatten had said 'Our task is to deny Burma to the Japanese.' 'Surely, Supremo,' said Leese, 'our task is to destroy the Japanese Army in the Field!' Leese was not splitting hairs, he was taken aback at the negative attitude. Mountbatten accepted the amendment, but never forgave Leese for the correction.

These, then, were the overall strategical plans:

Operation *Capital*. To advance via Kalewa with Fourteenth Army into the Mandalay Plain, with the first objective Yeu and Shwebo, both towns in the open country in the dry belt; and second, Mandalay itself. NCAC was to advance towards Lashio.

Operation *Dracula*, for the capture of Rangoon – intended to be carried out by troops from Europe – had to be dropped, as by November 1944 it was clear that the war in Europe would continue until well into 1945. As soon as it was known that *Dracula* could not be carried out, *Romulus* was planned in the Arakan. The object was to release divisions from the area. Four divisions were locked up in the Arakan, by a Japanese outflanking threat; and this threat could best be eliminated by the capture of Akyab Island, Myebon and Minbya. This done, the Arakan garrison of four divisions could be reduced to four Brigades, thus releasing valuable divisions from the area.

Leese quickly saw that it was necessary to expedite the advance towards Lashio, Mandalay and Akyab Island, and he was soon into his stride. On Sunday, 19 November, with Sidney Kent and John Stimpson he left Willingdon Airport, Delhi, at 0600 hrs for the NCAC area. At Myitkyina he was met by General Sultan, commanding NCAC, and General Davidson, commander of the US Tenth Air Force. Discussions went on until late at night, the party staying at Sultan's bungalow. Next day Leese and his party visited the HQ of General Liao, Commander of the Chinese Sixth Army. On to Mawlin for an afternoon with Frankie Festing's 36th British Division,[1] returning by air to Myitkyina. During their visits they had passed a lot of troops, and after a while Leese got them smiling and waving in Eighth Army fashion.

> 'The first time for hundreds of year,' he wrote to ML, 'that the peaceloving Chinese have had the desire for battle! We saw a lot of mules – very well looked after. This is a war of mules, porters and air supply – often not even jeeps.
> 4 Chinese Generals came to lunch, including a first-rate Army Com-

---

[1] Major General Festing (1902–1976) had served under Leese in 29th Independent Brigade. As Field Marshal Sir Francis Festing he was CIGS 1958–61.

mander, General Sun, who has had much fighting experience and talked very sensibly and with great understanding about leadership and battle.'

At 1000 hrs on 22 November he left Myitkyina by plane for Imphal. He soon had a piece of hardboard on his knee, reached for his writing paper, and was telling ML the news:

> Now we are on our way to see Slim, flying over acres and acres of jungle and hills. Desert. Beaches. Mountains. Jungle. Where shall we go next?

At 1130 they touched down at Imphal and were met by Slim. The day was spent in conference with Slim, Scoones (4 Corps), Brigadier Shepherd and Brigadier Kimmins. Leese visited Scoones' HQ in the evening and dined later at Fourteenth Army.

> 'We have had a great two days,' he told ML. 'It was most interesting to see Imphal, where Slim and Scoones took me round and showed me the battlefield of the siege last year. It was thrilling to see, and I got a good idea of the difficulty of the fighting and the daring outflanking movement by the Japanese . . . I spent most of the day in long conferences. I liked Slim. He is obviously a good commander, and has the confidence of an Army whom he has led to victory. He has the usual Indian Army complex, and I am sure he neither understands nor appreciates the British troops . . . Christie was in great heart and asked much of you. [Christison had been a friend of Leese at Staff College and would have met ML at cricket matches and on other social occasions]. He looked well and was glad to see me. His eyes dance about like car headlights on a twisty road. He runs an excellent show.
>
> Yesterday Christie took me for a drive to see the country of the Arakan. It is flat, and one mass of rice fields. Big chongs (creeks) intersect the land everywhere and are tidal – we are almost on the seashore. You see everywhere palms, flowering trees, barsha villages, Bengali and Burmese women in gay colours, often smoking pipes and cheroots. The men seem to do very little.
>
> Today we passed squadron after squadron of small red crabs rushing across the sand in formation . . . I met Lomax[1] who has commanded a division out here for some time. I liked him and thought he was intelligent and sound. I spoke to some 500 or so officers, English and Indian. We have found an Indian ADC, Captain Ishaq Mohd. He is in the 7/16 Punjabis. His father is a big landowner in the Punjab. Gen Lentaigne who succeeded Wingate came to see me today. I like him. John Stimpson is an excellent head ADC.'

28 Nov. OL to ML.

We were met [at Colombo] by Playfair, and by Wetherall the Ceylon

---

[1] Major General C. E. M. Lomax commanded 26 Indian Division.

General. We then motored the endless 3 hours to Kandy. It really is the
most crashing waste of time to sit down in the hills in that inaccessible
place. I am glad to say I have persuaded S[1] to cut down the conferences
for C-in-C meetings to leave more to be devilled out on a staff level. He
was very nice, and easy to work with. I hope he will cease to do so much
detail himself as he looks tired.

On 1 December five of Leese's ex-Eighth Army staff arrived from
England: George Walsh, Chief of Staff, Ion Calvocoressi who was to
become Walsh's assistant, Petre Crowder, to become Leese's liaison
officer, Mike Prynne, Intelligence, and Vic Cowdry, Leese's indefatigable Whizzer Pilot.

Leese liked Slim for his soldierly qualities. What Slim could not
forgive Leese for was his part in the victory at Alamein, or the tendency
of Leese, George Walsh and Dricky Bastyan at planning conferences,
to say 'Well, in Eighth Army we did it this way.'[2] They were all of
them too tactful to labour their desert successes, but to Slim, who had
suffered so much mental and physical pressure in the retreat through
Burma, even an occasional reference to desert victories was jarring
enough. Slim's comment about Leese and his staff speaks volumes for
his feelings:

> The staff, which he [Leese] brought with him, and which replaced most
> of our old friends at General Giffard's headquarters, had a good deal of
> desert sand in its shoes and was rather inclined at first to push 8 Army
> down our throats. No doubt we provoked them but while we had the
> greatest admiration for the Eighth Army, we also thought that the 14 Army
> was now quite something.[3]

Above all were the problems raised by Leese taking members of his
staff with him from the Middle East to South East Asia. 'Alex and I
were very concerned about Oliver taking all these people with him,'
Lord Harding told the present writer. 'It would be bound to make
things difficult.' Brigadier Sidney Kent reflected 'It was certainly
difficult. We received the minimum of cooperation. But if Oliver
hadn't brought anyone with him, his task would have been quite
impossible.' Colonel J. M. McNeill, ex-Eighth Army, had joined
Leese's staff, via 21 Army Group, as Colonel (Air). He recalls 'Only
two of us, Ian Spens, Brigadier RAC, and myself, were ever *persona*

---

[1] Leese was no longer referring to Mountbatten as U. He either wrote Supremo in
full, or simply S.

[2] Another of the main causes of friction was that Slim commanded Fourteenth Army
and all the rest until Leese arrived, so in a sense Slim was demoted by Leese's
appointment.

[3] *Defeat into Victory*. (Cassell).

grata at HQ, 14th Army, because, I presume, we had armour and air support to offer. Even then, all visitors had to bring their own lunch!'

On the surface everything was going well between Leese and Slim, the former making every effort to establish a happy relationship. To Leese's ADC's there was never any overt sign of friction. One incident however was a straw in the wind. Within a day or two of his arrival at Barrackpore, Petre Crowder, as Leese's Liaison Officer, found himself in conversation with Slim. He was a little taken aback when Slim suddenly barked at him 'Well, what do you think of 14th Army?' Before Crowder had time to reply, Slim supplied the answer himself: 'I think it's a damned good Army!' To judge by Slim's indignant manner, it was an oblique suggestion that there were people who didn't think so.

★

Fourteenth Army were increasing the tempo of their offensive. By 4 December a bridgehead was established over the Chindwin by the 11th (East African) Division and a 1000 ft floating Bailey bridge built in forty-eight hours. The original plan for *Capital* was an advance by 33 Corps to Yeu and Shwebo, assisted by an airborne operation, but Leese had to postpone this, as the Airborne division was not yet formed. Slim therefore altered his plan so that 33 Corps advanced on Yeu and Shwebo and 4 Corps advanced towards Mawlin with the object of joining up with 36th British Division, which was under NCAC control. The Chinese First and Sixth Armies under General Sun and General Liao respectively, were also achieving success.

3 Dec. OL to ML.

We shall shortly make John Stimpson and Petre Crowder majors.

4 Dec.

I stayed in one more day to keep George [Walsh] in the picture. It is a wonderful relief to have him once again.

5 Dec.

I had a more than helpful signal from O [Monty]. He is letting me have Fanny Steward [signaller] and Manners [gunner]. He has also given us one or two other people we asked for, so we are gradually building up a team. We had an amusing evening with Stratemeyer, our American air general.

On 7 December, Leese dined with Sir Richard Casey, Governor of Bengal, at Government House, Calcutta. The occasion marked a turning point in the Burma campaign. Casey was an Australian with a distinguished record in the first world war. Leese had known him in the Middle East when Casey was British Minister of State in Cairo and also a member of the War Cabinet. He was eventually to become Governor General of Australia.

During the evening Leese and Casey talked over future prospects.

'I shall always remember the look of horror on his face,' wrote Leese, 'when I told him that for 1945 our objectives were limited to a campaign to establish ourselves in Central Burma and to capture Akyab in the Arakan. This conversation confirmed the thoughts which were beginning to come together in my mind, and very soon I became convinced that the Allied Land Forces could achieve a lot more than we had planned for 1945, provided that we had sufficient air transport and landing craft. It really came down to the fact that, if we could obtain enough aircraft, we might well carry out the original *Dracula* operation [for the capture of Rangoon intended to be carried out by troops from Europe] with our own forces instead of a special force from home.[1]

From now onwards Oliver Leese was thinking in terms of Rangoon before the monsoon.

On 8 December, Dricky Bastyan and Peter Dunphie, Military Secretary, arrived. Leese's team was now complete. He talked to 600 officers about what was wrong and what was going to happen. He confided to ML that he might have been a bit 'over definite'.

Leese was now hoping that Margie would be able to come out to the Far East, but the War Office was not sympathetic, and eventually the project had to be dropped.

10 December was a busy day. He spoke to 800 British NCO's and men of his HQs for about fifty minutes, and then had a day of interviews and conferences until past midnight. He was up and working again by 5.45 next morning.

On 12 December he saw General Monty Stopford at his 33 Corps HQ, where he stayed for the night. 'Slim came over for the night. He is very good and I like him'. Leese's determined repetition that he likes Slim is illuminating.

On 15 December he attended the knight dubbing ceremony at Imphal, when Slim, Scoones, Stopford and Christison were knighted by Wavell, Viceroy of India.

It went off so well. It took place on an open space just below the HQs where Scoones and his Corps were during the battle. Above us were the

[1] Memoirs.

nearest hills reached by the Japs. Supremo stayed the night. In very good heart.

16 Dec.

We flew off this morning and I travelled in U's aircraft. Very comfortable. He very pettish with his staff, rather like a spoilt child, but overwrought and overtired.

Boy Browning had arrived at Kandy to take up his position as Chief of Staff to Mountbatten.

I am glad to get him out here, but I doubt if he can straighten out all the tangle at his end.

Leese met Lady Scoones and Lady Slim, also Lady Slim's son – 'a fine upstanding boy, just going to OCTU [Officer Cadet Training Unit].'

19 Dec.

We have just been to spend the day with Cowan and his Indian Div. They have been in the Burma fighting since 1941. A two hour motor drive across typical Madrasi country: flat, palm trees, rice, tanks, typical Hindu villages; some with ornate little temples. Picturesque colours on the women. The children with earrings and the red and yellow spot on their foreheads. Bullock carts everywhere; attractive barges with vast white sails on the canals – other barges pulled by sweating coolies.

Leese was certainly making impact: his energy was boundless. 'I met a Major who had been with him out East' wrote one senior officer, 'and he said his arrival was like a breath of fresh air coming up from the rear as guards supplies, mail, etc.'

Ion Calvocoressi, in a letter to Margie on 19 December, wrote:

His energy and stamina are quite fantastic, and I'm quite sure that there has never been a general who gets about as much as he does, or who gets to the bottom of things more thoroughly and unerringly. He never seems to get tired.

22 Dec. OL to ML.

On 20th we had an incredible house party [at Flagstaff House] and we dined at three large tables – Supremo, Boy B[rowning], General Stratemeyer, the American air general, Admiral Power, the Naval C-in-C, General Carton de Wiart[1] on his way back from China, Christie and Martyn, the Admiral

---

[1] Churchill's representative with General Chiang Kai-Shek.

who commands landing craft, to say nothing of innumerable Aides and Stooges. We then had one of the usual incredible conferences of about 40 people.

23 December 1944. Mountbatten to Leese:

My Dear Oliver,

I am writing to thank you for your kindness and hospitality to my party at your headquarters in Barrackpore, both on my way out and way back from the front. I felt our talks were of the greatest value, and, as I told you before, I am so delighted to find that we appear to see eye-to-eye on almost every matter.

I am sure that you would have been delighted to see from the latest peony[1] that there can now be little doubt about our reaching Mandalay before the monsoon. I thought you would be glad to know that wherever you had preceded me during my recent tour, you left behind a feeling of tremendous enthusiasm and confidence among the commanders, who volunteered this information without my even having to ask them.

I may say that you have inspired an equal degree of confidence and enthusiasm in all the members of my own party who have come into contact with you, and I include myself among that number.

This missive was signed 'Dickie' in the customary green ink. Leese's comment was that it was an odd sort of letter.

With the approach of Christmas, Leese was in his element. On Christmas Day itself, Holy Communion was celebrated on the verandah at 8 a.m., and at 10.30 a.m. there was a voluntary Christmas service in the grounds at which he read the lesson. The service was conducted by a Scottish Church Padre – 'a cross between Martin Luther and Harry Tate – he would give delinquents hell!'

From 12.30 onwards he went to eight Christmas Dinners; he presented the prizes at the sports; to everyone on his staff he gave a personal Christmas present. The evening ended with a display of conjurors, jugglers and magicians.

27 Dec. OL to ML.

Back home to dinner from Imphal, where we had an interesting 3 hours with Slim. I like him, and I think we shall get on well together.

Operations in the Arakan had been postponed until mid-December, because until then the ground would not be dry enough for tank operations. When Operation *Romulus*, to capture Akyab Island, did start, the efforts of Christison and Leese prevented a comic opera situation not normally associated with the British Army.

[1] Derived from the noun *peon*, which in India or Ceylon could mean an orderly or a messenger.

The occasion, wrote General Christison, was the capture of Akyab at the end of 1944.

This was the first amphibious operation by SEAC and Mountbatten wanted full Press and TV coverage. Frank Owen[1] had his Press men and camera men assembling in Calcutta, but my troops chased the Japs so fast down the Arakan that we got well ahead of schedule. Mountbatten, prompted by Owen, did all he could to stop me till all was ready, finally he sent a signal to Oliver Leese, 15 Corps being then directly under his command, which read:

Weather urgent cable. Waves 6 ft high on Akyab beaches. Consider operation should be postponed. Nevertheless I leave it in hands of Force Commanders.

These were Force W, Rear Admiral Martin, self and Air V. M. Earl of Bandon. Capt. Bush, Chief of Staff to Admiral, had intercepted the message and had turned H.M. ships and convoy about.

I got the Admiral to countermand the order, and we continued as planned. I told Oliver what I had done. He replied 'Go on and good luck, I'll defend you from Dickie's wrath.'

By 26 December, Christison's troops were overlooking Akyab Island. The original plan for a large scale assault some weeks later went by the board, for during the rapid advance, Intelligence reports showed that the Japanese were weaker than anticipated on Akyab Island. Christison, therefore, launched an immediate assault from the north, and on 3 January, 25 Indian Division carried out an unopposed landing, the Japanese having evacuated the island the day before.

Leese gave a summary in some detail of the pace of work he was maintaining in an account of the three days 27–29 December. At 7 a.m. on 27 Dec he left Barrackpore by air, arriving at Cox's Bazaar[2] at 9 a.m. for a conference with Christison. A three-hour conference and then he flew from Cox's Bazaar to Imphal for the three-hour conference with Slim already referred to. At 5 p.m. he left Imphal, arriving back at Barrackpore at 7.45 p.m. where he got into a bath and held audience with Ulick Verney, John Stimpson and John Green-Wilkinson, and signed all their papers. After this, dinner, then he left Barrackpore at 10.30 p.m. and slept in the aircraft.

At 2.30 a.m. 28 December, the aircraft took off, arriving Agra at 6.30 a.m. He visited the Taj Mahal, and had breakfast at General

---

[1] Frank Owen (1905–1979). A high-powered journalist who had edited the *Evening Standard* 1937–9, and edited the *Daily Mail* 1947–1950. Joined the Royal Armoured Corps in 1942. He was now editing the SEAC paper.

[2] Cox's Bazaar. A closely-knit collection of villages in the Arakan, south of Chittagong and overlooking the Bay of Bengal.

Scoone's house. At 9 a.m. he left Agra, arriving Delhi at 10.15 a.m. Here Leese and his party were met by Viceroy's Military Secretary and the party stayed at Viceroy House. During the day he had talks with General Auchinleck. He also met Colonel Fleming [Peter Fleming], General Pierse of Civil Affairs Burma, and Brigadier Desmond Young, a GHQ Staff Officer.[1] At dinner he met Basil Dean, representing ENSA.

At 9 a.m. on 29 December, he was en route from Delhi to Gwalia to visit Special Force. He was met by General Lentaigne, Wingate's successor, and they flew in a light aircraft to visit 77 Independent Infantry Brigade. He visited each battalion during the morning and lunched in the Brigade Mess. Then he flew to Meltone and spent the night with 77 Independent Infantry Brigade.

The new year opened propitiously with the victory at Akyab, and on 7 January, Leese handled a tricky press conference successfully.

'I always remember you telling me,' he wrote to ML, 'that my "smile" is my best weapon and armour – in fact I always remember that I am a Shirley Temple . . . I've got to go to Kandy tomorrow. It works out at 8 hours flying and 3 hours motoring each way.'

He expressed forcibly his dislike of the journey and of the unwieldy conferences. However, all went well.

10 Jan. OL to ML.

Lunched and dined with S who is very well and goes off today to meet the Lady Louis.

We have had a mass of high level conferences here. I brought George and Dricky for the first view of Kandy. All went very well and it was a very satisfactory visit.

I go to the Governor's house to dine with Supremo and the Gloucesters. It will be nice to see them again.

The Duke of Gloucester, several years younger than Leese, had overlapped at Eton with him. He was on his way to Australia to take up his appointment as Governor-General.

11 Jan.

Just going to see Peter Dunphie. He is a great success.

Colonel Peter Dunphie, who had arrived at Barrackpore on 8 De-

---

[1] Desmond Young had been captured in the Middle East; he later escaped from an Italian PoW Camp, and shortly after the war was to write the first biography of Rommel.

cember, had first met Leese just after the latter's appointment to
ALFSEA, when he came to Brussels to see Monty, and Leese said he
would like him to join his staff as Deputy Military Secretary. Colonel
Dunphie had been commanding a medium regiment on the Rhine,
and prior to that had been Military Assistant to Alanbrooke, in which
capacity he had rendered sterling service. This is how Colonel Dunphie
saw Leese as C-in-C ALFSEA:

> His sense of humour made it a pleasure to work for him. He really enjoyed
> a joke. I remember how delighted he was at an incident which occurred
> on one of his flights into Burma with an American sergeant at the controls.
> They made a very bumpy landing and as he left the plane, Oliver said to
> the pilot 'That was not a good landing, was it?' To which the immediate
> reply was 'General, anything you can walk away from is a good landing'
> . . . At his TAC HQ bungalow in Barrackpore he used to sit in an armchair
> in a small sitting room without a desk or even a table. He would sign letters
> on a piece of hardboard on his knee. All his senior staff officers walked
> across the gardens to the bungalow, carrying their documents – and trying
> to keep them dry in the rainy season. I well remember, as his Dep. Mil.
> Sec., when it was necessary for him to select a commander from a number
> of eligible and recommended candidates, I had to cover the floor with their
> personal files; then to gather them up and carry them back to my office.
> But it was no ordeal to visit the C-in-C at his TAC HQ, because he was
> such a charming person. He was always welcoming, friendly and helpful.
> He did not mind having an opinion presented to him that was not in accord
> with his own, and he delegated to me – and doubtless to others in their
> own capacities – a good deal of responsibility.

On 19 January, Joyce Grenfell and her pianist, Viola Tunnard, gave
an entertainment at Flagstaff House, and on 20 Jan 1945 she wrote up
her impressions, which in 1979 she most kindly copied out from her
Journal and sent to the present writer. The entertainment was an
informal affair arranged for the benefit of the officers, NCO's and men
of Leese's HQ staff:

> Last night V[iola Tunnard] and I dined with General Oliver Leese and his
> HQ Staff. Jimmy Boyle[1] organised it and arranged a piano for us to use
> afterwards . . . The evening went well. Jimmy Boyle and David Clowes
> fetched us in a magnificent car, with gadgets that responded to buttons i.e.
> the dividing screen rose with a hiss and retired with another. We were
> driven by a man who had driven Monty all over N. Africa. Such a nice
> face under his bathcap-like beret.
> The HQ is in a house that was once part of the Government House

[1] Lieutenant 'Jimmy' Boyle was an ADC. An energetic staff officer and witty companion, he died of cancer shortly after the end of the war.

summer property. We ate in a large white room at two white tables. Dark red roses in the middle; a general impression of light and gaiety. Drinks first with Oliver Leese in his own little sitting room. More roses. We approached it through his bedroom, and the sight of a battered panama hat, on a chest of drawers, adorned by an I Zingari ribbon, was endearing. He is a charming man. Entirely English of the best kind. Very tall, with a slight, almost non-existent stoop. Gentle eyes: kind. Like all people burdened with responsibility he has a certain distantness. But missed nothing at the same time. I sat between him and Ulick Verney, and V. sat between Jimmy Boyle and another General [This was George Walsh].

My romantic leanings found much in the whole set up. Very struck by the whole atmosphere of common intention; single-minded. One felt they liked each other, too.

Didn't know about the Brigade of Guards practice of calling its officers by their first names – General Oliver, for instance . . . We were about 20 to dinner including 4 civilians on a mission from the Admiralty or something equally unlikely.

After dinner V and I did our stuff. The General had invited all his drivers, batmen and orderlies to come in. They were our favourite part of the audience, except for David Clowes[1] who burst into his courageous wheezy laugh with flattering ease. The General listened with half an ear, but for the most part had his mind on other things. However he enjoyed Ernie [a Buckinghamshire village mother from a set of 3 sketches called Mothurr] and asked for 'Lily Marlene'.

Says much for the General that they [the other ranks] behaved completely naturally in his presence.

Ion Calvocoressi gave his own postscript to the party in his diary:

Jan. 19.

In the evening General Oliver had a large dinner party which I attended. Joyce Grenfell and Viola Tunnard came and performed after dinner. They were excellent. After they had all gone, the General strummed on the piano to Sidney and myself till 12.30.

He was in great form.

---

[1] David Clowes was ADC to Sir Richard Casey, Governor of Bengal. He had been severely wounded at Dunkirk.

16

MANDALAY AND RANGOON

The crown and climax of one of the most extraordinary campaigns in history.

The Times, on the capture of Rangoon, 2 May 1945

On 16 January 1945 Field Marshal Alanbrooke wrote in his diary: 'Boy Browning turned up from Ceylon this evening with a message from Olive[r] asking for additional aircraft for Burma'.

The result of Browning's visit was of supreme importance to Leese, whose talk with Richard Casey, on 7 December 1944, had confirmed his growing belief that Rangoon could be captured before the monsoon. Then, when all had been going well, bad news. At a time when Fourteenth Army was dependent on air transport for supplies, three of the transport squadrons were suddenly ordered to go out to China. The reason for this was the sudden advance of the Japanese who were threatening Chunking in the operational area of the American General Wedemeyer, who had taken over Stilwell's job as military adviser to Chiang Kai-Shek. Wedemeyer had no battle experience, and had become, as Leese put it, 'rather over-excited.' In addition to transport air squadrons Wedemeyer had demanded and received two Chinese divisions. This meant a severe check to the advance of General Sultan's NCAC, from which recovery was never made.

Leese had convinced Mountbatten of the importance of this check, and persuaded him to send Boy Browning to London with a strong request that the aircraft be replaced.

Alanbrooke's entry in his diary on 17 January reads:

Had a specially long COS[1] as we had Browning back from Kandy having been sent back by Dickie to plead his case for more transport aircraft from Burma Ops. There is no doubt that the ops there have taken quite a

---

[1] Chiefs of Staff Meeting.

difficult turn, and there is now a possibility of actually taking Rangoon from the North! One of the difficulties – aircraft belonging to the Americans, and that the conquest of lower Burma does not interest them at all. All they want is N. Burma, the air route and pipeline and road to China.

Browning's visit was highly successfully. The lost aircraft were replaced, and additional transport aircraft were supplied. For Leese this meant that there was a chance of achieving the impossible. Tactical mobility in jungle fighting is afforded by air supply, which makes it possible to execute the manoeuvres necessary to outflank points of enemy resistance; and it was thus possible to checkmate the Japanese technique of establishing road blocks on every road and track.

'I now felt confident,' wrote Leese, 'that we had a good chance to get to Rangoon before the Monsoon, and that it was a justifiable risk to attempt to do so. Accordingly I discussed the situation with General Slim and we appreciated that if we could force the enemy to a stand-up battle in the Mandalay Plain he might have a chance to defeat the northern wing in detail, and thus leave an open corridor for an open advance on Rangoon.'[1]

The possibility of taking Rangoon in May was something that had been beyond the wildest dreams of Mountbatten and his planners, and also of Slim, the limits of whose hopes had been to be established near Mandalay in September 1945. Neither Mountbatten nor Slim were lacking in determination, but so far as organisation was concerned, Mountbatten was not in Leese's class, and Slim had the reputation of being an extremely determined but orthodox fighting General.

Acceleramus, 'let's get a bloody move on!' had always been Leese's motto as a soldier. This he achieved by meticulous organisation. The use of transport planes to support the advancing Fourteenth Army, the diverse methods by which they could be loaded and unloaded, according to the terrain or the phase of the battle; these were matters in which his skill caused the Allied advance to achieve, within the next three months, a momentum that Mountbatten had not even contemplated. Leese had tended to be impatient of the Kandy administration from the first. There was excessive overmanning – the Staff at the Supreme Commander's HQ numbered about 7000 – and Leese was never able to understand the apparent inertia that this caused.

On 27 January, General 'Specs' Wheeler, Mountbatten's deputy, stayed the night at Barrackpore, and Leese let fly on the subject of lack of support from Kandy.

He wrote to ML:

[1] Memoirs.

We had a very tense night and finally after dinner – with George, Dricky and Ken [Ray] I told him precisely what I thought of Kandy and in particular his attitude towards the Army, in no measured terms. He had about an hour of it, so I hope by now our attitude to life is known, as I also told S exactly what I thought when he was here earlier in the week. Kandy tries to treat me like they were accustomed to treat Giffard. He was a charming, mild, good mannered man, with no battle experience – I told Wheeler that it was quite different now . . . He seem[ed] surprised. They never think anything out and they never offer one any resources in transportation, engineer services to help. The place is full of bright young things, the Marlene Dietrichs of their day, who produce a series of bright ideas, without any knowledge or responsibility. And the Army is always put in the unenviable position to prove that the idea is quite impracticable, with the resources available, then when S has agreed with one that the thing is off, they all try, including Wheeler, to discredit the Army – say that we will not take risks, and try to get S to reverse his decision backing us. But now we know the form, it will be easier. Also Boy is very alive to it and I think he will clean up the whole system. He knows O's and L's systems and I think we shall get it on a war basis. At present it is a cross between Hollywood and Judas Iscariot.

3 Feb. OL to ML.

This Kandy set-up is a great trial. Their trouble is that they never offer help, they seem to try and always put us in the wrong, and they appear deliberately to cast us with their subordinate formations. I expect it's more incompetence than ill will.

On 8 February he flew to Imphal to visit a vast ground organisation dealing with air supply.

Air crews, he explained, sometimes landed with supplies and sometimes dropped them; dropping having a twenty-five per cent wastage; and explained the logistical problems to be dealt with:

Everything has to be roped down in the aircraft. Petrol in barrels for landing. 4-gallon containers with parachute attached for dropping ammo, rations, canteen stores, ordnance stores. Engineer stores, forage for animals, Bailey bridging. The sorting and packing organisation for all this is a terrific work. Metal containers for fragile goods, silk parachutes for valuable fragile loads, cotton and sometimes jute ones for others, sometimes several parachutes to one heavy load. It is a great problem to see that each load is made up correctly; taken to the right aircraft.

Each day the battle may depend on some particular commodity. If a lot of fighting is in progress you want ammunition, if you are advancing quickly you want petrol and Bailey bridging. One Bailey bridge may need 30 aeroplanes. It needs a lot of highly efficient people and I think we have good men on the job. Dricky [Bastyan] is tackling it all very well, but he has a terrific task as his predecessor was a complete centraliser and did not leave us a proper system.

On 10 February he wrote to ML:

I think they are beginning to appreciate that my staff is good and out to help them. But it's a hard job, both to eradicate past feelings and prejudices; and to clear up the mess at our HQs while one is in the midst of one of the biggest administration battles we have ever had to cope with.

Of Mountbatten he wrote:

I am quite sure he undermines our authority and decries ALFSEA. But each time we grow proportionately stronger. He has no self-confidence and cannot trust anyone.

Mountbatten, he wrote, quite openly stated that he asked Leese's subordinates about his (Leese's) performance, and had even written to Slim saying that certain 'hold ups' in supply were Leese's fault.

It is so different to the old days with O and L. I doubt if he means to do it. It is his makeup and technique.

In his second letter of 10 February he wrote:

We have had most interesting visits to the flat Mandalay Plain. Light scrub rather like we saw in much of East Africa. A glorious change after the endless trees and jungle. It is glorious to be out in the open again, and good going for tanks. I wish we now had the Armoured Divisions that we had more than enough of in Italy.

On 14 February, Leese referred to

a visit from a Kandy Wren King, a rather flash and boring man. He comes over to verify some spy story by one of S's espionage systems, as to what we are doing on airfields. It's a jolly party.

20 February. OL to ML.

For Lunch today S arrived, like an avalanche, S had [as] usual asked all my subordinate commanders what they thought of me, and my staff! Quite indirectly, according to himself! Fancy telling me . . . He never stops, and looks very washed out. I don't think he's sure of himself and hence does not trust anyone to get on with his job. But you can't help admiring his never-flagging enthusiasm and energy, and he is very good with the troops.

On 24 February, Leese wrote with studied politeness to thank Mountbatten for his visit:

I would like to thank you very much indeed for holding your conference this time in Calcutta. My people have greatly appreciated meeting your staff and having the opportunity of working out our future plans so thoroughly with them: and it has been a great help to be able to do so near our own place.

I am very glad that you were able to spare the time to come out here and meet my Staff personally. I need not say how greatly they appreciated your visit.

Mountbatten replied on 26 February:

Thank you so much for your letter of the 24th February. I was on the point of writing to you to thank you for all your hospitality to Edwina and myself, and for arranging for the 'off-the-record' preliminary C-in-C meeting to be held in your room. I was particularly glad to bring up our fairly vast party to Calcutta, as I knew it would do all our party good to go to Calcutta, and I wanted to make a very clear gesture that I, for one, would not tolerate any more 'Kandy–Calcutta nonsense', and I felt the best way to give a lead was to make everybody come up to Calcutta.

Meanwhile, following Boy Browning's success in obtaining the aircraft, it was possible to plan positively for an advance on Mandalay. Slim's plan was to gain a bridgehead over the Irrawaddy, and then to strike eastwards to Meiktila with two infantry brigades of 17 Division and a brigade of tanks. The remainder of 17 Division was to be flown in by the American air commandos to Meiktila to open the airfields and provide a firm base.

All went well. On 19 February 17 Division passed through 7 Division's bridgehead, and in 72 hours reached Meiktila. They had cut the Japanese Army in two.

Thanks to Leese's sense of urgency and to his understanding of the situation, supported by the enthusiastic co-operation of General Stratemeyer, air transport was being used on a scale unprecedented in modern war.

'The air crews who delivered the goods,' wrote Leese, 'often made three or four journeys a day over hazardous jungle country, often flying in appalling conditions of weather. Many casualties were caused by these fearful conditions, and the risks were unflinchingly faced.'[1]

The Japanese commander, General Kimura, wanted to fight the main battle on the banks of the Irrawaddy, but events didn't go well for the Japanese, as 19 Division had broken out of their bridgehead and begun their advance on Mandalay: Gracey's 20th Indian Division had been fighting bitterly to link up with 2 British Division; 7 Indian Division

---

[1] Memoirs.

had captured Pagan. Kimura now tried a counter-offensive by abandoning the Arakan, weakening South Burma and reducing his forces facing NCAC in order to concentrate his troops in the Mandalay Sector, which he now realised was the vital one. He was too late.

Leese had planned for six divisions the task of destroying a force of eight Japanese divisions. However, he now had massive air superiority, security from air attack, and advantage in armoured strength in terrain where this could be exploited. Moreover the enemy opposition was deteriorating.

On 21 February, General 'Punch' Cowan's 17 Division had made its dash for Meiktila. 'Famous Indian cavalry regiments' wrote Brigadier E. D. Smith[1]

'drove Sherman tanks instead of horses – Probyn's Horse and the Royal Deccan Horse – with 116 Regt RAC [Gordon Highlanders] . . . for the first time in Burma, tactics akin to those adopted in the Western Desert were seen as the fast-moving armour went ahead.'

On 23 February, in a letter to Freyberg, Leese wrote that the battle for Mandalay had begun.

Now 4 Corps was under the command of Lt-General Frank Messervy, who had commanded 7 Armoured Division in the Middle East. He had some fine divisional commanders to support him. Major General 'Punch' Cowan led 17 Division with uncompromising dynamism. Major General Douglas Gracey had achieved wonders with 20 Division; he was to become C-in-C of the new Pakistan Army in 1947. Major General 'Pete' Rees, unorthodox commander of 19 (Dagger) Division,[2] diminutive in stature, fluent in several Indian languages, had won the DSO as a subaltern in the first war.

On 25 February Air Vice Marshal Keith Park had taken over as air C-in-C from Air Chief Marshal Guy Garrod, who had been in temporary command since the death of ACM Sir Trafford Leigh-Mallory. Keith Park was a New Zealander with a fine record. His No. 11 Fighter Group had borne the brunt of the fighting in the Battle of Britain. Park was a man of uncompromising views, especially where the role of the RAF was concerned, and he was not always to see eye to eye with Leese.

Leese was well aware of the paramount importance of taking Meiktila. The Japanese communications radiated from there; Meiktila was the advanced supply base for all Japanese forces in Burma, except those in Arakan. If Meiktila were captured, the whole

---

[1] *The Battle for Burma*. E. D. Smith. Batsford.
[2] The divisional sign was a dagger.

structure of Japanese defence in Central Burma was bound to collapse.

On 26 February Leese had written to ML saying that Slim's battle was reaching its crisis. He reported an excellent visit to Slim: 'He has a very happy HQ'. On 28 February, the attack on Meiktila went in from four directions. Major General Kasuya commanded a garrison of 3500 plus one regiment that had arrived fortuitously. He had strong well-sited defences and used all available men, including hospital patients. Two days and nights of savage hand-to-hand fighting followed. By the morning of 4 March, all Meiktila north of the railway had been cleared.

The tactics that had paid so well in the Western Desert had been used again with great success in terrain suitable for tank warfare. The steadily increasing tempo of attack was the result of planning to the last degree in all the vital components of the offensive. The Japanese were bewildered by the speed, drive and thrust of the ALFSEA forces.

Now came Leese's overall directive to Slim, Sultan and Christison, co-ordinating the next moves. NCAC and 15 Corps were to advance on the flanks of Fourteenth Army, while Fourteenth Army had the task of destroying the Japanese Fifteenth Army in the Mandalay area prior to the onslaught on Rangoon before the monsoon started.

Brigadier E. D. Smith has this to say of Slim's generalship:

'If the Imphal battle had shown the world that Slim had grown in stature as the commander of 14 Army, then *Extended Capital* proved without any doubt that he had entered the ranks of the truly great generals of World War II.'[1]

On 2 March, Leese was in Delhi where he had a long talk with Auchinleck. Leese wrote that Auchinleck 'is always quite charming to me'. Later, he lunched with the Viceroy and Lady Wavell. On 5 March, Leese was at Agra and while he was on the airfield, a signal arrived to say that Meiktila had been captured. The turning point of the campaign had been achieved.

As Leese himself had readily appreciated, the airmen did an enormous amount to make *Extended Capital*, the assault on Meiktila, possible. Making continual difficult and dangerous sorties, often in hazardous conditions, dropping supplies of ammunition, equipment, petrol and food, they flew the transport planes that Leese knew would provide the key for speedy victory.

'S arrived with 3 rather dim officers', Leese wrote from Delhi on 6 March. Next day Leese was at Monywa for conferences with Slim. On

[1] *The Battle for Burma*, by E. D. Smith. Batsford.

8 March he had discussions with General Dick O'Connor, GOC Eastern Command (India) at Government House.

12 March, OL to ML.

Sat next to Lady Wavell at dinner. S came in too. I remembered your 'Smile, smile, smile' and I think it will be easier. He is really very naïve.

Leese was fretting about the loss of momentum in the battle for Mandalay, although Pete Rees's 19 Division, advancing rapidly with an armoured thrust, had reached the outskirts of Mandalay on 7 March. On 15 March, he was writing 'These battles take a long time, and time is short before the monsoon.' The Ides of March had come, and there were seven weeks before the monsoon broke.

As the fighting in Central Burma moved from Meiktila to Mandalay, there was no doubt that Slim was a sick man. It was now three years since the loss of Singapore; during these years Slim had led his troops untiringly through times of disaster – from defeat to victory. The mental and physical strain in appalling conditions had taken its toll. In addition to this, about July 1944, Slim had had an operation for the removal of the prostate gland, and for a period of a fortnight General Scoones had taken over Fourteenth Army.[1] Slim had soon got back into harness and continued his fight against ill health and against the Japanese. Now, perhaps because of the quickening tempo, he was near to exhaustion. On 16 March an entry in the C-in-C Diary reads:

During the morning Lt-Gen Browniong, COS SACSEA [Chief of Staff to the Supreme Allied Commander South East Asia] *arrived. C-in-C held long discussions with him in the afternoon* [Browning also stayed for dinner]. *Late that evening the C-in-C decided to move up to Fourteenth Army a small Tac HQ.*[2]

'Boy' Browning had arrived with the specific intention of seeing Leese, to tell him that he (Browning) had just seen Slim, and that Slim was tired. Too tired, he felt, to keep a grip on the battle. Hence the long conversation with Leese, and hence Leese's decision to move up to Fourteenth Army.

Leese left Barrackpore on the next morning, Saturday 17 March, at 6 a.m., with George Walsh and other members of his staff. They flew to Akyab, and a quick conference was held with senior officers of 15 Corps. Next, Leese flew by L5, (American two-seater liaison aircraft)

[1] In a letter to his daughter Nina, referring to Slim's autobiographical work *Defeat into Victory*, General Scoones wrote 'The fact that after the Imphal battle, when IV Corps were sent out to rest, I was sent to command XIVth Army, while Slim had a prostate operation, seems to have been overlooked.'
[2] Author's italics.

with Vic Cowley as pilot, to visit HQ West African Division, then to TAC ALFSEA, where discussions were held with senior officers of Fourteenth Army.

When he met Slim the latter said that he wanted four months' leave as soon as Rangoon was taken. Leese considered this an astonishing request, and later said to Major Petre Crowder, his Personal Liaison Officer, that it was a bit much for Slim to ask for leave in the middle of a battle.

'There is no doubt Slim was a very tired man indeed,' wrote General Christison.[1] 'Gen. Boy Browning reported this to Mountbatten, and on liaison visit to Slim I was convinced he was about played out. We were great friends, yet he was rude, crotchety and off-hand.'[2]

On Sunday 18 March, accompanied by George Walsh and Dricky Bastyan, Leese left camp at 8 a.m. and went by jeep and L5 to visit the Inland Water Transport Organisation at Kalewa. The purpose of this was to give encouragement and logistic support to the boat-building:

'It is a great thrill to see this' he wrote to ML on 18 March. 'Boats of all sorts – barges, tugs, rafts, come hundreds of miles on lorries and trans-porters. Engines and parts come by air. Ship-building personnel come from all over India, and it is wonderful to see a vast small craft flotilla beginning to operate down the Chindwin. Boats assemble like mushrooms overnight.

On 20 March he heard from ML the sickening news that she could not come out after all. Leese wrote back suggesting that she join the WVS and possibly coming out with them: 'They are the best, the most efficient.'

He continued:

The battle is at its decisive stage, and I am up with a small TAC close to LI [Bill Slim – he had inverted the order]. We are in tents – George, Dricky, who leave tomorrow and are replaced by Sidney, John S[timpson] and a few others and the servants. It is nice to be in the open again. We are just off to see Pete Rees and his 'dagger' boys, and I will write to you later with news and chat. We had a big conference yesterday. Slim, Sultan, Christie, Stratemeyer. All went well, but it's a hard struggle with so many political and allied strains and pulls. I can fully realise what Marlboro had to compete with in the low countries.

[1] Letter to Ion Calvocoressi 23.2.79.
[2] Slim's diary entries for this period confirm General Christison's impression. The entries for 8 March and 23 March consist of the single word 'headache'.

In the evening of 20 March, flying from Mandalay to Manywa, he wrote again to ML:

A great day. We went back to Mandalay Hill to see a big air strike on the Fort. We were met, George, John S, and I by Pete Rees, a most colourful little man, in a red scarf, a very great personality, and very gallant, a great figure in his division. Mandalay Hill was captured by a Gurkha Bn, a great feat. It is very dominating, like Cassino – 1000 steps up, and temples, pagodas and Buddhas on every ledge as you go up . . . The Fort is like those at Delhi and Agra. 20 ft high red walls with battlements and inside the wall are earth banks 15 feet thick outside a 50 yd broad and deep moat. The guns were breeching it, firing direct at 200 yds range. Like the sieges of Seringapatham or Badajos.

After that we went to see Cam Nicholson's boys on the other side of Mandalay. I presented a Military Medal, approved today, to an AA Gunner, who had joined the Infantry. While I was there I got a signal that the Fort had fallen, and would I go back, so back we went as the sun began to set. We were met by Pete Rees again, and drove through and round the Fort. It was a great thrill.

Mandalay was taken. This was how Leese summarised the battle in the *London Gazette*:

By the 14th [March] the city had been cleared and Fort Dufferin invested. A gallant attempt by 98 Bde to storm the Fort failed, the attackers were held up by the thick weed in the moat. Old-fashioned siege warfare methods were then adopted, in order to avoid the casualties which a direct assault would have entailed; but even medium artillery, firing from 500 yards, and aerial rocket projectiles failed to break the massive walls, with their earth embankment. By the 19th March, however, the Japanese had had enough, and that night the remnants of the garrison attempted to escape through the ruins. The majority were intercepted and only a few got away. An immense quantity of equipment, chiefly ordnance stores, fell into our hands and 160 civilian internees were rescued. The capture of Mandalay was a fitting climax to a great advance.

Ion Calvocoressi's account, written shortly after the war had ended, less technical, was by no means lacking in clarity:

How well I remember in mid-March, when the battle of Mandalay was at its trickiest stage, Boy Browning coming back and saying to General Oliver that things were not going too well as Slim was tired. So off General Oliver [went] to the jungle and took control of the battle, and kept a firm grip on it, so that instead of stalemate, the fall of Rangoon became imminent, and it fell 6 weeks later.

Congratulations came thick and fast to Oliver Leese: a telegram from Alanbrooke; a letter from John Kennedy, Assistant CIGS, saying that it was interesting to see how things got a move on in SE Asia as soon as Oliver Leese arrived; General Giffard wrote to say 'It is thrilling to watch your progress which is really grand.' Auchinleck wrote – 'Good hunting to you, I hope you will soon be in Rangoon.'

Now that Mandalay had fallen, Mountbatten decided to hold a conference there. 'We go to TAC', wrote Leese, 'having heard that S cannot keep away from Mandalay. He is like a spoiled child.'

The conference was duly held. Major Petre Crowder who sat between Leese and Slim, remembers a frivolous exchange of messages between the two, to the effect that Supremo had only come to Mandalay to get his photograph in *Picture Post*.

On 24 March, Leese wrote to ML, referring to Mountbatten's highpowered conference at Mandalay, which included Slim, Sultan and Stratemeyer:

> S is really awful, but he has learned to hold a conference. He always talks about 'being straight'! I think because he is as crooked as a corkscrew himself.

Leese found it odd flying back to Barrackpore after a week in Camp which he had much enjoyed, especially the visits to so many troops, and seeing Christison and Frankie Festing again.

> But it is dull after our past two years, as Slim and most of the others are really strangers and we have very little in common. I think I am getting matters on to a better footing . . . But Slim is a bellyacher, and you know how good I am when I am bored.

28 March. OL to ML.

> Off to Monywa. I hope IL [Slim] will bellyache less this time. It is so boring.

Evidently the conference went smoothly, because on 29 March, OL wrote:

> IL was easier to deal with though I don't still enjoy it much. He has however a great reputation with everyone including the Americans, and I think he is traditionally difficult with his higher HQs. I have been the same!

30 March seemed to mark the zenith of Leese's relationships with Slim. Writing to ML, in the plane en route to Akyab:

> I had a long talk with LI [Leese, of course, meant IL] this morning. I gave him a syphon – with which he was pleased . . .

I am wearing our new sign – St. George's Cross on a shield, with inverted swords, surmounted by gold wings, on a light blue sky, above a dark blue sea! thus symbolizing the move of armies by air and sea – or, as some wags say 'the dash of the 8th Army to the rescue of SEAC'.

It now seemed unlikely that Rangoon would be taken from the north by land; Leese therefore decided that preparations for an amphibious landing were essential. The next day, Saturday 31 March, after discussions with Sultan and Stratemeyer, he flew to Akyab for talks with Christison, then on to Barrackpore. Late in the evening, accompanied by Walsh, Bastyan, Sidney Kent and John Stimpson, he left Barrackpore for Ceylon, his object being to put his revised plan before Mountbatten. This was to revert to *Dracula*, using air and sea attacks, and making use of Christison's 15 Corps for amphibious landings.

2 April, OL to ML.

I dined with S, Lady Louis, and Boy [Browning]. It was [a] frightful meal. She attacked me at dinner on hospitals and welfare and he after dinner on battles. I don't think they mean it but they never draw breath. They are very boring. She has done good work out here and all speak well of her.

The conference itself he described as difficult, and a 'very hard struggle to get my way, but think I have achieved.'

Ronald Lewin, in his biography of Slim, states that Leese procrastinated for 11 days after 19 March. However, the C-in-C's Diary for the relevant period shows him as ubiquitous and untiring, as he planned one of the most brilliantly successful offensives of the war:

On Tuesday 17 March he was fully occupied in connexion with the battle of Mandalay. He was then able to concentrate on planning for the assault on Rangoon.

Wed 21 March. Left Monya for Myitchi, where he met Lt Gen Messervy [4 Corps] and Maj Gen Mansergh [5 Indian Div]. The party then flew to Meiktila. The morning was spent with 17 Div. Flew back to Monywa.

Thurs 22 March. Met Mountbatten, Air Marshal Park and Maj Gen Fuller [DCGS] at 0730 hrs. Later Sultan and Stratemeyer arrived for conference on air supply. In the evening Mountbatten, Park, Fuller, Slim, Vincent and others dined at Leese's camp.

Fri 23 March. Left Monywa for Mongmit to visit 36 Div. 2-hour jeep drive to Mogok. Visited troops of 29 Inf Bde and 26 Ind Inf Bde. Stayed the night at Mogok.

Sat 24 March. Motored from Mogok to Mongmit, flew to Lashio, where was met by Gen Sun [1 Chinese Army]. Flew back to Monywa. Dined alone.

Sun 25 March. Flew from Monywa to Akyab, met by Gen Christison. Flew straight on to Ramree Island to aerodrome at Kyaukpyu. Visited HQ 26 Ind Div [Gen Chambers]. Looked round Sub area HQ, organisations around the aerodrome, including stockpiling arrangements for supply 14 Army. Flew back to Barrackpore.

Mon 26 March. Saw Walsh and Bastyan. After lunch saw Col Dunphie, Brig Manners-Smith and Maj Gen Walsh again.

Tue 27 March. A day of interviews and conferences in which Stratemeyer, Dick O'Connor, Dricky Bastyan and Peter Dunphie were especially involved.

Wed 28 March. Saw Walsh. Flew to Monywa with Gen O'Connor and Brigadier Kent. Conference with Slim in the evening.

Thu 29 March. Flew from Monywa to Monglong with O'Connor and Kent. Spent the day with 36 Div at Mogok. Flew back to Monywa.

Fri 30 March. Saw Slim in the morning. Flew from Monywa to Akyab with O'Connor and Kent. Conference with Christison. Flew back to Barrackpore.

Sat 31 March. Saw Sultan, Stratemeyer, Walsh and Ken Ray in the morning, Tyndall in the afternoon. Later visited Barrackpore airport and looked over the new signal aircraft, which had just arrived from England. Then at 2300 hours, accompanied by Walsh, Bastyan, Kent and John Stimpson, he left Barrackpore for Ceylon to see Mountbatten.

Meanwhile, at the Yalta Conference, the directive was issued to Mountbatten, ordering SEAC to defeat the Japanese in Burma and capture Rangoon. Mountbatten was now anxious to capture Phuket, an island off the Malay Peninsula, in the Andaman Sea, 700 miles south east of Rangoon. Leese did not want to sabotage Mountbatten's plan, but felt an attack on Phuket might warn the Japanese.

At the meeting of 2 April Leese asked for Mountbatten to support an amphibious operation against Rangoon, designed either to assist the advance of Fourteenth Army, or to capture Rangoon itself. Mountbatten was sympathetic towards the proposal. Power (Navy) and Park (Air Force) opposed it. Eventually Leese's proposal was agreed to, and Phuket was postponed.

Leese detailed 15 Corps with 26 Division as the assault formations to make the first landing in the Rangoon river.

During the early part of April Leese was having an extremely difficult situation to deal with, as he was not only fighting a determined enemy, he was also trying to convince Mountbatten, Keith Park and Power that his plans for the assault on Rangoon would work. Fortunately he succeeded, and the Japanese were defeated.

The weather, hot and humid in the weeks before the monsoon, did nothing to affect Leese's vitality. In his letters to ML he seemed mainly to be trying not to worry her about his problems.

'I sent you a ring with all my love for Easter,' he wrote on 4 April. 'It is a semi-precious stone – a cinnamon with Rangoon diamonds.'

6 Apl. A day for visitors yesterday – Desmond Young, the new India Public Relations Brigadier. A tough guy . . . and I think he will help us.

7 Apl. A glorious tepid bathe [Akyab]. Sandy beach. The sea azure blue like the Mediterranean.

9 Apl. Went to see Douglas Gracey's Division. They were in terrific form. He has done very well. He asked a lot after you.

On, in the oppressive heat, to Monya and thence to Akyab.

We have just had a conference with Christie. I drank 3 tin mugs of tea with Christie and have just had a glass of lemonade. We are all dripping – and using handkerchiefs like bath towels! We drink salt and water each day – to put back the goodness we sweat!

On 10 April Mountbatten visited Leese at Barrackpore, and a high-powered conference took place, including Stratemeyer, Air Marshal Coryton, commanding the RAF in Burma, and General Evans, commanding the Transport Aircraft. During discussions with Leese, Mountbatten countermanded Leese's instructions that no parachutists were to be used in the operation. Leese took this in good part, writing to ML that Mountbatten was quieter and more reasonable when alone with him.

On 14 April, Leese went from Barrackpore to Kyaukpyu for a conference of force commanders. There had been heavy fighting and evidence of heavy bombing. The Japanese had suffered 20,000 casualties in the area.

Our days are full of contrast – vehicles today for instance: our sleek black Cadillac limousine; *Lilli Marlene*, our Dakota; a L5 Light Aircraft and a jeep.

19 Apl. OL to ML.

Bumping along from Meiktila. Going to see Auk before he starts on a visit
to Home. I talked to the Worcester Bn., all stripped and resting, under
the shadow of a hill they captured yesterday after a tough fight. I passed
our old East Lancs friends [from 29th Independent Brigade], and waved
to those driving in their trucks, and then visited a Gurkha Bn resting –
their 10th day out of contact with the enemy since November. They were
in great heart and full of talk. I gave them two Military Crosses.

21 Apl.

On our way back from Agra. I stayed with the Auk, who was as nice as
ever, and is taking back the Mogra bracelet for you at the end of the month.
I think he will come and see you.

23 Apl.

We dined with Slim who was in good heart. He is an extraordinary devil.
He can never stop crabbing something. They have made him a jolly good
caravan, and all he does is to crab the fact that they have inlay work on
the wood! It is a kind of inferiority complex. But he is a good soldier and
he wins battles, and that is the main thing.

On 26 April there was a parade in the grounds of Flagstaff House, very
much a full dress affair, in which a Samurai Sword was presented to
Major General Stratemeyer on behalf of the troops of Allied Land
Forces. A Guard of Honour of the Royal Scots played after the ceremony.
Leese was very good at arranging a display with all the trimmings if he
thought the occasion suitable. The presentation to Stratemeyer was a
return for his enormous help in getting Dakotas as air supply planes
during the final assault on Rangoon. Speed was essential and Stratemeyer was able to cut red tape and get them quickly.

He always got on splendidly with Leese – rather to the annoyance
of Keith Park, who considered that Stratemeyer should have done
more to maintain air force independence.[1] Leese liked Stratemeyer
and chuckled over his foibles, such as carrying a dogwhip, and his
fondness for souvenirs. Hence the Samurai Sword.

---

[1] Tedder had taken a similar line with Monty over the invasion of Sicily; and Patton
had written that Tedder was more interested in producing an independent air force
than in winning the war. In a letter to Marshal of the RAF Sir John Slessor, Keith
Park complained that Leese had dominated Stratemeyer, adding 'Shortly after my
arrival [in SE Asia] I discovered that the Army Group Commander was virtually
supreme commander of the land and air forces in Burma.' Park told Stratemeyer that
the Army should state the problems or the effect required, and leave it to the air force
commander to decide the method of execution. It was said of Park that he could never
fathom Leese's pose as a gentleman farmer in uniform.

29 Apl. OL to ML.

We saw the Fort (Built in Madras in 1691) with the oldest British chapel in India. Clive was married there and Arthur Wellesley signed the visitors book!

Leese referred to Bastyan's work in administration – 'has had a terrible time sorting out the whole thing.' On 30 April – the day that Hitler committed suicide – Leese was scenting victory:

> 62 miles from Rangoon last night. It is really wonderful and there is now a good chance to bring it off before the monsoon. *It would be a wonderful triumph, as when I came out here it was never even thought of as a possible thing.*[1] . . . IL came to see me in great heart . . . Tomorrow we go to Kandy . . . how I hate it.

Judging the exact moment for the dash to Rangoon was of crucial importance. It was difficult to tell how a Japanese general would react, in comparison with a German or Italian commander. With the Japanese there came a moment when any form of higher control or signal communication ceased, and when this happened there would still be many Japanese fighting bravely in scattered groups. This was to happen in the assault on Rangoon.

Eventually, it was decided that the moment had come for Slim to make his dash against time, which entailed leaving thousands of Japanese troops on his flanks when he advanced, but the risk had to be taken. Pyinmana, Toungoo and Pegu were the vital objectives; Pegu, in fact, covered the last Japanese escape route.

During an advance of 260 miles in twenty days the Japanese were forced off the road and into the hills, and Leese wrote of the 'extraordinary situation in which our troops were down the road whilst the Japanese were walking out parallel to them in the hills on both sides of the road!' By this means thousands of Japanese were by-passed and could not get back in time to intervene in the battle. The Burmese National Army, which had been fighting with the Japanese, now turned against their former masters. General Aung San, its commander, surrendered, still in his Japanese uniform.

Meanwhile, Christison's 15 Corps went in according to plan with parachute and seaborne landings. The parachute landings were successfully carried out on 1 May, and the strategically important Elephant Point was taken. The seaborne landing, as planned, went in on 2 May: it proved to be just in time, as a storm arose two hours after the landing craft touched down.

Both the landings – on the east and on the west bank – were unopposed, and they took place in torrential rain. The troops now

[1] Author's italics.

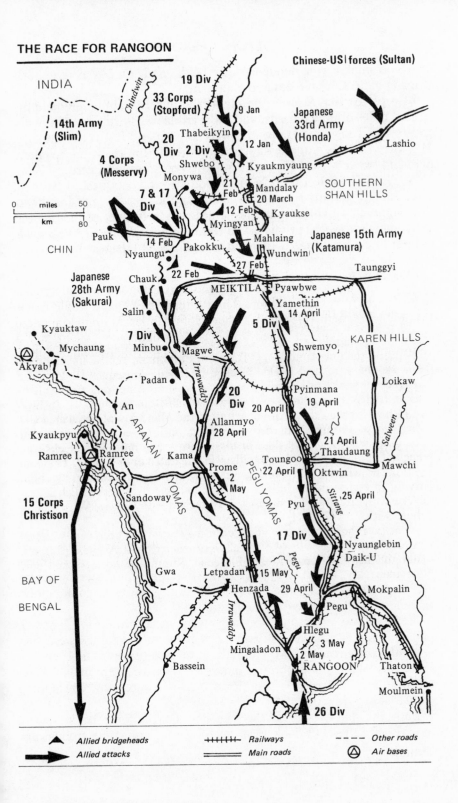

THE RACE FOR RANGOON

INDIA

Chindwin

19 Div

33 Corps (Stopford)

9 Jan

Chinese-US forces (Sultan)

14th Army (Slim)

Thabeikyin

20 Div 2 Div

12 Jan

Japanese 33rd Army (Honda)

Lashio

4 Corps (Messervy)

Shwebo

Monywa

Kyaukmyaung

SOUTHERN SHAN HILLS

0   miles   50

km   80

7 & 17 Div

21 Feb

Mandalay

20 March

CHIN

12 Feb

Myingyan

Kyaukse

Pauk

14 Feb

Nyaungu

Pakokku

Mahlaing

Wundwin

Japanese 15th Army (Katamura)

Taunggyi

Japanese 28th Army (Sakurai)

Chauk

22 Feb

27 Feb

MEIKTILA

Pyawbwe

Yamethin

14 April

Salin

7 Div

Minbu

Magwe

5 Div

Shwemyo

KAREN HILLS

Kyauktaw

Mychaung

Akyab

Padan

Irrawaddy

An

20 Div

20 April

Pinmana

19 April

Loikaw

Salween

Kyaukpyu

Ramree I.   Ramree

Allanmyo

28 April

Kama

21 April

Thaudaung

Mawchi

15 Corps Christison

Sandoway

ARAKAN YOMAS

Prome

2 May

PEGU YOMAS

Toungoo

22 April   Oktwin

25 April

Sittang

Pyu

BAY OF BENGAL

Gwa

Letpadan

17 Div

Nyaunglebin

Daik-U

Pegu

15 May

Henzada

29 April

Mokpalin

Pegu

Irrawaddy

Hlegu

3 May

Mingaladon

2 May

RANGOON

Thaton

Bassein

Moulmein

26 Div

| ▲ | Allied bridgeheads | ┼┼┼┼┼ | Railways | - - - - | Other roads |
| ➤ | Allied attacks | ═══ | Main roads | ⌂ | Air bases |

drove on inland over flooded paddy fields, and, on 3 May, the 36th
Brigade of 26 Division entered Rangoon.

4 Corps (Lt Gen Messervy) fought magnificently, but were held up
against miles of mined roads, and the terrible rainstorms flooded fields
and roads. Tanks and transports were halted, and it was not until 17
May that 4 Corps entered Rangoon. 'General Slim made an excellent
plan and never wavered from his purpse', commented Leese.

'So ended,' wrote Leese, 'a great victory – the conquest of Burma.
Here ended, too, my active service during the war . . . and thanks to
the magnificent fighting qualities and devotion to duty of the officers
and men whom I was privileged to command during these 3 years, we
did not lose a battle against Germans, Italians or Japanese.'[1]

4 May. OL to ML.

We have had our great triumph. We have out-generalled, out-manoeuvred
and out-fought the Jap and we have captured Rangoon.

It is a great achievement in 5 months, and a terrific relief to me, and
now we can supply 14th Army in a proper manner by sea and are no longer
reliant on the long land L of C [Lines of Communication] – its attendant
fair weather roads and tracks, blocked rivers and consequential complete
reliance on transport aircraft, so much of which is American, and liable to
be utilised away to other theatres at will with little or no previous warning.

14th Army won the decisive victory in the Mandalay-Meiktila area and
then broke through the enemy covering position at Pyante, south of
Meiktila. They then did their historic drive – 350 miles in 5 weeks – to
Pegu. The entire Jap army was either disintegrated or destroyed. They can
get out no wheels or supporting weapons, and they are wandering about
trying to escape in the hills . . . S has amoebic dysentery which is bad
luck, as the treatment is so beastly. I lunched with General Wheeler and
dined with Park [2 May].

The positioning at Kandy for the Burma battles has been very wasteful
in time and energy . . . We are all very excited – El Alamein, Tripoli,
Mareth, Sicily, Cassino, Rome, Florence, Rimini, Mandalay – and now
Rangoon.

[1] Memoirs.

17

A RAW DEAL

I feel very sorry about Leese as he was very able and completely straight and was doing his job excellently.
      Major General George Symes, Commanding Lines of
            Communication ALFSEA (Diary, 14 July 1945)

It is no good trying to hide the fact. We miss you like hell. I shall never know a happier relationship between commander and Staff Officer than I was privileged to know with you.
      Major General Edrick Bastyan, Chief Administrative Officer,
            ALFSEA (Letter to OL 18 July 1945)

I feel very sad the way things have gone. We were such a happy party . . . I should love to serve under you again.
      Major General R. H. Steward, Chief Signals Officer,
            ALFSEA (Letter to OL 10 August 1945)

The fall of Rangoon was not only a remarkable military achievement, but it meant that, as Pownall had put it, Britain had something in the shop window, that Burma had been re-conquered mainly by British leadership and British and Indian personnel, and would not be handed back to us by the Americans. Letters and telegrams of congratulations to Oliver Leese came thick and fast. In a letter to ML on 15 May he referred to receiving 'hundreds of telegrams on Rangoon'.

Few of the telegrams have survived, but the messages extant speak for themselves. General Alexander was 'delighted that things have gone so well'. General Sir Arthur Smitt wrote from Persia Iraq Command: 'Now that Rangoon has fallen it is a good moment to say how delighted I am. I was watching the race v. the monsoon, and wondered if you would pull it off. And now I see telegrams of congratulations to Mountbatten that ought to go to you.'

'You have had a wonderful success,' wrote Gort, 'and the boldness of your plan in conception and execution, well merited the victory which was destined to be your reward.' Bernard Freyberg expressed satisfaction in his enormous handwriting. 'It was a magnificent effort,' wrote Brian Horrocks, 'I never thought that you would "make it" before the monsoon started.'

Most memorable of all are the words of Major General A. P. Godwin-Austen, Quarter-Master General, India:

> My word! You have done marvellously! I do hope you won't think it impertinent of me to say that I feel your determination to launch the Rangoon party by sea, and your refusal to listen to the horde of dismal Jimmies, who must have talked interminably of 'the Monsoon' is to my mind one of the finest examples of high courage in a commander known in military history.

Having brought the war in Burma to a successful conclusion, Leese now gave priority to the planning of operation *Zipper*, the forthcoming invasion of Malaya. As amphibious warfare would again be necessary, Christison, who had done so well in the race for Rangoon, seemed the obvious leader for this operation. Slim had been on continuous active service in the Far East for three years, and possibly had not recovered from his prostate gland operation as quickly as he had hoped, and who at Mandalay had asked for four months' leave in England at the end of the Burma campaign, should obviously be given a less strenuous post. Leese therefore intended Slim to command the new army in Burma, where he would have plenty to do in the way of conducting mopping up operations.

On 3 May, the day after British troops entered Rangoon, Leese saw Mountbatten in Kandy. The latter agreed with Leese's ideas and gave him full authority to hold exploratory discussions with Slim and Christison. Leese suggested that Mountbatten, as Supreme Commander, should do this; Mountbatten however said that Leese should broach the subject with Slim, as Leese was Slim's superior.

On 4 May, Leese returned to Barrackpore, and on the same day Mountbatten wrote a somewhat odd letter to Leese:

> Please excuse pencil but I am writing this in bed as I particularly do not want to dictate this letter. Pug [Ismay][1] sent me a telegram last night asking me to send each Secretary of State the complete agreed combined Honour Awards lists for Burma and this I have now done.
>
> I have also sent a proposal line to CIGS urging that the final victory in Burma should be recognised either by your immediate promotion or decoration and urging the former. The CIGS makes a special point of my

[1] Major General H. L. (Baron) Ismay, Senior Staff Officer to Churchill.

writing to him from time to time to keep him in the picture. In general I have only favourable things to say; but I felt it incumbent upon me this time to inform him of our exchange of telegrams and subsequent interview.[1]

I would have preferred not to mention the incident to him at all since I consider the matter closed, but I have made this clear to him and purposely brought up the subject at the same time as my recommendation for your promotion, thus I hope placing the incident in its right perspective. I have told him how much I like you and that I am confident that when you have joined the other 2 C's-in-C in Ceylon, it will make things much easier. You have backed up theatre strategy extremely well and I am looking forward to our all conducting together a rapid and victorious campaign this year.

It seems apparent from the tone of this letter that Mountbatten intended to block Leese's promotion, that he wanted Leese to receive no award for his achievements in Burma.

The next day, 5 May, Leese wrote to Alanbrooke in connexion with the fall of Rangoon and with plans for the future. After some complimentary comments about Slim, Leese continued:

I think that both you and I realised at the same time the advisability to put an amphibious operation into Rangoon and I was very glad that you pressed for the postponement of the *Roger* Operation [Mountbatten's projected attack on Phuket]. It appeared then as if Fourteenth Army might get stuck between Rangoon and Mandalay. If they had been stuck in Central Burma with 150 or 200 miles to go to Rangoon during the monsoon, operations might have been terribly slow and costly.

I want to use Headquarters, Fourteenth Army, and Army Troops to control the operations in Malaya. Slim has been on continuous active service since 1941 and has been in Burma without a break since the finish of Field Marshal Alexander's operations in 1942. He has stood up to the strain well, but I do not think he has it in him to start off on another vigorous campaign with a completely new conception, without a rest. I have, therefore, asked you to allow me to transfer him from 14th Army to command the new Burma Army, which I intend to set up to control the operations and administration in Burma. I am not asking for a new staff as I am using 33 Corps as a basis on which to build the new Burma Army. I feel that if our propaganda is good, Slim can be built up as the conqueror of Burma and is the right man to set Burma on a sound footing for the future. Moreover there is still considerable fighting to be carried on in Burma.

I propose to put General Christison in command of Fourteenth Army. As you know I have been very pleased throughout with his handling of the operations in the Arakan. He is respected by everyone, and in view of his experience of amphibious operations against the Japanese, I would prefer to have him in command of the Army than to have out a newcomer at this

[1] Appendix C.

juncture. The necessity to get on at once with the planning for the Malaysia operations has been another factor which has influenced me in my decision to ask for Christison.

With regard to future operations Leese wrote that he intended to assault Malaya with Fourteenth Army, using 4 Corps as the assault Corps and 15 Corps as the follow up. Leese's letter was accepted amicably by Alanbrooke, who replied on 1 June: 'It was interesting to have your concept of future operations, particularly as it has given us greater detail of the units taking part. I hope it will be possible to provide you with sufficient resources for your Malayan operation.'

On 6 May, Leese flew from Calcutta to Akyab where he saw Christison on the way to seeing Slim at Meiktila, and indicated that he wanted Christison to command Fourteenth Army. Christison, believing that he had definitely been appointed Commander of Fourteenth Army, acting in good faith, informed his staff of his impending promotion, and they gave him the traditional farewell and congratulatory dinner. Leese's recollection of the occasion, years later, was that he had said Christison had as good a chance of Fourteenth Army as anyone else.

8 May. OL to ML.

I had a long talk with Slim and this morning we flew over to find Monty Stopford in a nice cool place on a lovely reach of the Irrawaddy . . . Monty was well and I talked to his BGS Scott and his AQ Jones. I liked them. I left them champagne to celebrate the Armistice in Europe – which we heard this morning. I also sent a bottle to Gracey – it seems unbelievable . . . when you look back on 1940–1942 out here it seems unreal.

The talk with Slim took place at Meiktila at 1500 hrs on 7 May. In this conversation Leese proposed to Slim what he had already outlined to Alanbrooke and Mountbatten, Leese going out of his way to let down lightly a subordinate who had always been difficult to handle. Leese, having told Slim his ideas, asked him to think things over, although he believed that Slim had definitely accepted the proposals by the end of the interview. Leese accordingly rang up Browning who was at HQ in Kandy, to tell him that the proposals had been accepted.

On 8 May Mountbatten, down with amoebic dysentery, conducted a conference in his bedroom.

10 May. OL to ML.

I think you may hear rumours about S and myself. Things have been very difficult, and, now that the land campaign is over, things may be easier. But I thought you ought to know, otherwise it might come as a shock to you, or you might get put in a wrong position, if things suddenly came to end. There is nothing to worry about, but I think you ought to know the form. I wish I could see the CIGS. We are so far away out here.

13 May.

En route to Bombay. We stay two nights at Bombay to see some generals, two nights at Quetta to lecture to the Staff College, two nights at Peshawar to visit some airborne troops. Then to Delhi, so we still cover a lot of ground. We have 'Hermes', our new wireless Dakota with us – so we are always in touch – so I hope we don't get recalled in the middle.

At Quetta, Leese stayed in their old house with Lt-General and Mrs Irwin. Irwin, Giffard's predecessor, had tried to sack Slim in 1943, but had been replaced by Giffard before Slim's dismissal had taken effect.

On 20 May, Leese wrote to ML en route for Kandy. 'Done the round of India in a week – Rangoon – Barrackpore – Bombay – Quetta – Peshawar – Lahore – Delhi – and now on to Kandy.' He was delighted at Margie's news that her brother John had been released after nearly four years as a prisoner of war.

On 21 May, Leese left Delhi for Ratmalana, Ceylon, and immediately motored to Kandy, where he dined with Mountbatten. He stayed the night at Main ALFSEA. On 22 May, he visited the new Tac HQ and later attended a luncheon party given by Mountbatten.

During the fortnight that had just elapsed much had happened behind the scenes – Slim had pencilled in his diary for 7 May 'sacked 1530', although it was not in Leese's power to sack Slim even had he wanted to, and it was to be expected that Slim, who was not exactly a raw recruit, would have known this.

In his biography of Slim, Ronald Lewin recalled that Colonel Denis O'Connor,[1] having been informed by Brigadier 'Tubby' Lethbridge, Slim's Chief of Staff, of the 'dismissal', later ran into Slim himself, and said how sorry he was. Slim replied:

Don't worry old boy. This happened to me once before, and I bloody well took the job of the chap that sacked me. I'll bloody well do it again.

Colonel J. F. Godwin, another of Slim's staff officers, wrote an account of the 'sacking' incident that certainly pulled no punches:

On reaching my caravan late in the evening, I was sent for by 'Tubby' Lethbridge, who straight away blurted out through a mixture of emotion,

[1] Lt General Sir Denis O'Connor.

anger and Scotch, 'Uncle Bill has been sacked. He wants to see all of us senior staff at 1000 tomorrow morning.'

On the next morning (9 May) Godwin reported Slim as saying:

> I have a very painful announcement to make to you, gentlemen. Two days ago, the Commander-in-Chief [Oliver Leese] visited our HQ as you know, and told me I was unsuitable for the coming operations, and could not command the 14th Army further. I can't tell you what a painful announcement this is for me to make to you when, as you will guess, I only have one ambition and that is to go on commanding the 14th Army, of which I am extremely proud, until the Jap is finally beaten flat. But that is not to be.

Slim continued that he had been offered Twelfth Army, adding the enigmatic statement

> I am telling you chaps now; I owe it to you who have helped me through so many tough spots before.

Slim concluded that he wanted no mention of the subject outside the four walls of the Mess, that there were higher loyalties than to him, such as to the Commander-in-Chief, to their King, to their country. If Godwin was reporting accurately, then Mark Antony could hardly have done better.

> 'Of course,' proceeded Godwin, 'we all wrote at once to the highest and most influential person we knew in Whitehall, saying that a monumental act of folly was being committed.'

Philip Ziegler quotes Godwin's comment: 'Oliver "Twist" and Mountbatten must be out of their minds. I never trusted that affected, silk-handkerchief-waving guardsman.'[1]

The news of Slim's 'sacking' soon reached Auchinleck, who saw Alanbrooke, who got in touch with Mountbatten, who gave his version of what had happened.

Three entries in Alanbrooke's diary at this time refer to the Slim affair:

> 17 May. After lunch at *The Times* back to W.O. for interview with the Auk about appointment of Slim to Burma command: Leese is going quite wild and doing mad things. Prepared a fair rap on the knuckles for him.

As General Christison has pointed out, the information regarding

[1] *Mountbatten*, by Philip Ziegler (Collins).

Leese's 'wild doings' could only have come from Mountbatten.

22 May. Auchinleck came to lunch with me and we had a very useful talk together.

23 May. Dinner with PJ and Lady Grigg, with Old Auchinleck dining also.

By the time Leese had arrived at Kandy on the evening of 21 May, the Slim story in various forms had been picked up, rumours had multiplied and the situation was out of control. Leese asked Mountbatten to back the original plan by which Slim would be sent on home leave and then return to take command of the Army in Burma, which was to be named the Twelfth Army. However, Mountbatten indicated that Slim should retain command of Fourteenth Army, asking Leese if he would keep Slim. Realising that Mountbaten was not going to back him up, Leese accepted the situation with a good grace, and it was agreed that Slim be confirmed in his command.

Having dined with Mountbatten on 21 May, when the position of Slim was discussed, Leese attended a luncheon party on 22 May with Mountbatten and Boy Browning. Ion Calvocoressi, as Walsh's assistant, attended this party, in which he found himself a very junior officer among twenty or so top brass. Mountbatten and Browning appeared:

'Oh, Oliver,' called Mountbatten, 'as you see, Boy and I are wearing the Burma Star ribbon. I've just had it flown out. I'm having a yard and a half sent to your HQ for you and your staff.'

'How very kind of you, Supremo,' said Oliver Leese. 'And when do the troops get theirs?'

'In a couple of months,' said Mountbatten. 'It's coming by boat.'

'Well thank you,' said Oliver Leese. 'In that case I and my staff will wait until the troops have got theirs.' Leese's reply would hardly have poured oil on troubled waters.

23 May. Mountbatten to CIGS:

On 3 May, Oliver Leese came to see me about future appointments of the Army and Corps Commanders in SEAC. He told me he considered Slim extremely tired after three years constant fighting in Burma and that Slim himself had on more than one occasion remarked what a strain it had been on him. He therefore wished to give Slim a job from which he could justifiably take three or four months leave and suggested he should be put in command of the Army in Burma which he suggested should be called the Twelfth Army. I authorised him to discuss the matter with Slim, on a friendly basis, and assumed that he would tell me if there were any difficulty, and in any case report back to me before approaching you.

23 May. OL to ML.

I dined with S [21 May] who is recovering from dysentery. He was very nice and gave me a first cut off the Burma ribbon. It is rather disappointing – not a vestige of green for the jungle, and rather like a second South African medal.

This may have been the occasion referred to by Ion Calvocoressi, Leese writing 'gave' instead of 'offered', so that ML would not be worried, or it may have been offered a second time, and he obviously could not refuse it twice.

On 24 May, Leese saw Slim at Barrackpore. It was the first time they had met since 7 May when the so-called 'sacking' interview took place. The interview of 24 May, according to C-in-C's Diary, was 'on past and future operations'. Slim was now supported by Mountbatten: Leese was making the best of a difficult job.

25 May. Browning to Mountbatten.

Leese has settled everything very satisfactorily with Slim. Latter returns Rangoon for three days before coming Delhi. Leese suggests Slim goes on month's leave with family to England. Am arranging their passage by air. Security must unfortunately be very tight as otherwise Slim would have had as he deserves great ovation in England.

It seemed, therefore, that everything had settled down. On 30 May, shortly before Slim was due to go to England on leave, Leese wrote an official letter to ML, asking her to do what she could to help:

This is to let you know that General Slim (the Commander Fourteenth Army), with Lady Slim, and his Military Assistant, Major Dan Munroe, will be home about 13th June. They will be in England from four to six weeks on leave. Would you please do everything you possibly can to help them while they are in England? Neither of them have been at home for many years, and therefore they are completely out of touch with people and with conditions in England in wartime.

I have booked them rooms at the Dorchester Hotel, and have asked Budget Loyd to provide an ADC and a servant . . . I am awfully anxious that after his past record everything possible should be done to help General Slim to have the best possible leave, and I know you will do everything you can for them.

On 2 June he wrote confidentially to ML on the same topic:

I interviewed a series of commanders in turn [This was at Viceroy House where Leese was then staying], finishing with IL before he goes to London. Be careful with him. He is very tired and wants a good rest – but I did not get it done satisfactorily and things got in a mess – and I bought it all ways! Partially deserved too! as I failed to bring off what was really the right decision – I can't tell you more. It has never been easy with him. He really resented my coming out here at all, and he has made things difficult all along for me and my Staff. He is almost a megalomaniac and compares himself very favourably with O. He can never resist having a dig at other HQs. As a result you can imagine that it has not been all 'fun and games' – dealing with S on one level and he on another. But he has put up a magnificent show and is a great figurehead with his men. And it is very necessary for him to be acclaimed in England. But don't expect him to be a friend of yours or mine – unless he wants something. We got on allright as soldiers – and I never had any trouble with him from that angle purely, though he is the world's bellyacher. A year with O would do him more good than anything else. His great attribute is that he is genuinely very fond of his troops. His worst enemy is his self-estimation and his complete lack of knowledge of the world.

Sandwiched between these two letters, he had written to ML on 1 June:

I have just got your letter – saying that you feel like blowing up about my 'Press'. I ask you most sincerely to be scrupulously careful not to do so. I have had a very difficult month for several reasons both with S and CIGS. It may be that things are now better, but, as I told you before, matters may come to a head, in which case the less publicity, etc., the better. I want particularly to warn you to be careful if an Honours and Promotions list comes out for Rangoon in which I am not mentioned. All these things are small in comparison to winning our battles, and so far I've managed that anyway, and now for the next!! After that Worfield and just you and I.

The Fourth of June was a date that as a loyal Etonian he would always celebrate, even during the war. 1945 proved no exception. He gave a small dinner party and sent the following signal to Eton, which was signed by Leese and Etonian staff officers at his HQ:

Hodie memorabile novem alumni Etonienses fideles sodaliter convocati apud ripam Hooglii, in calore incredibile sudentes, Rangoon jam revicto atque hoste Nipponico deleto, matrem nostram caram salutamus.

On 7 June, Mountbatten wrote a 2500-word diatribe to Alanbrooke in which he was obviously anxious for CIGS to sack Oliver Leese. Mountbatten's letter began with the statement that he had taken the opportunity of having long talks in his bedroom at the Viceroy's House with Christison, Stopford and Slim, in that order. To Christison he explained that Slim had been retained in command of Fourteenth Army on his (Mountbatten's) instructions and Mountbatten 'apologised for the position in which he had been placed.'

The talk with Stopford largely consisted of Stopford's account of a row with Slim, subsequently settled. Mountbatten then went on:

> Slim told me that Leese greeted him by saying 'Before we talk of anything else, I must tell you that I have decided to give Christison command of the Fourteenth Army and to ask you to stay on in command of the troops that will be left in Burma. I do not consider you capable of planning a large scale amphibious operation like *Zipper*, or of commanding the Fourteenth Army in such an operation; so I do not think it will be fair either to the Fourteenth Army or to yourself to leave you in command of it.'[1]

Slim, wrote Mountbatten, said that this had been a great shock to him, as he thought 'he hadn't done too badly'; not so badly, anyway, as to deserve being sacked in such ungracious terms. He asked permission to go on leave, and since he presumed there would be no other employment for him after supersession, he was quite willing to face retirement uncomplainingly. Leese begged him not to do this and urged him to think it over for three days and then let him know his decision as the changes would take place almost immediately. Slim said that nothing could possibly make him change his mind.

On 8 May, wrote Mountbatten, Leese wrote to him saying that he had seen Slim, Christison and Stopford, that everything appeared satisfactory. Slim was thinking it over, but Leese thought he was at least happy.

Mountbatten wrote that following the meeting between Leese and Slim, nothing happened for a few days, and that as force planning was to start in Delhi on 24 May, Slim sent a telegram to ALFSEA to say that failing instructions to the contrary, he (Slim) proposed to turn over to Stopford the command of the forces left in Burma, and to proceed to Delhi for further instructions as to his disposal by the 1st June.

> 'I rather gathered,' wrote Mountbatten, 'it was the wording of this telegram which caused the "leak", but since he had received these instructions one can hardly blame him for going ahead with what he understood was an irrevocable decision. He admits that the news appears to have spread like wildfire all down the Fourteenth Army. Indeed he told me that several

[1] John Stimpson writes: 'Whilst this was undoubtedly Leese's view, and proved by the facts, it is most unlikely that he would tackle such an interview with this initial assault. He would not have treated Slim in this manner.'

Corps, Divisional and Brigade Commanders wrote to him saying they no longer wished to serve under General Leese and wished to forward their requests for transfer. Slim replied that they were not to be stupid, that he relied on them to serve the new Fourteenth Army Commander as loyally as they had served him . . . The usual farewell dinner was given for Slim.'

Then Slim received the telegram saying 'It has been decided that you shall retain command of the Fourteenth Army.'

'He realised,' wrote Mountbatten, 'that Leese must have been over-ruled and expected that he would place his resignation in my hands. Slim was summoned to Calcutta and was very surprised to note from Leese's remarks that he had evidently allowed himself to be flatly over-ruled by me and had accepted it without demur. Slim refused however in the first instance to reconsider his decision. Leese gave him a letter from me asking him to stay on and Slim thought the matter over. He told me he had eventually decided to stay on so as not to let down the Fourteenth Army who had shown such trust in him and in order not to put me in the position of having to choose between Leese and himself.

'I asked Slim candidly whether he was really prepared to serve loyally under Leese in these circumstances, and he said "Of course I shall serve him with the utmost loyalty but I am afraid it will be without any confidence. I must also point out that my position will be extremely awkward in continuing to serve under someone who has once tried to sack me."

'I assured him of my personal trust and I should watch most carefully to see that he had scrupulously fair treatment. I asked him if he had any further troubles [a hilarious touch] and he replied that so far as he and his staff were concerned, they had nothing but trouble with ALFSEA, whose whole staff took the attitude "Now the Eighth Army is here, things are going to be done very differently." He told me that neither he nor the senior commanders trust Leese's military judgement.'[1]

Fortunately, wrote Mountbatten, he (Mountbatten) liked Oliver Leese, and since his row with him a month previously, followed by his over-ruling him over Slim's appointment, Leese was a changed man. If Leese stayed on in Kandy there should be no more difficulties. As he did give Leese full authority to discuss with Slim the matter of his future, Mountbatten wondered whether he himself should sack Leese, having already sacked Giffard.

Alanbrooke's subsequent Diary comments about Mountbatten are very unfavourable.

On 10 June, Leese wrote to ML from Rangoon, saying that he wouldn't be in touch for three days or so, as he would be visiting

---

[1] In his autobiographical work, *Defeat into Victory*, Slim has high praise for Leese as a military commander, and states that on the one occasion when they disagreed, events proved that it was Leese who was in the right.

troops in light aircraft, and wouldn't have time, and then he would be back just in time for 'S's Roman Triumph'.

I think it will be good, and he deserves it, and he will enjoy it like a child. He has asked over 30 official senior visitors of all the nations.

17 June. OL to ML.

Terrific victory celebrations [in Rangoon]. I met S at the Airport. He brought everyone you could think of – Power, Park, Wheeler, Sultan, Swayne and all the Kandy crowd. French, Dutch, Chinese – they opened Government House and brought in chairs and crockery and each night had over 40 to dinner. Really a very good effort.

On 19 June CIGS replied to Mountbatten, saying that Leese had lost the confidence of most of his senior commanders, and had managed to quarrel with Power, Park and Wheeler, that obviously Mountbatten himself had lost confidence in Leese, who should therefore be sacked.

'How did the CIGS learn all this?' General Christison said to the present writer (17.11.1980). 'He got the information from one man – Mountbatten. It was a pity he couldn't have gone out, got all three of them together, and said – "Look here, boys, what's all this about? Let's get everything straightened out!"'

It was unfortunate that when the affair was boiling up in England, Alanbrooke was obviously not at the top of his form. Excerpts from his diary during the period 6 June–20 June 1945 speak for themselves:

June 6. I feel very weary!

June 8. I had a difficult lunch with Anders at the Dorchester.

In the entries of 12, 13 and 14 June, 13 is entered as Sept 13, and 14 is entered as Dec. 14. The next entry reads:

June 18. Drafted letter to Mountbatten advising him to get rid of Oliver Leese who has proved to be a failure in South East Asia Command. It is very disappointing.

Alanbrooke noted on 19 June, 'Had long and interesting talk with Slim this afternoon,' and on 20 June 'Slim attended our COS meeting and gave us an outline for the proposed operations for the capture of Malaya.' This entry concluded with the words:

There is a definite time in a man's life when it is best for him to go into retirement. I am approaching that age.

Slim's diary meanwhile recorded a full time table. In addition to the

meetings referred to by CIGS, there was lunch with Lady Louis
Mountbatten on 19 June, and lunch with Lady Leese (Margie) on 20
June. On 22 June, there was a civic lunch in Birmingham and the note
'St P' followed by 'KES' indicated that he had visited at St Philips
Grammar School and King Edwards School, which he had attended
as a pupil.

22 June. OL to ML.

Off to Delhi.
   I think we shall stay with General Auk – [who had now returned from
leave] and so we should hear the home gossip. I shall be interested to see
him, as I don't think he helped us much when he was at home.
   S comes back to Delhi from Kashmir tomorrow and we shall have the
usual spate of meetings. I hope to go to Kashmir the next day, and I am
looking forward to a change.
   I got your letter about all the arrangements for the Slims. I am so
grateful, he deserves a good time and on the whole he will do us good out
here – if he does not overstate his case. He is a complete egoist, thinks
himself greater than O, and does not understand the meaning of the word
loyalty. But he is a good soldier, inspires his men with confidence, and
above all wins battles.

On 22 June Leese flew from Barrackpore to Delhi, staying the night
with Auchinleck with whom he dined. Next day, Saturday 23 June,
there was a conference with Auchinleck, and later a Supreme Commander's conference. Leese again dined and stayed the night with
Auchinleck. His only comments to ML (June 24) were brief and
deliberately vague:

We had a great party with the Auk – S – the Commander of Burma – Boy.
To dinner came Jack Swayne and Tommy Lindsell. We had a lot of
conferences.

It is fascinating to imagine the conversations at this particular time,
when Leese and Mountbatten were guests of Auchinleck.
   Leese now set out to Srinagar for a week's leave, with Ulick Verney
and Jimmy Boyle, as guests of the Maharajah of Kashmir, the party
staying in one of the Maharajah's guest houses. Most of the time Leese
spent in fishing and relaxing. On a couple of occasions he lunched and
dined with the Maharajah.

29 June. From Alanbrooke's Diary:

After lunch I had to go to PM at 3 p.m. to tell him that we should have to withdraw Oliver Lees [sic] from South East Asia and replace him by Slim. He kept me for an hour, but agreed to all I wanted.

We are now ordering Oliver Leese home, appointing Slim in his place and sending out Dempsey as the additional Army Commander.[1]

30 June. OL to ML.

I hope to stay here till the 3rd – go to Delhi for the night, and then on to Kandy.

It was on 2 July that the blow fell. Mountbatten's letter, dated 1 July 1945, delivered personally by an officer from Kandy to Leese in Kashmir, read as follows:

Dear Oliver,

I am afraid I have an extremely painful duty to perform and one that I had hoped, on purely personal grounds, I might be spared. From this opening remark you can guess what it is: namely that after consultation by letter with the CIGS, I find myself unable to retain your services.

I told you in Delhi that I intended to have a talk with Slim. He told me that he considered that you had categorically sacked him, and that in view of this he had been most reluctant to continue in command of the 14th Army, and had only done so out of the highest sense of duty. He pointed out that his position would be extremely awkward in continuing to serve under someone who had once tried to sack him, and that he could not see how mutual confidence would ever be re-established. It was thus clear to me that a position had been reached in which that complete trust between my two principal Military Commanders, which is a pre-requisite to successful ops, no longer existed.

In view of your longstanding successful record in High Command in this war, culminating in the capture of Rangoon, and since you did not yourself resign when I overruled you, I was extremely reluctant to take the decision that you should have to go.

I therefore placed the whole matter, as fairly and objectively as I could, before the CIGS, and have just heard his opinion, that he feels there is no alternative but to replace you at the earliest possible moment. I have therefore telegraphed to him that you are returning at once.

At the same time I telegraphed to the CIGS a strong recommendation that you should be offered a high and important military appointment consonant with your record and requested that this should be announced at the same time as the name of your successor is published.

The CIGS has offered me the services of Dempsey and I have agreed to the CIGS' suggestion to invite Slim to succeed you and Dempsey to succeed Slim.

---

[1] Ronald Lewin described Slim as 'bemused' when told of his appointment as Commander-in-Chief.

As I do not consider that Slim should have his much needed leave cut short, and as I do not think it would be fair to ask you to stay on in the present circumstances, I have arranged with the CIGS for you to go on leave to England as soon as you have turned over the command temporarily to Christison, to whom I have sent a letter, a copy of which I enclose.

I intend to let it be known, in due course, simply that you are going home on leave.

I hope you will believe how sincerely and deeply sorry I am that this situation should have arisen. I cannot close without expressing once more my sincere appreciation of the results achieved in the last 6 or 7 months of the Burma Campaign.

Mountbatten's letter to Leese is much milder in tone than his letter to Alanbrooke: it is almost apologetic. It seems evident that Mountbatten knew – and Leese knew – and Mountbatten knew that Leese knew – that Leese was 'carrying the can' for him.

On the morning of 3 July Leese, Ulick Verney and John Stimpson left for Barrackpore.

3 July. OL to ML.

My darling Margie,

We cut out Delhi and left Srinagar at 6 a.m. this morning. For at lunch yesterday a courier arrived with an urgent personal letter from S – telling me that he could not 'retain my services' – and that the CIGS had ordered me to return to London. A climax to the same old trouble with L which I thought was over. But S deliberately, I think, brought it up again with L – who apparently said that he did not see how he and I could have mutual confidence in each other again. I made a silly error in judgment and was carted above and below. But I bought it and I think that S meant anyhow to get rid of me. I've felt it for two months. I am very glad to leave here. It has been a horrid party with S and L. It has been intensely interesting and satisfactory in results. But I know I'm stale, and that, coupled with the difficult personal problems, makes it best to go. It is a pity however to get the sack. It will be awkward for a bit at home and I expect I shall buy a high level rocket or two – I am supposed to be coming home on leave and we hope to start on the 6th. We are determined not to blab and talk but it will be difficult to convince people. It will be lovely to talk things over together and see what the future holds out.

Too much should not be read into Leese's statement 'I know I'm stale', written to lighten ML's sadness. Of the four people most closely concerned with the Slim episode, Leese was the only one who was fully fit. Alanbrooke and Slim had both described themselves as being very tired, Mountbatten was convalescing from amoebic dysentery.

Leese was completely fit and had been working hard on plans for the assault on Malaya.

Having arrived at Barrackpore, Leese telephoned Christison: 'Get hold of a plane and come and see me in Calcutta at once. I can't say any more just now!' Christison wrote:

> I obeyed and found Oliver in his bath. 'Christie,' (with his characteristic snort), 'I've been sacked! You are to take my place at once, I'm for home. Brookie went to Churchill and told him the Indian Army wouldn't fight without Slim. "Who sacked Slim?" said Churchill. "Leese" said Alanbrooke. "Well, sack Leese." I gather I'm carrying the can for Dickie over this.'

6 July. OL to ML.

We had a hard two days at B/pore finishing off and packing. I only told George, Dricky, Peter Dunphie, Christie who is deputising for me and Ulick and John S . . . We kept up a very cheerful façade and I think we were fairly convincing. Anyhow no-one can say we either bellyached or bla-ed it about. I lunched both days at the Bengal Club to show the flag and make a change. George, Dricky, Ulick and I dined alone on the last night. They were so upset and so terribly nice. It is a pity that I should have been sent home, as there will be a lot of talk and gossip, but I'm sure it is for the best in the long run for me and for them. I expect we have some nasty moments ahead – but that is life, and we will ACHIEVE again – and in the meantime UPLIFT.

9 July.

I have thought a lot about my present position, and I expect a proper rocket from the CIGS. Whether they will employ me again for some time, one can't tell. One does not really know how much S has piled it on. But in the long run, I have a hunch that it is all for the best, I doubt if I would ever have got on with S, though funnily enough, I had got on better during the last 2 months – and he left me alone more – possibly as he meant to get rid of me, and I have a hunch that he did. It would also have been a rocky passage with L who had never been easy.

From Alanbrooke's Diary:

10 July.

At 6 p.m. poor Oliver Leese came to me having just arrived back. Very sad and repentant. He took it all wonderfully well. Ready to go back to private life or to lower rank, or anything that might suit best. Shall have a difficult job to find employment for him.

Major General George Symes, commanding the Lines of Communication, SEAC, was one of the first to hear the news about Leese.

General Symes had won a Military Cross in the first war. In the second war he had distinguished himself as a divisional commander, and while commanding the Lines of Communication troops had been visited by Leese on several occasions. He wrote in his diary for 14 July 1945:

> Met Christison who is acting C-in-C ALFSEA. Heard the story of Oliver Leese's departure:

> Slim was wont to remark that he was a tired man. Leese perhaps rather precipitately took him at his word, arranged for him to go at the conclusion of the Burma Campaign, and appointed Christison to succeed him. The latter went to Delhi and started planning the next operation. Leese notified the W.O. Then he saw Slim, said that he agreed with what Slim had said, thought he was too tired after six hard years to plan and carry out a fresh series of operations. Slim agreed and that was that. Then Slim started thinking it over, consulted Cowan and Gracie [sic] [brother Gurkhas] who persuaded him that (a) he wasn't tired and (b) it was a plot to sack him. Then Slim wrote to the Auk who was in London and said that he'd been sacked and had he got a job for him. Auk went to the CIGS and said why has the victorious commander been sacked . . .

> Well, I am sure that Leese is straight. He made a blunder in taking Slim at his word, and has now, most unfortunately, to suffer for it. I also know that, for all his popularity out here – which is *very* great – Slim is not straight. Had Leese known Slim better, he would have had it all in writing, so that Slim couldn't go back on it. Now, Slim is getting ALFSEA and Miles Dempsey is coming out to command 14 Army . . .

> Upheavals at this time are most regrettable and I'm extremely sorry about Leese as he was very able and completely straight and was doing his job excellently.

From Alanbrooke's Diary:

> 7 Aug.

> Seldom has a supreme commander been more deficient of the main attributes of a Supreme Commander than Dickie Mountbatten.

> 10 Aug.

> Started with a long COS attended by Mountbatten. I find it hard to remain pleasant when he turns up! He is the most crashing bore I have met on a committee, is always fiddling about with unimportant matters and wasting other people's time.

Alanbrooke was telling his wife, through his Diary, almost exactly what Leese had told *his* wife, through his letters, about Mountbatten. The CIGS would also have felt angry at having to sack Leese when he felt that the latter was being made a scapegoat. This feeling had increased very considerably after he had seen Leese on 10 July.

Leese's chief worry was about his Staff. 'I hope my boys will be allright' he said of his ADCs. To George Walsh, his Chief of Staff, he wrote on 11 July:

> I cannot leave without telling you again how deeply grateful I am for all you have done for me during the last three years. For me it has been a wonderful partnership from victory to victory. You have done a great job of work, and I cannot thank you enough for your loyalty, friendship, wisdom and devotion to duty.

On leave in Scotland, he wrote in similar terms to Ulick Verney, and concluded:

> I had a charming letter from FM Monty, saying how sorry he was, and inviting me to go and see him. I replied that I had better stay up here now, but would assuredly go and see him when I came south. You will be glad to hear that Margie, myself and 11 pieces of luggage, mostly of untold weight arrived here – O.K. We changed trains twice and buses twice. It was a great feat. I remained on terms with Margie, myself, porters and fellow passengers. I was quite secure in a cap and corduroy trousers – now the best dressed general in Scotland! I am quite down to earth, and, thank God, Margie and I can laugh again!

The news of Leese's recall was slow to filter through to England, but it was natural that some of his friends should hear, and one of the first to write to him was General 'Boy' Brooke, friend and mentor of thirty years, cousin of the CIGS:

> 'I dined with the CIGS last Tuesday,' he wrote on 11 August. 'As you know, he has had much to do with Dickie M. and quite appreciates the situation as regards you and him. He told me he was very sorry about it all, but of course could do nothing himself about it. He said that he thought you had taken it very well, and could not have behaved better – that he wanted very much to find you a suitable job, but that it was difficult in view of your seniority, and that he knew you wanted an operational one. Since then that does not arise of course, as from the news last night the Japs seem to have chucked their hand in. I'm sure he will do all he can for you as he is on your side.

When, a year later, Leese was leaving the Army, his friend Lord (Tim) Nugent, who at the time was Lord Chamberlain, referred to the Slim affair in these words:

> You have had a wonderfully successful career, my dear Oliver, without one blemish, and with only one set back that was clearly no fault of yours, and in that connection may I say that your conduct in that very distressing

affair which was none of your seeking has been superbly dignified throughout and has evoked in your many friends and admirers an even deeper
veneration for you.

The war in South East Asia concluded with the Sittang battles. On 6
August and 9 August, atom bombs were dropped on Hiroshima and
Nagasaki, and the war in the Far East ended on VJ Day, 14 August.

Slim returned from his leave and took up his duties as C-in-C
ALFSEA on 15 August. He had been promoted General before taking
up the appointment. In November 1945 he was offered and accepted
the appointment of Commandant Imperial Defence College, where he
found Major General 'Gerry' Feilden on his Staff.

Very soon Slim sent for Feilden. 'I believe you're a friend of Oliver
Leese' said Slim. Gerry Feilden said that he was. 'Well,' said Slim, 'I
thought that you might like to hear my account of what happened in
Burma before I succeeded him.'

'I know nothing about it,' said Feilden. 'Oliver has never discussed
it with me. It is nothing to do with me.'

Shortly afterwards Slim retired from the Army, but when in 1948
Monty retired as CIGS, Mountbatten persuaded Attlee to recall Slim
from retirement as Monty's successor. Slim was promoted Field
Marshal in January 1949. He subsequently became Governor General
of Australia. Leese kept in touch with Slim after the war, writing him
letters of congratulations on his various promotions and appointments,
which Slim acknowedged with staccato letters of thanks. It was an
impossibility for Leese to nurse a grievance, and, on becoming President of the British Legion, he invited Mountbatten to share his box
at the Festival of Remembrance.

Towards the end of his life Mountbatten wrote the script for a
television series on his career, which was produced shortly after his
tragic death.[1]

The following is an excerpt from the script of 4 November 1979:

Now I'd got rid of all four of my commanders-in-chief. But the new one
who came out, General Sir Oliver Leese, was a remarkable man . . . He
came with a great reputation. Unfortunately he came with a lot of Eighth
Army ideas, brought all his officers, and he tried to do a Monty and he
wasn't a Monty. He became very unpopular. He complained to me that he
wasn't getting enough publicity in my troop newspaper, the 'SEAC', and
wanted to take it over, to get more publicity. I refused.

I became more and more dissatisfied with him and when finally he made

[1] When the TV series was presented in 1979, Alanbrooke, Mountbatten, Leese and
Slim were all dead.

a complete botch-up of the reappointments after the campaign in Burma was over, when he tried to remove Slim from the Fourteenth Army and so forth, it was a bit too much. I told him to put back all the appointments, which he had to, he had to accept my over-ruling him. I wrote to Field Marshal Alanbrooke, the CIGS, to complain. I said 'I'd have sacked him but I sacked your last commander-in-chief. I can't go on sacking all your commanders-in-chief.' He replied, 'You certainly can, when they behave like this; go ahead.' So I sent him back. He was a broken man.

Following the broadcast, former members of Leese's staff were quick to defend their general. A letter from Brigadier Sidney Kent, Ion Calvocoressi, Ian Weston Smith and John Stimpson was published in *The Times*, although the names of Sidney Kent and John Stimpson were deleted.

After emphasising that Leese was carrying out Mountbatten's instructions, the writers concluded:

> The reappointments which had been put to Slim by Leese on Mountbatten's instructions at first with his (Slim's) agreement, ended in Leese's removal. To say he was a 'broken man' (although he might have felt let down) is bizarre to those who knew Oliver Leese . . .
>
> When Leese arrived in South East Asia in November 1944, he was amazed that the strategic plan for 1945, was solely to establish 14th Army in Central Burma. Having been urged by Churchill, personally, to recapture Burma speedily, he felt convinced that he must take Rangoon before the June monsoon.
>
> This was achieved, but to gain acceptance of this radical change of plan required his famous drive and initiative, which doubtless upset staff officers on the many headquarters. Any publicity he may have sought would have been not for himself but for his troops.
>
> We find it sad that the considerable contributions of this great soldier in the conquest of Burma should now be obscured by Lord Mountbatten's pursuit of his own infallibility.

Petre Crowder QC, who had been Leese's personal liaison officer in Burma, and later for nearly thirty years a distinguished Conservative Member of Parliament, wrote to *The Times*, associating himself with the letter:

> General Slim told Leese that he was very tired and asked for 4 months leave in England. Leese did not want to have an 'Absentee Planner' for the proposed invasion of Malaysia, he consulted Mountbatten who with the Dieppe Raid fresh in mind agreed.
>
> Accordingly he told Leese to ask Slim what he felt about it. There was no question of Leese ever trying to remove Slim [on his own initiative].

Petre Crowder's letter was not published, 'for reasons of space'.

It was not surprising that Leese, anxious to bring the campaign to a speedy and successful conclusion, had no room for an 'absentee planner'. Nor did he wish for Slim's removal. Leese's aim was the positive one that Slim should be built up as a conqueror of Burma, and remain in charge of the Army in Burma, where mopping up operations were necessary. Leese had not lost confidence in Slim. To use a cricket analogy: if a captain rests a fast bowler after a long and successful stint, it is because the bowler needs a rest, not because the captain has lost confidence in him.

This was the order of events:

1 Leese discussed proposals with Mountbatten, who instructed him to see Slim.
2 Leese signalled CIGS stating his proposals.
3 CIGS made no quick reply.
4 Leese saw Slim and Christison.
5 The news was leaked shortly after the Slim interview.
6 Leese saw Mountbatten, who didn't back him up.

What went wrong? Colonel Peter Dunphie advised Leese to wait for Alanbrooke's approval before taking any further action, but Leese said that time would not allow of any delay, and that as the first essential step, the Commander had to be nominated. General Symes felt that Leese should have checked that Slim didn't change his mind. General Christison considered that Leese, having been left holding the baby, 'should have bathed it and powdered it more carefully.'[1]

It was difficult for Leese working with Mountbatten and Slim. Mountbatten, with his flair for sacking commanders-in-chief, was not the easiest person to work with; both Mountbatten and Slim had a chip on the shoulder.

Mountbatten's father had been dismissed as First Sea Lord, in 1915. German by birth, he had been swept away in the wave of emotion that followed the outbreak of the first world war. The young Mountbatten determined to avenge his father by getting to the top of the ladder himself. An example of Mountbatten's style is given by General Sir Philip Christison:

On 20 Sept 1945, Mountbatten sent Browning to sound me out concerning the appointment of C-in-C Netherlands East Indies. Browning said 'Are you prepared to carry the can for Dickie? Things look pretty tricky. He'll back you from the wings, but full responsibility would rest with you. Dickie is not prepared to risk his reputation at this late stage.' I went to see Mountbatten that evening. He said 'Christie, you know how my father

[1] Comment to author, 17 February 1980.

was treated when world war came. Ever since that disgraceful episode I have lived determined to get to the top and avenge his memory. Nothing and no one, I repeat nothing and no one will ever be allowed to stand in my way. This Dutch East Indies business looks very tricky. I don't want to have responsibility for it directly. Will you take it on for me? I know you will do it well, and I'll back you all I can. I just don't want to fall at the last jump after all I've been through.' I said 'I'll go.'[1]

Slim's father had twice failed in business; Bill Slim, much to his credit, was determined to achieve success. After service in the Royal Warwickshire Regiment in the first war, Slim joined the Gurkha Rifles. He was a student at Quetta, and served as a staff officer for several years in India and Camberley. 'Must not allow himself to be cynical' said a confidential report in December 1927. His victories at Kohima and Imphal had established him in the front rank of British commanders.

Slim wrote his account of the 'sacking' affair in his book *Defeat into Victory*, but afterwards withdrew the chapter, in which he said that he hated to leave his Fourteenth Army while the war was still on; that on 9th May he told his principal staff officers, under pledge of secrecy, to make ready for the change of command, and that he told Mountbatten that he was prepared to continue serving under Leese.

Ronald Lewin in his biography of Slim makes no mention of Slim's prostate gland operation or of Leese going up to support Slim in the battle of Mandalay, probably because he didn't know of these matters. When Lewin wrote to Oliver Leese in 1972 to ask for his account of the affair, Leese replied on 1 December 1972:

It started when I flew to Kandy to discuss with Mountbatten, whether he agreed that Slim was tired after his arduous campaign and also that he was inexperienced in landing operations.

I suggested to Mountbatten that it might be best to leave Slim in command of the new Army which was to be formed to garrison Burma and to appoint a fresh commander to take on the landing in Malaya. Mountbatten told me to ask Slim what he felt about it.

I went to see Slim and I put the question to him. He seemed to me to raise no objections to the idea and I telephoned to Boy Browning, Mountbatten's Chief of Staff, and asked him to let Mountbatten know.

Early next morning I flew off to Quetta to speak to the Staff College and to visit my Base at Delhi.

Whilst I was in India a report got round that I had sacked Slim. This was not a fact, but the whole thing was exaggerated and very soon got out of control. As soon as I realised this I flew to Kandy to see Mountbatten.

[1] Letter to author 8 March 1980. General Christison was Allied Commander Netherlands East Indies 1945–1946.

He asked whether I was willing to keep Slim in command of 14 Army – I sent Slim a cable to this effect and flew back to my HQ at Barrackpore.

In reply to further questions from Ronald Lewin, Leese replied:

I quite see that *the evidence you have*[1] gives the impression that I sacked Slim. This too was obviously the opinion of Mountbatten, Alanbrooke and Slim. I respect these opinions and I only want to repeat to you that I went to see Slim with no intention to sack him. I thought, before I left him, that he accepted my idea. For that reason I telephoned Browning to this effect.

During the early months of 1973, Leese answered further letters from Ronald Lewin, and stated specifically that he did not blame Mountbatten for anything that went amiss. Lewin accepted this at its face value and informed General Christison that Leese had exonerated Mountbatten.

General Christison replied to Lewin, on 6 December 1978:

Surely as a historian delving for the truth, you cannot be so naive as to believe that this was other than loyalty to his superior. Leese was a Guardsman, fanatically such; and knowing him so well he would keep a stiff upper lip if he felt his superior was letting him down.

It is established that he had discussed removing Slim with Supremo, so the latter must have acquiesced. Indeed we know he did so as he told Leese to go about it carefully.

An intended visit by Ronald Lewin to Leese in the early summer of 1973 had to be cancelled, as the latter had to go into hospital for a leg amputation. However, even if Lewin had seen Leese, it is doubtful whether he would have learnt anything more, for the reasons that General Christison explained.

When Brigadier Michael Roberts, joint author of the official history of the war against Japan, was assisting Slim with *Defeat into Victory*, he wrote to Slim, who was in Canberra (18.12.1955) about a lunch time conversation with Christison.

Brigadier Roberts, who knew that Christison was a friend of Leese and of Slim and was not anti-Mountbatten, was impressed by Christison's statement that Leese had been 'dogsbody' right through, and also that Leese 'had, in a high degree the Guards tradition that you never questioned either at the time or after, an order given you by your superior officer in person, and that even if it was true that he carried out the unpleasant task and subsequently got "the rap" for it, he would not admit it.'

[1] Author's italics.

It was perhaps as a result of this letter that Slim decided to omit his chapter on the 'sacking' affair.

Certainly Leese took short cuts. For greater speed and efficiency he would consult direct with the Naval and Air Cs-in-C, which infuriated Mountbatten. He dealt direct with Indian divisions resting in India, as opposed to fighting in Burma, instead of doing it through Delhi.

'For my part,' wrote Colonel Peter Dunphie, 'I have always thought Mountbatten's part in this incident to be extremely devious. It would be no surprise to me if it transpired that he was not happy with Oliver and was glad of an opportunity – contrived or otherwise – to get rid of him.'

Philip Ziegler's comment, that the episode did not show Mountbatten at his best, is a masterpiece of understatement.

As for Leese, a man of simple and unpretentious patriotism, knighted on the field of battle by his sovereign in 1944, twelve months later he had been recalled from his command. If ever he reflected on Mountbatten trumping his sovereign's ace, it would only have been to comment 'Well, that's life!' and give his characteristic honking laugh.

Leese made the self-critical statement that he stupidly did not see Slim again the next morning. This may well have been a deliberate omission made either out of consideration or because Leese knew that he had spoken with his usual clarity and considered a further visit unnecessary. He was certainly anxious to treat Slim correctly.

On the evidence available it would appear that Leese explained his intended changes to Slim, who accepted them. The news spread like wildfire; Mountbatten backpedalled; Leese, 'carrying the can for Dickie', was sacked.

It was a measure of Leese's greatness that his demeanour, when, having returned to England, he reported to CIGS, so affected Alanbrooke that he remembered the occasion for the rest of his life:

'That interview,' wrote Alanbrooke, 'has remained vividly impressed on my mind, owing to the wonderful, manly way in which Oliver faced up to the blow that had hit him. There was not a word of abuse from him against anyone, or any suggestion that he had been roughly treated. And yet at the bottom of my heart I had a feeling, and still have a feeling, that although he may have been at fault, he had a raw deal at the hands of Mountbatten.'[1]

---

[1] *Alanbrooke*, by David Fraser (Collins).

18

POST WAR

In their brief holiday in Scotland Oliver and Margie had learned to laugh again. In mid-September they were at Tabley and Oliver sent for Ralph Warren to help out. Sergeant Lamb had now retired and was replaced by a young Guardsman named Errington. Ralph Warren found that in September 1945, life was going on at Tabley as in the days before the 1914–18 war:

> Vast numbers of servants, ruled by the butler. His word was law. I can still picture the scene to this day. At our dining table in the servants quarters everybody rose respectfully from the table as the butler entered – and only settled down when commanded to do so by him – and after Grace was said, of course.

For about a week, Warren was sorting out an accumulation of Oliver's papers and at odd times borrowed Margie's ancient bicycle to pedal down the long driveway, and then the two miles into Knutsford, to do some shopping for her.

Oliver soon after sent again for Warren, now on some vague form of extended leave, to come to Lower Hall, Worfield, where the latter's guide was William Buck, one of Leese's drivers in the Far East. Warren made several short walks to Davenport House, then functioning as a PoW Camp, to negotiate with the Commandant and his staff for some of the prisoners to work at Worfield to help Oliver in his new occupation as a mushroom grower:

> He often presided over a tea party he would arrange for the workers at the end of the day. I often wondered to myself what the position would have been if the war had finished the opposite way round.

Oliver was determined that in his next appointment he was going to be more with Margie. The posts of GOC, British Army of the Rhine, and GOC, British Troops in Palestine, were both on the *tapis*, but he preferred to accept the appointment as GOC Eastern Command. Captain Ian Weston Smith, an ADC during the Eastern Command period, was told at the time about the 'sounding out' by Oliver Leese himself.

> To the best of my recollection, Oliver's words went something like this 'They wanted me to take on Palestine or Germany rather than Eastern Command, but Margie and I want to get on with Worfield and for that plan a year at Hounslow fits in very well. Either of the others would have been a three year tour well away from Worfield.' This would have been a 'sounding out' conversation with someone he knew very well and who required nothing more – i.e. specific and definite. I felt too that there was an element of consolation in the idea – 'I know you had a rotten deal from Mountbatten, so here is something worthy of you' – which of course Eastern Command clearly wasn't.[1]

★

There are diametrically opposed views as to how Oliver was affected by the Slim affair. 'I am still a Lieutenant General and at least they can't take that away' he is reported to have said to his brother Alec a day or two after the return from Burma, and obviously before the 'soundings out' over Germany and Palestine. Some of his friends believe he was more bitter than he ever 'let on', the majority felt that he quickly dismissed it as over and done with. What is certain is that he carried out his task at Eastern Command with his customary ubiquitousness and drive. He was allowed a house, and took Long Orchard, two miles from Cobham, Surrey, motoring back each morning to the Command HQ in Hounslow. Ian Weston Smith said of him:

> I could prepare something for him with the utmost effort, and believed I had covered every possible aspect, every conceivable contingency, and in a few seconds General Oliver would point out a couple of details that simply hadn't occurred to me.

The *Army Commander's Tour Notes* were models of brevity and outspokenness. At Maidstone:

> The officers seemed listless and longhaired as the men seemed bored and dirty.

At Dover, the price of a sandwich (fivepence) was excessive. At Colchester Hospital:

[1] Letter to author 6.9.84.

The painting had begun this morning. Whether it would have begun if I had not gone down there I would not know. I wish to have a report each week on the progress made of the painting of Colchester Hospital for the next two months.

At an ATS[1] Camp:

I understand there are curtains coming from Welfare. Please have these gingered up, and also send down anything up to 200 pictures to assist in decorating the walls of the dining room and elsewhere. Welfare to let me know when this has been done. The girls are doing magnificent work, and I do not like the idea of their living in bad conditions.

In a Basic Education Centre:

Colonel Y is totally unfitted to command anything. The room they are working in is filthy and unkempt, and they have the most ghastly recreation room I have ever seen.

The picture was not always a gloomy one. Of a Physical Development Centre at Storrington he wrote 'I only wish that similar things were done for all backward boys in the nation'. There were always individuals to be helped: an officer who had lost a leg at Cassino; a sergeant released to read archeology at Cambridge; a second lieutenant applying for a regular commission.

There were three large garden parties on successive days: for Dominion troops; for Colonial troops; for the ATS – this last attended by the Princess Royal. On these occasions Margie, following Oliver unobtrusively, would sometimes tug at his sleeve to indicate someone a few feet away that he should talk to, or, indicating a distant bore: 'Look, Oliver, at least you can talk to him about cricket.' Oliver himself kept a fatherly eye on his young staff, jovially taking them to task with some such remark as 'I saw you talking to that pretty girl, now go and have a chat with the dentist's wife!' At one of these parties the diminutive General Juin decorated him with the medal of the Legion of Honour and the Croix de Guerre, but had difficulty in kissing him on both cheeks. Ian Weston Smith remembers how much Oliver valued Margie's opinion:

'Need I see So-and-So again, Margie?' he would ask, and 'No, Oliver, I think you've made things perfectly clear; it doesn't need any further discussion' – or 'Perhaps it might be a good idea; it would probably give him confidence.' More often than not, Margie's advice was accepted.

At the end of 1945 Oliver Leese had two suggestions to make to his staff

[1] Auxiliary Territorial Service. The women's branch of the Army. The ATS became the WRAC with effect from 1.2.49.

– officers and other ranks. One was that they all kept in touch with one another, at least once a year at Christmas, with individual accounts of the year's activities. The second was that half of the cottage wing attached to the Lower Hall be named TAC Cottage and be available for the members of his staff – and their families, for free self-catering holidays.[1] Both these ideas received warm support, the first was generally successful. Oliver's own Christmas card and Christmas present list, commenced in August of each year, was meticulously kept, containing several hundred names. Ion Calvocoressi and his wife Katherine were among those who stayed at TAC Cottage. 'The Lower Hall was great fun in those days,' wrote the former. 'You had to work if you went there! I remember, on a steaming hot August Bank Holiday, having to put fertiliser on a lot of cabbages. The evenings were most enjoyable, and then the General was at his funniest.'

In February 1946, Oliver went for a couple of days as the guest of Lord Justice Lawrence to attend the Nuremberg Trial of war criminals:

> On the whole they are an undistinguished looking bunch, especially Frank, Streicher and others of that ilk, who look the most common little brutes. Hess looks terribly ill, a ghastly colour and great paunchy eyes. Goering, still fat and podgy, had an obvious cold, but is very alive. Ribbentrop, grey-haired and old, but alive and took notes all the time. Keitel, Jodl, Doenitz and Raeder, dignified and taking it all in: in uniform with no badges of rank or medals. Von Neurath and von Papen the most distinguished looking.

The *pièce de résistance* of the day was the sudden production by the Russians of Field Marshal Paulus, the German Commander during the siege of Stalingrad. Oliver thought Paulus 'neat and tidy but old, and heavy rings under his eyes.' Paulus giving evidence against Keitel and Jodl he thought a shabby performance, unworthy of a soldier. But Paulus was probably heavily drugged.

After a year with Eastern Command Oliver decided to prepare himself for the rigours of civilian life.[2] Like many of his contemporaries, he felt that the training of the new Army should be in the hands of younger men. Arrangements were made, and accordingly King George VI received him at Buckingham Palace at 12 noon, 4 December 1946, on the relinquishment of his appointment as General Officer, Commanding-in-Chief, Eastern Command.

General Horrocks (Jorrocks) was saddened at Oliver's departure:

[1] While at Eastern Command Oliver and Margie went to Worfield at weekends, at first staying in the cottage wing. Later they moved into the Lower Hall itself.
[2] He fulfilled two civilian appointments after the war, each of twelve months' duration: President of the Old Etonians Association (1946–7), and High Sheriff of Shropshire (1958).

We have served together very happily in many places and I hate seeing the old links broken.

Bimbo Dempsey wrote on 23 January 1947:

I don't feel I can go on sitting at the top, playing musical chairs, any longer. I remember too well how you and I felt after the last war. The post war Army is going to be a tender plant, and we must see that the chaps who really matter get a proper run.

*

Oliver now returned with Margie to Lower Hall, Worfield, there to continue with his mushroom enterprise. As well as Bill Buck, Ernie Bishop and Gordon Davey were also there to help. Bill Buck had married a Worfield girl. Ernie Bishop, who had served with the Desert Rats from the time of Alamein, was a Worfield man; Gordon Davey, for several years an orderly to Oliver, had married Margie's lady's maid, Crowe. He became Postmaster in Worfield.

The mushroom enterprise soon became famous in military circles. Bernard Freyberg, now Governor General of New Zealand, started to buy mushroom spawn from Oliver on a regular basis. 'Jorrocks' wrote 'If you still hesitate about coming to the [30 Corps] Dinner, I will write to your wife and get her to use her influence, and failing this I will organise a raid on the mushrooms, so you see both your family and business life are at stake'; and Brigadier Desmond Young wrote to the German General von Ravenstein 'Did you meet Sir Oliver Leese, who lives just outside Wolverhampton and is now growing mushrooms?'

Concurrently with the mushroom business a market garden was being run, and Oliver was also starting to grow cacti and succulents.[1] Ernie Bishop needed help. The services of an ex-sapper sergeant were engaged; he succeeded in erecting a Bailey bridge over the river Worfe in place of a rickety wooden affair leading to the seven acre field that Oliver had taken over for his market garden projects.

Early in 1947 Oliver's old friend and mentor A. B. Ramsay (the Ram), master of the Lower School at Eton before the first world war, and now on the verge of retirement as Master of Magdalene College, Cambridge, was anxious for Oliver to be his successor. The latter was touched at being offered the post, but felt that the job was not for him and politely declined.

In May, 1947, the Kesselring affair blew up. Marshal Albert Kessel-

---

[1] Percy Thrower writes: 'Sir Oliver Leese exhibited his cacti and succulents at the first Shrewsbury Show in 1947 and continued for very many years.' Letter to author 22.10.1984.

ring, Oliver's opposing General in the Italian campaign, had been sentenced to death at a war crimes trial, in which he was held responsible for the shooting of 334 hostages in the Ardeatine Caves.[1]

The case at the time raised deep emotion. Oliver wrote a letter to the *Daily Telegraph*, saying that Kesselring had fought a clean campaign, and, that had the Allies lost the war, he himself would probably have been in Kesselring's position. This caused the Soviet Press to describe Oliver as 'a tender-hearted lady of the male sex.' Oliver himself received a stack of letters, mostly from ex-Eighth Army personnel, nearly all of them supporting the line he had taken. Kurt Hahn, imprisoned by Hitler in 1933, a British subject since 1938, founder headmaster of Gordonstoun, also wrote to Oliver supporting him, stating that Kesselring executed would be an ally of the nationalist menace.

Lilias Graham, a cousin of Margie's, wrote to her, on World's YWCA writing paper:

> Last week I was visiting a prison camp near here, and was asked to go and see Field Marshal Kesselring. He begged me to write and thank Oliver very much indeed for all that he has done, and is doing on his behalf, and to say that he is honoured and touched that Oliver should take so much trouble. So please give him this message. I thought Kesselring a very exceptional man. He was cheerful and chivalrous and quite free of bitterness against us. I felt very ashamed before him.

Finally Kesselring was reprieved and his sentence commuted to life imprisonment. He was released in 1952 on compassionate grounds, and died in 1960.

In 1947 Oliver was invited to become Colonel of the Shropshire Yeomanry. In the same year, his mother Violet, Lady Leese, died in her mid-seventies. A cheerful, equable lady, with a quiet sense of humour, she had lived the last years of her life chiefly in her London flat, and from time to time with her married daughter Betty Drake.

The old order was changing. Cuthbert Leicester-Warren was in poor health, and was finding the upkeep of Tabley too much for him: arrangements were put in hand, therefore, for Cuthbert and Hilda Leicester-Warren to move to Davenport, which Hilda owned. An advertisement appeared in *Country Life* announcing goods and chattels of Tabley House to be put up for auction: furniture, grandfather clocks, billiard table, sports rifles, golf clubs, a croquet set; much loved impedimenta of leisure – all awaited the auctioneer's gavel. This was the end of Tabley as a private residence. Two years before it was still maintained by a regiment of servants: butler, housekeeper, cook, footmen, ladies'

---

[1] The SS troops responsible for the massacre owed allegiance directly to Hitler and did not come under Kesselring's jurisdiction.

maids – who were brought their early morning tea by the chambermaids – tweenies, parlourmaids, gardeners, odd job men. Tabley House ceased to be one of the principal country houses in the north the same year that India ceased to be 'the brightest jewel in the Empire', and acquired independence: the days of the county families, like those of the British Raj, were numbered. Cuthbert and Hilda Leicester-Warren moved to Davenport late in 1947. Their son John took over Tabley House, and turned it into an independent school for boys from ten to eighteen. John had taken to teaching as a prisoner of war, and his idea was to start a school for boys who could not get into Eton. The school flourished until it closed in July 1984, owing to difficulties over renewing the lease.

At the end of 1947 Oliver and Margie went out to New Zealand to see the Freybergs. They stayed with them at Government House, Wellington – 'You and I can go fishing whilst our wives admire the scenery' Freyberg had written earlier to Oliver, though Margie was a good fisherman too. They spent Christmas with the Freybergs, and in January 1948 they visited Christchurch, where Margie recorded that Oliver was several times recognised enthusiastically. In February they were with Freyberg again. Margie loved New Zealanders: 'They are shy and reserved but not hypocritical and once they like you it's for always.' During a brief visit to Melbourne Oliver was offered the Governorship of Victoria, but pleasantly declined. They returned via India: Margie saw two *mem sahibs* behaving abominably to Hindu assistants in a flower shop. She recorded in her diary that these *mem sahibs* were the people who lost us our Empire.

Thoroughly happy as a civilian, Oliver kept up with his Army friends – Monty, Horrocks, Dempsey. He was often in contact with Anders and Lubomirski, acting as godfather to the latter's infant son. Patton had been killed in a car accident at the end of the war, but Leese maintained an affable correspondence with Mark Clark and with Stratemeyer: 'I never, throughout my military career,' wrote Stratemeyer on 30 July 1947, 'have had more pleasant associations than I had with you.'

Alex, now Field Marshal Alexander of Tunis, was Governor General of Canada from 1946 to 1952. He wrote to Oliver from time to time, with messages from Simonds, Vokes, Hoffmeister. He gave Oliver a hiliarious account of an incident in Los Angeles, where an American Civil War film was being produced. Alex, who was in uniform, was spotted by an irate costume manager, who exclaimed, pointing to Alex's medals – 'Hey, buddy, what wars are these meant to represent?'

From Major General Sir Miles Graham, an Eton contemporary of Oliver's – he had served under Monty in Egypt, and was his chief administrative officer in 21 Army Group – came a letter on 6 June 1947, referring to Slim's appointment as CIGS:

It is an absolute scandal that you should have been passed over. I have no doubt that he was an excellent Army Commander – but his successful campaign in Burma was not his campaign at all, but yours and without you in command he would still be unknown.

Slim was promoted to Field Marshal and filled the post of CIGS from November 1948 to the end of 1952, when he became Governor General of Australia.

★

Oliver's enthusiasm for cacti and succulent plants replaced his interest in mushrooms. In the course of a visit to France with Margie he had bought two barrel cacti in Paris. One they gave to a godchild, the other was dropped by mistake in the Champs Elysées. It had a permanent dent in it, but it proved to be the first plant in what eventually became one of the biggest cacti displays in the United Kingdom.

Oliver and Margie started their cacti venture on a small scale in a small greenhouse. Soon they decided to grow them commercially and had three more greenhouses. They joined the two British Cacti and Succulent Associations, and decided to arrange their displays as a piece of country, with all their pots buried, instead of in serried rows.

Their first success was in 1950 at Wolverhampton, when they won a silver medal. This was followed by gold medals at Southport, Shrewsbury and Chelsea – the first gold awarded at Chelsea for a display of cactus and succulent plants. In 1954 the Royal Horticultural Society staged an exhibition at Olympia for the first time for fifteen years, and the Leeses achieved another gold.

They developed a show ground at Worfield. There was a donkey, a children's playground, a museum of war relics, a collection of toy soldiers, a miniature cannon that Oliver delighted in firing, and the Doll's House that they had built up before the war, and added to during the war when Oliver sent things to Margie from Italy and the Far East. A great attraction was Madame Bruce's band, dressed in Spanish sombreros brought home from Spain by Oliver. Madame Bruce played Spanish music as long as she could bear, and then broke into Gilbert and Sullivan.

Alfred Randall had come as foreman in 1950, his wife later becoming housekeeper in Lower Hall. Randall learnt a good deal about cacti from Margie and became an expert. The business was now going from strength to strength. Oliver's assistants were normally daughters of family friends: Jennifer Beck and her cousin Diana; later, Penny Lloyd and Elizabeth Bache – they were known as the Garden Girls. Oliver claimed that the cactus was taking the place of the aspidistra; that it was a boon to people living in small houses and flats. He lectured to the Royal Horticultural Society in February 1955; in July of the same year he had a 3000 words article in the Society's Journal. There were chats with Percy Thrower on TV and Radio.[1]

Oliver and Margie made frequent journeys abroad in search of cacti – Arizona, Mexico, South Africa. Oliver never forgot the thrill of seeing his first saguaros in Tucson, thirty to fifty feet tall, standing like huge sentinels. Specimens, nine feet high, of Old Man's Head, from Mexico, helped to win many medals, and he was equally interested in the 250 species of mamillaria often less than two inches high.

John Sutton, who had fought at Arnhem with the Guards Armoured Division, and whose father had been at Eton with Oliver, came to know the Leeses well in 1952 when he was engaged to Ulick Verney's daughter, Carola, who stayed for three months at Worfield – she had been made a ward of the Leeses as her parents had to be away for three years. John Sutton soon became aware of Oliver's terrific explosive energy, and felt that Oliver had not been offered in civilian life a post commensurate with his ability.

Friends of Oliver and Margie used to say that wherever either of them was, the other wouldn't be far away: Oliver's eyes lit up whenever Margie entered the room. If Margie was away from Worfield for one or two days, Oliver was liable to explain to his guests 'You can't do that you see. Margie won't be here. No, it's no use, Margie won't be here.'

Carola Sutton remembers that the house was always packed at weekends with house guests, besides people for meals in the week. It was as if an overflowing river of people was going through the house. There were often at weekends half a dozen young men and an equal number of young women as house guests – and Margie was an indefatigable matchmaker.

Perhaps one night there would be a hunt ball. They would arrive back at Worfield in the small hours, and Oliver would cook buttered eggs for them – a culinary *tour de force* he had learnt as a fag at Eton. Then he sent them all off to their different rooms, telling them that they could sleep till eleven o'clock, although Oliver himself was always about again by eight.

He would say in the morning 'Well, did you enjoy yourselves?' When they said that they had Oliver would say 'Well, we'll do something for someone else tonight', so they might perhaps arrange something for the Legion, or a charity or something for the village. On Saturday nights it was always 'Breakfast at 9 tomorrow, Church is at half past ten.' Oliver took it for granted that they would all go to church – and they all did.

*

[1] Percy Thrower writes: 'Sir Oliver Leese perhaps did more for Cacti and Succulents than anyone else that I know. He and Lady Leese joined me in a number of Radio programmes, and Sir Oliver in several of my television programmes in the days of Gardening Club.'

Oliver's efforts to make a complete break with military affairs after the war never really stood much chance. He was still connected with the Shropshire Yeomanry, and Monty 'detailed' him to run the Alamein Reunion.

Eric Caswell, his assistant over the Alamein functions, found Oliver ready with sound advice when asked, but never interfering; he oiled the wheels by giving small luncheon parties at the Turf Club for the organisers – Vera Lynn among the guests – and was always ready to help by writing to anyone. Every year the 3000 tickets were sold out in a week or so: Vera Lynn was the great favourite, Marlene Dietrich and Anna Neagle were among the most popular performers at the Reunions.

> 'When Oliver took control,' wrote Ion Calvocoressi, 'as usual he went to immense trouble. He attended all the rehearsals . . . and took great trouble after the speeches were over, to go round all the bars and talk to the men, in particular the St. Dunstans men. I always had to lay on beer and sandwiches for his own former drivers, etc., who would always wait outside the 'Green Room' to have the chance of seeing him.

In 1948 the Government reorganised the Officers Training Corps, and the Combined Cadet Force was formed. This included Naval, Army and Air Force sections; contingents were formed in over 300 schools in the UK. Oliver was invited to become the founder President of the Combined Cadet Corps Association. His CCFA Secretary, Bill Newcombe, remembers that Oliver made more than adequate time to keep in touch with developments in the Association: 'He used to visit several schools each year, often being the inspecting officer at their annual Inspections.' He took every opportunity to meet and talk to CCF officers and brought public school and grammar school officers together.

In 1954 Alanbrooke was appointed Constable of the Tower of London, choosing Oliver as his Lieutenant. In view of the 'sacking' imbroglio of nine years before, Alanbrooke's action seems significant. 'Alanbrooke was always fond of Leese and respected him' wrote General Sir David Fraser, the Field Marshal's biographer. The post itself was for three years; it involved taking over from the Constable if he was ill. Oliver much enjoyed dealing with the Yeomen Warders.

Twenty-one-year-old Rosemary Jemmett had just been engaged as Oliver's secretary. With correspondence about mushrooms, cacti, cadet camps, Shropshire Yeomanry, regional British Legion activities, the Tower of London and the inevitable rounds of travel, she had plenty to do.

The work was hard, but Rosemary loved it, tapping away at the veteran Imperial portable typewriter that Ralph Warren had used in North Africa, and South East Asia. The Leeses treated her like a daughter, and Rosemary got on well with the domestic staff including the indefatigable cook-parlourmaid Mabel White – Oliver called her affectionately Ma Belle Blanche – who would think nothing of working a twenty-four hour day during the to-ing and fro-ing of cricket parties – late suppers at two in the morning, early breakfasts at four.

Rosemary worked with Oliver in a little office at Lower Hall. The room was panelled and painted white, the walls covered with corps and divisional shields and other Eighth Army and Coldstream mementoes. Oliver and Rosemary sat back to back – 'His huge desk and my tiny one'. At 10.30 there was a half hour break for coffee – Bovril in the winter. Alfred Randall would often come in, so that there was liaison between the office and the nurseries. Lunch was at one o'clock; whoever the guests were, Rosemary always had lunch with the family.

Cuthbert Leicester-Warren had died shortly after Rosemary Jemmett commenced work at Worfield, but on three or four occasions she paid monthly visits to Davenport to do Hilda Leicester-Warren's accounts – 'Generally a case of making out three cheques.' Rosemary would be given lunch, and every time she left, Hilda Leicester-Warren would give her a packet of chocolates, and the chauffeur would drive her home. Hilda Leicester-Warren died later in 1954, and after a short time her kinswoman Lady Boyne took up residence at Davenport.

Sergeant Alma 'Jack' Lambert, who had carried Oliver from where he was shot down on the battlefield of the Somme, about this time was grievously ill with cancer. Oliver visited him at his home in Sheringham, taking with him a tray with a miniature garden of half a dozen cacti. The burly soldier who once weighed over eighteen stone, was now less than a quarter of his original weight. Oliver stayed with him for three hours or so, and they talked of old times. Jack Lambert died a few weeks later.

1956 was the year of the ill-fated Suez venture. General Keightley, one of Oliver's old corps commanders in Italy, was C-in-C of the invasion troops. He made a point of seeking Oliver's strategic advice before setting out for Egypt.

Stanley Moore had been Vicar of Worfield for several years, but had moved to another parish in 1956. He was succeeded by the Reverend 'Tommy' Thompson after a career in the Merchant Navy, which culminated in his becoming Harbour Master of Rangoon. The living at Worfield was in the gift of Lady Leese, who had offered him the living, according to 'Tommy' Thompson, 'because he had done so well as a sailor!'

Shortly after his induction he was invited to a tremendous party at the Lower Hall. He went up the steps and through a door, and an enormous fist came out through the curtains. Oliver handed him a generous glass of whisky: 'There you are Vicar, that'll do you good.' In those days the Leeses gave twenty or thirty parties a year. Oliver threw a party every

Christmas after Matins. There was always a specially good attendance; (Worfield had a flourishing church with forty in the choir). The General's Cup was the main drink – a red concoction and relatively innocuous. There were occasional dances in the Village Hall. Once, when things got a bit out of hand, Oliver put an end to the proceedings and sent everyone home: 'the night the General stopped the dance' has become part of Worfield folklore.

In 1958 Oliver and Margie were working hard on their book *Desert Plants*. Oliver wrote the book in draft form; Margie checked, revised and herself wrote a few sections. The book was both comprehensive and successful. In the compiling of the book they received valuable help from Anthony Huxley, the writer, photographer and horticulturist:

> As the so-called cactus expert in *Amateur Gardening* I got considerably involved with Oliver Leese and visited his nursery several times to take photographs both for our own use and eventually to illustrate his book. I liked him and Lady Leese very much, and they were always most friendly and hospitable.
>
> However he [Oliver] was never any kind of botanist and I seem to remember having to do quite a lot of tactful work on *Desert Plants* in this respect – which I hasten to add he was only too pleased to receive. As the book suggests, he was a very good observer and his practical knowledge of growing the plants was by then considerable.

It became a Christmas routine to make up several thousands of miniature gardens of cacti and succulents. Rosemary despatched invoices all over the country, and two vans, driven by Alfred Randall and Ernie Bishop, would take them to London, via Birmingham, Oxford and Reading, and to the industrial towns of the north.

*

Cricket had always been one of Oliver Leese's great loves, and after the war he and Margie started going to Tests at Edgbaston, Trent Bridge and Old Trafford. He met Alex Hastilow, Chairman of the Warwickshire County Cricket Club, who asked him to become the Warwickshire President.[1] This he was delighted to do, and he held the office from 1959 to 1975.

In 1960 the first signs of Margie's fatal illness became apparent. She was examined by Professor A. L. (Pon) d'Abreu, who informed her that she had cancer of the breast. Margie took the news with fortitude. She was admitted to Queen Elizabeth Hospital, Birmingham, ironically

[1] He became the twelfth President, the Earl of Warwick having relinquished the post in 1959 on the grounds of ill health.

enough on 18 January 1961, the twenty-eighth anniversary of her wedding. She had surgery, and after starting a course of deep X-ray therapy was discharged home. For a while she appeared much better.

There were a couple of trips to Arizona and Mexico, calling on the way at Bermuda where they stayed a few days with Julian Gascoigne and his wife Joyce – Julian Gascoigne was now Governor of Bermuda. It was decided to sell Lower Hall Worfield, and build a smaller house in the village. Margie obviously needed to run a smaller establishment. The house belonged to the Davenport estate, and Margie wanted Oliver to have a house that he owned and that would be easy for him to cope with after she had died.

Oliver and Margie asked the architect Anthony Sanford, to help them get a prefabricated timber house built. Anthony Sanford first went to Worfield on 10 January 1961, to take instructions, and was shocked to be told by them that Margie had cancer, but got the impression that the idea of the new house took her mind off her misfortune. On 12 November 1963 they started moving their furniture into their new residence, Worfield House.

When the house was partly erected it was realised that a timber-framed structure did not provide much sound insulation between rooms. This was an important matter as Oliver wanted to discuss business in his office without it being overheard. The problem was overcome by filling the thickness of the timber partition walls with brickwork, and the fable was tactfully put about that this was being done so that what Tony Sanford called 'Sir Oliver's splendid barrack-room language' would not shock the servants.

Margie had apparently been in better health for nearly three years, but by 1964 she was obviously a very sick woman. An advanced Christian, she discussed her illness with 'Tommy' Thompson 'as though she was wondering whether to go to the Lake District or the Trossachs for a holiday.' She wrote to Ion Calvocoressi saying that the enemy was attacking her again, and that, should she die, Oliver would be shattered. She asked Ion if, in the event of her dying, he would get in touch with Monty and ask him to invite Oliver to stay at Isington Mill. When doctors at the Queen Elizabeth Hospital told Oliver that he had better face the facts and realise that his wife's days were numbered, he flew into a passion and said that a battle was never lost until it was won.

During the early months of 1964 Rosemary – now Rosemary Blackham, she had married in 1963 – spent a good deal of time keeping Margie company in her room, and Angela Moore, a qualified nurse, daughter of the former Vicar, was asked to look after her.

On 26 April, Anna Neagle with her husband Herbert Wilcox, visited the Leeses:

'I was playing at Wolverhampton,' wrote Anna Neagle, 'and Sir Oliver and Lady Leese invited Herbert and myself to lunch on our Sunday drive to the next date. Alas, Lady Leese was very ill, but she asked that we go up to see her. This was a rapidly deteriorating condition, and we were saddened to learn that she died shortly after our visit. Sir Oliver must have been desperately anxious but he made us most welcome.'

'Pray for me especially hard tonight' she had said to Mrs Randall the housekeeper, a few hours before her death. She died in Oliver's arms, on Thursday, 30 April 1964. There were flowers throughout the village on the day of her funeral.

Ion Calvocoressi posted Margie's letter, with an explanation, to Monty, who invited Oliver to spend a few days at Isington Mill. This Oliver did. 'He said to me afterwards, with his quizzy smile,' wrote Ion Calvocoressi, 'that it was typical of Monty to have shown him her letter and mine.'

After Margie died, Oliver could not bear to eat alone. There were visits to London: he would sometimes dine at Pratts, where members eat together at a long table; he was very well liked at the Turf Club – many of the waiters were ex-Eighth Army; sometimes he would take a couple of the Garden Girls there for lunch. He never had an evening dining on his own.

In the autumn of 1964 – Oliver was now seventy – he went to South Africa. This was to prove to himself that he could cope without Margie. It called for a tremendous effort on his part. He hired a car and drove from Capetown to Johannesburg, calling on cricket, Legion and horticultural friends on the way. David Brown was one of a quartet of Warwickshire Test cricketers invited to dine with him at the Mount Nelson hotel in Capetown: 'It was a marvellous place. Really delightful. You felt it had been built round Sir Oliver.' Up country Oliver stayed a couple of nights in Bedford, at the ranch of Victor Pringle, a member of one of South Africa's Scottish settler families, and was greatly excited when his host caught a monitor lizard, four foot six inches in length, and held it by its tail for Oliver to photograph.

In 1965 Oliver became President of the MCC. The Presidency is of twelve months' duration, from October to October, the President nominating his successor. He had been proposed by R. H. (Dick) Twining, who had captained the Eton XI in 1909. Twining had served with distinction during the First World War, and after the war played cricket for Middlesex.

Oliver was fortunate in that in his year as President he had Test Matches in Australia in the winter and in the summer the West Indians came to England. He went off alone to Australia, where for a time he was joined by Ion Calvocoressi. In Adelaide he stayed with Dricky Bastyan, who had been made Governor of South Australia. Ion Calvocoressi remembers buying 150 postcards for Oliver, which the latter sent out 'to almost everyone he knew, friends, godchildren, staff at Worfield and their children. My children and I had received many in the past, but I had no idea how thoroughly he went into it. Of course, he got on extremely well with the Aussies. I remember him walking round the ground at Adelaide, and he suddenly ran into Clarrie Grimmett, recognised him in the crowd, and started talking to him.'

On his way out, Oliver stayed in India and Hong Kong, and on the way back at Singapore, Kuala Lumpur, Bangkok and Pakistan, several places being visited for the first time by a President of the MCC. He also spent a few days in Japan, as he was developing an interest in bonsai trees in addition to his work on succulents. 'It was pretty cold in Tokyo' he wrote to his secretary, Diana Paterson, 'and I was lucky to have the extra overcoat belonging to the Ambassador . . . I don't think I like the Japanese any more after my visit.'

As President of the MCC Oliver had one difficult situation to deal with, when members challenged the committee's decision to demolish the Tavern and the old stand next to it and build a new complex on the site. After two general meetings at which Oliver took the chair, the proposal went through with slight modifications. When Oliver's turn came to relinquish the Presidency he nominated Sir Alec Douglas-Home as his successor. Sir Alec, Prime Minister in 1963–1964, had played for Eton in 1922 and occasionally for Middlesex.

*

In August 1965 Oliver met Frances Denby, whose husband, Dick Denby, had recently died of cancer. Oliver and Frances were introduced at a small dinner party by a mutual friend, Diana Beck. The next day Frances received a bouquet of long-stemmed roses by special messenger. They soon became good friends: they had both suffered a grievous loss, and as they met at Worfield, or at his London clubs, soon realised that they had many interests in common.

Thirty-three years old at the time she met Oliver Leese, Frances Denby had for several years run her Knightsbridge Kitchen, an organisation that combined Cordon Bleu standard with exceptional efficiency, catering for social functions, together with luncheon, dinner and cocktail parties in Central London.

In addition to her natural charm of manner, her gifts as a *raconteuse* and her flair for mimicry, Frances Denby had great initiative and powers of organisation which much impressed Oliver. Like him, she was a great traveller, and they soon started going on plant hunting expeditions together, each paying their own expenses.

Oliver asked her to act as hostess for him during his period as MCC

President in England, during the summer of 1966. Frances replied that she couldn't possibly do it, and knew nothing about cricket. 'Don't be so stupid' said Oliver. 'It's easy. Just read this,' and he gave her an enormous volume written by E. W. Swanton. After some misgivings Frances agreed to act as hostess and carried out her duties admirably.

During the summer of 1966 Frances Denby stayed as a house guest at the new house in Worfield, where Mrs Randall was acting as housekeeper and Alfred Randall foreman of the gardens. Oliver Leese's friendship with Frances naturally did not go unnoticed. Was this friendship, was it an *affaire*, or was there going to be a marriage? Oliver and Frances themselves were both highly amused at the excitement their relationship had generated.

On one occasion the Dowager Lady Boyne, who had been living in Davenport since the death of the Leicester-Warrens, came over to see them. Sitting down on a sofa she leaned forward, and taking a hand of Oliver and a hand of Frances in hers, she said with radiant confidence, 'My dears, it would be so much *easier* for everyone in Shropshire if you two would marry.'

Oliver showed great interest in Frances Denby's Knightsbridge Kitchen. At one of her cocktail parties he met Keith Erskine, Managing Director of Securicor, who offered him a seat on the board. Oliver accepted and was an active Director for several years. On another occasion, when a wedding reception was being catered for, he drove Frances and two or three of her assistants to the bride's home, where the reception was taking place. He enquired if there was anything further he could do.

'You can help with the washing up if you like.'

'Can I? Oh, what fun!'

Oliver put on an apron round his city suit, and, with a bottle of champagne beside him, attacked the pots and pans and plates and cutlery. After a while, the bride's father looked in at the kitchen, and saw Oliver, whom he did not recognise.

'Well, you're making a good job of things, my man!'

'Thank you sir,' said Oliver, towel in hand, and tongue in cheek.

'Would you like a glass of champagne?' said the bride's father.

'That's very good of you, but I've got a bottle of champagne here.'

The bride's father withdrew. Oliver, however, interested him, and he was soon back.

'Were you in the Army, by any chance?'

'Yes, I was in Eighth Army.'

'What was your unit?'

'Well, I'm Oliver Leese.' Collapse of stout party.

One of Frances Denby's assistants at the wedding reception was

twenty-three-year Judy Lampson, later to take on the running of the
Knightsbridge Kitchen. Judy had just survived the trauma of a broken
marriage, and she turned thankfully to Oliver and Frances, and the
happy atmosphere of their warm and affectionate relationship. For
Judy, Oliver became a father figure, Frances a sister, and she became
a frequent visitor to Worfield House.

Rosemary Jemmett and Diana Paterson had now married, and Cath
Brodie was taken on the strength as secretary. A cheerful, no-nonsense
Scot, she found Oliver 'a darling man', who astonished her with casual
instructions to telex Japan, and even, on one occasion, to drive a
three-ton truck in Central London. She was amused at his method of
dictation, when, after outlining in highly lurid language a letter that
he wanted written to some correspondent who had annoyed him, he
would invariably add the injunction 'put it nicely'.

*

The twenty-fifth anniversary of Alamein was in October 1967, and the
Sunday Times arranged for Monty, Oliver and a Staff Officer of
Monty's, Brigadier Hugh Mainwaring, to go to the site of the battle
with *Sunday Times* journalists and photographers, chiefly to record
and illustrate recollections of the battle. Freddie de Guingand under-
standably felt grieved that Monty had not wished him to be a member
of the party.

Before they went to Egypt, Oliver Leese and Frances Denby visited
Monty at Isington Mill. They arrived five minutes early for 4.30 tea.
Monty was sitting in a deck chair on the lawn apparently asleep, but
Oliver insisted on their remaining in the car until 4.30 precisely. At this
point Monty miraculously woke up, and explained what they were
going to do in Egypt. Monty remembered every detail of the battle, but
Oliver, Monty was horrified to discover, had forgotten a good deal.

'You're an absolute fool, Oliver, you don't remember a thing.'

'Well, I'm sorry, sir, but I've been doing quite a lot of different
things recently.'

Monty fished out half a dozen books on Alamein and handed them
to Frances.

'You must teach him about it,' said Monty. 'See that he reads one
of these for at least half an hour every day.'

'But Field Marshal, I can't do that!'

'You must. Can't have him disgracing me. By the way,' he explained
to Oliver, 'I'm going in uniform. You'll wear plain clothes.'

On 3 May 1967 they set off. Diplomatic relations between Great
Britain and Egypt had been broken off at the time of the Suez crisis
in 1956 and had not been resumed. The Arab press had been violently
anti-British. Colonel Nasser, however, President of the United Arab

Republic, had arranged that Monty and the members of his party would be the guests of the Egyptian Government during their stay in Egypt, Nasser offering to 'facilitate the visit in every possible way and provide cars, jeeps and helicopters as required.'[1]

The party arrived in Cairo at 7.30 a.m. on 4 May.

> 'As we emerged from the airport building,' wrote Mainwaring, 'we saw a long row of the largest Mercedes cars, police escort cars and motor cyclists, stretching far into the distance. On the bonnet of the car lent by President Nasser for Monty's use was the Union Jack provided by the Egyptian Government, the first to be seen in Cairo since the Union Jack had been hauled down at the British Embassy ten years before.'

Next day they flew in Nasser's personal aircraft to Alexandria, where they transferred to three Russian helicopters to fly to the desert. Nasser, at Monty's request, had closed the Western desert from Alexandria to Mersa Matruh to avoid the Press.

> 'From Alexandria,' wrote Oliver, 'we flew on in 3 helicopters, which remained with us for the ensuing week – together with some 10 motors and 10 jeeps, and two platoons of infantry to protect us from the British Press.'[2]

They flew on past Alamein Station to a new luxury hotel six miles beyond. There they had flats within a hundred yards of the sea. They set off about 7.30 every morning, either in helicopters, jeeps or motors, according to what they were doing. Everywhere they went had been cleared of mines by Egyptian sappers – there were still four million mines in the area, uncharted and unmarked. From the air the occasional gun-pit or trailer could be detected, and the stone sangars put up by the Indian division round Ruweisat. They found many points of interest, often with difficulty, such as the site near El Hamma where Monty founded Eighth Army HQ. They went to the Mitereiya Ridge, Ruweisat, Tel el Aqqaqir, Himeimat; they flew over the Qattara depression. Oliver also added to his collection of succulent plants.

Monty, aged seventy-nine (Oliver was seventy-two) was in very good heart, remembering everything and talking incessantly. Towards the end of the visit Monty went to see Nasser: Oliver was disappointed that he didn't take anyone with him, as he would have liked to have met Nasser. On the Sunday of the visit Monty laid a wreath in the Alamein British Cemetery, where there are 7000 graves and records of another 5000 who were killed elsewhere. Brigadier Hugh Mainwaring wrote of 'standing beside him, with Oliver Leese on his right and me

---

[1] *Three Score Years and Ten.* By Hugh Mainwaring. Printed privately by S. G. Mason (Chester) Ltd.
[2] Round Robin letter 7.6.67.

on his left, in silence to pay tribute to our friends twenty-five years after they had died that we might live.'

Less than a month after the Alamein party had returned to Britain, the 6-day War of 5–11 June 1967 erupted between Israel and Egypt. The Israeli preemptive strike, which destroyed the bulk of the Egyptian air force on the gound, virtually settled the issue in the first three hours of the conflict. Neither Monty nor Leese had any idea that this war was on the stocks, and they had seen no concentration of troops anywhere. There had been plenty of evidence that Nasser wished to resume friendly relations with Britain.

Oliver and Frances were invited to join in Monty's eightieth birthday celebrations on 17 November 1967. Frances made him a birthday cake which she took to Chelsea Hospital on the afternoon of 17 November. Monty was visibly affected, and said 'Nobody has ever made me a birthday cake before.'

Soon he became the Field Marshal again.

'You two are to get married,' he observed crisply. 'That's an order. Frances, you heard what I said?'

Oliver beamed into the middle distance, and Frances replied 'Field Marshal, you are not my Commanding Officer.'

'You're to get married,' repeated Monty. 'Both of you. And I'll make the speech at the wedding reception.'

Oliver's friend, General Sir Frank Simpson (Simbo), now Governor of the Royal Hospital, Chelsea, gave a dinner party at the Governor's residence to mark the occasion of Monty's eightieth birthday. Monty, in wayward mood, had previously announced that he wasn't going to ask Freddie de Guingand. Eventually he did invite him. Freddie now said that he wasn't going. It was Oliver who persuaded de Guingand to see reason, and all was well. Among the fifteen guests at the dinner – *The Times* described it as a 'spirited gathering' – were Field Marshal Lord Harding, Major General Sir Francis de Guingand, Major General Sir Miles Graham, Brigadier Hugh Mainwaring, General Sir Frank Simpson, Brigadier E. T. (Bill) Williams, Captain John Henderson (Monty's ADC) – and Lt-General Sir Oliver Leese.

Monty stayed the night at the Hospital, during which time thieves broke into his house, Isington Mill, stealing gold, silver and jewellery. His Field Marshal's baton was stolen, too: this was the biggest blow.

*

In the world of cricket, Oliver's adopted county of Warwickshire were always good value to watch.[1] Oliver as President would often entertain

---

[1] Warwickshire won the Gillette Cup in 1966 and 1968 and the County Championship in 1972.

players, officials and distinguished guests to dinner at Worfield, or, more informally, to a barbecue party – he was also President of the Worfield club, and delighted in the village game.

Once, when the West Indies were over, at a barbecue, Tommy Thompson was talking to Wesley Hall, the West Indian fast bowler. Oliver, in his capacity as genial host, came up to them and said to Wesley Hall 'What are you doing talking to our Vicar?', then, turning to Thompson, said 'Do you realise this man's a Catholic?'

'Look, General,' replied Wesley Hall, 'being black is bad enough, don't make me a Catholic as well!'

Ion Calvocoressi used to go down to the Lower Hall to help them before the Tests: 'He had the most interesting people to stay, such as Douglas Jardine, R. E. S. Wyatt, Gubby Allen, Harold Gilligan and Ian Peebles.' Two cricket-loving prime ministers figured among Oliver's guests, Sir Alec Douglas-Home and Sir Robert Menzies, the Australian Premier. Sometimes Oliver would bring his own team to play the village.

'He was a splendid person,' said Colin Cowdrey. Mike Smith, Warwickshire and England captain, recalled 'The players appreciated him. He was a one-off character.' Alan Smith, Warwickshire captain, England wicketkeeper, and later Warwickshire Secretary, valued Oliver's friendship: 'He was a great enthusiast who enjoyed the ambience of the game.'

Leslie Deakins, a great cricket personality, Warwickshire Secretary from 1944 to 1976, saw in him an outstanding President, who regularly attended annual general meetings, and from the chair inspired membership, officials and players alike.

'In particular,' wrote Leslie Deakins, 'one recalls his exhortations to fielders that "catches win matches". It was typical of the man that he should appreciate so clearly that whilst the batsman and bowler might hold the centre of the picture, it was the fielders who could turn the tide and so often did.'

*

Oliver was very much the Squire of Worfield. Once Oliver rang up the Vicar and said 'Tommy, I want you to come down and have dinner with me. I want to talk to you (a) about my soul, and (b) the British Legion. 7 p.m.' Oliver was concerned because he was to see the Archbishop in connexion with the Festival of Remembrance, and there was to be a new Service.

He had many friends in the Worfield area who would come round for visits: Bill Fea, a director of GKN, and his wife Nan; Ian Beddows, who fought at Alamein as a young subaltern, and his wife Veronica – Ian worked with Oliver in connexion with Church and British Legion affairs; Harry Parker, a farmer whose land was separated from the Lower Hall grounds by the tiny river Worfe.

Of his friends from Tac HQ, Dricky Bastyan, and his ex-driver Joe Colliton he would see on his trips to Australia; Ken Ray in South Africa. With Sidney Kent, John Green-Wilkinson, Ion Calvocoressi, John Stimpson, Petre Crowder, Ian Weston Smith, Vic Cowley, he exchanged correspondence and visits.

From 1967 onwards Oliver and Frances used to go overseas from January to early March, selecting their destinations partly to see cricket and partly to visit areas where cacti and succulent plants were growing:

'If possible,' wrote Frances Denby, 'to visit countries with a risk of trouble, e.g. Aden, where we always had to have an armed escort, and were shot at collecting plants, Israel, where we were dined by the generals of the '67 war. He was their hero of desert warfare, they could not believe he was on a private visit. Rhodesia, to stay with Humphrey Gibbs, we had to turn out our luggage on to the road on the border.

Lusaka, only allowed into the country with escort to see the Cathedral. Petra, we were the only people in the city. Troops came in for firing practice. Oliver solemnly went on writing postcards, with a stiff whisky.'

They went to the West Indies when Mike Smith's team was there; they saw cacti in Trinidad and Jamaica, and found time for a short visit to Venezuela. There were journeys to South Africa – once to Madagascar and on to the Canary Isles, returning via Morocco and Gibraltar; visits to SW Africa and Namaqualand, to virtually inaccessible places where few English people had been. In 1967 they left England in September for four weeks of the South African spring. There had been good rains and hence many spring flowers. They were in touch with Professor Rycroft of Kirstenbosch, and through his guidance they saw spectacular masses of wildflowers, in Namaqualand and in the Karroo.

In November 1968 they went to Southampton to cross the Channel on the *Queen Elizabeth*, at the beginning of her last voyage. 'We thought it would be fun to have caviar and see the ship' said Frances Denby. While they were on the deck, a man's voice, delightedly incredulous, called 'It can't be you, Oliver!' It was the Canadian General, Guy Simonds, who had learnt so much from Oliver in Sicily.

In 1969 General Anders invited Oliver to the Service which he was organising at Cassino to mark the twenty-fifth anniversary of the capture of the Monastery. Anders by now was a sick man. He died the following year and was buried in Cassino among his Polish soldiers. Oliver attended the Memorial Service in Westminster Cathedral. At the end of the Service one of the congregation was heard to exclaim

'There's Oliver Leese! I haven't seen him for a long time. I must have a word with him!' It was Mark Clark. The two chatted for half an hour about the events of a quarter of a century before.

*

In 1962 Oliver had succeeded Major General Sir Richard Howard-Vyse as President of the British Legion. Captain David Coffer was General Secretary and Gordon Shepherd was Oliver's Personal Assistant. The emphasis during Oliver's Presidency was on increasing membership and Poppy Appeal Collection. Oliver did much to change the Legion's image from what he described as that of 'old boys clanking medals and quaffing beer.' Girls in mini-skirts selling poppies proved a highly popular innovation. By 1969, the year before he retired, the decline in membership had been halted, and an increase of 50,000 new members had resulted through the development of well organised clubs.

> 'My own most vivid memory' wrote Gordon Shepherd, 'is of Sir Oliver's deceptively languid demeanour, and his personal magnetism. Very rarely indeed did the mailed fist emerge from the velvet glove, and when it did so it was always with good reason, and devastating for the individual concerned! He inspired devotion from all Legion staff who came into contact with him and to me he stands head and shoulders above any other person I have met.[1]

Oliver's biggest responsibility was during the Remembrance period, beginning with the visit of the Queen Mother to lay the main cross in the Garden of Remembrance outside St Margaret's Church in Westminster. He attended many rehearsals of the Festival of Remembrance, and on the Saturday morning visited the main poppy selling stands. Of the Festival itself he wrote:

> Each year I had to go up to the stage and speak the 'Exhortation'. You had to stand at attention – so you could not read the words, which were only too easy to forget. It was the most tense and moving moment in the Service, when the poppies were falling from the ceiling high up in the Albert Hall, and one false move by me could have spoilt the effect of the vital moment in the Service.[2]

After the Festival at the Albert Hall, Oliver would take the chair at a VIP Dinner of some sixty people at the Dorchester, making a speech to which the Prime Minister and Leader of the Opposition would reply.

Oliver spent his seventy-fifth birthday on 27 October 1969, in Paris.

[1] Letter to author 5.2.1982.
[2] Memoirs.

There were pre-dinner drinks with Christopher and Mary Soames at the Embassy, followed by dinner at Maxim's.

In the New Year, Oliver and Frances went to South Africa, Judy Lampson going with them. There was the usual stay at the Mount Nelson Hotel in Capetown, and the quest for Army friends, cricket and cacti. This was at a time when the South Africans' policy of apartheid was causing considerable repercussions in the cricket world.

The South African Prime Minister, John Vorster, refused to accept Basil d'Oliveira, a Cape Coloured, who had played cricket for Worcestershire for a number of years, as a member of the MCC team to tour South Africa in 1968–69. The MCC had promptly cancelled the tour. In 1970 it was South Africa's turn to tour England, and when Oliver wrote to Leslie Deakins, the Warwickshire Secretary, on 2 February 1970, the fate of the tour was very much in the balance:

> The feelings about the 1970 tour are very mixed. I kept on saying that we at Edgbaston had so far agreed to try and play the first Test Match at Edgbaston, and that we intended to do all that we could to achieve this . . .

> The Prime Minister, Mr. Vorster, sat behind us. I was introduced to him and spoke to him. He sat quite isolated, and I thought that rather stupidly none of the cricket hierarchy 'made much' of him. His elections are just coming on and he has an outspoken right wing party to compete with, and I was not at all surprised when they refused Ashe[1] a visa. The stupid thing is that Mr. Vorster thoroughly enjoys his cricket, and yet he is doing everything to isolate his country in international sport. It is sad because they play sport well and are worthy rivals. We've done everything in MCC to try and help them, in the Test Match world, but if they go on like this, it seems to me that we might very well soon let them stew in their own juice, till they learn some sense in the modern world as it is today.

★

From 1970 onwards he gradually gave up his jobs. This was largely because of circulation trouble in his right leg. 'His first collapse' wrote Frances Denby, 'was after a British Legion dinner. We got home and he collapsed on the floor, insisted on going to the Parade at the Cenotaph the following day to march with the men to the tune of "A Long Way to Tipperary"'.

Soon it was necessary for him to have a wheelchair. This he found very frustrating and he was occasionally listless. Frances was remarkably successful in finding occasions to cheer him up. Once Bill and Nan Fea were astonished to find Oliver, of all people, at Glyndebourne: Frances had arranged a picnic.

[1] A black American tennis player. He won the US Open Championship in 1968 and the Singles at Wimbledon in 1975. He later became non-playing Captain of the American Davis Cup team.

On another occasion he went with Frances and Cath Brodie to hear
Marlene Dietrich give a performance at Wolverhampton. Oliver had
met her in connexion with the Alamein Reunion in 1963 and wanted
to renew old memories, and she invited him to see her in the green
room after the show. Word of the general's intended visit had quickly
got around, and when they reached the theatre, half a dozen ex-
servicemen were soon on the spot to carry Oliver, in his wheelchair,
up several flights of spiral staircase, to the auditorium. She sang her
bitter sweet melodies to the delight of the audience in general and
Oliver Leese in particular, who soon had tears trickling down his
cheeks. At the end of the performance he was wheeled into the green
room, where Marlene Dietrich came forward to greet him, putting her
arms round him and kissing him as he sat in his wheelchair.

'Oh, Marlene, you were wonderful!'
'Oh, Oliver, Oliver!' lamented Marlene Dietrich. 'All our friends are
gone: Noel Coward is gone. 'Emmingway is gone. Only you and I are left!'
Oliver wept anew.

Eventually, in the summer of 1973, Oliver was told that amputation
was necessary. This was a risky business, as he was seventy-eight, but
he decided to go through with it.

'I'm not going to die, Frances,' he said, 'there are so many things I
want to do.'

The below knee amputation of the right leg was performed by Sir
Frederic Ashton on 4 June – of all days! – at The Queen Elizabeth
Hospital, Birmingham. The operation was successful, and when Ion
Calvocoressi visited him and asked how he was, Oliver replied 'Oh,
the leg's all right, but my backside isn't half sore now I have been in
bed for so long!'

Frances Denby recalls

After the operation he had to go and be fitted for an artificial leg. He saw
all the young people there with amputations, he visibly drew himself up
straight and said we would go on for lunch at the Plough, where we had
champagne, and he said we must neither of us ever complain about this
blasted leg, he was so lucky to have had such an active and interesting life.
If ever we felt miserable, we must think of all those young people who had
not been so lucky.

Recovery was quick; a month later he was able to officiate at the
opening ceremony of the new Worfield cricket pavilion, and unlocked
the door from his wheelchair.

About this time Frances Denby bought Dolwen, an eighteenth
century farmhouse on the Welsh border, a few miles from Oswestry:

We were intending to use it as a change from Worfield. He asked where I would want to live after he died, and would I keep the two houses? I said I would only keep Dolwen, so he suggested that Worfield House should be sold, and we should live at Dolwen. In this way he settled his affairs, and was able to give to his friends many of his treasures in his lifetime.

I arranged the house to give him as much independence as possible, [with a bedroom on the ground floor], which gave him an incentive to recover from the operation. We gradually increased our time at Dolwen, he enjoyed exploring new country. The staff at Worfield were wonderful, but he was almost over looked after, he hated being thought of as an invalid.

Oliver sold the wooden house at Worfield. 'Now I've got some money, Frances,' he said, when the sale had been completed, 'I'm going to buy myself a present.'

'And what's it going to be?'

'I'm going to get myself half a dozen pairs of pants at Harrods.'

Subsequent trips to Harrods, in a wheelchair, caused havoc among the shoppers when the Leese motorhorn – an old-fashioned rubber taxi horn – cleared the way for his progress down the aisles.

Oliver's eightieth birthday celebrations began with a dinner party at the Capital Hotel, for London friends, after the Alamein Reunion. Oliver, still a schoolboy, had strawberry ice cream made for the occasion. There was also pink champagne. On Sunday, 27 October, his actual birthday, there was a luncheon party at Worfield House, for local friends. 'We ate at a large table in his bedroom' wrote Frances Denby, 'the only room large enough to lay the tables, which I dressed with his Coldstream Guards figures.' In the evening the whole village was invited to a bonfire party at Worfield. Oliver, at last taken by surprise, was presented with a colour television: they had made a collection in the village.

More and more of his time now was spent in the house on the Welsh border. His travels, no longer world wide, were normally confined to the immediate vicinity at Dolwen. Like George Berrow he soon developed a liking for the fascinating village nearby: often he accompanied Frances in her Rover down the three-quarter-mile stony track between high hedges that led to the village square. Here Frances would do her shopping, while Oliver, looking out from the car window, would chat to the old timers: 'There's an old Army Corporal that lives in Dolwen now,' one of them was heard to observe, 'there's nice he is!'

That he retained his zest for life until a day or so before his death speaks volumes for the nursing of Frances Denby, who gave him sympathy, and, also, the understanding, perhaps more than understanding, that delighted him. She never seemed tired in those last months. Above all, in the last years of his life, she gave him a happiness that otherwise he would not have known.

On 24 March 1976 Monty died. Oliver in any case could not attend his funeral, so Ion Calvocoressi represented him in St George's Chapel.

In October 1976, Oliver managed to get down to the Royal Festival Hall for the last of the official Alamein Reunions, at which the guest of honour was the Prince of Wales. Monty had gone, but Oliver was still there, and the veterans raised the roof when he made his appearance. When, finally, the curtain fell on this last celebration of an epic victory, the Prince of Wales linked hands with Oliver at the singing of 'Auld Lang Syne'.

His diary for 1977 recorded nearly 200 social engagements, mainly small luncheon, tea, dinner or drinks parties at Dolwen. Birthdays of friends, including ex-servants, were meticulously recorded; a list of Christmas presents for his friends; his own appointments with the doctor, and Luke's, the border terrier, with the vet. As had been his lifelong custom, he had crossed out each day when it was over; an indication that it belonged to the past. The diary spilled over into 1978, the hand more shaky. In the last entry, for 5 January, he recorded the birthday of a friend.

It was evident by the end of 1977 that Oliver had not long to live, and Judy Lampson, who had stayed at Dolwen for Christmas, was back again on New Year's Day to help Frances look after him.

On the night of 15 January Oliver suffered a severe heart attack, and Dr Gwynn was called. The next morning Oliver said to Frances:

'Was I ill in the night?'

'Yes you were, Oliver.'

'Was it a heart attack?'

'Yes, it was.'

Oliver considered this.

'Oh, so that's what a heart-attack is like, is it? I've often wondered.' When Dr Gwynn called later in the morning, Oliver apologised profusely for having a heart attack at so inconvenient a time. He became gradually weaker. Jenny Beck, Cath Brodie, Rosemary Blackham visited him. He would talk lucidly and then doze off to sleep. Ian and Veronica Beddows visited him on Friday 20 January: he recognised them and smiled. Elizabeth Bache came over for lunch on Saturday the 21st. He spoke to her cheerfully and lucidly for a quarter of an hour and then dozed off. Later in the day there was another heart attack. 'On the 21st evening' said Frances Denby, 'he drifted into unconsciousness, holding Judy's and my hands, at peace with the world, and died as I was making the usual cup of tea at 8 a.m.'

Field Marshal Lord Carver read the lesson at the funeral service in Worfield Church, and the bugler who sounded the last post on that wintry, gusty day, had performed the same office when Monty died. Oliver Leese was buried in the Leicester-Warren family vault, which was also the final resting place of his wife Margaret.

On 7 April 1978 a Service of Thanksgiving took place at the Guards Chapel. It was a joyful service, the music played by the Band of the Coldstream Guards. Rimsky-Korsakov's superb *Glory* brought the service to its exciting conclusion, and to the outgoing voluntaries of the Regimental Slow March and the Regimental Quick March. Outside, the General's friends exchanged their favourite Oliver stories, then went their ways, musing on remembered things from the varied drama of his life – the guns of Alamein; buttered eggs at Eton; wild flowers in the Karroo; Stukas at Dunkirk; the shadows falling at Edgbaston; transport planes over Burma; Arizona; 'Lili Marlene'; the Somme; parties at Worfield; the Festival of Remembrance; the last Alamein Reunion.

A few months later, memorials were unveiled, in the Coldstream Cloister of the Guards Chapel and in the Parish Church of St Peter at Worfield.

19

LAST POST

Oliver Leese has not received the credit that is his due as one of the greatest fighting generals of the Second World War. This is partly because he shunned publicity, and partly because others have been given credit for his achievements.

Like many of his contemporaries, he left the Army shortly after the Second World War, but was almost unique in that he started from scratch and quickly reached the top of a new profession – horticulture – gaining a world wide reputation as a collector and grower of cacti and other succulents. With these and other wide ranging pursuits he remained extremely active until the time of his leg amputation, when he was nearly eighty.

A brigadier at Dunkirk, he was a divisional commander for eighteen months, a corps commander for two years, an army commander for nine months and an army group commander for eight months – five spheres of responsibility in as many years.

He acquitted himself splendidly at Dunkirk as Deputy Chief of Staff to Pownall, and, as his successor during the last three days of May 1940, he took a lion's part in the saving of the British Expeditionary Force. In little over a year (1941–1942) he formed and trained the Guards Armoured Division.

Commanding 30 Corps he achieved the breakthrough at Alamein and led the 1500 mile pursuit to Sfax: in Sicily he showed maturity and wisdom over the Monty–Patton contretemps, achieving order out of potential chaos, and coming out of the affair with his reputation further enhanced.

Some of his contemporaries (e.g. Harding, Urquhart, Gascoigne) consider that it was as a corps commander that Leese reached his peak. However, his staff point out the unquestioned success he achieved in higher commands. An army commander has more independence and therefore more responsibility; his decisions will not be purely military.

Political and diplomatic matters arise; it is important to have a good relationship with military leaders of Allied nations. Leese had no sooner taken over Eighth Army than he was faced with an irate Anders pointing to a map of post-war Europe, in *Eighth Army News*, in which Poland didn't appear. Leese, through sheer good will and the honesty of his approach, together with the amazing gimmick of Eighth Army French, won the cooperation of Anders and took Cassino. He carried out one of the greatest hoaxes in military history by transferring the main part of his forces from East to West Italy in a fortnight's odyssey that was unobserved by the enemy: later he brought off the same stratagem in reverse.

He was regarded with particular affection by the Poles from Anders down – as he had been by the Scots and Commonwealth divisions in the Middle East; he was always on the best of terms with Juin and the Free French. He had a very good relationship with the Americans; with Mark Clark after some difficulties, but he got on like a house on fire with Eisenhower, Patton, Bradley, Gruenther, Lemnitzer and Bedell Smith. In South East Asia his partnership with Stratemeyer was one of the major factors in the successful race to Rangoon. He brought his active career in the war to a brilliant conclusion, reconquering Burma five months ahead of any previous – and less – schedule.

Burma conquered, he was recalled to England following a misunderstanding that was none of his making. There followed an appointment in England – more important appointments in Germany and in Palestine he refused as they would entail further separation from his wife.

*

What are the essentials of a commander? Montgomery, in conversation with Bernard Shaw, said that you have to make quick decisions, adding 'As long as fifty-one per cent of your decisions are right, you'll succeed.'

Leese never shirked quick decisions: a high percentage of them were right. Monty's opinion of him is expressed clearly to Alanbrooke on four separate occasions from North Africa: 'The best of the lot is Oliver Leese, who is quite first class'; 'Oliver Leese has been quite first class'; 'he is a very valuable officer, he is easily the best I have'; 'Oliver Leese is first class, Horrocks is very good, Lumsden is poor;' – and in his diary he wrote 'my best Corps Commander was Oliver Leese.'

'Dricky' Bastyan wrote of him:

So far as I was concerned, in both theatres [CMF[1] and SEAC] Sir Oliver was a fine commander to work for. He made quite clear what he wanted and trusted me implicitly to see that the logistics worked to give full support to his plans. He never interfered or asked needless questions. On my part I knew that if and when the need arose I could approach him personally. Often when we would meet, unexpectedly, in Italy, we would get out of our jeeps, and he would invariably say 'All going well?' To which I would reply 'Yes' – or 'Bit of a problem over (something or other that was always the unexpected) but we have it under control.' With a few simple words each would proceed on his way.

Kirkman on Leese:

As soon as we had taken over in the Cassino area, Leese established himself in a tactical HQ, within almost walking distance of my HQ. This was in the Monty tradition, but unlike Monty I do not remember him often visiting my divisional commanders, nor do I think he used ADCs or Liaison officers to discover what was going on in the forward area . . . What he *did* do was to have a fairly long telephone conversation with me in the evenings before dinner time, not necessarily about any particular problem, but I suppose to find out any local news, how I was getting on, etc.

I rarely consulted Leese about the tactical decisions in 13 Corps, but, having made any decisions of any importance was always careful to tell Leese.

Considered individually any of the examples of initiation coming from Corps rather than Army would be perfectly normal practice, but taken over a six monthly period they suggest that Leese can be criticised for not himself sufficiently directing the Army's plans and future policy. Later Keightley experienced similar reaction.

Contrast with Monty directing operations himself, Monty exercising a very close control of operations, the initiatives for fresh moves coming from him; Leese, prepared to accept ideas from his subordinates, and anxious to support and encourage them. Both systems worked. A commander, to be successful, must to some extent develop his own technique to suit his own personality, and you can argue that Leese did just that.

Gregory Blaxland, military historian, ex-Eighth Army liaison officer, does not think Leese quite pulled it off in his opening efforts to raise morale by Monty-style visitations, 'a thing that had of course become infinitely harder in the slog up Italy than when backs were to the Nile and the prospect of spectacular achievement bright. Monty himself had failed to arouse his troops to anything like the same pitch of enthusiasm when confronted with mud, mountains, and endless river-lines.'

Leese's opening attacks, says Blaxland, in both the Liri Valley and Gothic Line battles were masterpieces of planning and brilliant

---

[1] Central Mediterranean Forces.

examples of how to take the enemy by surprise when options were extremely limited, but he failed to appreciate the problems of exploitation and was far too optimistic about what armour could achieve.

It has sometimes been said of Leese that he tried to be Monty instead of being himself. Two relevant factors should be examined. First, Monty taught the art of generalship to his subordinates, especially Leese, Horrocks and Dempsey. As Leese worked for six months in close relationship with Monty, he naturally put some of his master's precepts into practice – such as visits to troops, pep talks, essentials of plan known right down – these methods were copied by Leese to good effect. Why not?

Second, as General Kirkman emphasised, Leese's system as an army commander was his own. Far from being an imitation of Monty's, it contrasted with it. As Kirkman said, both systems worked, and Leese's system was quite definitely his own.

★

The story of the so-called sacking affair has already been dealt with. It cannot be stressed too strongly that Leese did not try to sack Slim, that he couldn't have done so even if he had wanted to, and that the affair was none of his seeking. What does stand out like a star in the darkest night is Leese's magnanimity over his treatment. To have been recalled, shamefully and humiliatingly, as his only reward for playing a major part in one of the most brilliant of Allied victories would have embittered almost anyone. That he was able to shrug it off, almost with compassion towards his chief detractor, was one of the greatest personal achievements of his life.

★

In 1946 Freddie de Guingand, Britain's most successful Chief of Staff this century, wrote his war memoirs, *Operation Victory*. He did not have Oliver Leese in mind when writing his comments in generaliship, a factor that makes them nonetheless apposite in connexion with the subject of this biography.

Thus:

> If it is decided to employ a successful commander in a new theatre it is a decided advantage if he can take certain key officers with him. In fact where possible 'teams' should be kept together. They are so obviously more efficient.

In his six points for generalship de Guingand emphasises that the general should know his stuff; be known and recognised by his troops; ensure that troops are given tasks within their powers; see that subordinate commanders are disturbed as little as possible; command by personal contact; be human and study the human factor. Leese scores high marks on all six, but de Guingand's 'Ingredients of the big man' are what might well be an admirable summary of Leese as a commander:

a He should be able to sit back and avoid getting immersed in detail.
b He must be a good picker of men.
c He should trust those under him and let them get on with their job without interference.
d He must have the power of quick decision.
e He should inspire confidence.
f He must not be petty.
g He should not be pompous.

*

Leese's weaknesses were often the extension of his positive qualities: his desire to get on with the job could lead to corner cutting and impatience. One rather sedentary brigadier complained to Monty about Leese's language when reprimanding him. 'I don't care what he calls you as long as he wins his battles,' replied Monty.

He could be intolerant. He liked people to be intelligent and amusing; he was liable to be especially intolerant towards non-games-players. Lord Tweedsmuir, Ian Weston Smith and Bernard Bruce have all said that he would occasionally be intolerant of a person without reason: it was no use telling him so, however tactfully.

In civilian life he was frequently described as the perfect host. He was not always the perfect guest. When Leese was on a visit to New Zealand, Sir Bernard Fergusson (Lord Ballantrae) who was then the Governor General, found him off-hand and unpunctual.

These flaws did not detract from his essential greatness. Oliver Leese was a nonesuch. It was Julian Gascoigne who said 'He was completely unlike any other general, any other guardsman, any other soldier.'

Major General G. P. B. Roberts remembered him for his encouragement and inspiration.

Lorne Campbell, VC, was impressed by his complete calmness and confidence:

An impression heightened in a rather untidy world of shorts and bare knees or often scruffy trousers, by his invariably smart appearance in a Guard's Officer's Khaki plus-fours and beautiful stockings which could have come straight from Turnbull and Asser.

The Canadian General Burt Hoffmeister on Leese:

I received a signal to report to 8th Army HQ. Sir Oliver adjourned a conference on my arrival and gave me his undivided attention for the allotted time. As I recall his words: 'I just wanted you to come down so that I could acknowledge and thank you personally for the great work done by you and the 5th Canadian Armoured Division in the Gothic Line battle': he then went on to give me his appreciation of the contribution we had made to the Army plan. At the conclusion of our meeting he handed me copies of the previous day's London papers and a box of sweets from Groppi's.

The next signal that Hoffmeister had from Leese 'was to the effect that I had earned a vacation and that his personal aircraft would be available to take me to Cairo.'

Colonel S. Zakrzewski, Polish Corps, shortly after the capture of Ancona:

> I stood near my armoured car giving some orders when a British officer came and asked me to see his General, who was in his staff car not far away. I recognised General Leese and reported the tactical situation to him. The General shook my hand and said 'Well done, Carpathians, well done indeed, thank you!' After a few friendly remarks he went on his way. It was not customary to shake hands in the army, and to be visited by an Army Commander. I was very impressed.

Brigadier Maurice Lush, as chief political officer, Tripolitania, was responsible for the administration and welfare of the civilian population as the Eighth Army, driving the enemy before them, occupied the territory:

> Oliver Leese was, to me, the ideal of a British officer; intelligent, competent; resourceful; compassionate; open to sensible suggestions; understanding; willing to listen and to learn; a born commander; a great soldier; a splendid friend. I wish I had known him better.

Many of his young officers are now grandfathers. Some *obiter dicta* about their General Oliver:

Ion Calvocoressi: He was the greatest person in my life. He showed us how to get things done, how to achieve things.

Ian Weston Smith: He was a very unorthodox soldier. A bit of the rebel in him. Able to summarise within minutes the fighting ability of a division. His capacity to make himself understood was his great strength. Not interested in money, honours, pomp, ceremony.

Lord Tweedsmuir: The people who loved Oliver really did. If ever there was a realist it was Oliver.

Vic Cowley (Whizzer Pilot): I adored Oliver. Anything he did, it worked. A father figure. Such a wise chap.

General Sir John Gibbon (Ex-30 Corps): Very good at putting it across and being seen where it would do good. He built up an efficient military team which became a family circle. He brought us a cartload of victories.

To Bill Fea, a Worfield friend, who knew him well

> It was one of his many great qualities that he had friends everywhere and in every walk of life. And for many of us our feelings went beyond friendship; respect for his personality, admiration for his achievements; gratitude for his generosity, and untold kindly acts – yes, all of those, but more than that – we loved him.

Oliver Leese liked people of all ages, a fact which was demonstrated in his taking the children of the village by coach to see the illuminations at Blackpool, and by his warm good fellowship, in his basket chair in the field on Guy Fawkes night, surrounded by everyone in Worfield.

'How lucky he was,' said Hilary Leese, 'that there were two such women in his life as Margaret Leese and Frances Denby.'

His greatest virtue was integrity.

A last word from Maurice Lush:

> If ever the trumpets sounded on the other side, they were for Oliver.

Appendix A

THE JEALOUSY TRAP

Written by Field Marshal Lord Harding with special relevance to Leese and Mark Clark

I remember in summing up at the end of an exercise run by Southern Command in the early 'thirties, where I was then a junior staff officer, the C-in-C, General Romer, made the point that friction between senior commanders was a very serious menace in war – friction or jealousy, call it what you will – this had developed between Oliver and Mark Clark, and still more so between Kirkman and Mark Clark. I am sure that Oliver started off with the best of intentions in regard to the inter-army cooperation, but as time went on I fear he fell into what, for want of a better description, I call the 'jealousy trap' to which all senior commanders are vulnerable, prompted mainly I think by Kirkman and probably some members of his staff also and quite rightly jealous for the prestige and public image of 8th Army. In consequence, inter-army relationships became more difficult, in spite of Al Gruenther's[1] valuable work as an emollient, and it was a good thing that in the final campaign the main axis of the armies diverged – 8th Army NE and 5th Army NW.

1 April 1983

---

[1] Mark Clark's Chief of Staff.

Appendix B

BEFORE CASSINO

PERSONAL MESSAGE FROM THE ARMY COMMANDER

Great events lie ahead of us. All round Hitler's Germany, the Allies are closing in: on the East, the victorious Russians drive on – in the West, the British and American Armies are massed to invade.

– Now in the South, the Eighth and Fifth Armies are about to strike.

Side by side with our French and American Allies, we will break through the enemy's winter line and start our great advance Northwards. Our plan is worked out in every detail – we attack in great strength, with large numbers of tanks and guns, supported by a powerful American Air Force and our own Desert Air Force.

The peoples of the United Nations will be watching the Eighth Army. Let us live up to our great traditions and give them news of fresh achievements – great news such as they expect from this Army.

We welcome gladly to our ranks those Divisions whose first fight this is with the Eighth Army. We send a special message to our Polish Corps, now battling beside us to regain its beloved country.

I say to you all – Into action, with the light of battle in your eyes. Let every man do his duty throughout the fight and the Day is ours!

Good Luck and God Speed to each one of you!

(signed) OLIVER LEESE
Lieut.-General

ITALY,
MAY, 1944.

Appendix C

THE BATTLE OF THE TELEGRAMS

★

Telegrams between Leese and Mountbatten shortly before the fall of Rangoon. Mountbatten used Leese's telegram to block the latter's promotion.

Personal Mountbatten information Playfair from Leese.

8. From repeated enquiries lately received here I can only assume you are not fully satisfied with administration my command. I am fully satisfied liaison between my staff and service and CAS (B) is good and both are making the best use of the very meagre capacity at present at their disposal and have plans in hand to improve situation as soon as further capacity offers. Moreover repeated enquiries calling for detailed replies on matters for which I am responsible waste valuable time which my staffs cannot afford with operations in their present state. I shall be grateful for assurance that my position is understood and that these enquiries will cease.

Personal Leese from Mountbatten
Your telegram, Paragraphs 1 to 7, noted.

2. Paragraph 8. I have only carried out one Civil Affairs tour since I have been here at the end of which I very naturally sent you my telegram.
3. I must point out that although you are responsible to me for the administration of Burma the ultimate responsibility to H.M. Government is mine. It is at their insistence that most of the repeated enquiries have been made. I did not however immediately jump to the conclusion that they are dissatisfied with my conduct of affairs.
4. I must make my position perfectly clear. When I require information from a subordinate Commander-in-Chief, whether for H.M. Government or for myself, I shall apply for it and trust that in future I can

count on the same loyalty from you as H.M. Government expects from me.

5. Finally, I must inform you that you acted in an improper manner in repeating a telegram containing your paragraph 8 to your MGGS at Kandy.

Earlier in the campaign Mountbatten himself had sent an offensive telegram to CIGS on the subject of a replacement for Pownall, containing the expression 'if the Army cannot from their resources assist me with a suitable Chief of Staff' – which drew from CIGS the comment that he took exception to the tone of the telegram.

Appendix D

REFLECTIONS ON THE SLIM AFFAIR

by General Sir Philip Christison

You might, I think, consider the paradox created by Alanbrooke's decision to appoint Leese. Had he promoted Slim, the senior and very successful commander, he would have had to find a new commander for 14th Army – someone who would be as popular with his troops and of equal calibre to Slim . . .

Had Slim been promoted I have no doubt Leese would have followed Montgomery as CIGS and not Slim who had already retired. Such is fate.

I consider Leese fell down on his 'man-management' when he did not take the course of ordering Slim to take convalescent leave after his prostate operation. Had he done so all would have been well.

From communication to author, 3.3.83

BIBLIOGRAPHY

Relevant sections of the Official Histories have been consulted. The following is a brief list of other books that have been helpful:

Barnett, Correlli *The Desert Generals*. Kimber 1960.
Blaxland, Gregory *Alexander's Generals*. Kimber 1979.
Blumenson, Martin *Mark Clark*. Jonathan Cape 1985.
Bond, Brian (ed) *Chief of Staff. Diaries of Lt-Gen Sir Henry Pownall*. Leo Cooper 1972 and 1974.
Carver, Michael *El Alamein*. Batsford 1962.
Carver, Michael *Harding of Petherton*. Weidenfeld 1978.
Churchill, Winston *The Second World War*. Cassell 1948–1954.
Crimp, R. L. *The Diary of a Desert Rat*. Leo Cooper 1971.
Douglas, Keith *Alamein to Zem Zem*. Oxford 1979.
Fraser, David *Alanbrooke*. Collins 1982.
Graham, Dominick *Cassino*. Pan/Ballantine 1972.
Guingand, Major General Sir Francis de *Operation Victory*. Hodder & Stoughton 1947.
Guingand, Major General Sir Francis de *From Brass Hat to Bowler Hat*. Hamish Hamilton 1979.
Hamilton, Nigel *Monty, Vols I, II & III*. Hamish Hamilton 1981–1986.
Hart, Basil Liddell *History of the Second World War*. Cassell 1970.
Horne, Alistair *To Lose a Battle*. Macmillan 1969.
Hough, R. *Mountbatten, Hero of our time*, Weidenfeld 1980.
Jackson, W. G. F. *The Battle for Italy*. Batsford 1967.
Jackson, W. G. F. *The North African Campaign 1940–1943*. Batsford 1975.
Leese, Oliver and Margaret *Desert Plants*. Collingridge (USA) 1959.
Leese, Sir Oliver *Cacti*. Ward Lock 1973.
Leslie, Shane *The Oppidan*. Chatto & Windus 1922.
Leslie, Shane *The End of a Chapter*. Constable 1916.
Lewin, Ronald *Slim, the Standardbearer*. Leo Cooper 1976.
Macmillan, H. *The Blast of War*. Macmillan 1967.
Majdalany, F. *Cassino*. Longman 1957.
Montgomery, B. *A Field Marshal in the Family*. Constable 1973.
Montgomery, B. L. *Memoirs*. Collins 1958.

Nicolson, N. *Alex*. Weidenfeld 1973.
Orgill, Douglas *The Gothic Line*. Heinemann 1967.
Pack, S. W. C. *Operation Husky*. David and Charles 1977.
Pyman, H. *Call to Arms*. Leo Cooper 1971.
Richardson, Charles *Flashback*. Kimber 1985.
Slim, W. *Defeat into Victory*. Cassell 1956.
Smith, E. D. *Battle for Burma*. Batsford 1979.
Young, Desmond *Rommel*. Collins 1950.
Ziegler, P. *Mountbatten*. Collins 1985.

UNPUBLISHED MATERIAL

Letters of Sir Oliver Leese to his wife.
Memoirs and Private papers of Sir Oliver Leese.
Lt-Colonel Hilary Leese's notes on the Leese family.
Operations of 1st Guards Brigade August–September 1916.
Ulick Verney's account of the retreat to Dunkirk and other papers.
Ion Calvocoressi's War Diary.
Ian Weston Smith's account of the Sicily campaign.
Army Commander's Diary (Eighth Army) 3 Jan 1944–2 Oct 1944.
C-in-C's Diary (ALFSEA) 1 Nov 1944–10 July 1945.

INDEX

Adair, General Allan, 90–1
Akarit, battle of, 130–31, 197
Akyab, 212–13
Alamein, battle of, 93–115, 141, 149, 157, 189, 195, 275, 276, 286
Alamein, First battle of, 95
Alamein Reunions, 268, 282, 283, 284, 285
Alam Halfa, battle of, 95
Alanbrooke, Field Marshal Lord (CIGS November 1941–June 1946), 63, 84, 85, 86–7, 89, 113, 123, 154, 156, 179, 186, 192n, 195, 196, 197, 201, 202, 217, 226, 230–37, 238, 239, 240, 242, 243, 245, 246, 247, 248, 249, 250, 251, 253n, 254, 255, 257, 287; comments on OL receiving a raw deal, 258; chooses OL as Lieutenant of the Tower of London, 268
Alexander, Field Marshal Lord, 31, 63, 82, 84, 95, 99, 101, 114, 123, 125, 128, 129, 133, 144, 151, 154–56, 158–59, 163, 172–74, 176, 177, 179–84, 187–89, 191, 193, 194, 201, 201n, 235, 237, 265
Allfrey, Lt-General, 149, 154, 155, 164, 164n
Amery, L. S., 62, 62n, 189, 189n, 197
Anders, General, 154, 157–59, 165–70, 174, 178, 181, 182, 246, 265, 279, 287
Anderson, General, 117, 123, 128
Anzio, 155, 156, 157
Aplin, Sgt Major, 29
Army Formations
    Allied Land Forces South East Asia (ALFSEA), 220, 223, 225, 239, 244, 245, (NCAC 203, 204, 209, 217, 222).
British Expeditionary Force (BEF), 60–85
11 Army Group, 195, 202
21 Army Group, 147, 176, 208
British and Commonwealth Armies:
First, 117, 123, 128, 139, 161
Second, 129, 147, 149
Eighth, 40, 95, 111, 112, 115, 122, 125, 129, 130, 138, 144, 147, 148–50, 152, 154–56, 159, 161, 171, 173, 174, 176, 177, 180, 183, 190–93, 208, 228, 245, 269
Twelfth, 240, 241
Fourteenth, 203, 204, 208, 209, 217, 224, 225, 234, 237, 238, 240, 244, 245, 254, 256
Corps:
4th, 209, 222, 234, 238
5th, 154, 182, 185, 192
10th, 117, 130, 155, 156, 162
12th, 86
13th, 54, 162, 164, 165, 170, 184, 185
15th, 203, 204, 224, 228, 238
30th, Chapters 8–11; 165, 192, 263
33rd, 209, 210, 236
Divisions:
Guards Armoured, 86–92, 97, 106
1 Armoured, 130, 189
4 British, 164, 165–66, 185
4 Indian, 101, 155, 158
6 Armoured, 164
7 Armoured, 122, 124, 125, 222
8 Indian, 165
15 Scottish, 88–9

army formations – *cont.*
17 Indian, 221, 222
19 Indian, 222, 224
20 Indian, 221, 222
26 Indian, 229, 234
36 British, 228
44 (Home Counties), 125
50 (Tyne & Tees), 73, 129, 143, 149
51 (Highland), 86, 111, 114, 119, 122,
    123, 125, 131, 138
78 Division, 142, 155, 164, 168
Brigades:
1st Guards, 22, 32, 161
22nd Armoured, 122
26th Indian Infantry, 228
29th Infantry, 86, 228
231st Infantry, 135
Units:
11 Hussars, 122, 131
Other Commonwealth formations:
9 Australian Division, 101, 108
Canadian Corps, 156, 169, 185
1 Canadian Division, 135, 149
5 Canadian Armoured Division, 291
2 New Zealand Division, 101, 107,
    122, 155
1 South African Division, 101, 107
United States formations:
US Fifth Army, 148, 152, 155, 156,
    157, 161, 164, 171, 183, 184, 192
US Seventh Army, 141, 186
French formations:
2nd Army, 66
9th Army, 66, 69, 70
German formations:
10th Army, 172, 173
Afrika Korps, 115, 118, 119
90 Panzer Grenadier Division, 159
Arnim, General von, 127
Ashton, Sir Frederick, 282
Asquith, Luke 162, 165, 193
Attlee, Clement, 98, 189, 189n, 253
Auchinleck, Field Marshal, 198, 223,
    227, 231, 240, 241, 247, 251

Bache, Elizabeth, 266, 284
Bacon, Sir Edmund, 35
Baldwin, Stanley, 39
Balfour, General Sir Victor FitzGeorge,
    126, 137, 140
Bandon, Air Vice Marshal, Earl of,
    214
Barrackpore, 203, 204, 205, 209, 212,

213, 214, 215, 224, 227, 228, 229, 230,
    236, 242, 247, 249, 250, 257
Bastyan, Lt-General Sir Edric, 149, 150,
    153, 155, 162, 164, 165n, 186, 191,
    205, 208, 210, 214, 219, 225, 228, 229,
    232, 250, 272–73, 279, 287–88
Beck, Diana, 266, 273
Beck, Jennifer, 266, 284
Beddows, Ian, 278, 284
Beith, Major (Ian Hay), 35
Belisha, Leslie Hore, 43
Billotte, General, 66, 68, 70, 74
Birks, Major General H. L., 47, 47n, 49
Bishop, Ernest, 263, 270
Blackham, Rosemary (née Jemmett),
    268–69, 270, 271, 275, 284
Blakiston, C. H., 9, 10, 11, 13, 18, 20
Blaxland, Major Gregory, 152, 159n,
    165, 165n; assessment of OL, 288–89
Boer War, 3
Bonsai trees, 273
Boyle, Jimmy, 215, 215n, 247
Boyne, Lady, 269, 274
Bradley, General, 137, 141, 142, 287
Bridgeman, Robert (2nd Viscount), 5,
    5n, 7, 31, 36, 63, 71, 72, 74, 77, 82
Brodie, Catherine, 275, 282, 284
Broke, P. V., 11, 19
Brooke, Major General Sergison, 32,
    32n, 43, 62, 89, 252
Brown, David, 272
Browning, Lt-General Sir Frederick, 65,
    65n, 202, 211, 217, 218, 219, 224, 225,
    226, 228, 241, 242, 247, 255, 256, 257
Bruce, Bernard, 97, 98, 99, 165, 290
Buck, William, 259, 263
Burges, Major Guy, 28
Burma Campaign, 194–234
Burns, Lt-General E. L. M., 157, 169,
    178, 181
Butter, David, 149, 153, 154, 156, 160,
    174, 176, 182

Cacti, 266–67, 268, 276, 279, 281, 286
Calvocoressi, Ion, 102, 102n, 122, 123,
    126, 127, 134, 142, 147, 147n, 150,
    151, 155, 157, 159, 160n, 161, 161n,
    162, 165, 167, 175, 176, 177, 181, 182,
    187, 187n, 208, 211, 216, 226, 241,
    242, 254, 262, 268, 271, 272, 273, 278,
    279, 282, 284; assessment of OL, 291
Camberley, Staff College, 31, 144, 195,
    197, 198, 256

Campbell, Brigadier Lorne, VC, 120, 131, 290
Carne, Colonel James, VC, 87–8, 87n
Carrington, Charles, 22
Carter, L/Sgt, 23–4
Carver, Field Marshal Lord, 108, 109, 120–21, 131–32, 284
Casablanca, 133
Casey, R. G., 114, 114n, 209–10, 217
Cassino, 155, 158, 159, 160, 161, 163–79, 189, 279
Cator, Major General, 32, 32n, 37–8
Cavan, Field Marshal the Earl of, 174–75
Cazalet, Victor, 12, 12n, 136, 136n
Chamberlain, Neville, 62, 73
Charlton, Warwick, 154, 158, 159
Christison, General Sir Philip, 31, 203, 205, 207, 210, 211, 212, 213, 225, 225n, 227, 228, 230, 236, 237, 238, 240–41, 244, 246, 249, 250, 251, 255, 256n, 257
Churchill, Winston, 62, 69, 73, 74, 78, 79, 84, 95, 113, 122, 123, 124, 127, 133, 156, 160, 170, 172, 177, 187, 188, 195, 196, 197, 200, 203, 247–48, 250, 254
Clark, General Mark, 148, 149, 152, 155, 156, 158, 159, 160, 161, 170, 171, 172, 173, 175, 176, 177, 178, 178n, 185, 187, 192, 265, 280, 287
Clowes, David, 216, 216n
Colliton, Joe, 68, 88, 126, 191, 279
Corap, General, 66, 69, 70, 74
Cowan, Major General D. T., 211, 222, 251
Cowley, Victor, 181, 208, 225, 279; assessment of OL, 291
Crawley, Cosmo, 88
Crawshay, Major Jack, 68, 83
Crerar, General Harry, 150, 150n, 151, 154
Crowder, Sir John, 7
Crowder, Petre, 208, 209, 225, 279
Crowe (Mrs Hilda Davey), 34, 38, 126, 263
Cunningham, Admiral, 134, 134n, 137

Daily Telegraph, 246
Davey, Gordon, 263
Deakins, Leslie, 278, 281
Dempsey, General Sir Miles, 31, 129, 149, 155, 248, 251, 263, 265, 289
Denby, Frances, 273, 274, 275, 277, 279, 281, 282–83, 284, 292

Dieppe Raid, 200, 254
Dietrich, Marlene, 268, 282
Dill, Field Marshal, 40, 69, 76, 77, 78, 79, 82, 85, 95
Dolwen, 282–83, 284
Dorman-Smith, Major General E. E., 31
Drake, Betty (née Leese), 3, 264
Dunkirk, retreat to, 61–86, 286
Dunphie, Colonel Peter, 210, 214–15, 229, 250, 255, 258

Eastern Command, 260–61
Eastwood, Lt-General Sir Ralph, 65, 65n, 66, 68, 70, 72, 75
Eden, Anthony, 83
Edward VII, 1
Eighth Army French, 170–71
Eighth Army News, 150, 154, 158, 287
Eisenhower, General Dwight, 117, 125, 128, 130, 133, 144, 148, 197, 198, 287
Elizabeth, the Queen Mother, 43, 280
Elizabeth II, 24
Erskine, General, 125, 128
Eton College, 7–14, 28, 29, 30, 35, 160, 197, 243, 265, 267, 272, 273, 285

Fea, Bill, 278, 281, 292
Feilden, Major General Sir Randle, 91–2, 196, 253
Fergusson, Sir Bernard (Lord Ballantrae), 290
Festing, Field Marshal, 206, 206n, 227
Finch, Colonel John Wynne, 38
Fleming, Peter, 88, 88n, 214
Fraser, General Sir David, 268
Freyberg, General (Viscount), 101, 102, 105, 109, 111, 112, 114, 123, 158, 159, 161, 170, 174, 222, 236, 263, 265

Gamelin, General, 69, 73
Gandhi, 58
Garrod, Air Marshal, 202, 202n
Gascoigne, Major General Sir Julian, 96–7, 96n, 98, 102, 105, 111, 112–13, 128, 271, 286; opinion of OL, 290
Gell, Harry, 16, 17
George III, 13
George V, 13, 38
George VI, 43, 79, 178, 180, 181, 182, 197, 262
Georges, General, 66, 70
Gibbon, General Sir John, assessment of OL, 292

Gibbs, Mr., 4
Giffard, General, 195, 198, 202, 204, 219, 226, 239, 245
Gladstone, W. E., 1, 11
Godwin, Colonel J. F., 239–40
Godwin-Austen, Major General, 236
Golding, Cyril, 185–86
Goodhart, A. M., 11
Gordon-Lennox, Lt-General Sir George, 71, 182–83
Gort, Field Marshal Viscount, VC, 62–84, 136, 195, 235–36
Gothic Line, 185, 187, 188, 189, 190–91, 191n, 192
Gott, Lt-General 'Strafer', 95
Gracey, General Sir Douglas, 221, 222, 230, 238, 251
Graham, Lilias, 264
Graham, Major General Sir Miles, 196, 265–66, 277
Grant, Colonel Charles, 27, 28, 29
Graziani, General, 94
Green-Wilkinson, 35, 99, 100, 103, 106, 136, 149, 153, 191, 197, 213, 279
Gregson-Ellis, Major General, 31, 64, 65, 71, 72, 74, 81
Grenfell, Joyce, 215–16
Grigg, James, 197
Gruenther, General, 160, 287
Guards Armoured Division, 86–92, 197, 286
Guderian, General, 66, 74
Guingand, Major General Sir Francis de, 111, 113, 125, 134, 142, 275, 277; his six points of generalship, 289–90

Hall, Wesley, 278
Hamilton, Nigel, 73n, 130, 139n, 141, 141n, 146, 201
Harding, Field Marshal Lord, 31, 120–21, 124, 159, 173, 174, 176, 182, 183, 184, 186, 208, 277, 286
Hargreaves, Constance (Later Constance Leese), 2
Hargreaves, Reginald, 2
Hargreaves, William, 1, 1n
Hastilow, Alex, 270
Head, Viscount, 62, 62n
Hiroshima, 1, 253
Hitler, Adolf, 42, 62, 73, 138–39, 158, 170, 175, 186, 232
Hitler Line, 159, 168, 169, 174
Hoffmeister, Major General, 188, 265;

assessment of OL, 290–91
Hogg, Quintin (Lord Hailsham), 29
Home, Alec Douglas, 273, 278
Horrocks, Lt-General, 84, 96, 99, 101, 117, 127, 130, 132, 155, 236, 262, 263, 265, 287, 289
Hough, Richard, 200
Hull, Field Marshal, 48, 50, 51, 189
Huntziger, General, 66
Huxley, Anthony, 189

Ironside, Field Marshal, 73, 74, 76, 79, 84
Ismay, General Lord, 40, 69, 236, 236n
Italian Campaign, 146–93
Italy, 41–2

Jackson, General W. G. F., 128
Jon (Cartoonist), 109
Juin, General, 177, 187, 261, 287

Kandy, 196, 198, 199, 200, 202, 203, 205, 206, 207, 211, 214, 217, 218, 219, 220, 221, 232, 234, 236, 239, 241, 245, 248, 256
Kasuya, Major General, 223
Keightley, General Sir Charles, 163, 164, 178, 182, 187, 269
Keith, The, 82, 83
Kennedy, Major General Sir John, 40, 156, 157, 163
Kent, Brigadier Sidney, 125, 126, 147, 153, 159, 165, 165n, 172, 174, 175, 177, 191, 197, 198, 203, 208, 216, 225, 228, 229, 254, 279
Kesselring, Field Marshal, 133, 139, 144, 151, 155, 172, 263–64, 264n
Kimura, General, 221, 222
King-Hall, Commander Stephen, 54, 54n
Kirkman, General Sir Sidney, 149, 154, 155, 157, 159, 162, 164, 165, 166, 169, 170, 181, 183, 184, 192; assessment of OL, 288, 289
Knightsbridge Kitchen, 273, 274–75

Lamb, Sgt Jack, 62, 68, 80, 82, 147, 165, 191, 259
Lambert, Sgt Alma (Jack), 22–3, 24, 269
Lampson, Graham (Lord Killearn), 178, 182
Lampson, Judy, 275, 281, 284

Laszlo, Philip de, 34, 35, 36
Leese, Alexander, 3
Leese, Gertrude, 2
Leese, Lt-Colonel Hilary, 292
Leese, Joseph, 2
Leese, Sir Joseph, 2, 6, 15n
Leese, Lady Margaret (née
  Leicester-Warren)
  ancestry, 34; early years, 34–5;
  marriage, 37; travels with OL, 37–43;
  her letters from Quetta, 50–60; her
  letters to OL (1940), 66, 67, 70, 71–2,
  73, 75, 76, 77, 78, 79, 81; OL spends
  leave with her, 146; lunch with the
  Churchills, 197; in Scotland, at Tabley
  and in Worfield with OL, 259; in
  Worfield, 263; their life in Worfield,
  267; writes Desert Plants with OL,
  270; first signs of illness, 269–70;
  travels abroad with OL, 270; illness
  and death, 271–72
Leese, Lt-General Sir Oliver, Bt.,
  Ancestry, 1–3; Boyhood 3–14;
  Ludgrove, 4–7; Eton, 7–14; joins the
  Coldstream Guards, 15; goes to
  France, 17; wounded at St Julian, 18;
  sent home, 18; second journey to
  France, 19; wounded in face, 20; wins
  DSO and severely wounded in battle
  of the Somme, 20–5; recuperates and
  is posted to Bushey, 25–6; Adjutant of
  3rd Bn, Coldstream Guards, 27–8;
  Adjutant at Eton, 29–30; student at
  Staff College Camberley, 31–2;
  returns to regiment, 32–3; marries
  Margaret Leicester-Warren, 37;
  administrative officer, London
  District, and promoted Brevet
  Lieutenant Colonel, 38; G2 at War
  Office and in Southern Africa 40–1;
  commands First Battalion, Coldstream
  Guards, succeeds to baronetcy, 42;
  experiments in amphibious warfare,
  43–4; Chief Instructor at Quetta,
  46–60; Deputy Chief of Staff with
  BEF in France, 62–85; prepares
  blueprint for evacuation to Dunkirk,
  73; commands 29th Infantry Brigade,
  86; commands 15 Scottish Division,
  88; appointed to form and command
  Guards Armoured Division, 89;
  commands 30 Corps in Egypt, 93;
  leads breakthrough at Alamein,
  107–15; advances to Tripoli,
  Medenine, Mareth, Akarit, Sfax,
  116–32; commands 30 Corps in the
  invasion of Sicily, 133–45; takes over
  command of Eighth Army from
  Monty, 148; his humour, casualness in
  dress, outgoing manner, 152–54;
  moves Eighth Army westward towards
  Cassino, 159; breakthrough Gustav
  and Hitler Lines following the battle of
  Cassino, 163–74; relationship with
  Mark Clark, 177–78; knighted in the
  field, 181; prepares and carries out
  Operation Olive, 183–87; breaks
  through the Gothic line, 188–89; takes
  over command of Allied Land Forces,
  South East Asia, 198; his impressions
  of Mountbatten and the HQ at Kandy,
  201; his long journeys, 205; meets
  Slim, 207; plans swift advance to
  Rangoon, 210; obtains transport
  planes, 217–18; Mandalay taken, 226;
  Rangoon taken, 234; hears from
  Mountbatten, 236–37; writes to
  Alanbrooke, 237–38; talks with Slim,
  alleged 'sacking' of Slim, 239–47;
  recalled to England, 248–53;
  aftermath, 253–58; appointed GOC
  Eastern Command, 260; retires from
  the Army, 262–63; grows cacti and
  succulents, 266; organises Alamein
  reunions, 268; appointed founder
  President of CCF, 268; Lieutenant of
  the Tower of London, 268; President
  of Warwickshire County Cricket Club,
  270; death of his wife, 272; President
  of MCC, 272; meets Frances Denby,
  273; Director of Securicor, 274; visits
  Alamein with Monty, 275–77; attends
  Monty's eightieth birthday
  celebrations, 277; overseas visits with
  Frances Denby, 279; President of the
  British Legion, 280; right leg
  amputated, 282; moves to Dolwen,
  283; attends last Alamein Reunion,
  284; death, 284; his achievements and
  character, 286–92; his gift for
  friendship, 292
Leese, Peter, 3
Leese, Violet (née Sandeman), 2–3, 20,
  24, 25, 264
Leese, Sir William, Bt., 2, 3, 6, 8, 9, 15,
  15n, 16, 24, 42

Legge, 2nd Lieutenant, 16, 17, 17n
Legh, Piers, 178, 182
Leicester-Warren, Cuthbert, 34, 35, 36, 48, 52, 57, 58, 59, 74–5, 264, 265, 269
Leicester-Warren, Hilda, 34, 35, 59, 264, 265, 269
Leicester-Warren, John, 35, 36, 238, 265
Leigh, E. C. Austen, (the Flea), 19
Lemnitzer, General, 287
Lentaigne, Brigadier, 204, 207, 214
Leopold III, King of the Belgians, 63, 66, 79
Leslie, Shane, 11, 14
Lewin, Ronald, 228, 239, 248n, 256, 257
Liddell, Alice (later Alice Hargreaves), 2
Liddell Hart, Basil, 43, 43n
'Lili Marlene', 181–82
Lilli Marlene (Dakota), 197, 205, 230
Llewellyn, Colonel Harry, 125, 125n, 126, 126n
Lloyd, Penny, 266
Loos, battle of, 21, 38
Lower Hall (Worfield), 37, 44, 53, 259, 262, 263
Loyd, Major General H. C. (Budget), 19, 19n, 26, 31, 38, 54, 63, 83, 83n
Lubomirski, Prince Eugen, 158, 159, 167, 265
Ludgrove, 4, 5, 6, 7
Lumsden, Lt-General, 62–3, 84, 105, 109, 111, 112, 113, 114, 287
Lush, Brigadier, 122; assessment of OL, 291, 292
Lynn, Dame Vera, 268
Lyttelton, Canon Edward, 7–8, 9

Macfarlane, General Mason, 64, 94
Macmillan, Harold, 7, 12, 160, 162, 170, 190–91, 191n
Magdalene College, Cambridge, 263
Mainwaring, Brigadier Hugh, 275, 276, 277
Mandalay, 206, 212, 218, 222, 224, 226, 234, 236
Mandalay Plain, 220
Mareth Line, battle of, 123, 124, 125, 127, 130
Margaret, Princess, 43
Mary, Queen, 13, 38
Mary, Princess Royal, 35, 261
Mavers, Leslie, 182
McCreery, General, 31, 114, 155, 156, 162, 164, 166, 181, 191

McGrigor, Admiral, 137, 143
McKinley, President, 1, 1n
McNeill, Colonel J. M., 208
Medenine, battle of, 125, 127
Meiktila, 221, 222, 223, 224, 231, 234, 238
Menzies, Sir Robert, 278
Messervy, General, 222, 234
Milne, Christopher, 4, 4n
Mitford, Unity, 57, 57n
Monckton, Lord, 6, 84
Montgomery, Field Marshal Lord, 31, 47, 63, 69, 80, 84, 94, 96, 101, 105, 111, 112, 113, 114, 116, 116n, 117, 119, 122, 124, 125, 127, 128, 129, 130, 133, 134, 135, 138, 139, 141, 141n, 144, 148, 149, 150, 151, 155, 156, 157, 159, 164, 172, 174, 193, 196, 197, 198, 201, 201n, 209, 243–45, 247, 252, 253, 265, 272, 275, 276, 277, 284, 285, 286, 288, 289; informs Alanbrooke that OL needs a rest, 146; congratulates OL on victory at Cassino, 176; opinion of OL, 287
Moore, Prebendary Stanley, 93–4, 269
Morshead, Major-General, 100–101, 108, 112
Mountbatten, Admiral of the Fleet, Lord, 136, 138, 139, 144–45, 191, 195, 197, 199, 200, 202, 203, 204, 206, 208n, 217, 220–21, 223, 224, 225, 227, 229, 230, 235, 238, 239, 240, 241, 242, 243–45, 246, 247, 250, 251, 252, 253, 253n, 254, 255, 256, 257, 258, 260; letters to OL, 196, 212, 221, 236–37, 248–49
Munster, 5th Earl of, 77, 77n
Mussolini, 42, 94, 139, 182

Nagasaki, 253
Nasser, Colonel, 275–76, 277
Neagle, Dame Anna, 268, 271–72
Nuremberg Trials, 262

O'Connor, General Sir Richard, 31, 94, 95, 195, 224, 229
Operations
  Anvil/Dragoon, 176, 177, 186
  Battleaxe, 95
  Capital, 202, 206
  Crusader, 95
  Diadem, 159, 163, 168
  Dickens, 159
  Dracula, 202, 206, 228

Extended Capital, 223
Husky, 133–45, 146
Olive, 192
Overlord, 168, 180
Roger, 237
Romulus, 202, 206, 212
Supercharge, 113, 114
Torch, 117, 123, 128
Zipper, 236, 244
Oppidan, The, 11
Owen, Frank, 213, 213n

Paget, General Sir Bernard, 197
Park, Air Chief Marshal Sir Keith, 222, 228, 229, 230, 231, 231n, 234, 246
Patch, General, 186
Paterson, Diana, 273
Patton, General George, 121, 135, 137, 138, 141, 141n, 142, 144, 178, 265, 286, 287
Pearl Harbor, 194
Pegu, 232, 234
Picture Post, 227
Pienaar, Major General, 101, 109, 112, 119
Pirow, 41, 41n
Playfair, Major General, 202, 202n, 207
Powell, Anthony, 30
Power, Admiral, 211, 229, 230, 246
Pownall, Lt-General Sir Henry, 31, 62, 63, 64, 66, 70, 72, 73, 81, 195, 198, 199, 202, 235, 286
Prince of Wales, 284
Pringle, Victor, 272
Pyman, General, 48, 50

Quebec Conference, 176, 195, 202
Quetta, 44, 45–60, 62, 73, 75, 98, 203, 239, 256

Ramsay, A. B. (The Ram), 11, 263
Ramsay, Admiral Sir Bertram, 137
Ramsay, Maule, 77, 77n
Randall, Alfred, 266, 269, 270, 274
Randall, Grace, 266, 272, 274
Rangoon, 210, 217, 218, 225, 226, 227, 229, 230, 231, 235, 236, 237, 242, 243, 245, 246
Ray, Colonel Ken, 98, 174, 191, 205, 219, 229, 279
Rees, Major General, 222, 224, 225, 226
Ridley, Lady, 23
Roberts, Major General G. P. B., 290

Roberts, Brigadier Michael, 257
Rodgers, Pte, 24
Rommel, Field Marshal, 66, 94, 95, 109, 113, 115, 125, 214n
Roosevelt, President, 133, 176
Royal Horticultural Society, 266, 267
Rudnicki, Major General, 166, 167

Sainsbury, Cpl, 23, 24, 25
Sandeman, Albert, 2
Sandeman, Maria Carlotta, 3, 16, 24
Sandys, Duncan, 165, 166
San Marino, 39, 190
Sardinia, 133
Scoones, General, 207, 210, 213–14, 224, 224n
Scott, Major General O'Carroll, 47, 48–50, 73, 200
Shepherd, Gordon, 280
Sicily, 40, 133–45, 286
Simonds, Major General, 135, 155, 156, 157, 265, 279
Simpson, General Sir Frank, 38, 80, 81, 277
Singapore, 47, 95, 194, 273
Slim, Field Marshal Lord, 195, 203–205, 207, 208, 208n, 209, 210, 218, 220, 223, 224, 224n, 225, 225n, 226, 227, 231, 232, 236, 237, 238, 239–40, 241–43, 244, 244n, 245, 245n, 246–52, 253, 253n, 254–58, 260, 265, 266, 289
Smith, Alan, 278
Smith, Major General Sir Arthur, 235
Smith, General Bedell, 124, 124n, 135, 287
Smith, Brigadier E. D., 222, 223
Smith, Ian Weston, 133, 139, 140–41, 254, 260, 279, 290, 291
Smith, M. J. K., 278, 279
Smuts, Field Marshal, 176, 176n
Somme, battle of the, 21, 25, 29, 39, 269
Stalin, 176
Stalingrad, 195
Steward, Major General, 209
Stilwell, General, 204, 217
Stimpson, John, 152–53, 159, 175, 191, 197, 198, 200, 203, 207, 209, 213, 225, 226, 227, 228, 229, 244n, 249, 250, 254, 279
Stirling, Colonel David, 97, 119, 120
Stopford, Lt-General Sir Montague, 43, 43n, 75, 210, 238, 244

Stratemeyer, General, 202, 203, 205, 209, 211, 221, 225, 227, 228, 229, 230, 231, 265
Succulents, 266, 273, 276, 286
Sultan, General, 204, 205, 206, 217, 223, 225, 227, 228, 229, 246
Sun, General, 207, 209, 229
Sunday Times, 275
Sutton, Carola (née Verney), 267
Sutton, John, 267
Symes, Major General, 250, 251, 255

Tabley House, 34, 35, 36, 67, 69, 70, 71, 74, 75, 76, 79, 126, 140, 259, 264, 265
Taylor, Derief, 168–69
Tedder, Air Marshal Lord, 134, 134n, 231n
Tehran Conference, 176
Thomson, Prebendary, 269, 271, 278
Thorne, General Sir Andrew, 65, 65n, 86
Thrower, Percy, 263n, 267n
Times, The, 3, 12, 36, 254, 277
Trinder, Tommy, 154, 155
Tuker, Major General Sir Francis, 49, 101, 158, 160
Tunnard, Viola, 215, 216
Tweedsmuir, Lord, 165, 166, 174, 290, 291
Twining, R. H., 272

Ultra, 127, 155
Umberto, Crown Prince of Italy, 162, 162n, 188
Urquhart, Major General, 102, 135, 286

Verney, Ulick, comments on Dunkirk, 63–81; 88, 147–48, 152, 160, 161, 165, 171, 175, 178, 182, 191, 197, 203, 213, 247, 249, 250, 252
VJ Day, 253

Vokes, Major General, 162, 193, 265
Vorster, John, 281

Wake-Walker, Admiral, 82
Walsh, Major General George, 98, 102, 103, 113, 121, 122, 126, 127, 135, 138, 140, 147, 148, 153, 156, 162, 164, 165, 165n, 178, 186, 189n, 191, 205, 207, 209, 214, 219, 224, 225, 226, 228, 229, 241, 250, 252
Warre, Edmond, 8
Warren, Ralph, 99, 103, 147, 259, 268
Wavell, Field Marshal Lord, 198, 210, 223
Waterloo, battle of, 42, 76
Wedemeyer, General, 217
Wells, 'Bummy', 29
Weygand, General, 73, 74, 75, 76, 84
Wheeler, General, 202, 204, 218, 219, 246
White, Mabel, 268–9
Wilcox, Herbert, 271–72
Williams, Sir Edgar, (Bill), 113, 277
Williams, J. W., 167, 167n
Wilson, Field Marshal Lord, 152
Wimberley, Major General, 31, 101, 102, 105, 108, 111, 119n, 120, 125, 131, 144
Wingate, Major General, 203, 214
Wolseley, Field Marshal Lord, 94, 198
Worfield, 60, 66, 72, 104, 161, 243, 260, 266, 267, 269, 271, 273, 274, 278, 282, 283, 284, 285

Yalta Conference, 229
Young, Brigadier Desmond, 214, 214n, 230, 263

Zakrzewski, Colonel, 291
Ziegler, Philip, 200, 240, 258

NOTE. As stated on Page 96, OL had devised a simple code that he often used when writing of senior generals:
Alexander (L)
Mark Clark (AL)
Monty (O)
Bill Slim (IL)
For Mountbatten (Supremo) he wrote, at first, U, and afterwards, S.